Indian River County Main Library
1600 21st Street
Vero Beach, FL 32960

DROP DEAD ON RECALL

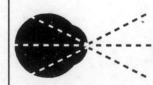

This Large Print Book carries the
Seal of Approval of N.A.V.H.

AN ANIMALS IN FOCUS MYSTERY

DROP DEAD ON RECALL

SHEILA WEBSTER BONEHAM

THORNDIKE PRESS

A part of Gale, Cengage Learning

Detroit • New York • San Francisco • New Haven, Conn • Waterville, Maine • London

GALE
CENGAGE Learning·

© 2012 by Sheila Webster Boneham.
An Animals in Focus Mystery.
Thorndike Press, a part of Gale, Cengage Learning.

Thorndike Press® Large Print Mystery
The text of this Large Print edition is unabridged.
Other aspects of the book may vary from the original edition.
Set in 16 pt. Plantin.

LIBRARY OF CONGRESS CATALOGING-IN-PUBLICATION DATA

Boneham, Sheila Webster, 1952–
  Drop dead on recall / by Sheila Webster Boneham.
    pages ; cm. — (Thorndike Press large print mystery)
    ISBN 978-1-4104-5634-2 (hardcover) — ISBN 1-4104-5634-X (hardcover) 1.
Animals—Fiction. 2. Large type books. I. Title.
PS3602.O657155D76 2013
813'.6—dc23   2012044216

Published in 2013 by arrangement with Midnight Ink, an imprint of Llewellyn Publications, Woodbury, MN 55125-2989 USA

Printed in the United States of America
1 2 3 4 5 6 7 17 16 15 14 13

For Roger, because living with a writer can be murder, and for the real-life Jay, my sweet babboo.

ACKNOWLEDGMENTS

Writing and publishing a novel is a bit like training a dog. It takes time and dedication. It's fun and it's messy. It's a labor of love, and although it sometimes feels like a one-woman show, the end result depends on many people. I can't begin to thank everyone — the many authors whose work I've loved and from whom I hope I've learned a little; members of several writing groups; my teachers, my students, my readers. If I haven't named you here, please know that I appreciate your time and comments. I don't always do as I'm told, and any errors that remain are mine, all mine.

Some individuals have, naturally, been more prominent in the development of this book than others — I owe you all! Writer and physician Ronda Wells has been along for this whole ride, and did her best to keep me honest about medical issues. My obedience training friend Linda Wagner read early drafts and made brilliant suggestions. My agent, Josh Getlzer, not only found this series a home, but became a good friend in the process. As a bonus, he's a very funny guy. Thanks to Terri Bischoff, my editor at Midnight Ink, for having faith in the books, and the rest of the crew for making it happen. Special thanks to author Susan Conant, whose own work inspired me not only to try writing mysteries, but to enter my first obedience trial two decades ago. And last, but never least, my profound thanks to the dogs and cats and other critters who have inspired and informed my work, enriched my life, and keep my feet warm while I write.

LIST OF CHARACTERS

Dog owners	Animal, breed
Abigail Dorn	Pip, Border Collie
Connie Stoppen- hagen	Poodle trainer
Francine Peterson	Border Collies
Janet MacPhail	Jay, Australian Shepherd (Aussie) Leo, orange tabby cat, Domestic Shorthair
Giselle Swann	Precious, Maltese
Greg Dorn	Percy, Poodle
Rhonda Lake	Eleanor, Golden Retriever
Suzette Anderson	Fly, Border Collie Mimi, Shetland Sheepdog
Sylvia Eckhorn	Tippy, Cocker Spaniel
Tom Saunders	Drake, Labrador Retriever
Virginia Scott (Ginny)	Border Collies

Other characters
Bill Bruce, Janet's brother
Bob Bradley, competition judge
Chet MacPhail, Janet's husband
Collin Lahmeyer
Eckhorn twin daughters, Lizzy and Meg

Homer Hutchinson, detective
Jade Templeton, Shadetree asst. manager
Jo Stevens, detective
Goldie Sunshine
Marietta Santini, Dog Dayz owner
Mrs. Bruce, Janet's mother
Neil Young
Norm
Paul Douglas, DVM
Tommy Saunders, Tom's son
Tony Balthazar, show chair
Yvonne Anderson, Suzette's sister

Other breeds in the book
Beagle
Chesapeake (Chesapeake Bay Retriever)
Collie
Curly (Curly Coated Retriever)
English Shepherd
Flat-coat (Flat-coated Retriever)
German Shepherd, German Shepherd
  Dog
Lab (Labrador Retriever)
Malamute
Pomeranian
Poodle (Miniature Poodle, Toy Poodle,
  Standard Poodle)
Rottweiler
Sheltie (Shetland Sheepdog)
Shih-tzu

St. Bernard

Toller (Nova Scotia Duck Tolling Retriever)

"Old dog trainers never die,
they just drop on recall."

BUMPER STICKER

1

Someone outside the competition ring laughed, but I didn't think Abigail Dorn was fooling around. I wasn't sure I'd ever seen the woman smile, and from all indications, she thought obedience competition was as serious as a heart attack. Whatever she was doing now, though, had nothing to do with winning.

Abigail had keeled over at the judge's signal. Pip, her Border Collie, had come flying when Abigail called, then dropped to the grass twenty feet out on her "Down!" command. According to American Kennel Club rules, Abigail should have called him again when the judge gave the signal. I'm no expert on the finer points of scoring, but I was pretty sure that falling flat on her face was a serious handler error. I mentally smacked myself for my irreverent thoughts, though, as it became more obvious with each crawling second that something was very wrong.

Ringside chatter had hushed to a low, sporadic hum, and the only other sound I could hear was the soft huff-huff of my own dog panting at my side. I shifted my focus from Abigail's prone form to Bob Bradley, the judge, who was peering at Abigail over the top of his glasses. Either he was too surprised to move, or he didn't want to interfere in case Abigail tried to fix her *faux pas.*

Greg Dorn, Abigail's better half, dashed by me and vaulted the collapsible fence that defined the ring. "Abby!" He knelt beside her, rolled her onto her back, slid his left arm under her shoulders, and raised her upper body off the ground. Abigail's startled gaze fixed on Greg's face, and her right hand twitched as if it wanted to reach for Greg but couldn't be bothered. As she began to gag and choke, Abigail's face slowly darkened to muddy mauve. Greg squeaked, then cleared his throat and yelled, "Help me!" to no one in particular.

His squawk shook me out of my stupor, and I signaled Jay, my Australian Shepherd, to get into his crate. Abigail appeared to need more help than Greg or anyone else on the show grounds was likely to provide, so I began to fish through my dog-show tote

16

for my cell phone. Then I noticed that The Hunk with the Big Black Dog was already dialing. I caught his eye, pointed toward his phone, and mouthed, "Ambulance?" He nodded, so I left my phone wherever it was hiding among water bottles, freeze-dried liver, cracker crumbs, and other dog-show sundries. No wonder the darned thing didn't work half the time. I made a mental note to add bag cleaning to my To Do list. If I could find it.

I turned back to the ring. Greg had unzipped Abigail's jacket and was going through her pockets, pulling them inside out. Empty. He said something to Bob and one of the ring stewards, a tall blonde whose wrinkled forehead and wringing hands played counterpoint to the grinning Golden Retriever on her sweatshirt. The steward ran to the scoring table, grabbed a white box with a red cross on the lid, and rifled through the contents. I zipped my jacket a little higher and wiped a wind-induced tear from the outer corner of my eye.

The Hunk appeared at my side and said, "I'm sure she'll be fine." I felt the moisture on my fingers and realized he thought I was upset about Abigail, which of course I was, but not to the point of tears. "You're friends, I take it?"

"I sort of know her, but not that well." I didn't feel pressed to add that Abigail had never shown me any reason to want to know her better, nor would she have been amused by my easygoing approach to obedience trials. Abigail was there to win, and I was there mostly to play with my dog.

The steward ran back to center ring empty-handed, and I wondered what she'd been sent to find. I couldn't hear what they were saying, but Greg was growing more and more agitated, and Abigail more and more purple. Greg scanned the clusters of people standing around the ring, locked onto me, and appealed for help with wide eyes. Not sure I could offer much, I scurried into the ring, wishing all the way that I'd taken that first aid class I'd been thinking about for the past few years.

Funny thing, memory. I've forgotten for years to sign up for that class until it was half over, but my mental image of the fear in Abigail's eyes is as clear as yesterday. That look, and the sound coming from her throat, like the long squeal of air escaping the taut mouth of a balloon. My heart pounded in my ears like hail on a metal awning, and I had to lean over to hear Greg.

"Her EpiPen. It has to be here. She always has it with her." His voice was pitched high and tight, his enunciation precise.

"What?"

"Epinephrin. She's allergic to bee stings. She carries an epinephrin kit."

That took a moment to sink in. Then an image slithered from the shadows of my mind, a hazy vision of Abigail and Pip at the gate, beside the steward's table. The image cleared, and in my mind's eye I saw Abigail set a small bag on the steward's table next to her white dumbbell, which the steward would collect when the time came for Pip's retrieves.

A cold stab of adrenaline set me in motion, and I reached the steward's table at a dead run. The bag was there, pale turquoise, with a machine-stitched Border Collie jumping a striped bar over the initials A.D. — Abigail Dorn — on the side.

I grabbed the bag and turned back toward center ring, ripping the zipper open and pawing through the contents. A baggie stuffed with freeze-dried liver. A narrow leather leash. A plastic cylinder with a syringe inside, "Epinephrin" blazed along the length of the tube in red. My fingers closed around it and I raced back to Greg and offered him the EpiPen.

"Open it!" He lowered his wife's head and shoulders gently onto the grass.

I tossed the bag behind me and gaped stupidly at the thing in my hand. "How?"

Greg pulled his arm from under Abigail, his face so red and drawn that I thought they might need twin stretchers for the family Dorn. "Twist the top! Pull it out!"

I pulled the syringe from the cylinder, and Greg snatched it from my hand. The raw panic seemed to leave him and he moved with quick assurance, pulling the cap off the end of the cylinder and tossing it behind him. He positioned the syringe with the business end jutting past the heel of his hand and plunged it into her black-clad thigh with a force that made my eyelids twitch. Greg held it there for what seemed like forever, then lifted the injector to eye level, glanced at the end, tossed it to his side, and looked back at his wife.

Abigail's mouth hung slack and a thin ribbon of drool traced a line from the corner of her lower lip across her cheek to her ear. Her eyelids were half-closed, the visible parts of her eyes white. She gave no sign that she felt the blow or the needle, no sign that she felt anything at all.

2

A hint of movement tickled my peripheral vision, and I turned toward it. Abigail's Border Collie, Pip, stood on the spot where he had lain down a heartbeat before Abigail fell. He rocked from one front paw to the other, head thrust down and forward, ears at full alert, and watched the drama unfold around his mistress. He took my eye contact as permission and, shoulders lowered in a Border Collie crouch, ran to Abigail's side, shoved his nose under her limp arm, and whined. My mind tried to hang on to the hope that, when help arrived, everything would be fine, but my heart knew that hope was in vain when Abigail didn't respond to her dog.

I squatted beside Greg, ignoring the crackle of protest from my left knee. "What can I do to help?"

Greg tipped his head forward and let go of a long breath. He paused, then said, so softly that I almost missed it, "Take Pip."

I stood and retreated to the steward's
table, retrieved the leash that lay beside
Abigail's turquoise bag, and softly called to
Pip. He looked at me, then at his mistress.
Greg touched the dog on his shoulder and
spoke to him, and Pip reluctantly stood up.
He swiped Abigail's cheek with his tongue,
then trotted to me, sat, cocked his head to
the right, and lifted his neatly trimmed left
paw. I clipped the leash to his collar and led
him out of the ring and over to my chair,
weaving through the small crowd that had
gathered to watch. He craned his neck
toward the ring and whined softly, but came
with me.

The Hunk with the phone joined me
outside the ring. We'd never officially met,
although we had nodded to one another at
dog shows and I'd seen him at one or two
obedience training sessions. "The ambulance is on the way. They said five or six
minutes, so they should be here any time
now." He held out his hand. "Tom Saunders. You're Janet MacPhail." It wasn't a
question.

"I am." I was too focused on the warm,
firm hand grasping mine to come up with
anything more clever, but in any case he
had me pegged — Janet MacPhail, admirer

of fine dogs and reasonable men. In that order, with possibly a few other things between the two.

In the ring, Greg was holding Abigail again, but he seemed a lot calmer, or maybe he was in shock. I decided I had to take that first aid course the very next time it was offered so I'd have a bit of a clue in the next emergency. I heard the faint cry of a siren somewhere to the south, and when I looked past the obedience ring toward the sound my eyes focused on a parade of freight cars marching across the road just south of the fairgrounds. "That might be a problem," I said, nodding toward the train.

Tom followed my gaze and clucked softly. He pulled his cell phone from his belt, dialed 911 again, and told the dispatcher about the train. Then he turned back to me.

"What were they looking for in there? What did he give her?" Pip leaned against my leg as I told Tom about the epinephrin.

He turned toward the tableau in the ring. "Hunh. That should have worked by now."

"That's what I thought." As my brain groped for the memory of something I'd read about epinephrin, Tom shifted topics.

"We need to find a show official." He turned and covered the four or five yards back to his crate in about two strides and grabbed his show catalog. "Tony Balthazar is show chair. I'll find him." He smiled at me, the sort of knee-liquefying smile I don't see all that often anymore except in the movies, and in spite of the circumstances I felt a long-forgotten butterfly twitch to life in my belly.

Tom stopped at the ring. I watched the steward in the Golden Retriever sweatshirt speak into a walkie-talkie, then say something to Tom. He turned and loped toward the big-toppish tent that housed the show officials when they weren't roaming the grounds. *Nice rear assembly,* I thought. I felt a mild twinge of guilt, considering Abigail's plight, but I couldn't help evaluating Tom's retreating posterior, and putting it in terms of canine structure was second nature. If I were interested in complicating my life with a man, he'd be one who understood the comparison as a compliment.

I stroked Pip's silky head and looked into his black-brown eyes. We set off for the calf barn, a sprawling white building on the edge of the fairgrounds where the Dorns' equipment was set up. "You'll have to stay in your crate for a while, Pupper." Pip glanced over his shoulder at the ring and whined, but then trotted beside me in the opposite direction, panting and grinning and waving his white-tipped tail. His nose lifted and twitched as we stepped into the barn and its faint bovine memory of last summer's 4-H fair. A siren warbled off to the west, muted but growing louder and more shrill with each wail.

We passed a cluster of six huge crates, five of them occupied by adult Malamutes, the sixth by a half-grown pup. Two were sitting, three standing, one lying down, but all of them listened intently, heads tilting side to side to locate the sound, ears twitching, a faraway look in all twelve eyes. Thick gray fur poked out between the wires of the crate walls where the big lupine dogs leaned against them.

Toward the center of the barn I found a collapsible metal crate with Pip's nameplate on its top-of-the-line white epoxy-coated door — "OTCh MACH CH Paragon's Pip UDX." Obedience Trial Champion, Utility Dog Excellent. In other words, a helluva competition dog, with top-level titles in obedience and agility, and a breed champion for good measure. Pip's also a helluva pleasant dog to be around. You'd think that would be true of all obedience stars, but it isn't. Like so many human celebrities, some top dogs are nearly perfect in the competition ring and thoroughly obnoxious outside it. Not their fault, of course. Some of their owners are just so caught up in the pursuit of titles and high scores that they neglect to teach basic canine-to-human etiquette. Whatever I thought of Abigail and her own behavior, I had to admit that her dogs were mannerly and happy.

"In you go." I slipped Pip's collar off and checked the water in the stainless-steel bucket attached to the crate door. I was laying his collar and leash on a green folding canvas chair next to a show catalog with "Dorn" scrawled across the cover when I felt the little warning hairs on the back of my neck stand up, an unwitting response to the distinct sense that I was being watched.

I glanced around. I saw only one other person in the building, and all I could see of her was the back of her jeans and marigold sweatshirt, and a flash of what I took for a red hat as she disappeared out the other end of the barn. I went back to what I was doing, but the feeling lingered and grew, and unease skittered up and down my skin.

3

The creepy sensation that I was being watched stuck with me as I secured the door to Pip's crate, so I took another look around the calf barn. Across the aisle, a pink plastic pet carrier no bigger than a boot box sat on a grooming table. A pink plastic sign hung on the wire door, "Precious" etched into it in white, and a pink plastic tote bag slouched to one side. Bright black eyes monitored my movements from beneath curvaceous white eyelashes and a topknot adorned with a tiny pink bow. A Maltese. About six pounds sopping wet. He spun in a happy circle when I made eye contact, and I let go of the breath I hadn't known I was holding. "Hi, Big Guy." I couldn't bring myself to call him Precious. "You know you gave me the willies?" The little dog panted happily and I could swear he winked at me.

I refocused on the Dorns' area. *Strange,* I thought. *One crate, one dog, one chair.* Greg always brings his miniature Poodle, Percy, along, and I couldn't remember Abigail ever coming alone to a dog show. *God forbid she should carry her own equipment.* So where were his dog and his stuff?

Suzette Anderson bustled to her crate, which was set up next to the grooming table that held Precious the Maltese. She pulled a bottle of spring water from a cooler, poured half into a bowl for her Border Collie, Fly, and took a swig. Suzette and Fly both watched me, and Suzette swiped a tissue across her mouth. "You know, she's probably back on her feet by now and bitchin' that you took her dog away. Ms. Drama Queen probably pulled this to cover her bad run."

I thought about the color of Abigail's stricken face when I gave Greg the EpiPen. I didn't think Abigail had been "pulling" that, but decided to let Suzette blather for the moment. When she seemed to be finished, I said, "I really wasn't paying attention until she fell. She had a bad run?"

"She was all over the place. Couldn't walk a straight line. Maybe she had a little too much Rescue Remedy." Some people swear by teensy doses of this blend of alcohol and flower essences to dull the sharp edge of competition nerves. "You know, like Stoli to

28

the rescue?"

In all the time I've been around dog shows, I've only once seen anyone obviously soused at an obedience trial, and she sure wasn't a top competitor. I must have looked skeptical, because Suzette said, "She was way off. Seriously. And I wouldn't put it past her to turn an off day into a major drama. You know how she can be."

"No, actually, I don't know her very well."

The howl of the ambulance was close now, and a single tone, true and clean as the ring of a tuning fork, rose behind me and slid upward a quarter tone at a time until it met and mingled with the siren. Some primitive nerve in my body leaped into survival mode, and screamed at me to run for my life, but my modern brain resumed control, replacing fear with a sense of wonder. A second tone chimed in, then a third, and more, until all six Malamute voices merged in a timeless song. I turned and saw them, chins tipped up, ears back, eyes squeezed tight in . . . what? Remembrance? Desire? A prayer? The building around us seemed to fade to white, and I could imagine that aria rolling across the land ten thousand years ago when wolves hunted and glaciers gnawed out the ravines and lake beds of northern Indiana.

Suzette's less melodious tune yanked me back to the present. "Trust me. Abigail's a major drama queen." She slugged down more water. "Anyway, I'm sure she'll be fine. Probably ate something that disagreed with her." She glanced at some food-smeared trash sitting on top of Pip's crate and wrinkled her nose.

"Greg thinks she reacted to a bee sting."

"Could be, I guess." She tossed her water bottle back into the ice chest and pulled her long blonde braid over her left shoulder. "Come on, Fly, let's go see how we did," and off she jogged, her black and white dog bouncing and barking beside her.

I closed my eyes and let the song of the Malamutes wind around me for another moment before I followed Suzette back to the ring. When I arrived, Bob Bradley was hunkered down talking to Greg, who still held his wife. She was definitely not back on her feet. I had the uncharitable thought that this was the first time I'd ever seen Abigail with her mouth shut for more than three minutes, which is how long the dogs have to stay put in novice obedience while their handlers watch silently from across the ring. I recanted mentally, though, as I thought of the scene in the ring and the clear signs that Abigail was in deep trouble.

4

The ambulance turned into the fairgrounds at the far end of the grandstand. As its final notes waned, the last strains of the canine accompaniment drifted away on a gust of spring wind. Tony Balthazar paced in circles just inside the gate, his agitation punctuated by a string of lollipop-colored triangles slapping the fence behind him or riding horizontal on the wind. After a quick word with the ambulance driver, Tony hopped onto his golf cart, wheeled it around with as much spin as he could squeeze out of the electric motor, and led the way. A quarter mile into the fairgrounds he braked, hopped off the cart, and pulled apart two sections of the portable wooden fencing that defined the western perimeter of the competition ring.

Two EMTs sprinted past him through the gate. Greg spoke to them while they checked that Abigail had a pulse and was breathing. One of them opened Abigail's mouth, inserted a tongue depressor, and checked her throat. The EMT looked like a fourteen-year-old gymnast, tiny and quick, with blonde hair pulled into a perky ponytail. She wasted no motion and no time. Neither did her partner, a muscular dark-skinned man with shaved head, who was busy inserting an IV into Abigail's arm.

Greg and the blonde EMT both checked their watches. The EMT fished in her bag for a moment and came out with a syringe and drug vial. She loaded the syringe and emptied it into Abigail's arm. By then the driver had arrived with the stretcher.

Bob Bradley guided Abigail's distraught husband out of the way. As he rose into a wobbly stand, Greg glanced around. "Where's the dog?" he asked, scanning the ring and surrounding area, his eyes widening as his head turned. "Where's Pip?" The last word was barely audible.

I hurried over and laid my hand on Greg's arm. "You asked me to take Pip, remember? I put him in his crate."

He didn't seem to understand, if he even heard me, so I tried again.

"Don't worry about Pip. If you and Abigail aren't back before I leave, I'll take him with me. You can pick him up on your way home, or he can stay the night."

I had always liked Greg and now I felt sorry for him, although I'd always been flummoxed by his devotion to Abigail. She was no more considerate of him than she was of anyone else, at least not in public. It was always "Greg, do this! Greg, you did that wrong!" I'm not a big fan of electronic bark collars on dogs, but there were times I'd thought of strapping one to Abigail's elegant neck to stop her yapping.

Greg nodded, his focus on the stretcher bearing his wife. "I don't understand. The epinephrin should have worked by now." He glanced at his watch. "It's been twenty minutes since the first shot, twelve since the second." His voice cracked and he cleared his throat.

The EMTs pulled the bed of the stretcher up, locked it into position, and wheeled it the few feet over bumpy grass toward the ambulance, where each picked up an end and slid it into the waiting vehicle.

I touched Greg's arm. "If Abigail isn't back on her feet tomorrow, I'll pack up your stuff and take it home with me. You do what you need to do. Now go."

And off he went, the panic back and bright in his eyes.

I watched him climb into the ambulance, and when it reached the fairgrounds exit, I turned back to the ring, where Bob Bradley and Tony Balthazar conferred. Then Bob stepped toward the spectators and asked for everyone's attention. "Folks, we're going to take the lunch break a little early. We'll resume this class in one hour, at eleven o'clock, and bump the other classes back accordingly." He looked like he could use something a tad stronger than the water and soft drinks offered in the judge's tent. Maybe a quart of Rescue Remedy would help.

5

I sank into my blue canvas folding chair, stretched my legs out in front of me, and looked around. Tom's chair and his dog's crate were empty, and I mentally slapped myself for noticing. What did I care? As if he could read my mind, Jay stared at me from the crate beside my chair and sneezed. "I do not care where they are," I said, and he sneezed again.

With the unscheduled break, and six more dogs to do their individual runs, plus the group stays, the Open class wouldn't finish before noon. The crowd had scattered as soon as the ambulance pulled out, and only a few people and pooches remained outside the obedience ring.

I opened my cute new purple soft-sided cooler and pulled out a bottle of water and a carrot. Jay watched expectantly while I opened the bottle and took a drink. I glanced at the water bucket hanging inside the door of his little home away from home. He had plenty of water. I took a little bite of the carrot and watched a thin glob of drool trickle from the corner of my dog's lips, then unzipped the roof opening enough to slip the carrot through. Jay gripped it delicately with his incisors, dropped it onto the floor of the crate, and gave me a "Thanks!" look as he licked his lips. Then he got to work, attacking the carrot in the center and taking bites along the length as if it were a cob of corn. Every one of my dogs has had a personal carrot-handling technique, like people with sandwich cookies.

I pulled a fleece throw from the back of my chair, unfolded it, and draped it over myself to cut the wind. The lilacs blooming on the perimeter of the fairgrounds perfumed the air, and a hint of early honeysuckle blew in from time to time. I heard clapping and whooping from a distant ring. Most of the dogs were frisky in the cool air, but the wind was a few degrees too cool for a sedentary naked ape. The polar fleece helped.

I rested my head against the back of the chair and shut my eyes for just a minute. Three quarters of an hour later, I snapped back to consciousness when I heard Jay sit up in his crate. He gave me The Look.

"You need to go out, Bubby?" Jay cocked his head, so I pushed myself out of the chair and reached for my leash as I unzipped the crate. Jay waited. I can't say he was patient, but he knew better than to bolt through an open door with the alpha bitch — yours truly — in the way. I fastened the leash to his collar, then calmly said, "Free," his off-duty signal. He squirted out of his crate and bounced straight up to look me in the eye. Down. Up. Down. Up. His feet never touched me. "You big goof." He stopped bouncing and grinned at me, eyes bright and butt awriggle. I grabbed a plastic bag and stuffed it into my pocket. "Off we go!"

We spent about twenty minutes walking around the field east of the parking area. Jay sniffed everything, stopping to mark several Canadian thistles, a couple of fence posts, and a concrete block half hidden in a clump of wild something at the east edge of the field. He also did a little organic recycling, and as I stooped to collect his deposit in my plastic bag, I thought about Abigail.

Why didn't the epinephrin work as quickly as Greg thought it would? Was it an allergic reaction after all, or something else? I couldn't remember ever seeing Abigail look anything but in the pink. In fact, I had the impression she was something of a health nut. Not that I'm opposed to being healthy, but there are limits to how much pleasure I'll forego or pain I'll endure. Don't even think about feeding me tofu unless it's camouflaged in hot and sour soup!

Could Abigail have had a heart attack or a stroke? She was young and in great shape, but it was possible. Could it have been a seizure of some sort? I guessed we'd know soon enough. I checked my watch and figured we had time for Jay to get a drink and rest a few minutes in his crate and for me to run to the porta-potty before we needed to warm up. And there might be news from the hospital by now.

6

"Anything?" Tom Saunders and his dog had returned by the time I got back to the obedience ring.

"Not that I've heard." I caught myself checking him out again, and not just because of the way he wore his jeans. I'd seen Tom a few times training at Dog Dayz, and competing at obedience trials with his black Labrador Retriever, Drake, who now stood at the man's knee, his tail waving gently. I guessed Tom was about my age, early fifties. Life had roughed him up enough to add interest. Laugh lines radiated from his eyes, and an intriguing scar like a question mark divided his chin a tad left of center. Silver highlights ran through his collar-length brown hair and moustache, and he had that knee-melting smile and knew how to use it.

"Gotta get over there. Drake qualified." He grinned again, and trotted his big dog to the gate, where the ring steward was assembling the class qualifiers. I was admiring both rear views when I noticed Tony Balthazar standing near the gate, listening to his cell phone. His forehead furrowed and the corners of his mouth went rigid as he tucked the phone back into his pocket.

"Hey, Janet! What's up? Why was that ambulance here earlier?" Connie Stoppenhagen was coiffed and polished, as always, as if she'd just stepped off a movie set. She's the only dog-show person I know who never has dog spit or paw prints on her clothes, or a hair out of place on herself or her dogs. She shows Poodles, toys and miniatures, with great success. We'd been friends ever since we met in my veterinarian's waiting room a decade ago. "Someone get hurt?"

"They were doing the drop on recall and Abigail Dorn collapsed."

"Isn't the dog supposed to be the one who drops?" Connie cocked her head and blinked at me, looking for a laugh, but having seen Abigail I wasn't amused. "Sorry. That was bad."

"Uh-huh."

"Well, if it had been anyone else, I wouldn't have thought it, you know."

"I know." I did, too. Abigail didn't exactly go out of her way to make friends.

"I'm surprised to see Greg here."

40

"He always comes to Abigail's events."

Connie didn't look capable of snorting, with her perfect strawberry-blonde hair, un-smudged makeup, and tailored peach suit, but snort she did. "Where have you been? They're separated, and I gather it's not all that friendly."

"Hunh." I digested that information. "I did wonder about the setup when I crated Pip."

"Maybe Greg's here on his own showing Percy?"

Connie obviously didn't spend much time around the Dorns.

"I don't think Percy is into obedience. Abigail's always harping on Greg to 'train that damn dog.' "

"Ah, but that's what harpies do, is it not? Gotta hand it to her, though. Passing out in the middle of an exercise certainly is a creative way to dodge a bad score."

There it was again. Maybe Suzette wasn't just being snide earlier. "I thought she and Pip had been doing great."

"They have, but she told me this morning that she felt all discombobulated. Said she tripped over Pip while warming up, and he'd been shy of her on left turns ever since." Connie commented on an Irish Set-ter gleaming like a polished penny in a distant ring, then picked up the Abigail thread again. "She did seem really agitated this morning. She kept tripping and dropping things. Nerves, I guess."

Connie's comment didn't make sense to me. Abigail had competed, and won, against the best obedience dogs and handlers in the country. "But this isn't a big trial. Why would she be nervous?"

"Who knows? She doesn't like to lose." She crinkled her nose. "But who does?" She glanced at her watch and said she'd see me later.

Bob Bradley had finished checking his scores, and was inviting the qualifiers into the ring. He led a round of applause for the stewards, the overworked, undervalued volunteers who keep things rolling. Then Bob, a history professor at Indiana University, explained that to qualify a dog must earn more than fifty percent on each exercise and one hundred seventy out of two hundred possible points. "In other words, dogs have to get a solid B to pass, whereas my students at I.U. only need a D." That got a few chuckles.

Bob glanced at the paper in his hand. "Seven of the ten dogs in this class qualified. Good job, folks!" There was more applause, a couple of whoops, and a series of staccato yips from an appreciative Sheltie. Then Bob identified the four dogs who got the highest scores, including Tom and Drake with a respectable 192 and third place.

First place went, not unexpectedly, to Suzette Anderson and her Border Collie, Fly, with a fabulous 199, which probably put them out front for their zillionth High in Trial award, given to the dog with the highest score from the regular obedience classes. Suzette also trained at Dog Dayz, where Jay and I train, and I knew from the newsletter that she and Fly were kicking butt this year.

As Bob finished handing out ribbons, Tony shuffled into the ring and mumbled, "Congratulations to all the winners and qualifiers." He cleared his throat. "Um, I have some rather bad news, I'm afraid." He coughed. "I just spoke to Mr. Dorn at the hospital, and, umm, I'm afraid that, umm, uh, Mrs. Dorn, the lady who became ill here in the ring a little while ago, uh . . ." He made a strangling sound and dabbed his glossy forehead with a crumpled hanky, then squared his shoulders and continued. "Umm, she passed away en route to the hospital."

In the dead calm that followed I saw Suzette Anderson smiling at Fly.

7

Rumors raced around the show grounds like whippets in a field of bunnies. A woman from Illinois told me that Abigail had a stroke. Heart attack was a popular option, and aneurysm got a few votes. Some people thought Abigail had an asthma attack. Several who were ringside when Abigail went down suggested diabetic shock, thinking the injections were insulin, although no one remembered ever seeing Abigail with any medical paraphernalia. Anaphylactic shock from a bee sting got only one vote (not that I was keeping track). Oddly enough, no one asked me what was in the syringe I had retrieved for Greg. I guess they didn't want to confuse themselves with facts.

Suzette Anderson strolled over with Fly and asked what I'd heard. Her eyes and nose were red and moist, and she fiddled with a sodden tissue while I told her about the epinephrin. "That's odd. I was with Abby when she had to use her EpiPen a couple of times. It worked really fast." Suzette dragged the back of her hand across her wet cheekbone. *Give me a break,* I thought, recalling the potshots she'd taken at Abigail earlier. She went on, "She probably died of plain old hard-headedness. I'll miss her, though." *Yeah, right.* She stroked Fly's cheek with the backs of her fingers as they walked away, and although I was skeptical about Suzette's claim to sorrow, I was also surprised to feel a wave of sadness and regret wash through me. For a moment my sense of generalized loss was so sharp that I couldn't move. I took several deep breaths as memories of my own lost loves and opportunities beat and prodded the folds of my heart. Jay, always alert to my moods, uttered a low whine and brought me back to the present, and I got him out of his crate to warm up.

Our class went off without a hitch, and Jay earned the second of the three legs required for his novice obedience title. I hoped he'd get the third one, and the title, the next day. Then on to the fun stuff, jumping and retrieving.

By 2:30, the obedience classes were finished and the stewards were tallying scores for special awards. The temperature had climbed into the low seventies and the wind had softened, so I stripped off my sweater in favor of my newish lime-green T-shirt. I put Jay in his crate and asked the people seated next to me to keep an eye on him for a few minutes. They were from Indianapolis and I didn't know them well, but had seen them at enough shows to know they wouldn't let anyone mess with my dog. Then I headed for the calf barn to check on Pip.

Various thoughts drifted around my mind like fog as I tried to make sense of Abigail's sudden death, but the instant I stepped onto the concrete floor of the barn they made way for a new concern. A woman stood by Pip's crate with a leash in her hand. I recognized her yellow-gold sweatshirt, and the improbable red hair I'd mistaken for a hat when I saw her leave the building earlier. She struck a momentary deer-in-the-headlights pose, then hustled out the other side of the barn. "Hey!" I yelled, picking up my pace as I passed the crated Malamutes, but she vanished between two motor homes.

Everything around the Dorns' equipment seemed to be the same as when I was there earlier. Still, people lurking around other people's dogs give me the willies. Especially when they act weird about it. Dogs are stolen occasionally, and certain extremist groups have been known to "liberate" dogs at shows, as if the life of a stray scrounging for food and dodging traffic and coyotes and other hazards of "freedom" were better than regular meals, a warm bed, and love. Not much I could do except be sure that Pip was secure, but I'd find out who she was.

I took Pip out for a quick pee, then crated him again and started organizing the Dorns' belongings. The scant remnants of Abigail's breakfast — a few bits of bagel, a plastic container with the remains of a creamy spread chock-full of green twiggy things — sat on top of Pip's crate alongside a half-finished bottle of organic apple juice. *As opposed to inorganic apple juice,* I mused. There were also some crumpled bits of paper towel and a slicker brush with black fur captured in the aluminum tines. I looked for a trash can as I pulled the fur from the brush. Failing to find one, I tossed fur, bottle, and towels into a large fuschia and yellow canvas tote bag stowed under Abigail's chair. Like the little bag Abigail carried to the ring, this one had a Border Collie and "Dorn" embroidered on the side.

I opened the plastic container and sniffed at the spread. It smelled strongly of dill, and something else, something I couldn't identify and not all that appetizing. It reminded me vaguely of a mouse nest I'd once pulled from an unused electrical box in my grandfather's garage. I crinkled my nose and assumed it was one of Abigail's famous health foods. Then I remembered that I hadn't eaten, and wondered whether the vendor by the grandstand had any bear claws left.

There was no place to rinse the plastic container, so I made sure the lid was tight, and tossed it into the tote. In my jacket pocket I had a padlock that I sometimes use on Jay's crate if I'm worried about someone opening it. I slid it around the bars of the door and frame of the crate and snapped it shut, then slipped a bit of freeze-dried liver to Pip and told him I'd be back as soon as I collected my own dog, equipment, and van.

Most competitors had cleared out by the time I got back to the obedience ring, but a few were watching the final awards ceremony. I stepped up beside Tom and was surprised to feel another little flipflop in my gut. "What's up?" Suzette and her dog were in the ring, Fly's leash in one hand and a nice big blue and green rosette and stainless-steel water bucket stuffed with dog biscuits in the other.

Tom filled me in. "Suzette and Fly got High Combined." That's for the dog with the highest combined qualifying scores from the Open and Utility classes. "We're waiting for High in Trial. Probably Suzette."

"And High in Trial is . . ." I wouldn't have thought it possible, but Suzette pulled the corners of her mouth back even further as Bob Bradley slid his glasses halfway down his nose and searched his score sheet. Her face froze, though, when Bob announced that the High in Trial dog was Rhonda Lake's Golden Retriever, Eleanor.

Rhonda had given the sweet young Golden to her husband of thirty-two years Christmas before last, barely a week before a drunk driver made Rhonda a widow. For a time, Rhonda was paralyzed by grief, but training and loving Eleanor helped her focus on life and the living again. The whooping and clapping from the spectators who knew the story announced how thrilled nearly everyone was for her.

Everyone, it seemed, except for poor Suzette, knocked out of High in Trial by a rank beginner and half a point. I heard someone behind me stage whisper, "Ooh, she didn't see that coming. Got rid of Abigail and still got whupped."

I was turning toward the voice when Tom diverted me. "Will we see you tomorrow?" He grinned at me, and I surprised myself by wishing I'd put on some makeup. I couldn't seem to find my tongue, so I nodded, then watched him and Drake walk away, not sure whether that tingle under my waistband was disappointment or relief that he was leaving.

It took two trips to get Jay and all my stuff back to my van so I could get back to the calf barn. Pip was stretched out on his back, legs akimbo and neck bent around the corner of his crate, but he flipped himself over and gave a hello woof when he saw me. I unlocked the crate and fastened the leash to his collar. As I shut the crate door, the big fuschia and yellow tote bag caught my eye, and I decided to take it home and run the container with the smelly spread through the dishwasher. No point letting it turn green and fuzzy, a metamorphosis known to occur distressingly often in my refrigerator.

Tom's smile stretched bigger than life across the screen of my memory as I loaded Pip and the tote bag into my van, but the soundtrack in my mind didn't match the picture. All I could hear was, *got rid of Abigail and still got whupped.*

8

My class was first in the ring at 8:30 Sunday morning, so I was back at the fairgrounds early. Pip was enthusiastically sucking cheese out of a hollow sterile bone when I snapped the padlock onto his crate in the calf barn. Then I got Jay and a chair from my van and arrived at the obedience ring in time to warm up and watch one performance before I took my customary three deep breaths and we stepped into the ring.

We got through all the individual exercises in good shape. Jay's heeling wasn't perfect, but I've seen uglier. He kept all four feet planted for the stand for examination, letting the judge's hand touch his head, shoulders, and croup as I stood six feet away and watched. And his recall was snappy, although he forgot to sit in front of me and circled behind me into heel position a little ahead of schedule, losing a couple of points. Unlike Abigail and Suzette and other stellar handlers who strive for perfect 200s, I consider a passing score to be good enough.

We were on the home stretch, two and a half minutes into the three-minute down-stay, when a baby started to cry somewhere off to my left. Jay works with kids in the Allen County Public Library's Paws to Read Program, and unhappy children distress him. He stood and turned toward the sound, then looked over his shoulder at me, turned again, lay back down, and let out a long sigh as he rested his chin on his crossed paws and apologized to me with loving brown eyes. I longed to touch him, and to tell him that there was always the next trial, and did just that as soon as the judge sent us back to our dogs. Compassion outranks competitiveness in my book.

Connie Stoppenhagen stopped by to see how I'd done. She looked spectacular as ever, her pale lime jacket setting off her strawberry-blonde coloring to full advantage. She was helping me squeeze my folded chair into its canvas bag when I asked, "Do you know who that woman is with the crayon-red hair?"

Connie gave the chair a final shake and turned to find the object of my curiosity. "Oh, her. Francine something. She's Pip's breeder. Abigail introduced us last year."

"I saw her in the barn yesterday, looking at Pip. I guess that explains why." I thought about Francine's startled reaction to my arrival. "It was kind of odd, though. She had a leash in her hand, and took off when I showed up. I padlocked Pip's crate after I saw her there."

Connie leaned toward me and lowered her voice. "*She's* kind of odd. Abigail seemed to get on with her okay, but she's, I dunno, cold. Sneaky." Connie adjusted the rubber band holding her entry numbers on her arm and continued. "Peterson, that's it. Francine Peterson. I've heard she's very competitive, and hard on her dogs if they don't do well." She looked at something behind me and raised her chin as if to point. "You have company. Call me later."

"Leaving already?" Tom and Drake had come up behind me, and that unsettling flutter went off inside me again when I heard Tom's voice. I was beginning to get tired of myself.

"Yep. We're done. Jay broke the down stay, so we NQ'd." Meaning we had earned a non-qualifying score.

"I'm sorry." He signaled Drake to lie down. When he smiled at me, the tanned skin around Tom's eyes crinkled into happy lines. "Are you sure you won't hang around for awhile? We could grab a bite to eat."

I swear, I got my tang toungled and started to stutter. "I, uh, . . ." *Get a grip, woman!* "I'd love to, but I promised to shoot a friend's kids this afternoon."

Tom's eyes sparkled. "Is that legal?"

I smiled. "It is when you use a camera."

"Ah, so you're a wildlife photographer."

I could fall for this guy if I wasn't careful. Nice rear view and a sense of humor to boot. He went on. "I should have Drake's portrait taken." He bent toward his dog, and Drake squinted his eyes and shoved his glossy black head into his best friend's hand. "We'll have to set something up. If you're willing, of course."

That goofy tingle somewhere south of my belly button cried *ready, willing, and able, and I could even take some pictures,* but I kept my mouth in line and mumbled what passed for assent. Then I bade him farewell and took my dog, my blushing face, and my dirty mind to my van. From there I set off to get Pip and the Dorns' belongings from the calf barn. Since the place had been thoroughly cleaned after the baby bovines left the 4-H fair the previous summer, I never expected to step in deep doodoo.

9

When I got to the calf barn to collect Pip and the Dorns' equipment after my class on Sunday, show chair Tony Balthazar was talking to a guy in rumpled tan chinos and coffee-stained shirt. The knot of his tie was tipsy and the day's growth of whiskers so fashionable with some actors these days just wasn't working for him. He was scribbling in a little notebook as he talked to Tony, but when I reached for Pip's crate he started toward me. "Hey! Whaddya think you're doing?" Tony tagged along, worry lines etched into his face. Tony must have inherited his chronically wrinkled brow from his wife's Pugs.

I was about to reply when Giselle Swann huffed into the building. "I'll take Greg's things home with me!" she wheezed. In contrast to her lithesome name, Giselle was about five-foot-one whichever way you measured. She was fond of stretch pants a size too small and three shades too bright, and huge tent tops with ruffles or fringes. Her hair always had that not-quite-clean lankness of a day too long between shampoos, and she peeped furtively from under brown bangs that straggled like spider legs over her eyebrows and into her lashes. I'm not exactly svelte and stylish myself, but Giselle takes frump to a whole new level.

" 'Fraid not." Scribble Man shoved the notebook and pen into his pants pocket. Giselle narrowed her eyes at him and twisted the fringe of her day-glo yellow poncho into tight little wads, and Scribbles hooked his thumbs into his front belt loops as he rocked on the balls of his feet. "I can't authorize release of this property to either one of you."

I'd had enough. "Excuse me, but who *are* you and how is this dog your business?"

He parried, and upped the volume. "And you are?"

"Wondering who *you* are and why you're yelling at me." I was also trying to ignore the indigo stain that was expanding with astonishing speed over his pants pocket.

"Detective Homer Hutchinson. Call me Hutch." *As in Starsky and?* Janet Demon whispered into my left ear, meaning David Soul, the first Hutch, not the recent what's-his-name remake. *In his wildest dreams!* Her angelic counterpart cautioned, *Shhh. He's a boob, but he's probably armed.*

"Detective Hutchinson, this 'property,' as you call him, is a living, breathing dog. You can't just put him on a shelf somewhere until you're ready to deal with him."

"And your name . . ." He reached into his pocket. "Aw, shit!" He shuffled backward, gaping at the pen, notebook, and hand he'd withdrawn from his pants. All three glistened dark blue. He pinched the pen between the thumb and index finger of his other hand and threw it into the aisle of the barn.

Giselle clasped her hands to her breast, and Tony wove from foot to foot and coughed. I was rather proud of my self-control when I asked, with barely a snicker, "Who *can* authorize release of the dog?" I wasn't leaving Pip with the cops, and I wasn't leaving him with Giselle. She has enough trouble managing her own teensy dog. I don't know what she'd do with a bundle of Border Collie energy.

"I can," said a voice from behind me. "Detective Jo Stevens. What can I do for you?"

Jo Stevens was about my height, 5'4", but a good forty pounds lighter at maybe 115 dripping wet. She was also twenty or so years younger. Her hair was brown, like my own, but unlike mine, her short do was tidy. She probably doesn't have to fend off gray with monthly touch-ups, either. She wore navy slacks and a white broadcloth shirt, the cuffs folded neatly over the sleeve hems of a fine-gauge navy cardigan and hitched toward her elbows, baring strong, tan forearms. Her badge hung from a black cord around her neck, and a holster bulged against her right hip. I knew in a heartbeat that in a dicey situation, I'd want her on my side.

Detective Stevens glanced at her colleague, a twitch playing along her lip. "Go clean up, Hutchinson." Scribble Man shuffled off, muttering something about brand new pants and dangling his inky hand and notebook out to his right to dry.

I introduced myself and explained about Pip. Giselle gave her name as well, and insisted again that she could and should take everything with her.

Detective Stevens pulled a cell phone from a black leather holster and hit the speed dial. "Hold on," she nodded at me, and walked away a few steps. Giselle schlumped over to her grooming table, the one bearing the Maltese I'd chatted with earlier, and lifted the crate and captive dog onto the floor. Still puffing, she began packing up the grooming table and other stuff scattered around her setup.

I stepped closer to Tony Balthazar. "What's going on?"

Tony dabbed about a quart of sweat from his forehead with a wrinkled hanky, then wadded it up and stuck it back in his pocket. He looked like he needed to get back to sitting on his golf cart. "I don't know. They didn't really say. I guess they need to be sure nobody steals anything." He cast a quick glance over his shoulder at the detectives, and lowered his voice to a near whisper. "I don't like having all these cops around. It doesn't look good."

And having someone drop dead at a dog show does? "No one knows they're cops, Tony."

Before I could ask any more questions, Detective Stevens rejoined us. "Ms. MacPhail, my lieutenant checked with Mr. Dorn. You can take the dog with you."

Giselle piped up, "Did you tell him I could take the dog?"

"Yes, ma'am. He said Ms. MacPhail should take the dog." Giselle scrunched up her crimson face but didn't say anything more, and the detective turned back to me.

59

"I'll need your name, address, and telephone number." I fished a creased business card out of my jacket pocket, smoothed it as best I could, and handed it over. She jotted something on the card, slipped it into a notebook she carried in her breast pocket, and handed me her own card. "Okay, Ms. MacPhail, you can take the dog, but nothing else. We need to hold the decea . . . , uh, Ms. Dorn's property until cause of death is determined." Her face softened. "And I'm sorry for your loss."

That took me by surprise. I hadn't thought of Abigail's death as a personal loss, but realized that it was in an odd way.

Stevens continued. "Don't touch anything as you get the dog out."

I thought about that for a moment. "Nobody touched her, you know. She just sort of fell over." She had an unwavering gaze that undoubtedly served her well in her line of work. It was all I could do not to confess to my one flirtation with larceny, nicking that Milky Way from the Waynedale Pharmacy when I was eleven. Instead, I squatted next to Pip's crate and opened the door. Forty pounds of Border Collie bowled me over and straddled me as I lay on my back in the dirt, whole body wagging and tongue slurping at my face. By the time I got him off me, stood up, and brushed some of the dirt from my backside, I felt a whole lot better.

Detective Stevens laughed and started to walk away, but turned back, glancing quickly at Giselle and then at me. "Ms. MacPhail, don't let anyone else have that dog without my go-ahead."

I was halfway home when Detective Stevens' directive to "take the dog, but nothing else" echoed in my head, and I pictured Abigail's tote bag resting in my living room, and her plastic food container, now spiffy clean and drying in my dishwasher.

10

I whacked the snooze button on my alarm clock a few too many times Monday morning and had to hustle my bustle to feed Jay and Pip and Leo, my cat, load my equipment, and get to my 8:30 appointment. I wasn't sure what to expect other than one litter of Cocker Spaniel puppies and another litter of "people puppies" — not a litter, just twins, and really, I like kids, but at this point in my life I'm glad I don't have to deal with diapers. The backyard and litter-box offer poop aplenty, thank you very much.

The news was playing on NIPR — Northeast Indiana Public Radio — and I listened through three lights as I waited to turn left onto Coliseum from North Anthony. "Abigail Dorn, 37, heir to the Aunt Ellie bakeries, died Saturday. She was competing in a dog show at the Allen County Fairgrounds when she collapsed. Cause of death has not been determined."

I sipped my V8 Splash and thought about that. *How could a healthy young woman who was, as I recalled, a bit of a health and fitness nut, simply drop dead? On the other hand, who would kill Abigail, and why? I know she wasn't exactly warm and fuzzy, but . . .* A honk from the SUV threatening to caress my rear bumper brought me back to earth and I turned the radio off so I could think and drive. The human passions aroused by canine competition could inspire murderous fantasies, but had someone really followed through? Or was I watching too many *Law and Order* reruns?

Sylvia Eckhorn and her buff and white Cocker Spaniel, Tippy, answered their door. Sylvia was barefoot, decked out in gray leggings with a hole in the left knee and a once-pink sweatshirt, food and what I hoped was just baby slobber arrayed across the front. She obviously hadn't found a comb before she captured the bulk of her frizzy blonde hair in a clip. Tippy was in better shape, grinning and wriggling her well-groomed fanny at me. From the back of the house I could hear a shrieking kid and barking puppies, and a human male asking if his lunch was packed. "Janet!" Sylvia grinned at me. "You're on time! I should've known you would be."

First the dog show, now the photo shoot — two days in a row, and look where punctuality got me. I decided not to read that time management book that lurked somewhere in the pile on my coffee table. Better to just take it back to the library and pay the fine. "How 'bout I unload my equipment and you take care of what you need to do?" Sylvia looked relieved at my suggestion. "Just show me where we're going to do this."

"Oh, you're the best! Thanks! Right in there." She waved a damp hand toward a room to the right of the front foyer and disappeared down the hall to the kitchen.

A couple of trips later I had my camera, lights, and a few props unloaded. My cell phone vibrated in my pocket, but I didn't answer. I checked the light in various parts of the room and decided on a spot opposite the front window. Sylvia's grooming table was set up there, so I moved it to the side of the room where several crates were stacked. In a normal person's home, this would be the living room. For Sylvia, it was the dog room. Half the people I know decorate this way — Modern Canine.

Tippy checked everything I carried in, then trotted back to the kitchen. I took advantage of the lull to pull my phone out and check the message. "Ms. MacPhail, this is Detective Jo Stevens. Call me." I felt a twinge of concern as Abigail's totebag and food container popped into my head again, but quickly decided the call had to be about releasing Pip to Greg, and that my return call could wait until I finished with Sylvia's crew.

I settled into a well-worn armchair, the room's only furniture meant for people other than a bookcase stuffed with dog books and magazines. I picked up an old copy of *Dogs in Review* from a pile by the chair and leafed through it, my photographer's eye taking in the stunning photos of top-ranked dogs and rising stars while my conscious thoughts frolicked elsewhere. Abigail couldn't really have been murdered, could she? Now that the thought had taken root, it wrapped its tendrils around my mind. But I saw Abigail go down, and no one was anywhere near her. She warmed her dog up before the class, and then was in the ring . . . How? And why? And most of all, *who would do such a thing?* There had to be another explanation.

Sylvia bounced into the room, bounce bounce bouncing a tiny replica of herself on each hip and singing a ditty about love and family and kisses. She was altogether too cheerful for this time of morning.

All three Eckhorn women had round faces with polished-apple cheeks, cheery baby blues, slightly too-high foreheads, and kewpie-doll mouths, all framed by swirling layers of frizzy curls that gathered the morning light into golden halos. They bounced to a stop, and all three started to laugh. I couldn't help but join them.

"Look, girls! Auntie Janet has come to take your pictures! Won't that be fun?" One of the girls smiled at me and giggled. The other blew spit bubbles.

"Man, Sylvia, it seems like only yesterday that you were showing Tippy with that big belly in front of you. How old are they now?"

"Ten months on Saturday. Amazing, huh?" She grinned. "Okay, then, I'll get them dressed for the photos. Do you want to play with the puppies while I do that? They're in the kitchen."

Now I ask you, who in her right mind would not want to play with seven-week-old puppies?

Sylvia's husband, whose name escaped me, waved a slice of toast at me as he ducked out the service door into the garage. A television on the counter explained how I could have mildew-free bath tiles with practically no effort on my part and a greasy plate by the sink alluded to the mapley bacon scent that lingered in the kitchen.

The Eckhorns' breakfast nook was temporarily modified into a puppy nursery, and five of the cutest pups ever whelped wagged their nubby little tails at me while Tippy sat beside the pen, grinning and panting with maternal satisfaction.

"Nice job, Tippy!" I scratched behind the happy spaniel's ear, and reached for one of the pups, a buff and white with a lozenge, or dot, smack between the ears. I peeked underneath. "What a handsome little man!" Tippy put her front paws on my knees and sniffed her son's behind. I nudged her off before she made him pee or worse, then pressed my nose against the side of the puppy's head and inhaled the rich, warm, clean-puppy scent of musky love with a trace of milk. I held him a few inches from my face and we gazed into each other's eyes, his big round brown ones bringing to mind an ancient Joan Baez song about a stranger whose "dark eyes melted my soul down."

I was settling him back into the puppy pen when the news came on. The lead story was Abigail's death. A photo of Abigail that had to be twenty years old filled the screen as the announcer gave essentially the same story I'd heard on the radio earlier. Except for the punch line, delivered by an oh-so-sincere young reporter who spoke on camera in front of the Fort Wayne City-County Building. "Police decline to comment on the cause of Ms. Dorn's death, but a source in the department confirms that detectives are investigating a person of interest."

Detective Stevens' message echoed in my head as a summons, and the presence of Abigail's tote bag in my house took on gargantuan proportions. I had removed evidence from the scene of a crime and washed it away in my dishwasher. An irrational but ominous chill curled around my heart.

11

Sylvia saved me from my thoughts. She bounced back into the room with the girls, bedecked now in frilly pink dresses, white lacy anklets, and shiny black Mary Janes. Big floppy pink satin hair bows completed the look. It was time to do some work, and anyway, I hadn't done anything wrong. At least not on purpose. I shoved my fears to the back of my mind.

Sylvia wanted portraits of each of the girls and of the two together as well as pictures of puppies and of puppies and kids. She wisely suggested we start with the girls one at a time, since the more players we put in the picture, the more we set ourselves up for chaos and mess.

"Hang on, I have a prop that's perfect!" Sylvia plopped the girls onto the carpet and ducked into a room down the hall. She reemerged, a white wicker chair with a rose-chintz seat cushion in one hand and a white

Boyd's bear with a pink hat in the other. I set up the chair and my lights and grabbed my camera. As I tell my photo class students, when photographing kids and pets, be ready and be quick.

"We'll do Margaret first." Sylvia settled the first baby into the chair and placed the bear in her arms. "Meggie, what're you doing?" she chirped, just as baby number two howled in outrage. I let Sylvia deal with the screeching child on the floor and started shooting the one in the chair. Meggie gave me a perfectly timed series of sweet-baby poses, smiling at me, smiling at the bear, smiling at her mom and unhappy sibling, kissing the bear's nose, patting the bear's cheek with her dimpled pink hand, hugging the bear.

"Sylvia, this kid has a future in modeling."

Sylvia dodged a baby fist. "Meg's a good baby. She always seems to know what to do to please us." She cooed at her sweet daughter as she twisted her bottom lip free of the other one's grasping little fingers. "Did you hear about Abigail Dorn?"

I told her what I knew.

"Oh, you were there." She gazed at me in wide-eyed sympathy. "Suzette called me last night. She said Fly is in the lead now —

70

number one Border Collie in obedience. Fly and Pip have been neck-and-neck all year, you know."

"I knew they were close."

"Suzette's thrilled, of course. She and Fly have worked their tails off, and having Abigail and Pip to compete with all the time was tough." Her eyes widened. "Oh! I don't mean she's thrilled that Abigail is dead!"

"No, of course not." *Ha!* Janet Demon elbowed my left ear.

"No, really, she's very upset." *But not too upset to relish her dog's rise in the rankings.* "Abigail wasn't well liked, though." Sylvia sucked her lower lip into her mouth and a tiny wrinkle formed between her eyebrows. "Lots of people couldn't stand her."

"She didn't offer a lot to like, did she?"

"Oh, I think she was kind of insecure. People who demean the good things in other people's lives usually are." I waited while she seemed to consider something. "Abigail made all sorts of nasty comments to me when I got pregnant."

"Really?"

"Really. But I understood."

"You did?"

"Oh, sure. You know, she and Greg tried for years to get pregnant. Spent a fortune on doctors and tests. You probably didn't know them then, but they lived next door to my folks, and Abigail talked to my mom all the time." She pushed a rebellious curl back behind her ear and shifted topics. "She was a great dog trainer, but not very humble. A bad winner, you know what I mean?"

"She did have a way of ticking people off."

"Worse, she hurt people, and sometimes it seemed like she did it on purpose." Sylvia hesitated before saying softly, as if to herself, "But that doesn't mean . . ." She let the thought trail away. "I'm sorry. Better to remember the good."

"Well, her dog is certainly well behaved." I couldn't think of anything else that endeared Abigail to me.

"Oh, yes, she was devoted to her dogs. And she donated a lot of time and money to Border Collie rescue and health research."

"Oh?"

Sylvia nodded. "She didn't talk about it. But several BC rescuers have told me about her donations. She was very generous." She settled a sky-blue gaze on me. "She was also very kind to me when my parents died. I was off at nursing school when my dad crashed his plane."

"Oh, God, I'm so sorry. How awful." I

didn't know what else to say, and felt my eyes go hot and moist with that all-encompassing sense of loss I'd felt when Abigail was taken away in the ambulance. "I guess there's a lot most of us don't know about each other, even after years and years."

Sylvia broke the silence that followed. "Ready for Elizabeth?"

Somehow, it came out more like a warning than a question, and my well-honed photographer and dog-trainer instincts screamed *uh-oh* in my head. I lifted Meg from the chair, put her on the floor, and gave her a keep-the-baby-busy gadget with knobs and flaps and noisemakers.

Unlike her sister, Elizabeth evidently was not interested in modeling. She bawled and stiffened her little legs as Sylvia tried to position her in the chair. She flailed her arms, catching Sylvia a good one in the eye. When her little fanny finally hit the chair cushion, she glared at Sylvia, then at me, then at her happy sister on the floor. Sylvia tried to use the lull to our advantage, placing the bear in the kid's arms and cooing, "Oh, Lizzie, look at the nice lady bear!" Lizzie glared at the bear, grabbed its ear in one chubby little mitt, and heaved it straight up. The term "evil twin" was becoming more meaningful by the second.

We spent another ten minutes trying to get the little darling to cooperate, but by the time she started to wind down her face was blotchy and streaked with tears and snot, and the pink bow hung limp and lopsided from her wildly willful yellow mop.

"Maybe you could buy several poses of Meg and pretend some of them are Elizabeth?" I wished out loud.

"That'll work." Sylvia scooped the girls up and disappeared down the hallway, calling over her shoulder, "There's coffee if you want some. I'll be back in a minute." I poured myself a wonderfully hazelnutty cup of coffee, gazed at the snoozing puppies, and wondered if Sylvia was crating that kid with a chew bone to gnaw on.

The puppies behaved themselves, probably because they had just stuffed their tummies and were ready for naps. I got individual and group shots, and a few more of the puppies with Tippy, whose nub never stopped wagging. Sylvia retrieved good twin Meg, who giggled with delight as she held each puppy in turn on her lap for some lethally cute kid-and-puppy pictures. She was starting to nod off by the time Sylvia snuggled her into the chair with Tippy for the final shots.

By ten o'clock I had packed all my equipment and pointed my van toward home, thinking that in the future when I have regrets about not having kids, I could always spend a half-hour with Lizzie for therapy.

12

I try not to swear too often, but was sorely challenged as I stood outside the front door of my house fishing for my keys. They were somewhere in my purse, trapped under a bag of pizza-flavored treats (for dogs), my wallet, a half bag of dark-chocolate-covered raisins (for me), Jay's pin brush (which I sometimes borrow since I never seem to have a comb of my own, and hey, I bought it at Sally's Beauty Supplies), assorted scraps and wads of paper, and an 18-inch plaited kangaroo-leather leash that cost more than a gourmet dinner but is soft and pliant as cashmere. Finally I freed the keys and opened my front door.

"Okay! okay! Settle down!" Jay goes through nearly every canine greeting maneuver in the book whenever I come home. He knows better than to jump on me, at least not when my hands are full, but it's still a chore getting by him and his Joyful

Demeanor.

I dropped my purse by the door, let Pip out of his crate, and ushered both dogs out the back door. There was no place to crash, so I shoved a pile of *Nature Photography, Dog World, Front and Finish,* and assorted other magazines, credit card offers, and ad flyers off the couch. I pushed the one decorative pillow I own, a tapestry number with a blue merle Aussie on it, into the corner, and plopped myself down. Despite my mother's lifelong instruction to the contrary, I propped my feet on a corner of the coffee table and scanned the library books scattered there to remind me of my latest self-improvement project. All eight volumes would teach me — so the jacket blurbs claimed — to stop procrastinating and get organized. If I ever got around to reading them. Self-help guru Cheryl Richardson, whose books I actually had read at my friend Gina's suggestion, might say the expired due dates were "a clue from the universe" that I wasn't ready to stop procrastinating. Maybe later.

I was thinking about returning Detective Stevens' call when Leo sauntered in. He hopped from the floor into a crouch on my torso with one silky motion, and began kneading the flesh over my sternum, flexing the toes and claws of one front paw, then the other, through my sweatshirt and, just barely, into the skin beneath. He purred brilliantly and gave me a cat-love look through half-closed amber eyes. I stroked his satiny orange felineness from crown to tail, and the bustling world slid away. Leo tucked his paws under his chest and settled into me, and we both hovered somewhere near sleep until a barkfest broke out in the yard a half hour later when Jay and Pip announced the arrival of the mail truck. I got Leo off my lap and myself off the couch and to the front door just as the carrier reached for the bell. Not my regular guy, but a grumpy substitute who lost no time on small talk before launching into a rant about the car parked in front of my mailbox. "If I didn't have this for you to sign for, I wouldn't have delivered today 'cause of that car."

"What car?" The street in front of my mailbox was clear.

Although Grumpy looked toward the mailbox, he didn't seem to notice that no car sat in front of it. "Don't see many Yugos these days. All fell to bits, more'n likely. Foreign made, ya know."

I signed for the delivery, waved at old Mr. Hostetler across the street, and went inside, wondering if anyone I knew drove a Yugo, assuming there had been one by my mailbox. I went to the kitchen and let the dogs in, grabbed a cold blueberry bagel and a diet root beer from the fridge, sat down at the kitchen table, and took a quick glance at the *Parade* magazine from the day before. I'm not a news fiend, but I do like to keep up with Parade's version of celebrity gossip, Marilyn Dos Savant's latest mind bender, and Howard Huge's weekly exploits. I have my priorities.

The bagel was rubbery so I divvied it up between Jay and Pip, and then got to work. When I tell people I'm a freelance photographer, they seem to think I lead a glamorous life, bounding off to exotic locales and tramping around with my cameras and native bearers, striking all sorts of fascinating poses as I set up the perfect shot. It's true, I do get to travel a bit, set my own hours mostly, and carry mountains of stuff along. I also spend a lot of time opening envelopes, processing orders, e-mailing proofs and mailing prints, contacting publishers, mailing photo CDs, e-mailing whatever, and filing, filing, filing. If I made more money, I'd hire an assistant. As things stand, I'm all I can afford. The benefit of doing it all myself is that I'm reminded that I am actually working when I photograph beautiful things.

I polished off my soda, piled the outgoing mail on a corner of the table, popped the empty can into the recycling basket in the pantry, and looked out the window into my backyard. The dogs were stationed at the back door, eyes wide and gleaming. Pip's tail waved, and Jay's entire rear end wriggled. "Okay, boys, let's go play ball." They started shouldering each other for first dibs on barging out the door, so I made them sit and stay while I opened it. They whined and squirmed, but both held the stay until I released them. It makes for a much safer egress, since bouncing down the back steps on my butt hurts a lot more than I remember things hurting thirty years ago.

An assortment of dog toys obscured a lounge chair on the patio. I'd put them there on Friday to save them from the lawnmower and there they had stayed while we ran back and forth to the show all weekend. I found Jay's favorite Jolly Ball, a thick blue bouncy sphere about the size of a soccer ball with a handle molded of the same thick rubbery material. I also pulled a reasonably ungummed-up tennis ball from the pile for Pip. I pitched the blue ball toward the back of the yard with my right hand, and the tennis ball wildly to the left. Ambidextrous I am not. But dogs don't care how goofy you are as long as they're having fun, which these two were. Pure, unadulterated, ball-crazed fun. Perfect role models, if we only pay attention.

When the edge was off the canine energy, I abandoned my pitching station, left the boys to their own devices with balls and a tug rope, and surveyed the modest flower garden at the back of my lot. Buds on my bearded irises and peonies were beginning to split open, and the mounding foliage of coreopsis, coneflower, black-eyed susans, and catmint made colorful promises. The daffodils were finished and the lilacs beginning to droop, but full-blown late-blooming tulips glowed like watercolors and the edge of the bed smiled with violas. With all due respect to Emily Dickinson and the things with feathers, I think hope is the thing with petals that blooms within our hearts.

Poofy white clouds lazed across the warm blue sky, and the thermometer on the back fence read seventy-five degrees. June would arrive in less than a week, bringing warmer temperatures, and I couldn't help wondering what else might heat up in the wake of Abigail's death.

13

"Janet!" My neighbor, Goldie, waved across the fence at me. "Whatcha up to?" Goldie was grinning, but pale violet half-moons under her eyes accentuated the pallor that had me worried about her the past few weeks.

"Just enjoying this glorious spring day." That's the thing about northern Indiana — spring is fickle. She grants us only a few balmy days, making the move from bone-cold, windy, rainy post-winter to sticky-hot summer in one nimble leap. Days with reasonable temperatures, soft breezes, and no rain arrive not in packs, but as lonely strays, and you'd better enjoy them while you can.

"How's the garden?" I asked.

Goldie's garden. I've never seen anything like it that wasn't sustained by an army of paid laborers. Grass walkways wind from one plot to another with such craft that the small yard expands in your mind until you think you've walked through acres of flowers rather than a simple suburban lot. And if ever a person's yard reflected the person herself, Goldie's does. The exuberant, joyful profusion of colors mingle in unexpected combinations that, to a casual eye, might suggest chaos. But under it all is a rich and deep foundation built on discipline and strength, nurture and ruthless culling.

"My babies are starting to peek from under their earthy cover!" She laughed from deep inside and threw her head back so that the wide rim of her straw hat hit the top of her spine and popped from her head, revealing thick braids crossed and fastened into a crown of silver. Little stray hairs sparkled around it in the warm light. She caught her hat and tapped it back in place. "Ain't I poetic?"

"You're a wonder, Ms. Golden Sunshine." That's her name. Honest. Goldie has several years on me, so she was old enough in the sixties to be fully immersed in the counter culture. Née Rachel Golden, she went off to San Francisco in '68 with flowers in her hair, and called herself "Sunshine" for a while. When she went back to school, she liked hearing her professors call "Golden, Sunshine," so she went to court and reversed the names for real. She's been Goldie Sunshine ever since.

Goldie had seen an article in the paper about Abigail's death. "They didn't say what she died of. Do you know?"

"No, I haven't heard anything except rumors and speculation."

"A shame, a young woman like that." A dark cloud seemed to pass through Goldie's expression, but it was gone before I was sure I saw it.

"I know. And the more I think about it, the less sense it makes."

Leo hopped up onto the fence post, and Goldie bent toward him for a nose bump and nodded. "It's hard to make sense of a friend's death."

"We weren't friends. Actually, I didn't like Abigail very much. Didn't know her well, never really wanted to. But I had the impression she took good care of herself. How could she just fall over and die like that?"

"So, then, what? You think someone bumped her off?"

"Bumped her off? You watching B movies again?" As if to vouch for the complexity of the human spirit, Goldie, passionately and loudly anti-war and pro-human-rights, loves murder and mayhem on the silver screen and has a huge collection of murder mystery tapes and DVDs. I returned to her question. "I don't know. It's possible, isn't it? Maybe someone poisoned her."

Goldie raised her eyebrows. "Who's been watching B movies?" She adjusted a pin in her braid and grew thoughtful. "It happens, Janet. Sometimes people just die. Death doesn't have to make sense."

I met Goldie's gaze and registered again that the circles underneath her eyes were darker than usual, and the sharp blades of her cheek bones more prominent, so I asked again, as I'd asked just about every day for a month or so, "Are you okay?"

She let out an odd little sound that might have passed for a laugh if I hadn't known her so well. "Oh, yes, just didn't get much sleep last night. Stayed up late baking bread."

Meaning she wasn't going to tell me what was wrong. But we've been friends long enough that I knew there was something. I'd have to try again later, or just wait until she volunteered the information. For the moment, I changed the subject. "So what's new for this year in the garden?"

"Witch's garden." She gestured toward a newly planted circle of earth in the middle of her yard.

"Witch's garden?"

"Yep. Really another herb garden, but the ones used in witchcraft through the centuries. You know, belladonna, wolfsbane, that sort of thing. 'Double, double, toil and trouble . . .' " She let out a silly cackle. "Maybe I could stock the garden with newts and bats." Leo hopped up onto the fence post, and Goldie slipped a hand along the length of his body. "See? I even have a familiar."

"Long as you don't use the stuff."

"Nah! I'm no witch, 'though I do like the Wiccan Rule of Three. See here — I've painted it onto a sign for the gate to the witch's garden." She pointed to a colorful wooden sign, rimmed with a garland of greenery and a smattering of raspberry foxgloves and some blue blossoms I couldn't identify. Gothic letters spelled out: *Whatsoever ye shall do for good or evil shall come back to you three-fold.*

I know a few witches who would do well to learn that rule.

14

Monday night Jay and I went to Dog Dayz. It's the biggest dog training school in northeast Indiana, and the busiest. I slipped my Caravan into the last available parking space, and decided when I walked into the building that every member was there with at least two dogs. News travels fast in the dog world, and the place was abuzz with rumors, facts, gossip, and questions about the weekend's events. People seemed to think I had the inside scoop since I'd taken Abigail's dog home, but honestly, Pip hadn't told me a thing except that he enjoyed his dinner and really liked fetching tennis balls.

Marietta Santini, owner and drill sergeant, called the group practice ring to order at seven o'clock. In the adjacent ring, Suzette Anderson was working Fly on hand signals, and several other people I knew only by their faces were working on various commands. "Dogs on the inside! Ready! Forward!" Marietta's upbringing as an army brat had not gone for naught. "About turn! Halt! Forward!" I was waiting for the night her smoke-graveled drawl ordered us to "present leashes!" I have to say, though, that for all her brusqueness with people, I've never, ever seen her be rough on a dog.

She ran us through a snappy routine of forwards, fasts, slows, about turns, halts, and circles for ten minutes, then had us line up along one wall. "Sit your dogs! Leave!" A chorus of "Stay" sounded down the line, and we humans walked away. A few green dogs needed their people close and attached by the umbilical cord known as a leash. The rest of us scattered higgledy-piggledy ten, twenty, thirty feet from the line of canines.

"Before we get to other announcements and brags from the weekend, I'm sure many of you have already heard the sad news about Abigail Dorn. You probably remember Abigail working her Border Collie, Pip, here. For those of you who haven't heard, Abigail died over the weekend."

A murmur ran through the group, and a short, plump woman with a face and hairdo much like those of her Shar-pei, wheezed, "That's so sad! What happened?"

I didn't hear Marietta's explanation. Tom Saunders and Drake had walked in and I was busy thinking, *Now, that's my kind of male. Strong, graceful in a muscled masculine way, with — what do they say in those romances? — raven hair edged with a hint of silver.* Tom wasn't bad, either.

Right on cue, Tom shot me one of his grins. He sat Drake between Jay and a Golden Retriever, told him to stay, and walked across the ring to stand next to me. My cheeks felt warm, and a few other parts heated up as I became reacquainted with hormones I'd forgotten I had.

My brain wasn't entirely disabled, though, and I heard someone half whisper, "No great loss if you ask me" and another someone reply, "No kidding. Guess her karma finally caught up with her dogma."

I also managed to register that Marietta was calling for a moment of silence. People training in the individual practice ring stopped what they were doing, and Suzette and Fly strolled over to the wooden fence between the two rings. Everything got very quiet for about five seconds, and then Fly started to bark.

"Now, Fly, stop that!" Suzette addressed the yapping dog in a stage whisper. *Yip yip yip,* Fly replied. I watched the fingers of Suzette's right hand ball into a fist, pop open, and spread, over and over. Every time they opened, Fly yipped. And I happen to know that Suzette's command to shut the dog up is *Quiet,* not *Now, Fly, stop that.*

Tom waggled his eyebrows, Groucho style. "Subtle."

I was about to answer when Marietta congratulated Jay and me on our success on Saturday, and went on to acknowledge other members' victories, large and small. "And the really big brag is two in one — Fly is a new Obedience Trial Champion and Utility Dog Excellent." She stopped and looked around the room. "Where in the heck are Suzette and Fly? They were here a minute ago."

She was right. Suzette was nowhere in sight.

Marietta shrugged and got us back to work for a few minutes, then lined us up for recalls. Somewhere behind me I heard snippets of conversation about the long-standing rivalry between Suzette and Abigail, but what got my attention was a breathy, "I didn't think Suzette meant it when she said she'd like to kill her."

15

Giselle Swann waddled over and took the spot behind me in line, distracting me from the accusatory gossip about Suzette and Abigail. Precious, her minuscule Maltese, watched her warily from the end of his leash, a pink bow tilting his silky white topknot to a rakish angle. I thought of asking why he wore one topknot, like a Shih-tzu, rather than the conventional two that most Maltese wear, but I was afraid she'd take that as criticism, which I knew Giselle did not appreciate, however constructive it might be. No, she would take my question as an attack on her person.

Precious. I like to think that in the community of dogs he was known as "Spike" or "Ratslayer." It might make up for the pink bow. He kept a close eye on his mistress, not so much attentive in an obedience sense as observant in the self-preservation sense. Some people say dogs don't reason, but those are people who haven't observed dogs and other animals very closely. I know the little guy had a pretty good idea of what would happen if Giselle toppled onto him. I put Jay in a down stay, and the little white fluffball came up and sniffed a greeting while Jay wriggled his rear end in reply.

Giselle peered at me from under her stringy bangs, her body listing to the left as if she were ready to duck and cover. "Hello, Janet?" It sounded more like a question than a greeting. Except for our encounters at the weekend dog show, Giselle hadn't spoken to me in months, not since our last online dust-up over a dog training issue. I couldn't help but wonder why she seemed so eager to talk to me now.

"Hi, Giselle. How are you holding up? I know you and Abigail were pretty close."

"Oh, okay. Not bad? You know, I feel pretty sad for poor Greg? But okay. You know, not too bad."

"Yeah, rough for Greg." I tried to make eye contact, but she dodged me. "Kinda rough for Abigail, too."

Giselle blinked and shuffled, hoisted Precious, and enveloped him in her massive arms. "Oh, sure, of course? But," her voice went dreamy, "she's in a better place."

"I hope they have obedience trials there. I

don't think Abigail would find harps and clouds all that heavenly. Anyway, I'm not sure she was quite ready to go."

Giselle shot me a look I couldn't interpret, then lowered her gaze again. "I just wanted to let you know I'll take care of Pip for Greg?" Was she asking or telling? "You don't need to bother?"

"It's no bother. I think Greg is okay with this arrangement for a few days. Besides, Pip and Jay are having fun together." She tried to sneak a sidelong look at me, but I caught her and she looked at the floor instead. "But thanks for offering."

We'd reached the head of the line and it was my turn for a recall, giving me an escape. The obedience rules say that "The dog must come directly, at a brisk trot or gallop, and sit straight, centered in front of the handler." I told my dog to stay and walked the forty feet to the other end of the ring. When I called him, Jay came running, failed to brake, hit me in the chest with his front paws, and dropped into a sit in front of me with a grin on his face. Fine with me. I'll take happy over precise any day, as long as I don't end up on my butt.

I got a bottle of water from my bag and was just swiping my sweatshirt sleeve along my mouth when I heard Tom's voice behind me. "Nice recall. Brownie points for staying on your feet." He was grinning that grin again, and my stupid knees wobbled. Then he shifted his gaze to my lovely dog. "Jay's really shaped up in the past year." He murmured something to Drake, and the big dog lay down, rested his graying chin on the cool linoleum, and closed his eyes. "I remember when you first got him."

You do?

Tom hunkered down and let Jay sniff the back of his hand, gently stroking the underside of the dog's chin with the other. "You look great now, Pal! Shows what love can do." He turned to me and winked a wicked wink.

Whoosh! Blood rushed to my face. Tom was so busy petting Jay that I doubt he noticed my reaction, and I managed to get a grip on myself and babble, "He was seventy-three pounds when I got him. His breeder had already taken ten off him. He was so fat he couldn't roll over, had no training, and was afraid of other dogs, too. Now he's fifty-four pounds and as sweet and confident as can be."

"His breeder let him get into that condition?"

"Oh, no! She sold him as a puppy. The people who bought him decided four years later they didn't want him. Thank God they brought him back to the breeder. She was furious about the shape he was in, but thankful they didn't just dump him somewhere. I saw him a couple days after she got him back, when she had me take some photos of her other dogs, and I couldn't get him out of my head. I'd just lost my old Aussie, Rowdy. It took me a month to talk her out of Jay."

"Some things are meant to be." He stood up and I found myself falling again into eyes so brown they made my mouth water. After maybe a minute, maybe a month, Tom asked, "Have you heard any news about Abigail?"

Earth to Janet. "No, nothing, except that they aren't sure what she died of."

"Not bee allergy?"

Giselle was watching us from across the ring. She stopped when she noticed me noticing her.

"Apparently not. Actually, I wondered about that when the epinephrin didn't work. It should work really quickly, as I understand it. And besides . . ."

"It should have," Tom cut me off. "But I suppose other factors could affect how well it worked. I know just enough about commercial drugs to be dangerous."

Commercial drugs, I wondered. *As opposed to what?*

16

I had Tuesday morning free, so after I fed the dogs, Leo, and myself (in that order) and pooper-scooped the litter box and the back yard, I settled into my new green Adirondack-style chair that sat outside the ring of shade from my enormous red maple. The chair is actually periwinkle blue, but it's made of recycled milk jugs, so I love it double. I wrapped my fingers loosely around my mug and inhaled the musky sweet steam of blackberry sage tea and savored the moist heat against my palm. I had the latest copy of *Nature Photography,* the membership roster from Dog Dayz, and my cell phone. Jay and Pip were playing "toss and tug" with a big knotted rope, and Leo was honing his claws on a landscape timber backed by purple and orange Jolly Joker pansies that slow-danced in the breeze.

I leafed through the magazine until 8:30, then dialed the Dorns' number and counted thirteen rings. No Greg, no "leave a message after the beep." The dogs bounded over when they saw me hang up, panting and wagging and eager to slobber on my clean sweatshirt. I blocked with a bent knee and a firm, if frantic, refrain of "Off! Off!," saving myself from drool and paw prints but slopping tea all over myself.

The dogs suddenly spun toward Goldie's yard, ears alert, Pip's fully erect and Jay's folded over about a quarter of the way from tip to base. They blasted over to the fence and shoved their black noses into the space between the pickets. Jay's short little nub directed his fanny in a wriggle, and Pip's long, lush plume swung back and forth.

"Good morning, Mr. Jay! And good morning to you, handsome boy. I'm sorry, I've forgotten your name already, but I haven't forgotten your toast!" Jay has a morning ritual of fence talk and toast with Goldie. Not a leftover morsel, mind you, but a fat slice of Goldie's home-baked flavor of the week, toasted lightly and polished with a thin gloss of jam made from one of Goldie's raspberry vines. This morning she brought two slices, neither of them for me. Maybe I should slobber and wriggle my fanny too.

Leo stopped his claw sharpening and

studied the goings-on at the lot line. He trotted over, leapt to the top of the fence and onto the ground beyond, and began meowing and rubbing against Goldie's legs. "Ah, Leo! Good morning to you. Come on, we'll get you a fix, too." I hauled myself out of my chair and walked to the fence, watching as Goldie and Leo strolled through one of the herb beds and selected a tender new sprout of catnip. Leo never helps himself to Goldie's cat-drug stash, but waits for her to serve him as is his divine right. He took the morning's tribute and trotted to a patch of lawn, where he chewed a bite of the herb, slid the top of his skull through the leaves, then his ears, neck, shoulders, and back, and began the whole sequence again.

Goldie turned to me and said, "I need to run to the co-op for some flour and stuff. Want to go?" Her face was pale in the morning light, and the dark circles I'd noticed the last couple of weeks still hunkered under her eyes. I was about to say yes, thinking I could press her about her health if I had her captive in the car, when my phone rang. A pang in my gut reminded me that I hadn't returned Detective Stevens' call. I nodded at Goldie and spoke into the receiver, expecting a summons to police headquarters.

It was Suzette. She wanted to have some pictures taken of Fly, so we set a time and I turned off the phone.

"Actually, I wanted to leave a note for Pip's owner at his house. He's not answering the phone and the machine is off. I want to be sure he has my number. We can do both."

17

I bagged a half pound each of organic rolled oats (for homemade dog biscuits, the only thing I bake) and licorice all-sorts (for me) from the bulk bins at the Three Rivers Food Co-op. I was adding up the price tags on the stuff in my cart as I rounded the end of the aisle and pulled up just short of a crash. "Oh! Tom! What a surprise!"

Tom Saunders stood in front of a display of garden seed packets. "Janet! Hey! What's up?"

"Running some errands. You? You're not working today?" I caught myself wishing for the second time in so many days that I'd taken time for a dab of makeup this morning, at least a bit of shadow and mascara. I could have changed out of my tea-stained apparel, too. *You slob,* scolded my guardian angel. *Get real,* countered the little demon. *If you're looking for a fashion plate, it ain't me, babe.* "I'm on a Monday-Wednesday-

Friday schedule this semester." I remembered then that I'd heard he was a professor, although I didn't know whether he was attached to the Purdue or Indiana University side of the joint Fort Wayne campus.

"What do you teach?"

"Anthropology."

"Oh." I could have sworn someone told me he worked with plants. "Somehow I got the idea you were in botany."

"I am, sort of." He grinned. "Ethnobotany."

Recalling his comment about commercial drugs, I would have pursued the topic, but Goldie rounded the end of the aisle, asking something about which essential oil I liked better for a spring potpourri, lilac or lily-of-the-valley. She stopped and got a tricky twinkle in her eyes when she saw Tom. I introduced them, and she offered her hand. He looked a tad startled when she held on longer than strictly polite and gazed into his eyes. Then they grinned at one another, and she let him go.

"It's great to see you, Janet." That struck me funny since he was still grinning at Goldie. "Unfortunately, I have a faculty meeting in half an hour." He and Goldie both nodded, as if they shared a secret. Then Tom turned his baby browns to me, reached out and squeezed my shoulder, making several parts of my body contract. "See you soon."

As we watched him walk to the check-out line, Goldie leaned into me and said, "Not bad!"

"Yeah, I guess." My face was heating up again. "I barely know him."

"Ha! But you'd like to!"

"Don't be silly."

"Me? Silly? You're the one who's drooling! And frankly, it's about time. They aren't all like Cheat."

"Chet." Goldie and I had played the Cheat/Chet game for years. "It has nothing to do with Chet." She was right, of course. It had everything to do with cheatin' Chet and his escapades. "I'm just not interested. I like my freedom." *And my sanity, credit rating, and bank balance, modest though it is.*

Goldie rolled her eyes and made a rude sound.

"Oh yeah?" I couldn't come up with anything intelligent for the moment. "And what, pray tell, was that business with Tom's hand?"

"Just checking."

"Checking?"

Goldie is not merely a New Age seeker of enlightenment. She's been this way since the sixties. For all I know, she was born this way. More than once. "Feeling his energy," she shrugged as she plunked both flower oils into her basket and furrowed her forehead. "I know him from somewhere." Then she grinned at me. "Hey, girlfriend, go for it!" She adjusted her glasses halfway down her nose and spun the seed display rack.

"I'm not interested in going for anything!" I glanced into Goldie's cart and did a double take. She must have had thirty bottles of vitamins and herbal concoctions. Saw palmetto. Green tea. Cat's claw. Stuff I'd never heard of. *What's up with that?*

I couldn't think of what to say, so I read the names on the seed packets she was studying. Alyssum. Bachelor's buttons. Calendula. Castor bean. "Castor bean? Aren't these poisonous?"

"Deadly."

"And they sell them?"

"Oh, my dear, lots of plants are poisonous. Castor plants are gorgeous big things. Just don't eat the seeds."

"Seems a bit casual to me."

"Oh, heavens, we're surrounded by toxic plants. Did you know that rhubarb leaves are poisonous? Tomato leaves too. Daffodil bulbs. Lily-of-the-valley. Here — foxglove — poisonous." She pointed to a packet of *Digitalis purpurea,* then another with blue flowers like those painted on the Rule of Three sign in her garden. "Monkshood too. Deadly. Used to be known as wolfsbane. Those yews in front of every other house in suburbia? All toxic. Shall I go on? And then of course there are the wild poisonous plants — jimsonweed, the hemlocks, pigweed . . ."

"Okay, okay. I get it. Remind me not to piss you off."

18

"Holy moly," said Goldie. We had just pulled up in front of the Dorns' house, one of a handful scattered around this slick new subdivision. The nearest neighbor was a block away, although not for long. Streamers of fluorescent orange tape flapped from stakes in the lot next door.

The front of the Dorns' house was all glass, taupe-tinted brick, and putty-colored woodwork. The double front door was one of those snazzy jobs with an intricate full-length pattern of clear leaded glass set into a frame of rich, luminous cherry-stained wood. The landscaping, mostly shrubs and groundcovers and saplings, was professional and neat, but lacked the joy and passion of Goldie's plot of ground. The path to the door was fancy aggregate set in concrete and hemmed on both sides by brick to match the house. It struck me as a swanky piece of impersonal architecture, but not a home to comfort those within, the expensive, hard facade of the house not unlike the face that Abigail herself had shown the world.

An engine roared somewhere nearby but out of sight, and as I stepped from the car a noxious blend of gasoline and new-mown grass surged into my nose and planted a blade of pain in my skull. I was scurrying toward the front door and trying not to inhale when a boy of about fourteen pushed a beat-up mower around the corner of the house. He waved at me through the blue fumes, mowed to about ten feet from me, and cut the engine. The silence was deafening. The boy shoved a shock of brown hair off his forehead. "Mr. Dorn isn't here right now."

"Any idea when he might be back?"

"No. Not for a while, I guess. He paid me in case he doesn't get back before I finish. He had to go to the store, for the new locks, I guess."

I guessed I'd leave a note, and the kid nodded, restarted the mower, and roared away to where the yard met a raggedy lot aglow with early yellow sweet clover. There he turned and disappeared toward the back of the lot again.

Why did Greg need new locks? According

to Connie, he and Abigail were separated. Had she changed the locks? I filed my questions away for later, finished the note, and went to the front porch. There was no storm door, so I wedged the scrap of paper into the frame around the leaded glass, hoping he'd see it there, and returned to the car.

"Speaking of toxic plants." Goldie nodded toward the ratty vacant lot next door.

"What?"

"Right there. Poison hemlock."

"As in Socrates and death by hemlock?"

"Precisely. The stuff with the purple stems. Grows all over in waste areas. When it's in bloom it's easy to mistake for wild carrot, you know, Queen Anne's Lace, or for wild parsnip. If in doubt, think 'hemlock is hairless.' Wild carrot has little hairs on the stems and leaves, hemlock doesn't. Not that you're likely to be collecting wild carrot, although it is pretty in a late summer bouquet." She spoke faster. "I remember a field near a lake, now where was that? I can't remember, but this field was like a gigantic bouquet of Queen Anne's Lace and ironweed and black-eyed Susans. Oh my, that white, purple, and yellow combination was exqui . . ."

"Shit!" I was about to turn left from Greg's street onto Rothman Road when a green car with cancerous rust patches squealed around the front of my van from the right, nearly taking my left headlight as a souvenir. I slammed on the brakes.

Goldie twisted in her seat. "Don't see many of those anymore."

"What? Idiots?" My stomach heaved from the adrenaline surge.

"Yugos. And I've seen that one before."

"Yeah?" I made myself resume breathing. "Well, I hope I never see it again."

"So you don't know whose it is?"

I glanced at her. "Why would I know tha . . . ?" The grumpy mailman shuffled into my thoughts. "Wait a minute! The mail-man said there was a Yugo parked in front of my mailbox yesterday. That's weird."

"Weirder still, it drove by three or four times while I was waiting for you back there."

19

I'd been home about half an hour when the doorbell rang. The canine welcoming committee was in the backyard, so Leo trotted to the front door and meowed at me to see who was there. He's not the most patient character in the world. I picked him up and pulled the door open.

"Ms. MacPhail. You never returned my call."

"I, uh . . ." I gestured for Detective Jo Stevens to come in. "I meant to. I've been busy."

"I have a few questions."

Like why did you tamper with evidence? I glanced at the magazines, books, videos, and unopened mail on the couch and coffee table in the living room, and suggested we talk in the kitchen. When I put Leo down, he promptly rubbed against the detective's leg, leaving a streak of short yellow hairs on her navy slacks. She bent to pick him up and settled at the kitchen table, rubbing his head. "Nice cat."

"His name is Leo. Thinks he's a lion." I picked up the carafe from the coffee maker in one hand and the teapot in the other and waggled them at her.

She asked basic getting-to-know-you questions while I set Mr. Coffee to work. I'm not particularly paranoid, but couldn't help but wonder if this was her way of putting me at ease before the interrogation, or if she was genuinely interested in my work and my furry family. I sat across the table from her, and watched her reassemble her expression as she slid Leo gently to the floor. By the time she sat up she was all business again.

"Where's your sidekick?" I asked.

"Hutchinson? He had other things to do."

Like play tiddlywinks, whispered Janet Demon. As if she knew what I was thinking, Jo added, "He's not as dopey as he acted the other day." I withheld further comment, and she got back to business. "What do you know about the circumstances of Ms. Dorn's death?"

Something twisted in my chest, but I worked at staying calm.

"I saw her fall, but I don't know anything else except what's been on the news." I studied her face, and decided she must be a heck of a poker player. "You're investigating her death?"

"Just asking a few questions."

"You don't think she died from a bee sting?"

"What do you think?"

"I don't know what to think." I didn't add that the more I learned the more confused I got. "She was in great shape and as far as I know had no other health problems. The two doses of epinephrin should have snapped her out of an allergic episode. I guess I think it makes no sense."

"Did Ms. Dorn have any enemies?"

I didn't like the direction the conversation was going, but what could it hurt Abigail now if I passed on what little I knew? If someone did kill her, maybe something I said would help the police figure out who. "I don't know about enemies. She wasn't very popular."

She pulled her beat-up little pad and a pen from her breast pocket, wrote something, then looked me in the eye, her question clear if unspoken.

I went on. "You know, there's always gossip. I've heard little snippets. Abigail was well known among dog people, and it's been a shock. Someone you know dies suddenly, people are curious. Concerned." *Nosey.*

"And what's the gist of the gossip?"

"I don't know that there is a gist. People want to know what happened. Some think Abigail died of a heart attack or a stroke." *Or meanness.*

Jo didn't seem very interested in that kind of gossip. "She had enemies?"

Enemies again. I retrieved a couple of clean mugs from the dishwasher, and poured the coffee, using the time to think. *Don't say too much, Janet. You don't have any real information.* But I couldn't rid my mind of the disembodied words I'd heard at Dog Dayz: "I didn't think Suzette meant it when she said she'd like to kill her." Or the memory of Suzette herself, signaling her dog to bark during Abigail's moment of silence. I set the mugs on the table and pulled a pint of hazelnut creamer from the fridge door. "Sugar?"

She shook her head. "Love this stuff though!"

"Do they know what killed her?"

"I can't comment on the case."

I took too quick a slurp of coffee, burning the tender spot behind my upper incisors, and struggled not to show the pain.

She jotted something on her pad. "Ms. MacPhail, were you . . ."

"Would you mind calling me Janet? Ms. MacPhail makes me want to put my bifocals on and my hair in a bun."

That seemed to relax her, and she told me to call her Jo. She smiled, leaned back in her chair, and set her pen down on the table. "Could I have more coffee? I woke up this morning with a headache and I think this is helping."

I poured her a second cup and asked if she'd like some aspirin, but she said she'd already taken several more tablets than medically advisable. The caffeine would have to do.

Jay barked outside the back door. I was halfway there when he and Pip exploded into the kitchen. "You're too smart for your own good, Bub." Jay danced around me. "I'm going to have to change this handle back to a regular doorknob. I just had it put on a couple weeks ago, and he's figured out how it works. As you can see."

I looked out the door before I closed it. The sun was hidden behind a bank of thunder heads, the patio freckled with raindrops. Fortunately, the dogs had stayed under the awning and were dry, because they were soon mugging Jo. She stroked both heads, one with each hand. "Nice dogs. Border Collies?"

"The black and white one is. That's Pip. He's — or he was — Abigail's dog. The one I brought home from the show. The other one, Jay, is an Australian Shepherd."

"Beautiful color." She ran her fingers down Jay's shoulder through black and gray and silver waves.

"It's called blue merle."

"I miss having a dog." She sounded wistful. "Wouldn't be fair though. I'm gone so much." She glanced at her watch.

"Jay, settle." Pip apparently knew the command, too, because both dogs sprawled on the floor, bellies flat to the cool vinyl, panting and grinning.

Detective Stevens picked up her pen and began to doodle on her pad. "So, you and Ms. Dorn were friends?"

"I wouldn't say that. We knew each other from dog training and competition. We train — trained — at the same place and . . ."

"Where is that?"

I gave her the address and phone number for Dog Dayz. "Anyway, I knew her and Greg, her husband, really just in the doggy context, you know, from training and shows."

"And who do you know who didn't like her?"

I'm afraid I allowed myself to guffaw.

"Sorry. Actually, I can't think of many people who liked her. Greg, of course. And I think Giselle and Abigail were friends."

"Giselle?"

"Giselle Swann. Remember the woman who wanted to take Pip home?"

"Ah, yeah, Precious." A barely perceptible tremor ran across her cheek. "And they were friends?"

"Yes, I think so. I know they often set their crates up together at shows. To be honest, I don't know either of them very well."

"And I take it there are people who actively disliked Ms. Dorn?"

"Abigail wasn't exactly warm and cuddly. Except with her dogs. Maybe Greg too, although I only ever saw her scolding him or ordering him around."

"Who else?"

"Gosh, I don't know. I mean, I don't know that I'd want to suggest that anyone I know hated her enough to kill her!" This conversation was not one I really wanted to continue.

"I didn't say anyone killed her." She gave me that poker face.

"Right." I fought off the urge to squirm in my seat. "There was a long-standing rivalry between Abigail and Suzette Anderson. But I think they were reasonably friendly outside the ring."

"What sort of rivalry?"

"They were both in the running for top national ranking in obedience with their Border Collies." I pointed at Pip. He was rolled onto his back, leaning up against the wall, his head back and tongue lolling out the corner of his mouth. "Believe it or not, you're looking at one of the top competitive obedience dogs in the country over the past two or three years."

"Yeah?" She gave me a look I couldn't read, but it made the base of my skull itch. "And now you have him."

20

"I have Pip temporarily, until Greg takes him." Here I was in my own kitchen, the heart of my little house, my cat purring, no bright lights in my eyes, knowing I'd done nothing illegal, at least not lately, and yet Detective Jo Stevens' questions were beginning to make me sweat. "In fact, with your permission I'll take Pip back to Greg today or tomorrow." Based on her non-reaction, I wasn't sure Detective Stevens had heard me so I rambled on. "Besides, obedience is a team sport. Pip's ranking is a result of their teamwork, his and Abigail's. It takes years to build that rapport between dog and handler."

The detective nodded. "So, this Suzette Anderson and Ms. Dorn had conflicts over national competition?"

"They were both hoping to qualify for the National Obedience Championship competition next January. Both their dogs were in the running for top-ranked Border Collie of the year. But obedience people generally get along fine outside the ring. I mean, it's a sport where the results mostly depend on how you and your dog do on a particular day. Politics can enter in on some of the finer points, but mostly it's do or die." I sucked in a quick breath. "So to speak. I'm sure Suzette didn't hate her enough to kill her."

"Who else?" Jo was madly scribbling.

I was beginning to feel like a stool pigeon, but once I started to sing, I just couldn't seem to shut up. "I've heard that Abigail and Marietta Santini had some problems a couple years ago over a puppy sale that fell through."

"Who's she?"

"She owns Dog Dayz, where we train."

She wrote it all down.

"That was a while ago, and I don't know much about it, but I don't think it was that big a deal. I can't think of anyone else. I mean, as I said, lots of people didn't care for Abigail, but most didn't have any real conflict with her."

"What about her husband?"

"Greg doted on her."

"I heard they were separated."

"I heard that, too. But still . . . The guy

followed her like a puppy. He was right there when she collapsed, and he sent me for the EpiPen." *Of course, if he did poison her, he knew the epinephrin wouldn't help.* "He looked devastated." *Yeah,* a question nibbled at the edge of my brain, *but if they really were separated, why was he there?*

"He shows dogs too?"

"No. He has a little dog, but doesn't compete as far as I know. But he was always there for Abigail."

Jo's expression remained bland but for that slight tightening under her eyes that I'd seen before. It was enough to cast a new light on Greg's presence, and light makes all the difference to the nuances of a picture. *Picture this — estranged husband just happens to be at his wife's side when she keels over. He's a pharmacist. He'd know how to kill her. But Greg?*

We sat in silence for a moment as Jo wrote in her notebook. I was running my thoughts through a maze of images from the previous few days when one of them jolted me out of my seat. I reached for the pantry door, clearing my clenching throat.

"Uh, I keep forgetting about this . . ." I lifted Abigail's tote bag from the pantry floor and set it on the table in front of the detective. She took in the Border Collie and

"Dorn" embroidered on the side of the bag. When she looked at me, the blue of her eyes had turned cloudy and cold.

My cheeks went hot. "I'm sorry. I'm embarrassed. I, uh, I forgot I had it."

Jo shoved her chair back with her knees and startled the dogs onto their feet. She pulled a pair of gloves from a small pack on her belt and put them on. Jay and Pip watched me, no doubt waiting for the next game to begin. It wasn't one I wanted to play.

"This is Abigail's?"

I nodded.

"And it was at the show?"

I nodded again.

Jo gave me a "you moron" look, then reached into the bag. The first thing she picked up was the plastic container that once held Abigail's bagel spread. She pulled the lid open. "You washed this?"

My power of speech had taken a powder, so I nodded once more. The dogs gave up on me and lay down again.

Jo snapped the lid back onto the container and carefully laid it back in the bag. Then she fixed me with a new look. I wasn't sure whether it said, "How stupid *are* you?" or "Aha! I've caught you!"

"Get me a large plastic bag."

I did, and Jo carefully slid the canvas tote into the white plastic. She pulled off the gloves, shoved them into her pants pocket, and took a black marker from compartment on her holster and wrote something on the plastic bag. Almost as an aside, she asked, "Did you remove any other evidence from the crime scene?"

Embarrassment and fear bowed to anger at that. "I didn't know it was evidence or a crime scene. I was trying to help."

"I understand." She didn't sound like she did. "Did you remove anything else from the barn where Ms. Dorn's property was besides her dog and this bag?"

"No." Our eyes met for an uncomfortable moment, and my outrage began to fade.

We walked to the front door, and Jo pointed her pencil at three black leather bags stashed just inside the door. "Going somewhere?"

"What? Oh. A photo shoot this afternoon."

"You take that much luggage?"

I didn't like the way I squeaked out my reply, but couldn't seem to help myself. "Not luggage. Equipment. Two cameras, a tripod, some props."

She pocketed her pen and pad. "Don't leave the county for a while."

21

The rain continued for the next couple of hours, one of those bright rains under a sky full of light. A heavy cloud unloaded over Suzette's driveway just as I pulled in. The unsettled weather reflected the way I felt — sunny at first glance, a storm of anxiety raging within. I didn't feel much like taking pictures, but knew somewhere deep inside that it was better to focus on beauty and work than on my impending and unjust incarceration for tampering with evidence.

I gave the steering wheel a good whack with the heel of my hand, spat out an expletive, despite my efforts to clean up my language, and fished my cell phone out of my bag. Thus vented, I did manage to keep control of my voice when Suzette answered. "It's Janet."

"Scared of a little rain?"

"No, but my camera is. I'm in your driveway. I'll be in when this gully washer quits."

"I know. We're watching you."

Suzette and Fly were leaning over the back of a couch and looking out the window at me.

"So you are."

"It won't last long. Front door's unlocked. We're in the kitchen."

The rain put the Lassus Brothers' Handy Dandy Car Wash to shame, so I was stuck for the moment. I'd read and reread all the print matter scattered around the back seat of my van, so I stuffed all the wrappers, scraps, and food crumbs I could reach into a CVS bag I found under the passenger seat. That took up a minute or so. Nothing else to do, so I popped the angle of the seat back a few notches, switched off the radio, leaned back, and tried to lose myself in the rhythm of the rain. Maybe this was a sign from the Universe to start that meditation practice I'd been contemplating for the past decade. Maybe I should sign up for a class. Right after the first aid class I wanted to take. But I couldn't sign up for anything, trapped in the car as I was, so I just closed my eyes and listened as fat drops splatted against the windows and roof. I'd rather it didn't arrive when I have photos to shoot, but I do love a good rain.

How could I undo the damage I'd done

to myself? I couldn't blame Detective Stevens for being suspicious. Who but the guilty removes evidence and runs it through her dishwasher? Not that I knew at the time that it was evidence of anything but breakfast and dog brushing. My tear ducts threatened to self-activate from frustration so I squinched my eyes shut and beat the back of my head against the head rest.

Nothing like a good pity party once in a while. A good *short* pity party. Three head whacks and two deep sighs later I was cured of depression. And angry. *I didn't do anything wrong, and I'm not going to sit around while someone says I did.*

As if to lend meteorological support, the rain let up as quickly as it had begun. Watery clouds raced east toward Ohio, and the sun popped out, setting the rivulets and drops aglitter, bright as crystal, on the windows. When I turned toward Suzette's house, my heart leapt at the sight of a perfect rainbow suspended directly over the chimney. It took less than a minute to get my camera out, check the settings, and get a few shots. I half expected a flock of bluebirds.

Fly met me at the front door and bent herself into a donut, whining, "Pet me, pet me." The aroma of coffee drew me toward the back of the house, where I was nearly blinded by Suzette's kitchen. It looked like a can of sunshine paint had exploded. The ceiling, the walls, the cupboards and molding, the linoleum floor, even the frilly café curtains were all brilliant yellow.

"Cheerful," I said.

Suzette was standing on a yellow ladder-back chair, pulling a coffee cake off an upper cupboard shelf. "Have to hide all food items out of reach of Miss Counter Surfer there," she grunted, stepping down from the chair. "Could you flip the light on?" The sun had retreated behind another bank of clouds, and despite its hue, the kitchen was a little dark. Suzette slipped the coffee cake into the oven and glanced around the room. "Awful, isn't it?"

"Well . . ." I sat down at the table. Fly rested her chin on my knee and I massaged the backs of her ears until she groaned and pressed first one ear, then the other, harder against my fingers.

Suzette laughed. "Don't worry, I hate it. It was my aunt's place. She loved yellow. She died recently and left it to me, lock, stock, and barrel. I'm staying here until it sells. Already have an offer so I don't plan to be here long."

"You've had a lot of losses lately." *Includ-*

ing one major competitor.

"I just hope things don't really come in threes." As she spoke, Suzette pulled a ring from her left hand, and set it on top of a canister near the sink before she washed and dried her hands.

"Well, it looks like you're in for some good luck."

"Oh?"

I told her about the rainbow, and she gestured toward Fly. "That's my good-luck rainbow, right there."

The aroma of warm yeast and cinnamon had flooded the room, and Suzette pulled the coffee cake from the oven. Fly abandoned me and stationed herself at Suzette's knee, a look of utter devotion and hope on her face as she fixed the coffee cake with a Border Collie stare as if trying to will it off the counter. "So, do you think you'll be able to get some pictures without the sun?"

"No problem. A little cloud cover is good. No shadows or squints."

Suzette poured the coffee into delicate bone china cups with rose buds lacing the rims. I have my own grandmother's bone china dishes, but can't remember the last time I used them. I wasn't sure I ever had. They seem like relics of a more gracious time.

"Beautiful dishes, Suzette."

"Oh, thanks. I've been collecting bone china since I was in high school." She lifted her cup toward the light from the window. "I use them all the time. Don't see much point in having nice things but not using them."

"I'd be afraid of breaking them."

"I've broken a few pieces." She set the cup down. "But you can't live well without breaking a few things, can you?"

22

I watched Suzette slip a pearl-handled silver cake server under a too-generous piece of coffee cake and wondered if she included people among the things that had to be broken from time to time in order to live well. She slid the gooey cake onto a plate with a different rose pattern than on the cups, and set it in front of me. *That'll be way too generous to your butt,* nagged Janet Angel, but her evil twin reminded me that it would be rude to refuse. Especially when saliva was practically dribbling down my chin. Suzette told Fly to go lie down, which the dog did with a big "You don't feed me enough" sigh.

"I understand congratulations are in order."

Suzette had just put a big bite of cake in her mouth. She stopped mid-chew, alarm all over her face. She lifted her linen napkin to her mouth, chewed, dabbed, and asked,

"Congratulations? How did you know?"

"Everyone knows." I meant, of course, everyone who trained at Dog Days. Suzette paled a couple of shades, which I thought odd. "It's not every day that someone finishes an OTCH or a UDX, let alone both together."

"Oh, that." Her face changed colors again, this time to a lovely pale pink.

Oh, that? For two of the toughest, most coveted canine titles?

I plunged ahead. "I hear Fly's in the lead now for Border Collies?"

Suzette wiped her mouth and regained her composure. "Thanks. Yes, I think she's probably in first place. For now, anyway. It's exciting." Her voice was flat. "Really, I'm thrilled, but somehow it doesn't mean as much with Abigail and Pip out of the running."

Janet Demon blew a big fat raspberry in my left ear. She was getting pretty good at them. I ignored her. "Really?"

"Abigail and I were friends, you know." I didn't, nor had I realized until then what intriguing violet eyes she had. *Contacts?* "When they said she died . . . I froze, you know? It sounds crazy, but I was afraid to stop smiling." I thought back to the big grin on her face when Tony Balthazar announced that Abigail had died. Suzette sniffed and went on. "Like if I kept smiling, maybe it wouldn't be true, and if I stopped, I'd completely lose it. Which I did when I got in my car. I wasn't sure I could drive home." She pulled her braid over her shoulder and brushed her jaw line with the end. "Abigail could be a snot, but she was loyal to her friends and devoted to her dogs."

Suzette studied her nails for a moment, then went on. "You know what Abigail told me would be the best send-off she could think of? A song of joy sung by dogs." I thought back to Fly barking on cue during the supposed moment of silence at Dog Dayz. Suzette's eyes softened and the corners of her lips turned up. "So during Marietta's moment of silence, I decided to give Abigail what she wanted."

"Fly barking."

At the mention of her name, Fly walked over, glanced at me, and laid her satiny chin on Suzette's lap. Suzette nodded, then bent and kissed the top of her dog's head.

We sat in silence for a moment. A song of joy sung by dogs certainly beat the socks off a dirge. I began to wish I had known the Abigail beneath the prickly shell. I flashed back to the Malamutes howling along with Abigail's ambulance, and had the oddest

131

sense that their song lifted the dying woman's spirit in her final moments.

Suzette brought me back to the moment. "Everyone thinks I was jealous of Abigail, but if it hadn't been her and Pip, it would have been someone else. In fact, it is someone else by now. Several someones. I mean, if I didn't like competition, I sure as heck wouldn't show BCs in obedience."

"No, I guess not." Border Collies, with their brains and nose-to-the-grindstone work ethic, are among the most successful breeds in obedience and agility competition. They are also far too eager to work to make good pets for most people.

Suzette pushed a bit of coffee cake in circles around the cabbage roses on her plate. "I'm sure people will always think that Fly couldn't have been number one if Pip were still competing."

"Oh, I don't know about that. I thought you guys sort of flip-flopped back and forth in the standings?"

"Sure, we did, but Abigail and Pip were leading the past couple of weeks. We've had a little problem with straight sits."

"Well, jeez, as you said, it's not as if there's no other competition in Border Collies."

"True. But still. Abigail and I had our conflicts, that's for sure. But we were friends long before we were rivals, and we did try to keep that in mind." I was hoping Suzette would spill her guts, but she just waived a vaguely dismissive hand and laid her folded napkin beside her plate. "Whenever you're ready, we can try for some pictures before the next downpour."

I carried my plate and cup to the sink. As I set them down, I couldn't help but notice the ring on top of the canister. Who could miss the exquisite emerald-cut diamond snuggled between two smaller stones? My jewels pretty much come from the sales racks at department stores, so I'm no gem expert, but I'd hazard that the rock on Suzette's counter was a couple of carats.

I took nearly a hundred photos of Fly over the next three-quarters of an hour, and wrapped up the session with some terminally sweet candid shots of her smooching Suzette. A menagerie of thoughts had been frolicking through my mind the whole time, and as we were winding down I asked Suzette how well she knew Abigail's husband, Greg.

"Oh, Greg." I thought she started to sigh, but if she did, she stifled it. "I love Greg. He's a really sweet guy."

Whoa. Love? I was composing a follow up when Suzette diverted me with a question of her own.

"So, did you get some good ones?"

"I think so. We'll know for sure when I download them, but I think we even have some calendar-girl shots." I sell a lot of animal and landscape photos to calendar publishers. I clicked on the review screen and held my camera so that Suzette could see a few of the images.

"Great. When the puppies arrive I'll have you come take some more."

"Puppies? She's expecting?"

"No, not yet. But I'm planning to breed her after Nationals in January." That would be the obedience national championship, making the puppies ready for their photo shoot in late winter or spring, assuming Fly's hormones cooperated.

Suzette helped me lug my stuff around the house, through the gate, and into my car.

"So who's the lucky fella?" I asked her as I slammed the van door.

The high color she'd shown earlier flooded back into her cheeks. "Fellow?"

"Yeah. The stud."

Her blush deepened a shade before she recovered and gave her head a shake. "Oh, you mean for Fly."

Hey, there's your opening, so ask her about

134

that big fat rock, whispered my little demon, but goody two-shoes on my right shoulder reined me in with a gentle *Mind your own beeswax.* I settled for a nod.

"A dog in Virginia. Saw him last year at Nationals, and I like him a lot. Conformation champion, OTCH, MACH, working on his herding championship." Which would make him a champion in the show ring and in the three performance sports of obedience, agility, and herding. I felt tired just thinking about the work that went into earning all those honors.

"Well, let me know when the puppies are ready to model and I'll be here." I left her standing in the driveway, rubbing her engagement-ring finger as if it were missing something.

23

I contemplated Connie Stoppenhagan's revolting ability to keep her hair and makeup pristine even after her early morning run as I savored my toasted snicker doodle bagel with cinnamon-honey butter. I really do try to keep the calories down, at least for my first breakfast, and I should have in light of the coffeecake Suzette practically force fed me the day before, but Abigail's sudden departure reminded me that the future is an illusion. If I was destined to choke to death over my breakfast, it wouldn't be on a whole-grain gluten-free thing with tofu spread. Nope, I want a tasty life. Besides, I had more important things than calories and fat grams on my mind. I swallowed and said, "I feel so bad for Greg."

"Oh, I don't know about that," Connie replied.

I stopped mid-chew. "But he's always

136

been so devoted, and he put up with all her crap. 'Greg do this, Greg do that.' Even if they were separated, do you really think they'd split up for good?"

Connie sipped her tea before answering, and I wondered again how she kept her nails so perfect. "Abigail wanted a divorce. She was waiting until after the Border Collie Nationals in October. She didn't want her focus diverted since Pip was a serious contender for top national standing again this year."

"How do you know that?"

"I check the rankings every week."

That wasn't really my question, but her comment surprised me. "You do?"

"Sure." She looked at me. "Not just obedience. All the rankings."

"Oh." Of course she did. She was a seriously competitive dog person. "Anyway, I meant how did you know Abigail wanted a divorce?"

"She told me. We were set up next to each other at the Auburn shows."

"That was March! They've been separated that long?"

She shrugged.

"So what was he doing at the trial? He was Johnny-on-the-spot when she collapsed."

"Must have come to see someone else, 'cause he didn't come with Abigail. I saw her arrive. Poor thing had to carry her own crate and chair."

I winced at the sharpness of Connie's remark, then winced again as I remembered thinking much the same thing on the day of the show. "I guess most people won't miss Abigail all that much, but I can't believe anyone wished her dead."

"Oh, I don't know about that."

I gave her a "What are you talking about?" look.

"Greg, for one. He'll be sitting pretty now, that's for sure. The money was hers, you know, family money."

"No, I had no idea." I'd never thought about it.

"Her grandmother was Eloise Holtz. You know, Aunt Ellie's pastries . . ."

"Oh, yeah."

"Well, there was an article about her in *Fort Wayne Woman* about a year ago. It said that good old Eloise left her fortune to a son and a daughter, Abigail's mother. Abigail told me there were actually three siblings, but the old lady had some sort of falling out with the other daughter and wouldn't talk about her. That was Tom's mother . . ."

That woke me up. "Tom Saunders?"

"Yep. The article didn't even mention her. Anyway, the brother was killed in an accident of some sort not long before the old lady died, so Abigail's mother got everything. She ran the business for a while, then sold it for megabucks. When she died a few years ago, Abigail got the money. And now it's Greg's."

"But Greg doesn't need the money. He makes a decent living."

"He deserves it, living with that shrew all those years." The venom in Connie's voice pushed me back a few inches. "Don't know why he chose a drill sergeant instead of a wife."

I thought back to my own marriage. If I'd believed the comments I heard when it ended, instead of my own insider's view, I'd have thought I'd walked away from heaven on earth. "I don't think anyone else really knows what goes on between two people. He stuck with her a long time." Connie didn't respond. "Anyway, I can't see him killing her for her money."

"Who said he killed her?" Connie's eyes opened wide.

"Sorry. I thought you were suggesting that was a possibility." I didn't want to let Detective Jo Stevens' cat out of the bag, since it wasn't fully gestated. Still, Connie was always good for bouncing ideas around. "Anyway, I don't think they have her cause of death yet." I leaned across the table toward her. "But think about it. Abigail was young and in great shape. How could she drop dead?"

I watched in wonder as Connie wiped her mouth. How was it possible that her lipstick had stayed in place in spite of bagel, coffee, and napkin? "Happens all the time."

"It could, I guess. But still . . ." I thought of telling her about Jo Stevens' reaction to Abigail's totebag and its contents, but Connie went on before I could begin.

"Abigail thought Greg was having an affair. She hired a private investigator, but he said Greg wasn't fooling around." She went to the counter to top off our coffees. When she got back, she continued that line of thought. "Not that he didn't have opportunities to play around."

"He is a good-looking guy."

"Yep," she echoed, "a good-looking guy with a really snazzy ride."

I pictured Greg in his sleek red car. I'd only seen it once, and couldn't remember what it was. What do I know from cars? Something foreign and pricey.

"Actually, though, if anyone was fooling

around, my money would be on Abigail," Connie said.

"What makes you say that?" I asked.

"As soon as Greg moved out, Abigail got her hair cut and changed her whole look. Seems like new-guy behavior to me."

"Could be she just wanted a new look." I knew I wanted a new look. I just had no idea how to go about getting one.

"I suppose." Connie seemed to ponder the possibility. "Or maybe she thought she was competing with someone else, like she said."

I sipped my coffee and thought about that. "Did Abigail say who she thought Greg might be fooling around with?"

"She never mentioned a name, but if I had to guess . . ." She folded her hands together against the edge of the table. "No, I shouldn't speculate about such a thing. It will come out soon enough."

I berated her for holding out on me, but she wouldn't budge, so I said, "I still can't believe Greg would kill Abigail."

"Maybe he didn't. Maybe Su . . . uh, his girlfriend got tired of waiting and decided to get rid of the competition."

The image of a big fat diamond ring sparkled in my mind's eye. "Suzette?"

"I really couldn't say."

But you almost did say, I thought. "Suzette must be, what, fifteen years younger than Greg?"

"More like twenty. Not that most guys mind hooking up with younger women." She sounded disgusted. "Abigail knew Greg wasn't above cheating. That's how she snagged him in the first place." I wanted to pursue that little bombshell, but Connie preempted me. "Speaking of attractive men, Ms. MacPhail, what's up with you and Tom?"

"Tom Saunders? How do you know Tom, anyway?"

"He went to school with my big brother. They had a horrible garage band in high school." She crinkled her pert little nose in disgust. "Tom was at our house all the time. He making music with you now?"

"Don't be silly. I barely know him."

"Why, Janet, I do believe you're blushing!"

Before I could plead a hot flash, Connie glanced at her watch and started piling wrappers and cups onto her tray. "Gotta run."

I nodded, already drifting through a tangle of convoluted thoughts. Even if Greg were fooling around, why kill his wife? All those years with her acid words eating at him and

142

he'd never strangled her. Why now? Then again, inheriting from a dead wife might be better than losing a wealthy one through divorce. But we don't even know that she was murdered. And if she was, it might not have been Greg. What if Connie was right about Suzette? It wouldn't be the first time a lover waiting in the wings knocked off a spouse who held center stage too long.

24

When I got home from breakfast with Connie, the little red light on my answering machine was flashing. I sent the dogs out the back door and pushed the playback button. The first message was from an editor at *Dog Fancy* who wanted me to call back about some photos for an article on rally obedience. Then a message from Greg Dorn. He was sorry he missed me the day before, and he'd be home the rest of the day. He'd like to get Pip, so could I call him?

I brought the dogs in, checked their water, and sat down at the kitchen table with my cell phone. I punched in the number on Detective Stevens' card, then waited while the dispatcher connected us.

"Stevens!" The line crackled, then cleared.

"This is Janet MacPhail."

"Ah, Ms. MacPhail. Janet."

"Greg Dorn called and said he'd like his dog back. You told me to check with you first." She said that would be fine, then asked, "Do you have time to talk this afternoon? Say four o'clock?"

Oh no, not again, I thought, wondering vaguely whether I'd be arrested after the "removing evidence" incident. "I teach a class tonight at six. That would cut it a little close, depending on how long you need me."

"Where's your class?" I gave her the name of the junior high school. "You teach a junior high class at night?"

"Heavens no! I wouldn't want to teach a junior high class in broad daylight." I heard her chuckle, which was something of a relief. "It's a Neighborhood Connection class." She wasn't familiar with the Adult Education program of the Fort Wayne Community Schools, so I explained about the variety of non-credit classes they offer on everything from Windows to watercolors. We agreed to meet at the Firefly Coffee House on North Anthony at four o'clock.

Next I called Greg's number. On the fourth ring, a woman answered. The voice was soft, sultry, vaguely familiar. "Dorn residence." I asked for Greg.

"He's unavailable. Perhaps I can help you?"

"My name is Janet MacPhail. I'm taking care of Greg's dog. Who's this, please?"

145

"A friend."

I was starting to get peeved when I heard a scuffle on the other end of the line, and whispering I couldn't make out.

"Janet! It's Greg." He sounded even more annoyed than I was. "Thanks for calling back."

"Greg, how are you?"

"Not great. Getting by." His voice cracked for a second, then he went on. "I'd like to bring Pip home." Something scratched through the line and Greg said, "Hang on a second," and I heard more muffled discussion. All I could make out was Greg snapping, "Thanks, but that won't be necessary." Then to me, "Janet, I hate to ask, but is there any way you could bring Pip to me? I, uh, don't want to leave here right now."

I was more than a little curious about what was going on over there, and had a leash in my hand before he finished the sentence. "We're on our way!"

Twenty minutes later I pulled up in front of Greg's house, behind the decrepit Yugo that had tried to eat my fender on my last visit. Its right front tire rested halfway up the curb and its tail end was not quite out of the street. A peeling bumper sticker claimed, "My other car is a broom," and another boasted, "It's hard to be humble when you own a Maltese." No question whose car it was. I glanced in the open passenger-side window as I walked by. A book lay on the front seat, the top edge bristling with multi-hued slips of paper. *Spells for Lovers.* Another, *Magick Love Spells,* lay beside it. *Ho boy.*

Pip was all wriggle and whine from the van to the front door, and could hardly contain himself as we waited for Greg to answer the bell.

But it wasn't Greg who opened the door. It was Giselle Swann. She was wearing black over-stretched pants and the biggest black lace teddy I'd ever seen with a black cable-knit cardigan hanging, unbuttoned, over it. Her eyes were rimmed with black liner that narrowed them more than was natural, and she had a silver ring I didn't remember in her left nostril. It contrasted nicely with the brilliant raspberry gloss on her lips. Although my mouth may still have been agape, I was beginning to recover when Giselle reached for Pip's leash.

"Thanks so much, Janet. We so appreciate your bringing Pip home and caring for him." A blast of cheap powdery scent assaulted my nostrils and I reflexively lifted my hand to catch a sneeze, preventing Giselle from taking hold of the leash. *We?*

The little demon was back at my left ear. *What does she mean, "we"?*

25

"Giselle! What a surprise!" I sneezed once, twice, three times, fished a semi-used tissue from my pocket, and blew the rest of her powdery perfume out of my nose.

She ignored me and tried once more for the leash. "I can take Pip. Greg's tied up right now." I hoped she was speaking figuratively. Pip ducked backward, away from her hand, and let out a loud squeal as he rocketed through the door, bumped Giselle sideways, and pulled the leash from my hand.

"Pipper! How ya doin', guy?" Greg's voice mingled with Pip's whiney talk, and Percy the Poodle yipped in harmony. "Nice to see you, Pipper! Come on, want to go out and check your yard?" Greg fended off the bouncing Border Collie and invited me in. I squeezed past Giselle and followed Greg through an entrance foyer as big as my living room, emerging into a family room that easily accommodated the expansive leather sectional and chairs arrayed in front of a TV screen big enough for an IMAX. To the right a wall of roughhewn pale gray Indiana limestone extended from floor to ceiling, with a fireplace nestled beneath an arched opening. An enormous watercolor painting of a Border Collie working a flock of sheep graced the wall over the mantle. Behind the seating arrangements was a billiard table, and there was more than enough room to ensure that no one sitting in front of the television would get clobbered by a cue in play.

Two sets of French doors and the biggest window I've ever seen in a house made up the wall facing the fireplace. The doors opened onto a flagstone patio beyond which a lush lawn sloped to a pond that separated the Dorns' property from their neighbors. Most of the yard was open, but a picket fence surrounded the deck off the family room and enclosed a square of grass maybe forty by forty feet. Lawn covered the inside of the fenced area, too, except for a large maple in the center. A wide border of irises and peonies softened the outer perimeter. A gate opened from that yard into another, larger area where obedience jumps were set up.

Greg opened the French door and we all stepped out onto the deck and watched Pip and Percy race around their grassy yard.

"Thanks so much, Janet. It was a relief knowing Pip was safe and well cared for." Greg smiled, but there was a weight to his eyelids and a weary roundness to his shoulders.

"Yes," piped up Giselle, "it's good to have him home."

Greg's mouth tightened and he seemed to study his toes for a moment. Then he took Giselle by the elbow and steered her through the house and out the front door. I tagged along, unable to stop watching what looked like a bad accident in the making. Greg grabbed a suitcase-sized purse of brown and black plastic patchwork from atop an antique chest in the foyer, shoved it into Giselle's hands, and guided her onto the front porch.

Giselle turned back toward the house and shrugged her sleeve back into place. "I thought I might stay and make you some dinner, hon." Giselle took a baby step toward Greg and tilted her head coquettishly.

"No thanks." He closed the door, flipped the deadbolt, and turned toward me. "Sorry."

I sneezed into my elbow. "Nothing to be sorry about." I sneezed again. Apparently I was allergic to Giselle.

Greg pulled a box of tissues from a drawer in the antique chest and held it toward me. "Come on in and have some iced tea."

"I really can't stay," I protested, but I followed him to the kitchen.

He let the dogs in. Pip slurped up an enormous drink from a stainless steel bowl in one corner of the room, then settled himself, dripping happily, onto the gleaming white ceramic floor. Percy put his left front paw on my knee and pulled the right one up under his heart. What could I do but scratched his curly white chest? Greg put two glasses of iced tea on the table and settled into the chair across from me. "I do appreciate you taking care of Pip. Thanks."

"Are you doing okay, Greg?

"Yeah, I guess. Trying. It just doesn't seem possible that Abby's gone, you know?"

"I know." Though I'd never been widowed, I did know about loss and disappointment.

Greg put his hands on the table, turning his wedding band around and around with the thumb and finger of his right hand. "I miss her."

That took me by surprise. How could he miss her if he was leaving her — had already left, in fact? But then, the human heart walks a winding path. It occurred to me that it could be all for show, although I didn't get that vibe from him. But anything was possible.

"Give yourself some time."

"Yes. Time. There's always too much of the kind we don't want, isn't there? And not enough with the people we love."

We sat in silence for a moment. I couldn't think of anything useful to say, and knew in any case that words don't hold the lonely terrors of loss at bay as well as simple human presence. After a few moments I asked, "So, are you staying here now?"

"Where else would I stay?"

Well, this is embarrassing, whispered Janet Demon. *Let's see you get out of this one.* I couldn't help wondering, not for the first time, where that little voice was *before* I stuck my foot in things.

26

I was trying to backpedal after implying to Greg that he shouldn't be living in his own home. "I, uh, someone told me you and Abigail were separated."

"Who said that?"

Ho boy. "I must have misunderstood. I'm so embarrassed!"

Greg followed my gaze to the two new brass door locks on the counter. "My project for the afternoon."

"Lose your key?" My mouth was set on "blurt."

"No." He made it almost a question. "Oh, I see. You thought we were separated and figured she locked me out." My cheeks warmed up a tad. "No, that's fine. I can see where you'd think that. I actually did move out for a couple of weeks in March. We were having the floors refinished." I glanced at the mirror-like finish beneath our feet. "I'm deathly sensitive to the solvents. I got a

154

room and Abby and the dogs joined me there every night once the workmen left and she finished training." I thought back to what Connie had told me and began to grapple with the obvious fact that someone was a big fat fibber.

Silence hung between us for a moment, the next obvious question unasked. If Greg was in fact having an affair, could it possibly have been — or still be — with Giselle? Greg turned weary eyes toward mine. "You're wondering what Giselle was doing here, answering my phone and my door."

"Well, I, uh . . ."

"Yeah, I know. Good question. I've been asking it myself. She was in here when I got home. Abigail gave her a key last fall." The hand of sorrow squeezed his face, but he fought it off and won back control. "We went to the Border Collie nationals and Giselle came in to water plants and feed the fish." His delivery gained speed. "So I came home from walking Percy this afternoon and here she was. Says she just wants to help. She and Abby were friends so maybe she really feels she needs to step in for her sake or something, see that I'm eating and wearing clean clothes, I don't know. But I tell you," he sat back in his chair and ran his fingers through his brown hair, "that

155

woman drives me nuts."

"So you're changing the locks?" *Excellent plan,* I thought.

"I can't have her showing up here whenever she wants. I don't want to hurt her feelings, but it's my house." I wouldn't argue with that. "I guess I'll tell her I don't know who all has keys, so I need to make the house more secure since I'm gone a lot. Does that sound reasonable?"

"Perfectly." If Giselle were stalking me, I'd consider an armed guard and a brace of guard dogs reasonable. I thought about the witchcraft books on the seat of her car and wondered whether they included recipes for toxic brews. "The police wouldn't let me take Abigail's things home from the fairgrounds, you know. Her chair and crate and a few other things. Did you get them back?" I was gazing at Percy, who was lying in his open crate on a little synthetic wool pad, curly feet twitching in dreams.

"Not yet." He smiled toward his contented little dog. "Pip never uses a crate at home, so that doesn't matter. Poor Percy would be lost without his, though." The Poodle opened his eyes at the sound of his name, and Greg's comment gave me an opening.

"Good you didn't take him to the show."

He nodded, still gazing at his dog. "Yeah,

that was a fluke really. I went to work that morning to cover for one of the other pharmacists, but we got our dates mixed up. So when she showed up at work, I went straight to the fairgrounds to watch Abi . . ." He gagged on the final syllable, and we sat in silence for a few moments until he'd collected himself. Then Greg walked me to the front porch.

"Thanks again, Janet." He gave me a hug, and when we broke apart his eyes were glittery.

"Call if you need anything. Even just a friendly ear." He promised he would.

I turned the key in the ignition and glanced into the rearview mirror. The ubiquitous Yugo crouched in the street four lots down with the engine running. It looked like a giant reptile, unblinking in the sun, lying in wait. I couldn't see the driver's face for the glare on the windshield, but a heavy black-clad arm rested on the frame of the open driver's-side window, and a malevolent energy stirred the air.

27

I decided to swing by Mom's place before I went home. I tried to see her about once a week, but I'd let my filial duties slide a few extra days. She spent most of my last visit scolding me yet again for marrying Chet a quarter century ago. Not only did he not go to medical school like Neil Young, but he abandoned me. The fact that he did that when I gave him the boot for being a lazy, lying cheat seemed to elude her.

Mom came out the back door wearing blue and yellow striped capris and a white silk blouse with an imposing lace jabot. The buttons were one off, and the right tail of the blouse hung lower than the left.

"May I help you?"

"Mom! It's me, Janet!"

"Janet? Oh dear, I didn't know you without my specs." She giggled and slapped her thighs with both hands.

"Mom, you're wearing them."

She reached up and wriggled her glasses, leaving them slightly askew. She giggled some more. "So I am!"

I followed her into the kitchen, where my head nearly exploded as a miasma of pine-scented cleaner enveloped me.

"So, Mom, you been cleaning?" I flipped on the exhaust fan, propped the back door open, and raised the double-hung window as high as it would go.

"Cleaning? You think I need to clean up?"

"No, Mom, I wondered if you've been cleaning this morning." What I wondered was how she could breathe in there.

"No, I don't think so." I searched her eyes, but the woman I'd known all my life was nowhere to be found.

Nor were the accouterments I'd come to expect as part of her home, the home of my childhood. The kitchen counters were stripped bare and sparkly clean. The blue ceramic canisters were gone. Mr. Coffee was gone. The Little Red Riding Hood cookie jar that we'd picked out together when I was eight? Gone. Toaster? Gone. The tea kettle that always sat on the back burner of the stove wasn't there. The kitchen table, too, was clean and bare. The wooden napkin holder, the ceramic salt-and-pepper fawns, the restaurant-style sugar dispenser, even the red-checkered vinyl cloth. All gone.

"Mom, where is everything?"

"What?"

"Where is everything? All your things? From the counter and table?"

"Looks better, don't you think, Marsha?" Marsha was Mom's sister. She died a decade ago with her faculties intact, but her heart, not so much.

"Mom, I'm Janet."

She focused hard on my face. "Oh, Janet! It's so nice to see you."

I didn't know whether to cry or run away. Pending a decision, I opened the refrigerator. The milk was fine. All five gallons. The napkin holder was wedged in beside a quart of cottage cheese with an intact plastic seal around the lid and a use-by date a week gone. There was a bag of carrots on the bottom shelf. Next to the salt-and-pepper fawns. I grabbed some fuzzy green cheddar and Swiss from the butter bin. Mom sat at the table, humming and playing with the lace of her jabot. I dropped the cheeses into the garbage can under the sink and said, "Mom, I need to use the bathroom."

Chemical warfare had been declared on the bathroom as well. The weapon of choice here was chlorine bleach. I turned on the exhaust fan and cranked the small window open a few inches. She'd stripped this room to its bones, too. No towels on the racks. No soap in sight. Even the shower curtain was missing.

I opened the linen closet and was face-to-face with Little Red Riding Hood. I lifted her head and cape with not a little trepidation, and peered into the jar. Several cookie bits in the bottom, plus two bars of Ivory soap, a half-squished tube of toothpaste, three disposable razors, several packets of sugar, and a bottle of aspirin. I took two of those and swallowed them with a handful of tap water.

I went to the bedroom, picked the phone up off the floor (the night table was stripped), and dialed my brother's number. Bill works from home when he isn't flying around the world doing whatever it is he does. I've never been quite clear about Bill's "consulting" business.

"Mom?" Bill's caller I.D. was working.

"It's Janet."

"Oh, hi."

"Have you been in here lately?" I described the scene. Bill said he was in the house on Sunday and everything was normal. Even Mom, if I could believe Bill. "Well, it's not normal now. She can't stay here alone. She's going to gas herself."

He didn't reply.

"Look, I can't take her home with me. I teach tonight."

He grumbled, but said he'd be right over.

28

I went back to the kitchen. Mom was down on her knees fooling around with the contents of a cabinet. "Whatcha doing, Mom?" I leaned over and took a look.

"Oh, Marsha! How nice to see you!" She reached out and patted my leg. "I've been stocking up. The price of oil is going to go up, you know. I read it in the paper."

The cabinet was loaded with oil. Industrial-size bottles of corn oil, safflower oil, peanut oil. Two huge cans of olive oil, extra virgin. Whenever I see that term, I think of Agnes Baumgartner, a self-righteous little priss in every class I ever took in high school. Agnes, her pinched little face scowling over her buttoned-up white collars, was an extra virgin if I ever saw one.

"Mom, when did you eat? Shall I make you something?"

Her face lit up. "Cookies! Let's bake cookies!"

"First I think you should have something nutritious, okay?"

She slumped into a chair and leaned her cheek on her fist. "Okay. But I'd rather have cookies."

I opened the cupboard where she normally kept canned goods. The top shelf was bare. The next one down was crammed with condensed tomato soup. Say, sixty cans. "Mom, how about some tomato soup?"

"I don't like tomato soup."

"Great! Be ready in a jiffy." I pulled out a can and found a can opener and a whisk.

Mom was at the table folding and stacking sections of paper towels as she pulled them one by one off a roll, and humming fragments of something I couldn't quite piece together. My temples throbbed in time with my rambunctious thoughts. What did Detective Stevens want? What were we going to do about Mom? What was that song she was humming in spurts? What, or who, killed Abigail Dorn? And the question that slipped like a noose around my mind — am I really a suspect?

One problem at a time, Janet.

"So, Mom, Bill's coming over. Maybe you should stay with him for a few days."

"Oh, yes! I could help with the baby until Julie's on her feet."

Who in the heck are Julie and the baby? I bet Bill and his partner, Norm, didn't know them either.

I set the soup on the burner, and went back to checking out the cupboards. The shelf below the tomato soup was a hodge-podge of pastas, rice, coffee filters, dried beans and peas, an Englebert Humperdinck cassette, lentils, couscous, oatmeal, wheat germ, an unopened pantyhose egg, three packets of zinnia seeds, and a humongous bag of popcorn. I backtracked to the stove for some therapeutic soup stirring.

She's Come Undone. That was it. *Perfect.*

I opened the cupboard where the plates and bowls had lived since I was a little girl. Empty. "Mom! Where are your dishes?"

"Oh, I was tired of those old things. I gave them to Goodwill." Or maybe they were in the furnace room. I fought off the urge to beat my head against the edge of the cabinet, kept looking, and eventually found a ceramic mug among the soup cans.

"Soup's on!" I set the mug of soup and a spoon on the table and watched Mom tuck a paper towel into her collar. She tried to pat it flat against her chest, but the lace jabot fought back.

She slurped a spoonful of soup. "Mmmmm! Delicious! I love tomato soup!"

She was finishing off her third mugful when Bill banged in through the back door. "Hi, Mom. Janet." He glanced around the kitchen, eyes wide.

"George, you're home early." George was my father. He died of a heart attack in the middle of a Montana trout stream nineteen years ago.

"Mom, it's me, Bill."

"Oh, Bill!" She wiped tomato soup from her lips. "How was school?"

Bill and I adjourned to the living room and I filled him in while he tidied the cushions on the sofa. He finally ran out of excuses and promised to keep an eye on her until morning. "But this has to be temporary. I can't watch her every minute. And I leave in two weeks for Thailand." He was in full "all about me" mode by the time he got to his travel plans.

"You want some cheese with that whine, Bill?"

He glared into my eyes for a moment, then asked, "What's up with you?"

My overtaut tether snapped. "Well, let's see, my mother is losing her mind, I watched someone drop dead last weekend, and I'm apparently under suspicion for tampering with evidence. Otherwise I'm just dandy."

"The Aunt Ellie woman at the dog show? I wondered if you were there."

I nodded. He sat me down on the couch and heard the whole story.

"Look, if you need a lawyer, call Norm."

"Norm's a real estate attorney."

"He'll know who to call. You can't just pick a criminal defense attorney from the phone book."

My heart did a little tango as my brain screamed *criminal defense*?

Then Bill shifted our focus back to Mom, his tone softer. "It's time we get serious about other options."

"Right." A mix of emotions the size of a St. Bernard plopped onto my chest. "Listen, I need to get going. I'll call you when I get home from school tonight. Check out the cupboards while you're here."

Mom was at the sink, washing the mug. "Gotta go, Mom. Love you." I kissed her cheek.

"Okay, dear. Have fun. Be home by eleven."

29

I got to the Firefly Coffee House at 3:32. The place was quiet, so I figured I could do a little work before Detective Stevens arrived. I set my laptop on the table, bent to pull my notes from my bag, and dropped my favorite gel pen. I scooched down sideways to retrieve it. Big mistake. I slipped off the chair and gave myself a mild uppercut with the edge of the table, making my left leg straighten reflexively and scuttle the pen across the floor and under the legs of another table about ten feet away.

Two slick young guys in suits looked up from their laptops across the room, no doubt wondering why I was out unsupervised. I smiled at them and they pretended they hadn't noticed me. By the time I retrieved my pen and the shreds of my dignity, I no longer felt like doing anything constructive, so I went to the counter and ordered a large mocha latte. Caffeine and chocolate would do me good.

I was settling back into my booth when Jo Stevens walked in. "You're early."

"Yeah, I had the silly idea that I could get a little work done."

"Get the dog back to Mr. Dorn?

"Safe and sound."

Jo opened the file folder she'd brought with her and flipped a few sheets of paper over, exposing what appeared to be a print-out of an e-mail. "I have a few questions I thought you might clear up for me."

"Okay." I wasn't sure I liked the sound of that.

"I have some e-mails from the victi . . . er, Ms. Dorn's computer, and I don't understand them. Dog jargon."

"Okay."

She picked up the e-mail printout and pulled a pen from her breast pocket. "What does 'kurf' mean?"

"Kurf?"

"C-E-R-F."

I explained that the acronym is pronounced like *surf*. "Canine Eye Registration Foundation. It's an organization that registers the results of eye exams on dogs and tracks genetic eye diseases in the different breeds."

She nodded and made a quick note. "And

'ofa'?" She made it rhyme with *sofa*.

I choked on my latte. "Well, that one we call by the letters. O-F-A. Orthopedic Foundation for Animals. They keep records on a number of inherited problems in dogs, but usually when people mention OFA they're talking about hips. You know, evaluations of hip x-rays, testing for hip dysplasia."

She looked blank.

"Malformation of the hip joint. Causes arthritis and leads to lameness."

"That German Shepherd thing?"

"Not just German Shepherds. Lots of breeds, and mixed breeds, can have hip dysplasia."

"Okay. And AKC I guess is American Kennel Club?"

"Right."

"And NSDR?"

"National Stock Dog Registry. They register various stock dog breeds."

The blank look again. I was guessing she wasn't a dog person, though she had seemed comfortable enough with Jay and Pip bouncing around her.

"Border Collies, Australian Shepherds, English Shepherds . . . Breeds that traditionally work livestock on farms and ranches."

"Okay." She finished a note to herself,

shoved the e-mail back into her bag, then set her forearms on the table and leaned into them. "So tell me about breeding dogs."

"The birds and bees part, or the human social side?"

Jo smiled. "Human social. It can be a big deal, right? Big stud fees and all?"

"Some dogs do have pretty fancy stud fees, but not like, say, horses. Hundreds usually, not thousands. What are you getting at?" She didn't answer. "You need to be a little more specific. Details vary from breed to breed, place to place, person to person."

Jo let her shoulders relax and leaned back. "If the dog's value is in stud fees, why would someone turn down a stud fee?"

"Ah, well, first, you're starting from a faulty premise. To responsible breeders and stud dog owners, the dog's value isn't strictly financial. I mean, most people are happy when the dog brings in a little money, sure. For a dog with the right credentials, we're talking six to eight hundred dollars, maybe a thousand or a little more, in most breeds, maybe once or twice a year. Some dogs breed a lot more than that, but it's not the norm among responsible breeders. So we're not talking a fortune." I took another sip of latte, wiped the whipped cream off my lips, and went on. "Anyway, the bitch is important too . . ." The detective's eyebrows rose a couple of notches, so I explained. "Bitch — you know, female canine? Proper terminology. Like, you know, mare, hen, woman . . . I've been around dog people so long I forget that definition number one for *bitch* isn't canine for most people. But if we're talking about dog breeding, *female* sounds silly to me."

"Okay."

"Not that there aren't a few of the two-legged kind in the dog world."

She smiled again. "I bet. So back to why someone might say no to a stud fee on a dog?"

"If a responsible stud owner doesn't think the bitch has anything to offer the breed, you know, if she has major faults in terms of the breed standard, or hasn't passed the recommended screening tests for potential health or temperament problems, she'd probably turn her down. Or she might think the bitch is okay but not a good match for her dog. All dogs have faults, and you don't want to breed two that have the same faults themselves or in close relatives."

She scribbled furiously, and I went on. "Good stud dog owners also care about who owns the bitch and won't breed their dogs to any bitch whose owner they don't trust to do well by the pups."

"So you think Ms. Dorn would have been fussy about all this?"

"I think Abigail would have been very fussy, but . . ."

She cut me off. "It all sounds pretty judgmental. Lots of room for hurt feelings?"

"Sure, that can happen. Why the interest in dog breeding?"

"Part of the investigation."

"But Abigail wasn't standing Pip at stud."

"Must have been. That's what this," she tapped the paper with her pen, "is about."

"About using Pip as a stud dog?"

"Right."

Another little secret, whispered Janet Demon, ticking off all sorts of implications if that was the case. "When was it written?"

"Last week. Friday. The day before she died."

"Now that *is* weird," I said, mostly to myself and the table. Jo glanced up, then went back to writing in her notebook. So I told her, "Pip is neutered."

She stopped writing. "He's what?"

"The dog is a sucker for tummy rubs, and I'm telling you, he has no noogies."

30

"Can I ask you a couple of questions now?" I was revved up on caffeine and sugar by then and feeling a bit more comfortable with Detective Stevens.

"Sure. But I can't discuss the details of an ongoing investigation."

I remembered her telling me before that she was just asking a few questions. "Is it an investigation now?"

"Not exactly. But something isn't right."

"And the men in charge think you're hormonal for thinking that?" We shared a nonverbal female-bonding moment, and I said, "Windy and cool."

"What?"

"It was windy and cool on Saturday. No bees."

Jo's pupils dilated a notch. "You're very observant."

"I'm a photographer. I see things." I hesitated before asking, "What if she was poisoned? Would that show up?"

She sat up a little straighter and I swear I saw her ears prick forward like a terrier with a varmint in sight. "Depends. The effects of some toxins are obvious, but sometimes they have to know what to look for." She turned those cop eyes on me. "Why would you ask that?"

"What else? She wasn't shot or bashed in the head, and the bee-sting theory makes less and less sense."

"Why did you remove Ms. Dorn's bag from the crime scene and wash the contents?"

The blood raced out of my head, leaving me a little woozy. "I was trying to help Greg. I didn't know it was a crime scene!" The women at the table next to us stopped talking and turned to check me out. I lowered my voice and leaned forward into the edge of the table. "I didn't know it was a crime scene." The blood rushed back, and my temples began to pound.

"Of course not." She glanced at her watch as she stood and gathered her things. "Thanks for your time, Ms. MacPhail."

"Janet."

"Janet. I may need to speak to you again. You'll be around?"

"Sure, other than weekend dog shows. I

have my dog entered in a couple that are coming up." My head was settling down, but my stomach did a flipflop. "Am I a suspect?"

"There aren't any suspects yet. We aren't sure a crime has been committed. We won't know that until we have a cause of death."

And then she left, my peace of mind tucked into her pocket along with her nice little notebook.

My "How to Photograph Your Pets" class was a welcome respite — nary a word about murder. I showed slides of good and bad photos, and I reminded the class that I post tips online, including Janet MacPhail's #1 Rule of Photographing Pets: *Get down to the animal's level.* Don't shoot a picture from above. As I always explain, if you shoot from above, you'll get a big-head and teensy weensy paws. Your pet won't look too great, either.

Remember that, Janet, whispered the helpful little angel on my right shoulder. *Perspective makes all the difference.*

31

The next morning, I stopped at the pet supply store in Northcrest Shopping Center for dog food, and what should I spot in the parking lot but Giselle's beat-up old Yugo. A couple of new bumper stickers graced the hatch: *I ♡ my Maltese* and *If you can spell, thank a witch.*

I found Giselle examining tiny doggy duds. Precious popped his head out the v-neck opening of Giselle's wrinkled orange, yellow, and red poncho, his black eyes sharp beneath the purple bow that held his silky white topknot.

"Morning, Giselle."

Giselle flung a tiny denim jacket back at the shelf and clutched at Precious. She turned, took a step back, and peeked at me from under her bangs. "Oh, hi?" My fingers itched to get some grooming sheers from the next aisle and give her a trim. *Or you could get a big purple bow and give her a topknot so she could be precious, too,* suggested Janet Demon. Giselle probably thought I was smiling at *her.*

I left Giselle and wheeled my cart to the back of the store, where I wrestled a forty-pound bag of premium dog food into my cart and considered a visit to my chiropractor. I nearly ran over Giselle as I turned around. "Oops!"

"Oh, sorry, I'm sorry?" Why did everything she said sound like a question? Giselle still clutched Precious against her bosom with her left hand, but her right hand fluttered wildly. It patted her bangs against her brow, brushed something from her poncho, pulled Precious's purple bow slightly askew, back to her bangs, all in about four seconds. She didn't look at me.

"What's up?"

"Huh?" Eye contact! But only for a half second.

"Did you want something, Giselle?" *Perhaps a book on self-esteem?* The good Janet on my right gave my dark side a whack, reminding me to *Be kind, even if she begs to be disliked.* I took a deep, balancing breath and leaned my elbows against the handle of my cart.

Giselle took a good half minute to gather herself, but finally she whined, "Can I talk to you?"

That was the last thing I expected, and I wasn't keen on spending much time with Giselle, but something in her neediness got to me and I agreed to meet her at the Cookie Cottage across the parking lot.

I was borderline high from the warm aromas of baked goods, cocoa, and coffee wafting around the Cookie Cottage, but I had decaf, black, and an oatmeal raisin cookie. Virtual health food. I had to lose ten pounds. *Okay, twenty.*

"You sure Precious is okay?" It was too warm to lock a dog in a car.

Giselle deposited a large mocha with whipped cream and three big cookies — white chocolate and macadamia, double chocolate raspberry cream, and double chocolate mint chip — on the eat-in counter, then struggled onto the stool next to mine. I had a vision of Horton the elephant sitting on the bird's nest in my vintage Seuss. Giselle glanced toward the woman at the cash register, and, when she was sure she wasn't being watched, pointed down the front of her poncho. Precious was so quiet, I hoped he hadn't suffocated.

"Aha!" I watched a third of the double chocolate raspberry cream disappear in one bite. "So, Giselle, I don't have much time. What's up?"

"Oomph, I mwant a tell oo about Agail . . ." Mercifully, she stopped talking, finished chewing, swallowed, swigged her mocha, and started again. "I wanted to tell you, uh, ask you, about Abi . . . , uh, ask what about Gre . . . um . . ."

I still felt rather sorry for her, but something in her eyes urged caution. Dogs aren't people in fur coats, but our two species are more alike than you might think. Some individuals collapse in a submissive heap when frightened. Others bite. All my instincts told me I was looking at a fear-biter.

"What about them?"

"Um, uh, okay, Greg and I are, you know, friends?" Was she asking me? "I mean, you know, Abigail was my friend, too, so maybe it seems funny, but Greg and I are friends, you know, more than *friends,* and, okay, maybe you didn't know that when you came over and all, but," she broke off a huge hunk of the white chocolate and macadamia, "I thought you should, you know, know that so nobody gets, you know, embarrassed?" *Too late,* I thought as I watched her poke the cookie between her lips and tamp it in with her palm.

I finally got it. "Giselle, I have no interest

in Greg other than as a friend and fellow dog lover."

She munched on, staring at something in the vicinity of my navel. She didn't look convinced.

Just to make sure she got the message, I rephrased. "Giselle, I'm not romantically interested in Greg, and Greg's not interested in me." I didn't add that Greg didn't appear to be interested in her either. In the immortal words of Elvis and the good Janet murmuring in my ear, *don't be cruel.* I shifted the topic.

"Giselle, do you know anything about Suzette wanting to breed Fly to Pip?"

She washed the last of her cookies down with mocha and licked her lips, leaving a chocolatey smear at one corner. "Yes?"

"And?"

"Abigail wouldn't?" Apparently she didn't know that Pip couldn't. Was I the only one aside from the Dorns who ever gave the poor guy a belly rub?

"Do you know why?"

A little black nose poked out of the neck of Giselle's poncho. Giselle checked the clerk, who was busy and hadn't noticed, and patted Precious gently from outside the poncho. "All I really know is what was on the BC list." She meant one of the online discussion lists for Border Collie lovers.

"They discussed breeding plans on the list?"

"Not really?" Her spidery bangs veiled her eyes. "Abigail posted that somebody wanted to breed to Pip, but there was some problem with OFA or DNA or bad hips," meaning hip dysplasia. "She said it like, you know, disgusted that someone who should know better would breed like that."

"Did Suzette reply?"

She nodded and swallowed a bite of cookie. "Not right then. But everybody knew she'd talked about breeding Fly to Pip for a long time, so later she posted that people should check facts before spreading rumors."

"How come you're on the Border Collie list?" In all the time I'd known Giselle, she's had only tiny little boy dogs. Before Precious, the Maltese, she'd had Sweetie, the toy Poodle, and QT Pie, an ancient Yorkie.

"Oh, I dunno? I'm on a bunch of lists, maybe twenty or thirty? Just to, you know, learn stuff?"

Just to simulate a real life, you mean.

An hour later I was home and settled in to read my e-mail, but soon found myself on www.offa.org, the web site for the Orthopedic Foundation for Animals, or OFA. I hit the link to the searchable database and typed in what I knew about Fly. Her hips were rated OFA Excellent. So why would Abigail have claimed that she failed? I still had dial-up, and the search took a while, but I found Fly's siblings, parents, and their siblings, all with very acceptable ratings.

And what about that significant little detail concerning Pip's anatomy? Abigail had obviously kept his reproductive status to herself, which wouldn't be all that hard with a dog with nice long furry britches. But why?

I had no sooner signed off the Internet than the phone rang. Caller ID displayed my brother's cell phone number.

"Hi, Bill."

He pitched his voice high and talked way too fast. "Janet! It's Bill. Your phone has been busy for over an hour and your cell goes to voicemail. Is Mom with you?"

"What do you mean?"

"I'm at her house. She's gone!"

32

"Mom's gone! I've looked everywhere."

Well, now, Bill, not everywhere *or you'd have found her, huh?* "I thought she was going home with you."

"She refused."

Great. "Did you talk to her this morning?"

"Yeah. Around 7:30. I was supposed to take her to Scott's for groceries."

A terrifying thought hit me. "Is her car there?"

"Yeah, yeah, the car is here, and anyway, I took her keys a long time ago."

Thank God. My mind flashed on the massive stock of tomato soup and cooking oils in Mom's kitchen, but I decided now wasn't the time to ask how she got Bill to go along with those purchases if he was ferrying her on her shopping trips. I also decided it wasn't the time to ask why he left her alone in the first place, so I stuck with the essentials. "What time were you supposed to go shopping?"

"We said nine, but I didn't get here until a little after ten."

Two and a half hours. How far could a little old lady go on foot in a couple of hours?

I pulled up in front of Mom's house twenty minutes later. There was no sign of her, and Bill was still whining, "How could she do this to me?" I ignored the question, told him to stay put in case she showed up, and hopped back into my van. A glance in the rear view showed Jay standing in his crate with a "What? We're not getting out?" look on his face.

"Where are you going? Hey! She couldn't have walked to Scott's! It's too far!"

Bill was right, of course. It was more than a mile to the grocery store so unlikely that she'd go on foot. Still, Mom had been acting pretty darn weird lately. I drove as slowly as I dared, ticking off a couple of drivers behind me and scanning the area as best I could without leaving my lane. Nothing. I parked in Scott's lot, rolled all the windows down for Jay, and ran into the store. I made a quick tour, checking each aisle in turn, and started back to the door I came in.

"Morning!" came a cheery voice. Louise has been a cashier at Scott's for as long as I can remember. I haven't a clue what her last name is, but I do know that her son studies art at the University of St. Francis here in town, and her daughter is in the Air Force. Funny what we learn and don't learn about people.

"Have you seen my mom this morning?"

"Don't believe I have." Her freckled forehead crinkled under her brassy yellow bangs. "Something wrong?"

"Long story. Look, here's my card with my cell phone number. If she shows up could you please call me right away, and try to hang on to her until I get here?"

Louise lowered her voice and clucked softly. "She's been having some problems, hasn't she?" She didn't wait for an answer. "Sure, I'll keep an eye out." As I speed-walked to the exit I heard her add, "Let me know, okay, hon?"

I hit Bill's button on my speed dial as I rushed back to my van and surveyed the parking lot again. "Anything?"

"No, no sign of her." I couldn't tell which he was now, pissed or scared. Probably both. "How could she do this to me? I have better things to do with my time!" *Okaaay, pissed on the outside, scared silly on the inside.*

I opened the back of the van to check on

Jay. Even with the windows wide open, I don't like to leave him in the car on warm days. He lay quietly with his paws crossed, but stood when I opened the crate door. I clipped a leash onto his collar and put him in the back seat, something I rarely do. He's safer in his crate. But I needed someone to talk to, and he hardly ever back-seat drives.

I turned south out of the parking lot onto Maplecrest. I was about three blocks short of Mom's street when Jay started to bounce on the back seat, barking out the driver's side window and scaring the bejeepers out of me. "Quiet!" He switched to a high-pitched whine that I thought Memorex could have used in one of their glass-shattering ads for audio tape, then realized with some surprise that those ads were ancient history. Jay danced on the seat, his tailless bum gyrating like a hula dancer.

When my adrenalin leveled off and my brain started to function again, I realized what Jay was telling me. *Ohmygod.* There was a church entrance to my left and no traffic in the oncoming lanes. The van's tires protested mildly as I whipped them left into the parking lot. Jay bounced and wriggled and whined. I scanned the parking lot, lawn, and church entrance, but I couldn't see a thing. I got out and grabbed the leash as Jay

187

sprang into the front seat. He pulled me into a breathtaking run toward the church.

And then I saw her, prone and unmoving, as still as death.

33

A scattering of white dogwood petals glistened against dark mulch beneath the tree, and a heady blend of lilac and exhaust filled the air. All my senses focused on the scene before me, and the rest of the world receded in a blur.

Mom lay in a semi-fetal curl on a circle of grass ringed by hedges of forsythia, her head pillowed by her purse, the picture of peace under the stony gaze of St. Francis and his sparrow. She wore slacks the color of a good summer lawn, brown leather flats, and a white cotton sweater festooned with embroidered flowers. I gave her the sweater for her birthday, and hadn't seen her wear it before. She was so still.

Numb though I was, I felt the slack of the leash rise and go taut, the bite of leather against my fingers as Jay yanked me forward. Traffic whooshed and rumbled not twenty yards away, and birds murmured somewhere, not close, but not too far. We were moving fast, yet in my memory those seconds run long and languid. My heart expanded until it pressed all the air from my lungs, but still there was room for fear, and a forewarning of sorrow. Time stalled as I took in the prostrate form. Fear would have frozen me in place had it not been for my dog.

Jay had no qualms at all. He dragged me into the grassy circle, skidded to a stop, crouched low, and ran his velvet muzzle along Mom's arm and neck. Still whining, he covered the side of her face with short, hot swipes of his tongue.

"Oh my goodness! Laddie, stop that, you silly boy!" She opened her eyes and struggled to sit up. Laddie was her Collie. He died before I was born.

The spinning in my head slowed and changed directions. Mom was alive. From all appearances, she was well, physically at any rate. I pulled Jay gently off and had him lie down, then laid a hand on my mother's arm.

"Mom, what are you doing here?"

She flinched and swatted at me. "Who are you?"

I hooked my hands under her arms to help her to her feet. "Come on, upsy daisy."

She tried at first to pull away, then co-operated, sort of, and made it to her feet, swaying and swiping with moderate success at bits of vegetation clinging to her pants. I picked up her purse and Jay's leash, and off we went to the van. Once I had everyone safely locked into his or her spot, I called Bill at Mom's house and Louise at the grocery store, and got behind the wheel.

Half an hour later Mom was snoring softly in her own bed, Jay was sprawled on the cool linoleum by the back door, and Bill and I were still duking it out in the kitchen. The only thing we agreed on was that Mom wasn't safe on her own. Bill, of course, wanted me to take full responsibility.

"Look, I'll do the legwork, but you're going to have to help. If one of us is checking out nursing homes — that would be me — seems fair for the other to take care of her in the meantime." I moved into his line of vision and made eye contact. "That would be you."

I took his "Harumph" for agreement. The clock on the wall said it was 4:37, which meant it was probably about 5. Mom's clock had been twenty minutes slow for as long as I could remember. I'd taken my watch off when I was at the computer and had forgotten to put it back on, so I had to go with the guesstimate. "I've been asking around a bit already. If I get going now, I can probably stop at one or two places, you know, nursing homes, on my way home, and do some more research tonight." I neglected to mention that I had an agility class at 6:30. Dog-related activities had no status in Bill's world view.

Jay bounced and wriggled all over the kitchen in the hope of getting some dinner, while I changed into my running shoes and poured his rations into the fanny pack I use for training treats, adding some raw carrot slices and Colby-jack cheese cubes for variety. "You'll have to eat on the run tonight, Bubby," I told him.

I took a quick look at my e-mail, hoping the magazine editor had sent the contract for the photos she wanted. No such luck. I didn't see anything else that couldn't wait until later except one message from Greg Dorn's e-address. I opened that one and read.

"Janet, it's Greg. Greg Dorn." *Well, yeah, Greg, I sort of got that from the address at the top of the e-mail,* I thought, then mentally smacked myself for lack of compassion. The man was, after all, grieving. I read on. "I don't know what you think you're doing, but please stop asking about Abigail's personal affairs. Please. That's a job for the police, not her friends. Just let Abigail rest in peace."

34

I put Greg's message out of my mind when I walked into Dog Dayz twenty minutes later. People and dogs of all sizes and styles were arranged around the room in various poses and configurations. A Sheltie, a Miniature Poodle, a Beagle, and a Rottweiler were lined up at the back of one ring practicing a group sit-stay and watching their owners chatter to one another thirty feet away.

I set up my crate, put Jay inside, and went to see what was up with the gathering by the table that hugs one wall of the training room. Ten or so people surrounded it, oohing and aahing. A sheet cake held center stage among paper plates, napkins, and plastic forks, and although pieces had already been carved from its fringes, the design in the center was intact, a digital icing photo of Fly taking a jump, and underneath it the icing caption *Fly . . . Congratula-*

tions for soaring above the rest! A sign drawn in a rainbow of marker colors hung on the wall above the cake, announcing the reason:

New OTCH
Scotswool On the Fly
New UDX
#2 Border Collie in Open Obedience for last year!
In the running for #1 this year!

A big bowl of homemade dog biscuits sat to the side of the cake.

I checked out the room to see who else was there. Mostly I noticed who wasn't. Not that I really cared where Tom Saunders was, I reminded myself.

"Isn't it exciting?" Marietta Santini had stepped in beside me. "That makes four OTCH dogs who have trained here!"

Here and elsewhere, I thought, although I didn't say it. Truth is, most of the best trainers and competitors take classes, seminars, and lessons from anyone they think can teach them to be better trainers and competitors. But still, Suzette had been training at Dog Dayz since she got her first dog, a Shetland Sheepdog named Mimi.

There's nothing quite like having your peers admire your dog's achievements, and

Suzette was wallowing in the outpouring of congratulations when I walked up to the table. "Fly has a chance to be number one Border Collie this year now," I heard her say. *Now? As in now that Abigail and Pip are out of the running?* Despite what she'd said at her house, she didn't sound all that worried about Pip and Abigail's absence demeaning her standing with Fly. Suzette tossed a cakey plate into the trash, then picked up a clean paper plate and fanned her face with it.

"Is it hot in here, or is it me?" Her face was flushed, and tiny beads of perspiration glistened on her forehead. She folded the plate and shoved it into her back pocket. "I think I'll take Fly out to pee." They exited through the back door.

Suzette came back without Fly and I walked over to congratulate her a little more privately. *Who do you think you're kidding?* The Janet Demon was back. *You want to see if she says anything incriminating.*

Suzette's face was glossy with perspiration and pale but for two bright-pink spots on her cheeks.

"Are you okay?" I asked, putting my hand on her shoulder.

She swayed slightly. "Must be all the

excitement. I don't feel too great. I think I'm getting the flu or something. Think I'm gonna go home." She swayed again, and gulped down half a bottle of water. "I'm so thirsty." She finished off the bottle.

I put a hand on her arm to try to get her to sit down for a minute. "My God, Suzette, you're burning up!" I offered to drive her home, but she declined. "I just need some sleep. I already put Fly in the car." She started to leave, but turned back. "I need to talk to you. Was going to tonight . . . but . . ." She put her hand against the wall and panted. "God, I think I'm gonna barf." She squeezed her eyes shut and swallowed, then very softly said, "I'll talk to you tomorrow" and turned to leave.

I offered again to drive her home, but she waved me off. "Feel better!" I called to her back. Suzette raised her right hand in acknowledgment as she disappeared out the door.

35

Marietta Santini made her usual pre-class announcements, including an invitation to finish the cake so she wouldn't have to do it herself. I thought a few extra calories would help her long frame look a little less skeletal, but I kept my thoughts to myself. Then she picked up a beautifully wrapped package and looked around for Suzette and Fly, so I piped up. "Suzette wasn't feeling well and went home, but she asked me to thank you all for your support." People and dogs dispersed and resumed training, and I turned to find Tom and Drake standing behind me.

"Hi." Tom grinned. His brown, green, and white plaid shirt made his eyes look like melted milk chocolate, which I'm sure is why my mouth began to water. "How's your mom? I heard what happened." He squatted down and ruffled Jay's ears with both hands. "You're a genuine doggy hero, aren't you, fella?"

"Where did you hear that?" News always races along the dog-training grapevine like a pack of Beagles on a hot scent, but the speed of this transmission had to be record-shattering.

"Ran into Connie at the gas station on my way here."

"Gad. I talked to her less than an hour ago, on *my* way here."

"Your mom okay?"

I filled him in.

"So Jay saw her and barked?"

"He couldn't have seen her. She was lying on the ground in a little meditation garden there at the church." I caressed Jay's silky cheek with the back of my hand and felt the love from his warm brown eyes wash over me. "Sometimes they just know, don't they?"

Tom waited a heartbeat as he gazed into Jay's eyes and stroked the dog's soft cheek with his thumb, then stood and shifted topics. "Are you going to the funeral?" Abigail's service was at ten the next morning.

"Not much looking forward to it." *Talk about an understatement.* "But yes, I'll be there. You?"

"I have student conferences all morning, winding things up before finals, so it's not a good time to cancel." He paused, his eyelids drooping a bit and the corners of his mouth matching them briefly. Then his eyes regained their sparkle, and he said, "Hey! How about I take you out for dinner tomorrow evening and you fill me in?"

Some small, non-hormonal part of my brain registered how clever and cute that was — the grown-up version of the yawn-and-stretch arm-around-the-shoulder technique so well known to teenage boys of my generation. Some things never change, do they? You'd think the thirty years since he invited some lucky girl to the prom would make it easier to ask for a date.

A date? *Dinner with a friend isn't a date,* whispered one of my little friends. I wasn't at all sure which one, demon or angel, or whether she was right, but the point was moot in any case. I was on deadline to get some photos out to one of my publishers, so I asked for a rain check.

Tom nodded and smiled, but I thought his shoulders sagged a notch. He promised to cash the rain check soon.

36

I arrived at St. Hubert's around 9:45 and found small clusters of friends and family members in the lobby outside the chapel. I paid my respects to Greg, who greeted me as warmly as ever in spite of his "butt out" e-mail of the night before. Maybe he was out of his mind with grief?

Connie was standing outside the chapel, signing the guest book, so I joined her, greeting a few people I knew on the way. "Hey."

She put the pen down and turned around. She glanced at something behind me and curled her lip in a positively feline snarl.

Giselle had just emerged from the ladies room, dabbing at her face with what might have been a bright pink bandana, though it was so wadded up that it was hard to tell. Her skin was even more sallow than usual, except for a number of red blotches scattered across her cheeks and chins like cartoon cherries. She clumped into the group surrounding Greg, parting the well-wishers like a rhino through a herd of antelope. Her black stretch leggings reached half way down her calves, highlighting every roll and dimple along the way, and her faded black knit tunic clung to the ample contours of her torso. Fuschia roll-down socks peeked out between the fishbelly skin of her legs and her black canvas high-tops, underlining a huge crescent moon tattooed on the outside of her left calf. Black nail polish, eye shadow, and lipstick, and her trademark greasy hair, completed the look.

"Oh, Greg, it's so sad!" she sobbed, making an open-armed lunge toward the widower.

Even at that distance, I could see Greg's jaw muscles clench, and the crimson tinge of his cheeks made me wonder which was winning, his urge to flee or his urge to clamp his fingers around Giselle's throat and squeeze. Socialization trumped biology and he held his ground, fending off Giselle's proffered embrace by turning ninety degrees, as he might to teach a puppy not to jump up. He gave her a venomous glance, then turned toward the chapel and said to the other people gathered around him, "I think it's time."

The only comment I could conjure was, "Hunh."

"Right." Connie unpursed her lips and took my arm. "Come on, we may as well take a seat."

We sat down behind Marietta and several Dog Dayz members, about halfway to the front of the chapel, and I asked Connie if I'd missed any other excitement.

"Suzette's not here," she whispered. "Pretty tacky of her not to show up."

"She wasn't feeling well last night. Maybe she's sick."

"Even so, she could have made an effort out of respect for Greg." Connie lowered her voice further so I had to strain to hear her. "Let's face it, not many people are here because they loved Abigail. And Suzette and Greg . . . uh . . ." She shifted in her seat. "Anyway . . ."

"What?"

"I'm a blabbermouth. Forget it, okay?"

I was a bit put out, because in all the time I've known Connie, I've never thought she said or did anything by accident, and the sense I had now that she was trying to plant ideas in my head bothered me. "I don't know, I just don't see it with Suzette and Greg. But I guess it's possible." I rolled the idea around in my mind. "Do you really think they were involved?"

"I don't really like to gossip." *Yeah, right.* Connie leaned forward and said something to Marietta, and I decided to drop the Suzette and Greg issue until later. The morning sun cast shafts of gold and rose and heavenly blue through the stained-glass window behind the altar, washing the front of the chapel in shades of faith and hope. The altar itself was a simple affair of warm golden oak flanked by two simple sprays of white lilies.

The pews were filling quickly, and about half the faces were familiar. Sylvia Eckhorn smiled sadly at me. Many of the others were people I saw often at obedience and agility trials, and I mentally matched them with their dogs. I'd photographed lots of them, and although I couldn't remember most of the people's names, I never forget a furry face. There was Bullet's person, and owners of at least two canine Abbys, which I was sure Abigail would have enjoyed, and . . . you get the picture.

In the pew behind the family, among the blondes and brunettes, auburns and silvers, I spotted a head of incandescent red. Francine Peterson, Pip's breeder. She was leaning forward across the back of the other pew, toward the side of Greg's head, talking nonstop and chopping at the wood in front of her with the heel of her right hand. She had people's attention, and Greg looked none too happy about it.

Greg shifted in his seat and turned toward the jabbering woman, his hand held up in a "stop" gesture. I couldn't hear him, but saw him glare at Francine and round his mouth into "No!" before he turned his back on her.

Francine froze for a few seconds, then clambered over the people seated to her left, stumbled into the center aisle, and scurried toward the rear exit of the church. Her face was fury incarnate, and she was talking again, this time to herself. As she flew past us I caught two words that spilled like ice water down my spine: ". . . be sorry!"

37

A murmur swept the chapel in Francine's wake, and every eye following her retreat.

"Boy, you weren't kidding when you said she was odd."

"That was way past odd. That was certifiable." Connie resettled herself facing the front of the chapel. "Talk about bad timing. You'd think she could wait until his wife is in the ground."

"Wait for what?"

She combed back an errant lock of strawberry blonde with her manicured fingers. "To pester Greg about the dog."

"The dog?" I had no idea what she was talking about.

"She wants Pip."

"How do you know that?"

Connie leaned toward me, her blue eyes gone a dull gray. "I heard her talking to Greg before you got here. She said that as Pip's breeder she should get him back." A responsible breeder would be willing to take her puppy back at any age if he wasn't wanted by his owner, but I had seen the love between Greg and Pip and knew he was more than just Abigail's competition dog. He was family.

"What did Greg say?"

"He told her that Pip was staying right where he is."

Made sense to me. "Maybe she wanted to be sure he knew she'd take him if Greg didn't want him?"

"She wasn't asking, she was telling."

The pastor talked about Abigail's love of animals and her work with Border Collie Rescue, and Greg's brother offered a brief eulogy, mostly about Abigail's relationship to her dogs. It was fitting, upbeat, and twenty minutes long at the outside.

I couldn't see everyone from where we sat, but you'd have to be as deaf as the stained-glass saints to miss the mournful sobs and lamentations for "Poor, poor Abigail" emanating from Giselle's pew. Even the pastor was giving her "tone it down" looks, but Giselle was oblivious. And loud.

When it was all over and we were drifting out of the chapel, I whispered to Connie, "That was the most interesting assortment of music I've ever heard at a funeral." A young soloist from the choir had filled the chapel at strategic points in the service with his rich tenor renditions of *I Can See Clearly Now, I Hope You Dance,* and *Walking on Sunshine.*

"Greg said that Abigail left instructions with her will, including the music, and how she wanted to be dressed. Did you see her?"

"Uh, no. I'm not all that keen on viewing dead people."

"Her favorite black obedience slacks, and her 'Come Over to the Dark Side' sweatshirt." Connie grinned at me. "I guess the pastor had a hissy fit about that until Greg explained that the Dark Side means Border Collies."

"I bet." I was thinking once again that there must have been a side to Abigail that I'd never seen — a side I would have liked.

"She also wanted her favorite braided leash and photos of her dogs. I wonder what St. Peter will make of those when she presents them at the Pearly Gates?"

"Forget the Gates. She's going to the Bridge!" I meant the Rainbow Bridge, where pets are said to wait for their people to join them on the other side.

38

A half hour later, and despite Leo's assistance, I laced up my brand new ninety-dollars-on-sale running shoes. No question, they were comfy. I loaded my bouncing Aussie into the back of the Caravan and drove to the River Greenway trail head on North River Road. The sky was a clean robin's-egg blue, and the sign on the bank at Georgetown Square had given the temperature as sixty-seven degrees when I drove by on my way home from the funeral. A perfect day to find out whether my pricey new footwear made my back and knees feel better. Besides, a walk along the Maumee River would do us both some good.

Our goal was a mileage marker two miles to the east. Jay trotted back and forth at the end of his retractable leash, marking here and sniffing there among the violets and spring beauties skirting the paved trail. We startled a great blue heron from his fishing spot on a sandbar, and watched his heavy liftoff and slow rise against a backdrop of stout beeches and silver-trunked sycamores on the opposite bank.

I emptied my mind on the walk out, letting recent events go and reveling in the simple pleasures of a May day and companionable dog. Even without my other senses, my nose told me it was spring. The warm green scent of new-mown grass drifted to me from the farm to the north of the trail and mingled with the brown-black musk of damp soil and rotting bark. A pale, sweet, anonymous thread stitched itself in and out of the heavier scents, sweet and somehow disturbing. I had read somewhere that flowers want attention from both the loving bee and the scavenging fly, because both will carry pollen from bloom to bloom. So beneath the sweetness of tender blossom and heady scent lurks a hint of rot. Sex and death, entwined like lovers.

I watched the silky surface of the river to my right, wending its way northeast to Toledo and on to Lake Erie, lazy and brown, like thick, dark tea. My Zen skills, minimal at the best of times, were exhausted by the time we reached the two-mile marker, and Abigail, Greg, Giselle, Suzette, Tom, and crabby old Aunt Ellie played hot potato with my thoughts for the forty minutes back. Who stood to gain by getting Abigail out of the picture? Greg? He'd inherit her money, and be rid of the constant nagging. Still, by all indications Greg adored his wife. Unless Connie was right about him and Suzette.

An unwelcome question burrowed into my brain. What about Abigail's long-lost cousin Tom? Even with Abigail dead, he wouldn't get any of the family fortune, would he? Greg was Abigail's legitimate heir, and Connie mentioned a will, so what could Tom have to gain? Revenge? That didn't seem likely after all this time, but who knows how long vengeance can smolder in a human heart? I confess, I still entertain occasional revenge fantasies starring my ex-husband Chet, and it's been twenty years since he left me with three maxed-out credit cards, an empty gas tank, and an enormous sense of relief that he was gone. Perhaps Tom relished his revenge, as the proverb recommends, served cold.

Who else? Giselle? She's smitten with the widower, and she turned onto the road to Weirdtown long ago. But murder? Desire blurs people's vision, but could she really be so far off her rocker that she can't see that Greg just isn't interested?

And what about Suzette? Would she kill over dogs and dog sports? Or to get Greg away from Abigail? How about two with one blow? And there was the matter of Abigail's allegations about Suzette's bitch, Fly. But all Suzette had to do was refer people to the online resources. They could see for themselves that when it came to health screening for breeding, Fly was cleared for takeoff. It would have been easier — and safer — to kill rumors with facts than to kill Abigail. Were Suzette and Greg involved, as Connie suggested? Judging by the diamond ring by her kitchen sink and her confused reaction to my questions about Fly's intended consort, she certainly manifested all the signs that some sort of man-related business occupied her mind. But would Suzette kill for love?

Love. Hormones. What troublemakers. I was beginning to wonder if I was the only one *not* looking for a lover when a vision of Tom's broad shoulders and mischievous grin strolled into my thoughts. On its heels came an image of Chet before it all went wrong. No slouch in the good looks department, Chet. A cloud of sadness scudded across my mind. I shook off the sting behind my eyes and came back to the present, determined not to be sad, especially since I wasn't entirely sure what brought the feeling on.

We were almost out of the wooded portion of the Greenway when Jay darted across the blacktopped path and dove into some shrubbery, yanking me off the pavement. I sank to my ankle in soft, sticky clay, and the unmistakable stench of carrion crawled up my nose.

I fumbled with the locking mechanism on the retractable leash and finally clicked it into position, for all the good it did by then. "Jay! Leave it!" I panted, pulling him backwards out of the brush. He turned toward me with a glob of gray fur and disintegrating flesh in his mouth and a delighted gleam in his eye.

My left foot wrestled with the gooey clay for possession of my shoe, and lost. I stepped backward onto the pavement clad in two socks but only one shoe. I pulled Jay to me, snarled "drop it," and clamped a hand across the top of his muzzle. No dice. He gave me a "Go find your own rotten squirrel" look. I squeezed his lips against his teeth, trying to get him to drop the stinky mess so I wouldn't have to touch it. He loosened his grip, but not enough. I caught a lungful of air and held it, clamping my lips together and scrunching my nose against the stink. "Drop it!" I growled again, bending to grab the soft, wet mass from his mouth. I pitched it back toward the brush and shook my hand away from my body. "Yuch! That was disgusting."

Jay looked at me, and I told him to lie down and stay. He did, although he whined and gazed longingly toward the sprawl of crabgrass where the carcass had landed. I used my clean hand to search my pocket for a tissue. No luck. I swallowed the gorge that rose in my throat, and wiped my hand on a patch of grass, figuring it was better than nothing. I crouched on the pavement, reached cautiously toward my shoe, and took hold of the back of it. Pulled. It resisted at first, then began a slow slide toward me, and came free at last with a sucking plop. I fell back onto my butt and wrinkled my nose at the fat clump of yellow-gray clay that encased my no-longer-brand-new shoe.

Jay crossed his paws and squinted at me, panting and smiling. "Very funny," I said, using a stick to scrape off as much of the sticky gunk as I could. My sock was wet and muddy, so I peeled it off, stashed it in a plastic poop bag, and shoved my bare foot into my shoe. At least the inside wouldn't be ruined for now. I picked up the leash, released Jay from his stay, repeated the

"Leave it" command, and stomped toward the van. Nothing like a dead rodent and a pound of wet clay to cap off a nice walk on a spring day.

39

The thought of what might be dancing around on my squirrel hand had me itchy by the time we got home. I scrubbed and rinsed in the hottest water I could stand until my hands looked like lobster claws. Jay, ever the student of odd human behavior, followed my movements, brown eyes focused and ears pricked. He crossed his paws and grinned when I told him, "I know one dog who won't be kissing me for a week!"

Goldie would have pointed out that I was having a lovely time on my walk until I let my mind veer away from my own concerns and into other people's business. Still, I'm nosey by nature, so I settled in at the computer, checked my e-mail, and decided to find out a little about Tom Saunders, who was arguably making himself my business.

I started with a search for *ethnobotany*, which yielded an interesting assortment of links. Lots of websites devoted to saving the world's rainforests. Information for science teachers. New Age sites on herbs of all kinds. So he's a New Age conservationist? I googled Tom Saunders. *Googling Tom Saunders sounds like fun!* The little demon was back at my left ear. *Be that as it may, it wouldn't hurt to know something about him,* countered Little Ms. Cautious on my right.

I found his page among the university's faculty web pages. There was a nice shot of Tom in front of some enormous plant in a greenhouse, and a short biography giving his academic pedigree. B.S. in botany and chemistry from Purdue. Masters in anthropology, Indiana. Ph.D., anthro, Michigan. Dissertation title: *Flesh of the Gods: Ceremonial Use of Psychedelic Entheogenic Mushrooms in Oaxaca.* Whoa! I flashed back to reading Carlos Casteneda in my wild youth.

I went back to my search results and scanned the first page of links to see if there was anything else of interest. Mostly they went to conference sites where he was listed as a speaker, and some continuing studies courses from a couple years earlier, including one on native plants of Indiana.

At the very bottom of the list was an odd one, a six-year-old obituary for a Rachel Saunders. I clicked on the link. *Rachel Holtz*

Saunders, 68, died Monday at her residence in Fort Wayne. I skimmed over her two-paragraph biography, but read and re-read the rest. *Survived by a son, Thomas Saunders, of Fort Wayne, a daughter, Nancy Saunders Wilson, of Wilmington, North Carolina, a grandson, Tommy Saunders, of Bloomington, Indiana.* Since Tom was the only son, Tommy must be his son. College student? Bloomington is home to Indiana University's main campus, so it seemed likely. I realized with a start that I knew nothing about Tom's life away from dog sports, let alone his possible motives for, well, anything. There was also mention of a sister, Carissa Holtz Schwartz. That rang a bell. I ran to the kitchen and pulled the newspaper recycling bin from the pantry, fishing around for obituaries from the past couple of days. There it was, Thursday's *News-Sentinel* — obituary for Abigail Schwartz Dorn, daughter of Carissa Holtz Schwartz. I left the papers where they were and returned to my computer, backtracking to the biography for Rachel Saunders, where I found *Daughter of Eloise Holtz, founder of the Aunt Ellie's Bakery chain.*

So Connie was correct. Abigail's mother and Tom's mother were sisters, but Abigail's mother inherited Aunt Ellie's entire wad.

Ohmygod! my guardian angel screeched into my right ear. *Tom is an expert on poisons! Tom got screwed out of a fortune!* The little twerp was practically hysterical.

Oh please. The devilish voice of reason checked in. *Just because he could've and had a motive, doesn't mean he did.* Then again, it doesn't mean he didn't, either. I sat in front of the computer screen and batted the possibilities back and forth for a quarter of an hour. Jay snored softly, his chin warm and solid across my instep.

40

The rest of the afternoon passed quietly and I got a lot of work done. I even sorted a pile of papers and threw half of them away. The rest I piled back onto the desk. Okay, so I'm organizationally challenged. I'm trying, but recovery from lifelong messiness is a slow process. I've thought about hiring a professional, but I'd have to get organized first so she could sort me out. At four o'clock I fed Jay, and the two of us went outside for some fresh air.

"Janet!" called a cheery voice. "How are ya?" Goldie came to the fence. She peeled her dirt-encrusted work gloves from her hands and drew a forearm across her glistening forehead. The knees of her jeans were capped with drying muck and grass stains, and her faded denim shirt was rumpled and streaked with mud. She's the happiest looking woman I know, although I did notice that the delicate skin beneath her eyes still looked bruised, and dark hollows burrowed into her cheeks.

"Hey, what's up? How's the garden?"

"Grow, grow, grow."

"And you? Are you okay, Goldie? You look tired."

"Say, remember I told you I knew your Tom from somewhere?"

Okay, I thought, *so we're still not going to discuss how she is.* "He's not *my* Tom, Goldie." I could feel the heat rising in my face. *Damn!* "He's just a friend. That's all."

"Sure. I can see that in the way your face gets red when you think of him."

"I'm having a hot flash."

"My point precisely. It's time you put away your widow's weeds."

"I'm not a widow."

"My other point." She adjusted one of the pins holding her braids in place. "Anyway, I knew I knew Tom, but I couldn't place him. He used to have a beard. And of course he was younger since it was, what was it, ten years ago?"

"What? When?"

"Oh, when I took the class. And he was very good — great class, he did a wonderful job of pulling together material from different disciplines, you know, history, botany, psychology. He's an anthropologist, you know. Actually an ethnobotanist. Fascinating stuff."

"Yes, I know, Goldie. I mean, I know he teaches anthropology." I love her dearly, but getting information from Goldie can be like riding a luge down the rabbit hole. "What class are you talking about?"

"It was called, oh dear, it's been a few years, let's see," she stood silent for a moment. Her soft gray eyes seemed to look through me, then glinted in the sun as she found what she was searching for. "Yes! That was it! It was right before Halloween, you know. I think it was four sessions, but maybe only three. Wonderful class. He really knows his stuff."

"What kind of class, Goldie?"

"Oh, not a credit class. Adult ed. Lots of fun. That's why I decided to plant my new garden, been thinking about it ever since, finally getting around to it. Small world, huh?"

"Uh-huh." *Her new garden is a witch's garden.* I was starting to worry that I wouldn't like what she was going to tell me, but I had to know. "Goldie, what kind of class? What was it about?"

"The Witch's Garden." She waved an invisible wand through the air. "Taught it at that nursery out by Huntertown. Great stuff.

222

Love potions, poisonous plants, medicinals, midwifery, all sorts of stuff." She reached out and poked at some young leafy stems with her trowel. "Here we have some yarrow. When it blooms, I can make you a love charm if you like." She batted her lashes at me.

"No thanks. I'm charming enough." She giggled, and I steered us back to the subject at hand. "So he taught you about poisons?"

She laughed, a full-bellied Goldie laugh. "Not how to! But yeah, that was part of it." She spoke a little faster. "As I told you, lots of garden plants are toxic, and wild ones too. Fine line, you know, between curing and killing. Like, oh, digitalis. Foxglove. Also called Dead Man's Bells. Now, wouldn't that name go over big in a suburban nursery? Anyway, you know, a little can help a bad ticker, too much can stop a good one." She looked for something in the air over her head. "What was that show on *Masterpiece Theater* where the son knocked off his old mother with foxglove tea? Oh dear, let me think." She scratched her left temple with the back of her wrist in a futile attempt not to smear her face with dirt. "When was that? It was years ago. You'd have loved it. The hero had a way with dogs, tried to stop dog fighting and bear baiting and such."

My own heart was sinking as she spoke. What is it they say is needed to pin a crime on someone? Motive, means, and opportunity? Tom had them all. He knew his way around botanical toxins, that was clear. He was at the obedience trial when Abigail collapsed. Revenge could be a motive, but Abigail didn't disown Tom's mother, their grandma Ellie did. Still, Abigail did inherit the family fortune, and people hang onto all sorts of grudges. But would Tom do such a thing? More to the point, *did Tom kill Abigail Dorn?*

"Precious Bane." Goldie's voice pulled me out of my reverie.

"What?"

"That was the name of it. *Precious Bane.* Great story — it's a book too. You should read it. Wonderful."

Wonderful indeed. The first man to make me blush since Chet hit the trail might be a *real* lady-killer.

41

The Tri-State Border Collie Rescue Group's annual reunion cookout was the next day, and I had been invited to shoot photos. I drove into Foster Park from Old Mill Road, slowing to a crawl so I could savor the prismatic display of spring blossoms lining the roadway. Beyond the low beds of tulips, hyacinths, narcissus, and squill lay the perennial beds, now in various stages of spring growth. Grass walkways and graceful wooden benches backed by snowy dogwoods and cotton-candy cherry trees urged visitors to stroll, or simply sit and revel in the day.

I pushed my yearning for a quiet, contemplative escape from the turmoil of the past week to the back of my mind and drove to shelter house number one, a sprawling affair of limestone blocks set amid towering sycamores and oaks some thirty yards from the bank of the St. Mary's River. Two

Border Collies, a smooth-coated black and white and a rough-coated tri-color, were tugging on the two ends of a long knotted rope, shoulders low, rear ends high, tails waving. A dozen or so other BCs and their people mingled among the five picnic tables that dotted the grounds in front of the shelter house. Beyond them, near the river, a young man and his small blue merle dog entertained a knot of spectators with fancy flying-disk stunts, the wiry little dog vaulting from his owner's back, weaving between his legs, and racing away at a signal, always snagging the taxi-yellow disk in the air.

I gathered my camera bag and tripod from the back of the van, and walked toward the shelter house, scanning the crowd for a familiar face. Marietta Santini waved to me from one of the picnic tables, where she was talking to several people I didn't know. She came to greet me.

"Need help?"

"Sure, thanks. I have a few more things to bring over. Any idea where they want me?"

"Angie!" Marietta beckoned with a hand as she hollered toward a pair of women who were taping butcher paper to the picnic tables. One of them, a lanky blonde, wore faded jeans and a T-shirt with a row of Border Collie faces looking out over lettering that proclaimed her a "Proud Owner of a Rescued Border Collie." She stuck one last strip of tape to her project, and strode toward us as Marietta said, "Angie Yoder, Janet MacPhail."

Angie nudged a loose strand of hair away from her face with the back of her left hand, offering me her right. "Oh, the photographer. Great! People have been signing up for photos. I think about a dozen so far."

"Good to hear," I set my tripod down so I could shake her hand. "So, where do you want me?"

"Wherever. Pick a spot you like. I'll help keep everyone in order when you're ready." She started to walk back toward her taping project. "Help yourself to the grub whenever you're hungry, too. Gotta go finish the tables."

I picked up my tripod and explored the area, settling on a nice spot in light shade ringed by pink and white dogwood, a good backdrop for the mostly black and white dogs.

Half an hour later I had pots of tulips, daffodils, and pansies, a few loose cut flowers, my Radio Flyer red wagon, a red checkered table cloth, picnic basket with cheese, bread, and wine, all arranged in stations around my photo area. I just hoped none of the dogs ate the edibles. Or the inedibles, for that matter. The last thing we needed was another emergency.

I set off with my camera to get some candid shots and look around. I greeted a few people I knew, mostly by face or dog, not name, and a lot I didn't. I went into the shelter house to check out what was happening there. Someone had set up a table with several albums of photos, letters, newspaper clippings, and other miscellany documenting the history of Tri-State Border Collie Rescue, which covered parts of Indiana, Michigan, and Ohio. Some of the adopters had brought their own albums and framed photos of their rescued dogs.

A small table sat alone, draped in fabric printed with rainbows. A sign hung from the front that read, "In memory of those we couldn't help." I walked over there with some misgivings — nothing depresses me as quickly as the tales of wonderful dogs lost to negligence and cruelty. But whoever set up this memorial had kept it simple. An unmistakably Border Collie silhouette of black painted wood was fixed into a base at the back of the table. A small jar candle, ringed with tiny vases of dark blue pansies, flickered between the silhouette backdrop and a statement printed on creamy parchment held in a black wooden frame.

> We cannot save every dog in need.
>
> But we can help many through the Four E's:
>
> 🗸 example
> 🗸 education
> 🗸 effort
> 🗸 empathy
>
> Please help where you can.

The text was followed by the Tri-State's logo — a Border Collie silhouette in a heart — and their phone number, web URL, and email address. To the left were stacks of application forms for volunteers and potential adopters, and to the right a donation box and a pile of tri-fold brochures. I had shoved some bills into my pocket before I left home, so I pulled them out, extracted a twenty, smoothed out as many kinks and wrinkles as I could, and put it in the box. I stepped back from the table and took a few pictures of it. Then I turned to leave the shelter house, and found myself looking into Francine Peterson's gold-green eyes.

42

Francine had come in, like Sandburg's fog, on little cat feet, and she stood just beyond arm's reach from me. Her red hair seemed to fluoresce under the lights of the shelter house, and her expression was somewhere between casual hatred and venomous rage.

"Oh! Hi." My first two words came out about twice as loud as they should have, but I reeled my vocal cords back to normal volume as I went on, switching my camera to my left hand and offering my right to Francine. "Hi. We haven't met. Janet MacPhail."

"Yes, I know." She apparently also knew that I knew who she was because she gave me neither her name nor her hand. "You took my dog."

"Excuse me?"

"Pip. You took him."

"You'd rather the police had impounded him?" Angry as I was, little jolts of caution poked at me as I took in Francine's expression and body language. I squared my shoulders and straightened my spine — when faced with a predator it's a good idea to look big and strong. "I took him home to be sure he was safe. Now if you'll excuse me, I have work to do." I stepped past her and left the shelter house.

The rest of the day found me looking over my shoulder from time to time, but everything went smoothly. I photographed some thirty dogs, ate more than necessary but less than I might have at the lavish lunch spread, and had a wonderful time meeting the dogs and the people who loved them. Then I bought a stretch of raffle tickets, dropping them into lunch bags numbered for toys, treats, and a copy of *Rescue Matters: How to Find, Foster, and Rehome Companion Animals,* which was getting great reviews and I'd been planning to buy anyway. Didn't win a thing, but I did manage to avoid any further encounters with Francine, and saw her only once more, loading a dog into a beat-up van whose red paint had seen brighter days.

Suzette's absence was noted, although no one seemed to be sure whether she had planned to come or not. The only comments I heard about Abigail had to do with how much money and time she gave to Border Collie rescue and how much she'd be missed, confirming what Sylvia Eckhorn had told me about Abigail's generosity, and reinforcing my regret that I hadn't known her better.

I took hundreds of photos and made a foolhardy promise about when the proofs would be posted on my website. The afternoon flew by with only one minor mishap. An adorable fuzzball of a puppy pulled her leash out of her owner's hand, snagged a baguette from the picnic props, and ran in big fast loops known as "zoomies" among dog people. Bob Ziegler sent two of his working dogs after her, and they managed to corral her in the shelter house. Calm was restored, and the remains of the baguette split between Bob's dogs.

I was settling in at home about 6:15 when the phone rang. I let my electronic secretary get it while I called Jay back in from the yard and got a diet ginger ale from the fridge.

"Janet! Tom Saunders here. Nothing real . . ."

I grabbed the phone. "I'm here." I hoped he couldn't hear my stomach going boing boing!

"Oh, good! How are you?" We went through the dog-fancier greeting ritual — *how's the dog, how's training going . . .*

"Missed you at Dog Dayz on Wednesday." Another obedience practice night. "Everything okay?"

"I'm teaching a class on Wednesdays right now. Or was. That was the last class."

"What kind of class?"

"How to photograph pets."

Tom Saunders has a delicious laugh. "Nice to know you have diverse interests."

"Uh-huh. And pray tell, what do *you* do when you aren't at obedience training on Mondays and Wednesdays, agility practice on Thursdays, obedience, agility, and field trials on the weekends?"

"You forgot field training. Tuesdays and some weekends. You're not the only one with diverse interests." *My God, could this be my soul mate at long last?* I had a tiny twinge of terror in deference to my brief, disastrous marriage to Chet, but the fact was, ours was more a marriage of youthful hormones than of, as the sonnet goes, true minds. Tom broke the short silence. "So, is it a good class?"

"Class?"

"How to Photograph Pets."

Duh. "Sure. Lots of fun. No homework to

grade, interested students . . . I even have a Facebook page for it." I gave him the URL. "But you teach non-credit classes, don't you? So you know."

"Yes, ma'am. Starting one in a couple of weeks, as a matter of fact."

"Yeah? On?"

"Edible plants. Three sessions, one on edible garden flowers, one on edible wild plants, and a field trip."

"Not the witchcraft plants this time?"

"Have you been checking up on me?" There was a tease in his voice.

"No, no!" Even I could see I did protest too much. *Settle down. Yeesh!*

He let it go. "Actually, my training is in anthro with a botany minor. My research interest was — is — ethnobotany. But I think I already told you that."

"Plants in different cultures, right?"

"Pretty much."

"Sounds fascinating. You should meet my next-door neighbor sometime. Oh, wait, you did, at the co-op. And it seems she took a class from you once. She has the most fantastic garden. You should see it."

"How about you give me a garden tour?"

"We'd need Goldie if you want actual information."

"So, how about I buy you dinner tomor-

234

row evening and we go from there?"

Ho boy. That sounded like a slippery slope that I still wasn't sure I wanted to slide down just yet. But Tom, it turned out, didn't fight fair.

"You like Indian food?" he asked.

Better judgment aside, I never turn down Indian food. We agreed to meet at a little place on Coldwater Road. Its name changes about once a month, but the atmosphere is always relaxing and the food yummy. Stress makes me crave spices and carbs, and I had a hankering for *chana masala* and *mango lassi*. Janet Angel was tapping a toe on my right shoulder and giving me some nonsense about calories and heartburn, but Janet Demon outshouted her with her reminder that *You only live once — go for the spice!*

43

I exchanged instant messages with my online friend Randi, who offered a few observations about some of the characters we encounter in cyberspace. I always think of her as an "Aussie person," but suddenly remembered that she has two Border Collies as well as the Australian Shepherds, so I asked if she knew anything about the conflict between Abigail and Suzette.

Randogs: No. Not on any BC lists.
JanetFoto: ?
Randogs: Part of my 12 Step program.
JanetFoto: Curing yourself of the Internet?
Randogs: No. Toxic people.
Randogs: Did you check the bitch on OFA?

She was, of course, referring to Fly, not any of the human players.

JanetFoto: Yep. She's there, all clearances.

Randogs: Did you check the dog?

Meaning Pip, the dog, the male partner. Now why hadn't I thought of that? It never occurred to me to check Pip's records, but Randi's question gave me an epiphany. Abigail must have had a reason for having him neutered and keeping his reproductive status to herself. When we'd finished our chat, I typed in www.offa.org and searched the database for Paragon's Pip. There he was — hips OFA Good, elbows normal, other clearances in place.

I moved on to his relatives. Inheritance is rarely straightforward, and good breeders and smart buyers check to be sure that as many relatives as possible also passed their screening exams. Trouble is, you can't be sure what a lack of records in the database means. Some dogs are missing because they didn't pass the tests, some because they were never tested. But I would be very surprised not to find some of Pip's relatives there, considering his breeder's long history of breeding titled dogs.

I was very surprised. Pip's parents weren't in the database. I found only one sibling, and all that was listed for her was a clear thyroid exam. Could Pip have close relatives with hip dysplasia or other inherited health problems? Could Suzette have been the one who decided not to breed her bitch, Fly, to Abigail's Pip rather than the other way around? Abigail certainly wouldn't be the first stud-dog owner to retaliate with vicious gossip against someone who rejected her dog. If that were the case, I'm sure Suzette would be incensed. But enough to kill?

44

By six the next morning I was wide awake. I'm not prone to regular fits of morning exercise, but although I wanted to ask Connie about some things, I knew at this hour she'd be feeding and exercising her dogs, so I took Jay for a walk. It had been too long since I'd been out at the start of the day with an animal and not driving to a dog event or photo shoot. My right brain was whirling bits of information around like berries in a blender, but the other hemisphere savored the glow of dew on early summer grass, the sweet scent of honeysuckle reaching out from a neighbor's fence, the twitter and flit of finches, robins, and wrens. I almost forgot the inharmonious events that got me up so early in the first place.

When we got back, Jay sucked up his cup of kibble, tanked up on water, and plopped down for his morning facial from Leo, who, as always, gripped both sides of the dog's face in his paws and went to town with his raspy tongue. I knew that Leo would make sure that not a single crumb remained around Jay's lips, and that every hair on the dog's head was neatly licked by the time they finished. They were content, but I was getting more fidgety by the minute, and since Mr. Coffee was still dripping, it wasn't from caffeine. I picked up the phone at 6:55.

Connie declined at first, then agreed to meet me for breakfast. She had some grooming products I'd ordered — for Jay, of course — and would bring them along. She always orders my dog-grooming sup- plies at her discount price. I took a quick shower, arranged my curly wet hair into what I hoped would be a reasonable do when it dried, slapped a little eye shadow and mascara on, stuck some dangly silver and turquoise in my ears, and was out the door in twenty-three minutes.

I read the menu for the sixth time. I'd been there for a quarter of an hour and still hadn't decided between stuffed French toast, the farmer's skillet, or biscuits and gravy. Connie finally joined me, and I made the virtuous decision to have the fruit plate with banana bread. After we ordered, we somehow got onto the subject of childhood memories.

"Oh, you know what?" I had just finished recounting what I'd learned about Tom's background, none of which was news to Connie. She patted her fork against her scrambled eggs, "That brings back a vague image." She took a bite, chewed slowly, and made me nuts.

"What?"

"Nothing definite. But I have this sort of image of overhearing my mom talking about how sad it all was, something about Tom and his mom and . . ." Her pupils dilated a notch. "Yeah! I remember — she called old Aunt Ellie 'that mean old bat,' and there was someone else there, someone who said it wasn't right, no matter what, to cut off an innocent child that way."

45

Connie nibbled a piece of bacon and I chewed on the possibility that Tom Saunders might have had a hand in Abigail's death.

"But why would Tom kill Abigail? He wouldn't inherit from her, and besides, why now? He's what, fifty? Has a great job, nice house, good life, great dog. It makes no sense."

"More like fifty-five." Janet Demon and Janet Angel whispered in quick succession, *Oh, good, he's not a younger man,* and *What do you care? You don't want to get involved, remember?* I half ignored both of them and tried to pay attention to what Connie was saying about Tom. "Graduated with my brother." She leaned into the table and her eyes opened wide. "Maybe to avenge his mother? Deep hurts and all that?"

People do things you don't expect all the time, but the idea of Tom Saunders killing

Abigail in cold blood over a generations-old family feud just rang off key, and I told Connie, "Possible, I suppose, but I still don't see it."

She raised her eyebrows.

"Come on, Connie, you know the guy better than I do. It would take a real nutcase to hold a grudge that long." I knew I was talking a little too fast, hoping I was right without much real data to go on, and I felt my cheeks heat up. "Does Tom seem like a nut to you?"

"No, you're right, he isn't. I guess I watch too many movies. You know, screwed-up son raised by mother from dysfunctional family turns serial killer." She examined one well-groomed nail. "But you don't have to be crazy to want revenge. Happens to the best of us. Actually, if I were a detective I'd be looking at people linked to Abigail by dogs. She rubbed a lot of people the wrong way."

"Yeah? But that much? I mean, she wasn't very nice to be around, but murder?"

"Who knows? She hurt a lot of people's feelings, and attacked reputations, or sat back and watched other people attack them when she knew better, you know?"

"Funny that." I was thinking about what people had said at the Border Collie rescue picnic. "The rescue crowd seemed to really like Abigail."

"Yeah, well, they weren't competition, and they stroked her a lot because she donated gobs of money."

"I just wonder if some of us had the wrong impression. I know I never talked to her all that much, to be honest."

Connie set her coffee down with a thunk. "Okay, take Marietta. A couple years ago, Marietta was supposed to buy a pup from Pip's breeder, that woman you asked about at the show."

"Francine."

"Right. Pip sired the litter and I'm sure Abigail recommended the pups." I wondered if that was accurate in light of Pip's current reproductive status, but he could have sired a litter before he was neutered. Connie went on, "Marietta backed out of the purchase. She never said much, at least not to me, just that she wasn't comfortable with some things about the breeding. I think Francine got pretty nasty about it, kept the deposit and badmouthed Marietta. Abigail and Marietta were pretty good friends up until then."

"I heard a little about a puppy purchase falling through, but I didn't know Abigail was involved." I thought about it for a moment. "It's hardly a reason to kill someone."

"Abigail liked to spread crap around. Lots of accusation by innuendo, you know?" She crinkled her nose. "She and Francine both."

"And that's what she did to Marietta?"

"Someone posted on the Internet that Marietta was away from home day and night, and supposedly had a lot of dogs at her place. I always thought Francine was involved in that. Maybe Abigail too."

"Well, duh! Marietta runs a training school and boarding kennel." I was outraged. "She only has two dogs of her own, and they go to work with her."

Connie folded her napkin and laid it on the table. "Pay attention, Janet. It's the half-truths that matter."

I thought about that. "Okay, so she implied that the dogs Marietta boards are her own?" Marietta runs a lovely small boarding facility along with the training school, and usually has anywhere from five to twenty dogs in temporary residence. "But that's just silly!"

"Sure, if you know about Marietta's place. But you know how the Internet is. People get some half-baked accusation in their teeth and shake it forever. Marietta was pretty upset."

"I'm surprised she still let Abigail train there if she was involved."

"She had no grounds to give her the boot. Abigail's membership was undoubtedly paid up, and besides, Marietta used Pip's standing in obedience to promote the place. It all died down eventually. Anyway, Marietta wasn't the only one who didn't like Abigail. Suzette hated her guts."

Suzette didn't sound like she hated Abigail when I talked to her, I thought, but Connie knew them both better than I did, so I didn't comment. "Conflicts over obedience standings?"

"Nope. Okay, sure, I guess, but that wasn't where the real venom showed up. More breeding issues, I think." Her forehead creased. "Although what sort of breeding issues I'm not sure. I mean, dog or human, if you get my drift." Her left eyebrow lifted a notch and she went on. "I don't know too much, but I've heard things. I do know Suzette was angry about something to do with Fly. I think she asked Abigail about breeding Fly to Pip a while back, and Abigail had a rather public tantrum about it on one of the Border Collie lists."

There was that Pip-as-stud-dog problem again. "You know for sure that Pip's ever sired a litter?"

The space between Connie's eyes puckered. "Sure he has." Her tone suggested it was a really dumb question. "I told you, the pups Marietta looked at were his."

At least that's what Francine said.

I decided to let the subject drop. "Okay. So why did Abigail have a fit?"

Connie relaxed into the back of her chair. "Abigail claimed Fly had something shady in her genetic past and would sully Pip's reputation by producing pups with problems. I don't know the details, never looked into it. Not my breed, you know? But I heard that Suzette was fit to be tied."

"This was on the obedience lists?"

"I don't think so. I think it was on some BC list? Actually, though, I could be wrong. I heard about it from Giselle, so Abigail probably told her. They were friends."

"You talk to Giselle that much?"

"I groom her dog every few weeks, so yeah, we talk. Anyway, Giselle wouldn't be on a Border Collie list." But Giselle had told me she was indeed on the BC list and I was about to correct Connie about that when she laid a tip on the table, gathered her belongings, and stood to leave. "Hey, I forgot the shampoo and stuff. I need to run home before work anyway, so I'll bring it by your place in a bit."

I thought about our conversation while I fished out my credit card and decided I wasn't at all convinced that Abigail was the Dorn who held Giselle's interest.

46

I made a couple of stops, so it was half an hour later when I pulled into my driveway and spotted something on the porch. That wasn't unusual — I'm always getting packages of photos, publications, and what-have-you related to my work. But I could see from the driveway that this delivery had nothing to do with photography. It turned out to be a basket wrapped in crinkly pink cellophane and filled with what appeared to be homemade dog treats. A cluster of purple grosgrain ribbon ringlets hung from the rattan handle, and a tiny white envelope with "Janet" typed neatly in the center dangled from one curly strand.

I was unlocking the door when Connie's car pulled into the driveway and she hopped out with a plastic bag in her hand. She pointed at the basket. "Whatcha got there?"

As soon as Jay was out the back door, I pulled the gift card from the envelope and read the note typed there: "A small token for all you've done. G."

Leo stood on the table, leaning over the edge toward Connie, meowing and nosing around her pants pocket. Connie nudged him away. "I had some salmon treats in there earlier for training. The dogs love 'em."

I pulled off the elastic band that held the cellophane closed and took a whiff. Garlic and cheese — also very popular with the canine set.

"Who's it from?"

"Must be from Greg. I mean, he's the only one I've done anything for recently."

I pulled the cellophane down and picked out a biscuit. Definitely homemade, cut in the shape of a heart, and very fresh judging by feel and fragrance.

"Smells good enough to eat."

Jay popped the back door open and bounced into the kitchen. He made a bee-line to the table, dancing around, nose twitching, little bubbles of drool glittering along his lips. "Just one, Bubby!" I signaled him to spin to the right and twirl to the left, and rewarded him with the cookie heart. And a second one. I can be easy.

"I know Greg has a lot on his plate, but he's acting really odd. Why would he send me a 'take a hike' e-mail, then act like everything's fine and send me a gift?"

Connie's right eyebrow arched and I couldn't read the look in her eyes. "It's not all about you, Janet."

My jaw dropped and I stared at Connie as she pulled a tube from her pocket and freshened her lip gloss, oblivious to my reaction. "Greg's a nice guy. He probably just wanted to thank you."

She didn't seem to think he was so nice when she talked about his philandering earlier, but I didn't trust myself to say anything. I pulled the cellophane up and stashed the basket in the pantry closet, out of reach of Australian Shepherd jaws, then emptied the bag Connie had brought. Shampoo, conditioner, and finishing spray. "That's more gunk than I use on my own hair." I tried to smile at Connie, but my mouth wouldn't cooperate. She wasn't looking at me anyway. "Be right back."

It took me a minute to push bottles and toilet paper around to make room for Jay's new beauty supplies. By the time I got back to the front of the house, Connie was halfway out the door

"Hey! I need to pay you for the stuff."

She waved me off, calling "Later" over her shoulder.

I went to the kitchen and lifted Leo into my arms. What was that all about? Was I really self-focused enough to deserve the "not all about you" comment? And why *would* Greg give me a gift now? Ah, well, the Doors sang it long, long ago. *People are strange.*

47

Tom was already ensconced at a table and reviewing the menu by the time I got to the restaurant, whose name had changed again. It was the Bombay Inn this week. He stood, smiling, and sat back down across from me once I was seated. The sleeves of his chambray shirt were rolled to just below his elbows, and the blue fabric intensified the brown of his eyes. We went through the usual greeting ritual. At least I think we did. I was too busy trying to remember the steps to this dance. Besides, all I could think, if *think* is what I was doing, was *hubba hubba.*

A waitress, who spoke so softly I could barely hear her, interrupted us, setting a basket of black-pepper *pappadams* and a bowl of mint chutney on the table, and we ordered. Then Tom asked me about Abigail's funeral. "It was actually very nice. For a funeral." I filled him in on the details, including people's comments about Suzette's absence.

"It's not as if they were all that friendly," he said. "I suppose she could have come as a gesture of respect for Greg, but I doubt he even noticed."

"Abigail and Suzette were better friends than people realize. At least that was the impression I got from Suzette."

"Really?" He focused those milk-chocolate eyes on me. "Well, I'm sure Greg was preoccupied with other things, plus I imagine his own friends were there, and family from both sides."

Right. Of course, Abigail's cousin didn't show up, I mused during the momentary lull while we both nibbled *papads* and chutney.

"Did you know that Abigail and I were cousins?" How come everyone seemed to be reading my mind these days? What could I say? *Yeah, now I have been checking up on you.* Or maybe this would be a good time to ask if he killed her? *Nah!*

"My mom and Abigail's mom were sisters. But you knew that, didn't you?" I had an almost irresistible urge to squirm in my seat as if I'd been caught looking through his dresser drawers. "I'm sure Connie told you."

"I saw an obituary."

He raised one eyebrow. "For?"

"Okay, I Googled you." Why did that sound so sexy? I swore inwardly as I felt another warm red glow light up my face, and hoped it didn't show in the subdued light. "Your mother's obituary came up. But heck," I heard my delivery speed up but couldn't seem to rein in my mouth, "I barely know my own cousins. Just from Christmas cards and occasional phone calls, you know? They're scattered all over the country, hard to get together." I dished out some more verbal sedative until I noticed that Tom was leaning against the back of his chair and grinning at me. "Sorry." I took a big gulp of water to shut myself up.

"We were all here in town, but I didn't even know about Mom's family until I was pretty much grown up. She never mentioned them, and when I was a kid I never asked. Not sure why, although I have a hazy image of someone calling my grandmother an uptight, hypocritical old bag or something like that. I guess that killed my interest for a while." It didn't sound like anyone had anything very nice to say about old Aunt Ellie.

Our food arrived, and Tom leaned forward. "Sorry. Don't want to bore you with ancient family politics." He picked up a piece of *naan,* tore off a hunk, and scooped up a mouthful of *mattar paneer,* the peas and white cheese poking through the rich, savory sauce, and we embarked on other topics.

He talked about his fieldwork in Mexico and Peru. I talked about teaching in North Africa in the seventies, photo trips to Europe, Asia, the Arctic, one I hoped to set up to photograph feral dogs in Egypt. He told me about his son, Tommy, who would be starting graduate school in the fall. I realized later that neither of us mentioned spouses, and that I had no idea what had become of Tommy's mother. I found myself talking to him about things I hadn't thought about in years, and more than once I had to suppress the urge to shove the table out of the way and jump his bones right there in the restaurant. *Good thing I'm so disciplined,* I thought. *I'd like to be able to eat here again.*

48

The waitress cleared away the ruins of our dinner and served us steaming cups of fragrant spiced *chai.* The real thing, not the coffee-bar version. Talk shifted to high school, and Tom told me about the band he was in with Connie's brother, Jerry. "We practiced a lot in the big old barn on their grandpa's farm down near Ossian. I played drums." He mimed a drum riff. "We didn't really care about music, we just wanted groupies."

"Did you get them?"

"Nah. All we got were complaints from the neighbors. Said the racket upset their hogs." He chuckled. "Jerry's dad finally shut us down, much to Connie's delight."

"Connie didn't like the band?"

"She wanted to be in it. She used to show up for practice with a toy tambourine and get absolutely furious when Jerry wouldn't let her join in." He guided me further down memory lane. "It was their grandpa who got me interested in ethnobotany."

"I thought he was a farmer."

"Yep. Good old-fashioned Hoosier farmer. Corn, beans, hogs, feeder calves. But he knew his weeds. Used us kids to patrol the pastures for jimsonweed, hemlock, and the ever-popular wild *cannabis,* all hazards for his cattle."

"I can't see Connie traipsing around farm fields."

"It wasn't pretty. Whined all the way about getting her jeans dirty."

We talked the sun down, so the garden tour was off, but in spite of my reservations, I wanted to keep the giddy feeling a while longer. Okay, so maybe I was hoping to take this thing a step beyond the talking stage. *Might as well find out if the guy can kiss before you get in too deep,* whispered Janet Demon. I heard myself invite Tom home for a nightcap, then racked my brain trying to remember whether I'd left any underwear lying on the bathroom floor. *If I did, please be sure Jay didn't carry them to the kitchen,* which he did from time to time.

By the time I reached my van I'd exhumed all the questions about Tom that raging estrogen had made me forget. What was I doing, inviting a guy with a motive for murder into my home? I mean, hormones have made me do some dumb things in my time, and I'd been out with a few lady killers in my younger, wilder days, but as far as I know none of them were actual murderers.

And even if he were perfectly non-homicidal, what was I doing? I was dead sure I didn't want to put my heart out on another limb like the one Chet shoved it off. Not that I hadn't dated a few guys through the years, but it had been a while, and none of them had made my innards react like this. *Oh well,* I thought as I unlocked my van, *too late now.* I watched Tom open his car door, and my heart did a back flip when he turned and stabbed me with another of his killer grins.

49

We sat in the kitchen with mugs of black-berry sage tea, a plate of Goldie's anise-seed and almond cookies between us. I considered opening the bottle of Scotch I'd been saving, but decided I didn't need to mix alcohol with newly revivified hormones. Jay kept bringing his eyeless, one-eared squeakie bunny to Tom, who tossed it around the kitchen and into the dining room. There was a call on my answering machine, but I ignored the little red light.

"So, you enjoy these nature hikes?" I asked. Tom had just told me he'd be leading an educational outing on spring wild-flowers at Fox Island Nature Preserve the following Saturday.

"It's a nice way to get out for some fresh air and spread the gospel of nature appreciation."

"So, if you teach about edible plants, you must mention the inedible?"

He watched me with a look I couldn't read, and my cheeks went hot. Again. *Girl, you've done more blushing since you met this guy than you've done in twenty years.*

"Lots of toxic plants out there. Some lethal, some just nasty." He spouted off the Latin and common names for a whole string of plants that grow in Indiana, most of which I was surprised that I knew. "If you do any gardening, chances are you have poisons growing all around you."

"That's more or less what Goldie said."

He smiled at the mention of Goldie's name. I was about to ask him why when Leo sauntered into the kitchen. He took less than a second to size up our visitor before he sidled up to him, back arching and tail twitching as he deposited a film of orange hairs on Tom's beige slacks. Tom reached down and lifted the cat onto his lap. Leo gazed at him through squinted eyes and ran his motor loud enough that I could hear the purrrr purrrr from across the table. The man likes my cat and, more telling, my cat likes the man. *You're in serious trouble now, MacPhail.*

"Hello, Leo."

I didn't remember mentioning that I even had a cat, let alone what I called him. "How did you know his name?"

Tom massaged the back of Leo's skull and the cat looked practically orgasmic. "What else could a handsome leonine fella like this be named?" I was almost jealous, though of which of them I wasn't sure. "So tell me about Goldie."

"My neighbor with the garden."

"Right. The mystic at the co-op."

"Mystic?"

"I've known a lot of shamans, mystics, people of power. Your friend has the . . ." He paused, searching for the word. "Hard to define. Energy, power, charisma. I'm sure you've noticed."

I had indeed. "I thought you science types didn't believe in such things."

He lowered his eyelids and replied slowly. "You don't have to believe in magic to know that some people have something most of us don't. Or more to the point, they know how to use something inside themselves that the rest of us have forgotten about." It occurred to me that he might not be inclined to say that to a room full of college professors. I wasn't entirely sure what I thought about it myself, and decided to get back to rational conversation, if talk about friends killing friends can be called rational.

"So, we're surrounded by poisonous plants, huh?"

He gently lowered Leo to the floor and watched him stroll toward the living room. "Most of them won't kill you. Some would give you a good belly ache, or visions, but that's about it."

But a guy who knows what he's doing could use those plants to kill, I thought. *A guy like you.*

"Now, if I wanted to knock someone off with plants, there are only a couple I'd use." *There he goes again, answering my unspoken questions.* "I'd want to be sure that my victim was dead or beyond help before help arrived, and I'd want the symptoms to look like natural causes."

I hoped he couldn't hear the beating of my telltale heart.

"Janet, I didn't kill Abigail."

The temperature in my face must have spiked over the lethal level at that. I wanted to crawl under the table.

"It's okay." He smiled. "As you already know, I *could* have a motive, and I have the know-how. But I don't care about family history. Mom told me many times that we were better off without them. She liked to say they were dysfunctional before dysfunctional was cool. I didn't even know the old folks, and knew Abigail just to say hi. From what I know *about* them, I didn't miss

263

anything."

Janet Demon was back, whispering, *Other than a whole pile of money.*

50

Tom's eyes twinkled as he watched me stammer, "I don't know what to say. I'm sorry. Shit! I'm so embarrassed." I'd just as much as accused the man of murder. Nice move on a first date, if that's what this was.

"No need. It's a perfectly reasonable line of thinking. It just happens to be wrong." He changed the subject. "How's Connie doing through all this?"

"I dunno. I guess she feels bad for Greg. I don't think she and Abigail were all that close."

His eyes seemed to turn a shade browner. "No, I think that's a bit of an understatement."

"Oh?"

"Connie's a couple years older than Greg, but he hung out with her younger brother. She was a bit goofy for Greg way back when. Teenage crush mostly, although she kept it up into college. I always thought

Connie made more of small things than Greg ever meant, if you know what I mean."

I knew precisely what he meant. I'd misplaced a few crushes myself in my high-hormone days. I thought back to Connie's comments about what a catch Greg was. What was it she'd said? Something about a good-looking guy with a snazzy ride?

"Connie's brother Jerry and I went off to different colleges and drifted apart, but Connie used to call me at school. We'd get together when I was home. I guess I was sort of a big brother without the emotional baggage."

This was definitely a Connie I didn't know. But then my friend Gina is the only one of my current friends who knows anything about the Janet of thirty years ago, let alone forty, so why should I know more about Connie's younger years?

"She got married herself a year or so later. I had hoped she'd be happy." Tom looked thoughtful. "I think she was for a while."

"She was in the middle of her divorce when we met."

We sat in silence for what seemed a long time, and then Tom reached across the table and covered my hand with his, sending a zing up my arm and down to my toes, with several Tasmanian-devil-type spins en route.

"So, you said Greg left you a gift? Hard to imagine him baking dog biscuits, especially now."

"They look homemade, but I'm sure he must have bought them." I slowly withdrew my hand so my juices wouldn't boil over.

"Maybe someone made them for him."

I tried to stifle myself, but Tom must have seen my lips twitch.

"What?"

"Nothing." A giggle slipped through, and Tom leaned back, watching me from through slitted eyes and waiting for an explanation. "Giselle seems to have a thing for Greg, that's all. She'd have baked him biscuits if he asked."

"No kidding? Boy, he has 'em lined up."

"Has what lined up?"

"Girls."

"Hmm. Maybe I should take a closer look at Greg."

That killer grin again. "Or you could consider the road less traveled." *Whoa!* No one had flirted with me like this in at least a decade, or if they had I'd missed it. Queasy as it made me feel, I decided I didn't hate the feeling. I was still groping for something to say when Tom spoke again.

"So, let's see them."

"See what?"

"The biscuits."

I went to the pantry and reached for the top shelf, hoping that Tom wasn't watching my rear end as closely as I always watched his. I pulled the basket to the edge of the shelf and cautiously lifted it down. Something thumped softly at my feet, and as I lowered the basket I saw that the cellophane wrapper was torn open. Jay started toward me, his eyes focused on the floor in front of my toes. Tom intercepted him with one of those quick collar snags that come naturally to experienced dog owners, and in the same motion moved Jay to the back door, and out.

I held the basket to my side and looked down. "Ewwww!" A tiny corpse lay belly-up on my kitchen floor, glazed eyes open, little fists tucked up to its chest. I put the basket on the table and reached for some paper towels, thinking I'd entomb the body in the garbage. The outside garbage. *What is this, dead rodent week?*

"Hang on a second." Tom placed a hand on my arm as I moved toward the dead mouse. He turned the basket so that he could see the hole in the wrapper, and extracted a broken, or nibbled, biscuit through the hole. "Janet, did you say you gave Jay a biscuit?"

"Yes. A coup . . . Ohmygod! They're poisoned, aren't they?"

Tom and I gaped at one another for a quarter second longer, then both of us sprang into action with the precision that sheer panic can inspire. Tom carefully loaded the mouse into a plastic sandwich bag, the suspect biscuit into another. The back door sprang open and Jay burst in. "Down!" I snapped, and Jay dropped to the floor, his whole being focused on the bags in Tom's hands. "That's it! I've got to replace that damn handle with a knob he can't open!"

I called the emergency vet clinic and, surprised that my voice stayed as firm as it did, told them the basics and said we were on our way. I put a leash on Jay, grabbed my keys, and sprinted for the van. Tom brought the biscuit and the corpse.

51

We stayed until the initial treatment was over. It had been hours since Jay ate the biscuits, so there was no point trying to make him bring them back up. Besides, we didn't know positively that he'd been poisoned, or what the poison was if he had, although the mouse appeared to have bled out internally. They took blood from Jay for a liver function analysis, and administered fluids and vitamin K to counteract the probable anticoagulant and promote clotting. The vet commented several times on how cooperative Jay was throughout the ordeal. That's my good boy.

When we left the emergency clinic at 2:30 in the darkest morning I'd seen in a long time, Jay had a two-inch square of pink skin showing where they'd shaved his foreleg and shoved a catheter needle into a vein to pump fluid into him. He accepted all that without missing a beat, but when he realized

I was leaving without him, he put on his saddest-dog-in-the-world face and ripped out a piece of my heart.

Tom drove me home, solid and silent while I ranted all the way and into the house.

"How could anyone attack my dog? It's sick!" I punched the top of the table.

Tom said softly. "We don't know for sure yet that the biscuits were poisoned."

I glared at him. How could he be reasonable at a time like this? I wanted to punch somebody. "What if it were Drake?"

"Don't get me wrong, Janet. If the biscuits are poisoned and we find out who did it, I'd like a private turn myself with the lily-livered rat." The muscles in his jaw flexed, and his eyes were rivers of heat, at once gentle with concern and aflame with outrage, and something else, something that frightened me, something I wanted to hold and wrap around myself.

Something that ripped through the slender web of control that was holding me together. To my horror, my rage dissolved in a rush of tears. Tom wrapped an arm around my shoulders and steered me to the living room couch. Still holding me, he leaned over and shoved some magazines to the floor, clearing a spot for the two of us. He held me in his arms, and the spicy scent of soap and masculinity worked its way into my over-taut brain. We stayed like that until my well ran dry and my nostrils closed in protest. I went to the bathroom and splashed cold water again and again over my swollen eyes and nose. Then I blew my nose, wiped the mascara streaks out from under my eyes, and ran a brush through my tangled hair. A big hunk on the side of my head that had pressed itself against Tom's chest refused to lie down, even when I wet it, so I gave up and went with the half-nuts look.

By the time I rejoined Tom in the kitchen he had found the Scotch and poured me a double shot. "Drink this." The amber liquid burned its way into me, spreading from my core outward until my mind and limbs together were suffused with a muzzy warmth.

It took almost all the energy I had left to tell Tom, "I'd like to be alone for a while."

He nodded and stood to go. "Get some sleep if you can." His voice was thick with concern. I walked him to his car.

"Thank you." Two words, so often mis-used, so often all there is to say.

Tom hugged me again, and I almost recanted, almost asked him to stay. Instead, I stood alone in the waning night and watched him drive away.

The eastern horizon glowed with the blue-green light that comes before dawn, the sky above still indigo but for a slim silver crescent to the east. The sparrows and house finches that nest in the big blue spruce beside my garage twittered and stirred. I sat in the rocker on my front porch and wallowed in the loneliness of night until long strokes of tangerine and violet painted the day with promise. The birds began to flit in and out of the sheltering branches, murmuring good mornings. An occasional hint of hyacinth from Goldie's yard wafted over me on a light breeze.

I shivered, and realized that it wasn't just my heart that was chilled. I went in. My favorite prints, my handmade rugs, the carefully chosen hues of my walls tried to make me feel at home, but without my dog, this was nothing but a house.

I'd never be able to sleep, so I went to the kitchen to start a pot of coffee before showering. Leo lazed on the counter next to the telephone, and I greeted him in polite Cat with a mutual nose-bump. As I stroked his glossy body, I noticed the answering machine light still pleading for an audience. I pushed *Play,* crossed the kitchen to make a pot of caffeine, and listened to Marietta

Santini's voice, fast and pitched high.

"Janet, are you there? If you're there, pick up the phone." I was pushing the scoop into the bag of coffee and thinking it odd for Marietta to call when I froze. "Janet, it's awful. Suzette is dead!"

52

It was 5:45 a.m. I didn't think I should call Marietta that early, so I considered useful ways to fill some time. In the end I chose to sit on the couch with Leo purring on my lap, head-bumping my hand if it stopped fondling his neck and ears.

What the hell was going on? Two obedience people dead? And my dog poisoned. My Jay-Jay! Thank God the vet thought he'd be fine, but how could anyone do such a thing? I was a little afraid of what I might do when I identified the sneaky coward.

Greg? He wouldn't have baked those biscuits, would he? And if he didn't bake them, how could he poison them? How do you poison a hard dog biscuit? And why? It made no sense. Besides, I just didn't see Greg poisoning a dog. Me, maybe, if he saw me as a problem, but not my dog. So who baked them? Giselle? And if she did, why would she want to hurt my dog?

The blare of the phone jolted me to full alert, and I glanced at my watch as I reached for the receiver. Almost seven. I'd been sitting there for over an hour.

"Janet, it's Marietta. I wanted to catch you before you go out." She was talking very fast, as she did last night. "Did you get my message?"

"Just this morning. I was going to call you. What happened?"

"All I know is Suzette's sister Yvonne got worried when she couldn't reach Suzette Friday evening or all day Saturday, so she went over there and she found her dead, Fly standing guard, so she called me — she was frantic, waiting for the police, she could hardly talk." Marietta sounded like one of those speed-talkers who read the product disclaimers on air.

"But what happened?"

Marietta let go of a long breath and slowed down a bit. "I don't know. Yvonne was a basket case. By the time I got there, the police were all over the place. It was complete chaos. I didn't really get to talk to her. I just got Fly and brought her here."

"You've got Fly?"

"Yeah. Yvonne asked me to take care of her 'til she figures out what to do. Her kid is allergic to dogs so she couldn't take her

276

home." Her voice broke when she said, "It was suicide."

"What?" *What?*

"Hang on." I heard her blow her nose. "Sorry. Yvonne said there was a note, and an empty bottle of acetaminophen."

"A note?"

"Yeah. But Yvonne said she didn't read it. She said she couldn't stay in the house. She got out, and called the police."

Suicide? I didn't know Suzette all that well, but suicide didn't fit what I did know. Marietta continued. "You talked to her before she left Thursday night. Did she seem, you know, upset?"

"She just said she didn't feel well. God. Suicide?"

"It doesn't make any sense, does it? Everything was going so well for her."

"Yeah, Fly was certainly doing great." And judging by the ring I saw at Suzette's house, her love life must have been going great as well.

We both fell silent, but neither of us seemed inclined to break the tenuous human connection the phone line provided. My thoughts wandered hither and yon until Marietta sniffed and brought me back to the present. I'd remembered what Connie told me about the puppy deal, so at the risk

277

of being rude, I barged ahead. "Marietta, I need to ask you something."

"What?"

"What really happened on that puppy deal, you know, when you didn't get the pup sired by Pip."

"Oh. Well, I found out about some issues in the lines and took my name off the list."

"And Abigail was mad about that?"

"Abigail? No, of course not. She's the one who told me about the problems."

"Really?" If that was true, Abigail went up another couple of notches in my estimation.

"Yeah. She told me not to buy the pup, and she got my deposit back for me. Actually, I think she might have paid it out of her own pocket. She told me she was having Pip neutered, but wanted to keep it quiet to avoid a fight with his breeder."

"Pip was the problem?"

"Pip's whole family tree."

"So what? Hips? Eye problems? Epilepsy?"

Marietta said, "No no no. Worse," and paused. *Those are pretty bad. What's worse?* Then she told me. "Abigail didn't think the pedigree was right. She had him DNA-ed, and something was screwy, like his markers didn't align with supposed relatives. She was pretty sure that Francine was misrepresenting puppies as being from dogs she imported. You know, asking more for them, like that. Abigail said she was trying to nail it down, but since she had put me in touch with Francine in the first place, she gave me a heads up. Just asked me to keep it under my hat until she figured it out."

"Wow."

"Yeah, plus she said Francine could be a vindictive bitch, so she wanted me to be careful."

"Someone around here certainly is." I told her about Jay and the biscuits.

"Oh Janet! Oh no! Is he okay?"

"The emergency vet says he will be." I choked out the last three words as the emotional whirlpool sucked me down again. There wasn't much more to add, so I said goodbye to Marietta, then called Connie and told her what had happened. I barely registered that she'd be right over.

I closed my eyes, opened them, walked around, sat down on the couch, but I couldn't erase the images that cycled through the theater of my mind. Abigail on the ground, trying to live. The delicate pink skin of Jay's shaved leg, the IV needle stabbed into his vein. Greg's face, twisted by awareness that his wife might be dying. Suzette's beautiful diamond. My mom losing her faculties. Yvonne, finding her dead sister. Yvonne. Me. I closed my eyes to stop the tears, but they squeezed between my eyelids and ran like hot wires down my cheeks.

A soft presence materialized again on my lap, followed by light pressure on my chest and a bump to my chin. I opened my eyes. Leo lowered his chest to his paws and tucked his rear end down, letting his tail drape across my thigh. He snuggled into me, eyes half closed, motor revving, purrr purrr purrr. A smidgen of the tension gently rose from my heart like steam from a nice cup of tea.

53

I had pulled myself together by the time Connie arrived ten minutes later, but the glue holding my emotions was far from set, and when she came in and patted my shoulder, I reverted to a blubbering heap. Half an hour later we were hugging mugs of hazelnut cream coffee at my kitchen table, Leo gazing at us slant-eyed from the counter across the room.

"Who would do such a thing?" I wondered for the umpteenth time.

"Someone who doesn't like you. Or doesn't like you nosing around."

"I'm not nosing around."

"Sure you are." She blew on the surface of the steaming liquid in her mug and to a tentative slurp. "Need more cream." She stepped toward the fridge and started to reach for the door. She must have startled Leo out of a dream, because he arched his back and hissed at her, lifting a paw an inch off the counter and flexing his claws toward her. Connie hesitated. "What's with the cat?"

I jumped up and scolded. "Leo! What's the matter with you?" He settled back down, folded his paws under his chest, and stared up at Connie while she ran her hand over his head and down the back of his neck. "He's upset about Jay not being here. And he knows I'm upset."

Connie sat back down in her chair. "Anyway, you *are* nosing around. You've been asking a lot of questions."

"A lot of people have been asking a lot of questions! Someone died. Now two people are dead!"

"But Suzette killed herself."

The more I thought about it, the less inclined I was to believe it. My face must have given me away.

"Why are you such a skeptic? For all we know, Suzette might have killed Abigail to get Greg."

Anything was possible. Probable? I had no idea. The longer I live and the more I see, the less I seem to understand why people do anything.

"Anybody tell you what the note said?"

"No."

"Maybe she confessed. Maybe the guilt

was too much. Maybe she was afraid she was going to get caught. Who knows?"

I sure don't.

"Anyway, Janet, I'm worried about you. Suppose someone else *is* involved. If they think you're on to them, you could be in danger. I mean, somebody already poisoned your dog!" My eyes filled, but I got control before I fell into another crying jag as Connie continued. "Everybody's curious. But most people ask rhetorical questions. You ask like you really want to know. And you've been talking to the police a lot."

"No, I haven't."

Connie lifted an eyebrow.

"Okay, I have, but not a lot, and only because Jo . . . Detective Stevens . . . had some questions about the dog fancy. It's not like I know anything else!" I leaned across the table toward Connie, but she was apparently fascinated by something in her cup. "But why go after my dog?" Outrage straightened my spine and squared my shoulders. "I mean, that really pisses me off. He didn't do anything to deserve poisoned dog cookies. What kind of coward does that to an animal?"

"What better way to get your attention? You see it all the time. Not poisoned biscuits, but poison pen letters on the Internet, poison gossip in various groups. Somebody doesn't like somebody else, so they attack the person's dogs for being too big or too small or too hairy."

I stabbed the tablecloth with my spoon, inflicting a dribble of coffee on the blue cotton. "True. Every time she can't win an argument with me, Giselle posts snotty things about Jay to a couple of training lists."

"That note on the basket wasn't actually signed. 'G' could be 'Giselle'."

"She wouldn't!" I thought about Giselle at Greg's house and set my mug down a little too hard, sloshing more coffee onto the tablecloth. "I mean, why would she? It makes no sense."

"In case you haven't noticed, Giselle's not the most secure and balanced of individuals. And you know she has a crush on Greg Dorn." She snorted and rolled her eyes. "Like *that's* gonna happen. But maybe she thinks you're in the way."

I thought about my Cookie Cottage conversation with Giselle and her claim that she and Greg were more than friends. "Okay, but how is poisoning Jay connected to Abigail and Suzette's deaths? I mean, I can see Giselle doing something dumb to scare me, but kill Abigail and Suzette?"

"Who knows? The woman's a little off.

284

And she's into all that witch stuff."

I had to admit that Connie made some sense. And wasn't poison supposed to be a woman's weapon? But then again, Greg's a pharmacist. The more I thought about the possibilities, the more confused I grew. "Maybe it really was Greg." I told her about his e-mail telling me to butt out. "But it doesn't make sense. Even if Greg had reason to knock off good old Abigail, why would he kill Suzette? You said they were in love."

"He didn't. She killed herself. Or, if not, maybe Suzette found out Greg killed Abigail and didn't approve and he had to kill her too." Connie seemed to consider the idea, then went on. "But I don't see Greg doing anything violent. I mean, he spent all those years with the shrew without killing her." While I digested that little morsel, Connie stretched and stood up. "I have a Standard Poodle and a couple of mixed-breeds waiting." Connie has a grooming arrangement with my vet's office. They rent her space, and she keeps their clients looking spiffy. She has three assistants and a two-week wait for appointments. "That's my morning." And off she went.

54

When I got home, I made arrangements to transfer Jay to my regular veterinary clinic. Then I found Detective Jo Stevens' card under a pile of unopened mail on my kitchen counter, dialed her number, and was surprised when she picked up. I expected another machine. I wasn't sure she'd be interested in attempted dog poisoning, but she said that under the circumstances, she'd see me at my vet's office so she could take a full report. Leo rejoined me in the kitchen and wove himself in and out of my legs, rumbling like an Indy car. When I didn't pay sufficient attention, he sprang onto the counter and shoved his furry feline face against my cheek.

"What in the world got into you this morning?" I ran my hand down the silky path from his neck to the tip of his tail. "Are you worried about Jay?" He rumbled a reply, gently stroking my cheek with one soft paw and gazing at me squint-eyed. "Me too, buddy, me too."

I decided to do something mindless to pass a half hour, so I nuked a cup of leftover coffee, set Leo on the floor, and pulled out a box of miscellaneous photos I'd taken over the past several years. I'd been meaning to sort them for months. Okay, longer than that. Ah, well, no time like the present.

I made several piles — toss, file, give away, not sure. The giveaways were mainly candid shots of people and dogs, or just dogs. People are always tickled to get little photo surprises so I often keep prints like these to give away. After the fourth or fifth shot of folks from Dog Dayz, a half-formed thought began tapping at the back of my skull. I pawed through the toss and give-away piles and retrieved several photos.

Three of them were group shots taken at annual picnics sponsored by Marietta Santini for her Dog Dayz students and instructors. One was a shot of Greg and Abigail Dorn sitting together at an obedience trial. It must have been in Terre Haute. There was a Ferris wheel behind them and that's the only dog show I know of around here where you compete with carnival rides for your dog's attention. And there was one more photo.

It was a head shot of a Golden Retriever, and in the background, to the left, Greg Dorn and Giselle Swann stood side by side, their heads tipped toward one another as if they were talking. I picked up the photo of Greg and Abigail again. Someone had been standing behind and off to the right. All that was visible was a heavy leg clad in black and the angled and fringed selvedge of a brown wooly poncho. Giselle. I fanned the Dog Dayz photos out in front of me. One of them was of Marietta and Suzette mugging for the camera. Abigail was behind and to the side of them. She looked like she was sucking a sourball. The other two photos were group shots taken in the training building. Greg was in both of them, and so was Giselle, right beside or behind him.

The telephone shocked me right out of my chair. It was brother Bill.

"You have to do something about Mom."

"Hi to you, too."

"Hi. Happy now? She's nutty, Janet. You have to do something."

"*I* have to do something? She's your mother too, if I remember correctly." His barb had scored a direct hit, though, and I was struck by guilt for my failings as a dutiful daughter.

"Look, I'm in the middle of a big deal at

work. I have to go out of town next week, I told you that. So yeah, you have to handle this."

"Right. Okay, then. Talk to you later." I didn't bother to tell him that Shadetree Retirement Community had sent a letter saying they had a vacancy, and Mom was next up. I couldn't imagine how she'd moved to the top of the list so quickly, but I wasn't about to argue with the whims of fate and exquisite luck. I figured he was winding up for "Bill Maneuver #46: Explain once again why it really is all about him, and hang up," so I beat him to the disconnect. I'd fill him in later, after I cooled off. I grabbed Leo, who had hopped up in front of me, and rested my face against his furry skull. "I guess I'll have go stay with her or bring her here for a few days, huh, big guy?"

Leo bumped my chin with the top of his head. He poked at a pile of photos, re-arranged them with a few quick pats of his paws, and flicked one onto the floor. "Oh, no you don't." I lifted him off the table again and picked up the photo. It was an old one of Suzette's Sheltie, Mimi, standing on a grooming table at an indoor show. Where was that? I flipped it over, but I hadn't labeled it, so I studied the background again, focusing on the concession stand in the background. It was the Fort Wayne show, in the Memorial Coliseum.

Mimi had been gone at least three years, so how old was this photo? I looked for a historical time line on the ceiling, but all I saw was a cobweb mature enough to reproduce, so I started calculating on my fingers instead. I must have taken this shot at least eight years earlier, when Mimi was four or five.

Leo was back on the table. I scratched lightly behind his ears, mulling over the memories the photo brought back. Suzette was standing in front of Mimi, fluffing the dog's white ruff with a brush. Abigail and Connie stood behind the table, and all three women seemed to be laughing. I lay the photo back on the table. I dumped my cold coffee into the sink and put the mug in the dishwasher, thinking about the fragile natures of friendship and happiness.

When I turned back to the table, Leo said, "Mmrrowwwlllll," and placed a paw in the center of the photo of Mimi and friends. He flexed his toes just enough to touch the tips of his claws to the glossy surface and swept the picture off the table once more and chirped. This was, I assumed, a comment on my failure to acknowledge his right to toss bits of paper wherever he liked. He glided from the table to the chair to the floor, where he gave his paw a little flick. Then he trotted through the door and into the living room.

55

Jay walked into the examining room looking glum, but when he saw me, he crossed the remaining eight feet in one big wriggle-and-whine, telling me all about the weird things they'd done to him. He was a sight for dog-lonely eyes.

"How are you, Bubby?" I knelt in front of him and braced myself against the wall when he popped up, put his paws over my shoulders in a doggy hug, and slurped my face.

The emergency vet gave me some paperwork for Dr. Douglas, my regular vet, and raved about what a sweet dog Jay was while the technician removed the tubing from the IV catheter in Jay's right foreleg. "We'll leave the catheter in case they need to administer more fluids. It's taped down tight." I glanced at the tech, who was making kissy faces at Jay as she added another layer of tape to hold the catheter against his leg. "He's been leaving it alone, but if you want an e-collar, we can send one with you." E-, or Elizabethan collars, named for the big ruffled collars worn during the reign of Queen Liz number one, are used to keep animals from licking or biting at injuries.

"I have one in the car. Sometimes I need it for foster dogs. But I think he'll be fine until we get to Dr. Douglas' office." I was almost out the door when I had another thought. "Listen, don't destroy the mouse or the biscuit. The police may want them."

The vet said it might be too late, but she'd check.

Jay was elated to get out of that place, and not so keen on walking into another House of Sharp Implements and Offensive Odors. I had to coax him through the door, and he slunk down the hall to the examining room, dragging as far behind the vet tech and me as his leash allowed, head hanging and eyes as much like a Basset Hound's as an Aussie can manage. I sat down on the cold vinyl floor of the exam room and put my arms around my unhappy dog. We communed for a few minutes, Jay telling me all about his terrible night while I explained that he might have to spend another night here to make sure he was okay. I'm not sure I convinced him that it was the best option.

Both doors into the exam room opened. Detective Jo Stevens entered from the public part of the clinic and Dr. Paul Douglas came in from the behind-the-scenes part. I stood up, and Jay leaned against my leg.

When the introductions were made, Dr. Douglas began. "The mouse ingested an anti-coagulant, probably warfarin. According to the report from the emergency clinic, it bled out internally." He peered at me over the top of his wire rims. "You have mouse poisons out?"

"No, never. It had to be the biscuits."

Jo looked up from her notes. "I'm going to need the report on that mouse, and the biscuits and everything that came with them, especially the note. I also need a copy of your notes and lab tests." I explained that the mouse and biscuit were — hopefully — still at the other clinic, and the basket and note were at home. Dr. Douglas offered to photocopy the paperwork.

"You'll pursue this?" I asked Jo after Dr. Douglas left the room.

"I'll try. If we find that the biscuits are poisoned, I'll do what I can to find whoever did it and see that charges are filed. Don't know that the prosecutor will do anything, but . . ." She looked up from her notes.

"This is related to the deaths of Ms. Dorn and Ms. Anderson, isn't it?"

My eyes began to sting. "I guess it must be, but I can't believe anyone who loves dogs would try to poison Jay, no matter how much they hate me."

"Uh-huh." I had the distinct impression that Detective Jo Stevens thought people were capable of anything. "So why come after you?"

"No idea." But of course I did have some idea, courtesy of Connie. "Maybe whoever it is thinks I know something I don't." I stared at the detective for a moment while a spark of anger flared into flame. "But I think it's time I did."

"Don't do anything stupid. That's our job."

As soon as it was out of her mouth, Jo and I both started to laugh, and the release that brought kept us laughing longer than the joke really warranted. Finally, she said, "You know what I mean. Whoever tried to poison your dog was telling you to back off whatever you're doing. You could be next, so just be careful, and let us do the investigating."

Right.

Dr. Douglas came back into the room with several photocopies clipped together.

"I'll have my tech fax you the rest of the lab reports when they come in."

Jo stroked Jay's cheek. "So he's going to be okay?"

"I think so." Dr. Douglas reached for the leash. "Call me this afternoon if you don't hear from me and I'll let you know whether he can come home tonight or not."

56

I dug a tissue box out from under the back
seat of my van, but it was empty, so I had
to fish around in my tote bag for some tissue to wipe my eyes and blow my nose
before I could drive. I'd hoped to bring Jay
with me, but as it was, I arrived at Mom's
house alone. Bill's car was nowhere in sight
and I had to use my key, but I knew as soon
as I walked in that she was home. Her purse
was on the kitchen table, and the TV was
blaring in the living room.

"Hi, Mom."

She looked blank. "May I help you?"

"Mom, what's this?" I asked her, squatting beside her seat and touching the scarf
that was knotted at one end around her
boney wrist and at the other around the
wooden arm of her chair.

"Silk. And isn't the color gorgeous? It's
on sale today. I can let you have it for
$3.99."

"Lovely. I'll take it." I had to poke a pen into the knot to get it started, it was pulled so tight, but I got the scarf off my mother and then off the chair. Good thing Bill wasn't there. I had a blinding urge to put the thing around his booth-tanned neck, pull it tight, and knot it like a Chinese puzzle.

Mom picked up her knitting needles from the basket beside her chair. *Clack clack clack,* said the needles. *This isn't good,* said little Janet Angel. *Looney tunes,* said little Janet Demon. I wouldn't know a cable stitch from a purl, but I was pretty sure that she should have had those busy needles hooked up to some yarn. But then I've been known to make Mr. Coffee do his thing without benefit of water or ground beans, so who am I to criticize?

"Mom, I think you should think about moving."

"Oh, that nice young man told me not to move."

"Bill?"

"Was that his name?" The needles stilled and a stranger looked at me from behind my mother's eyes. "I don't believe we've met, dear."

"Mom, it's me, Janet."

"No, don't believe so." She went back to

her knitting, her mouth bowed gently up at the corners.

My cell phone rang, saving me from my second desperate urge in so many minutes, this one to grab one of the knitting needles and ram it in my right ear and out the left. It was Tom.

"How's Jay?"

I filled him in.

"And how's Janet?"

"Well, I'm scared for my dog, and mad as hell, and now I'm here with a woman who doesn't know me, planning to remove her from her home and lock her up and wondering what to do with her in the meantime. I was planning to take some of her things to the nursing home this afternoon, but I can't leave her alone. Otherwise, I'm dandy. And you?"

Twenty minutes later, Tom walked in the door, gave me a hug, and sent me on my way. "Don't worry about it. I brought something to read, and I can always hold the yarn for her if I get bored." If he didn't quit winking at me, I thought, I was going to have a permanent hot flash.

I arrived at Shadetree Retirement Home with a box of photos and knickknacks, a new bedspread in Mom's favorite shade of violet, and a suitcase full of her clothes. Jade

299

Templeton, Shadetree's assistant manager, helped me arrange the room.

"This will make it much easier for her to adjust."

"If she recognizes any of it." The last three words came out in a squeak as all the emotions of the past few days surged through me in one great whoosh. I sat down on the bed and burst into tears. I hadn't cried so much in years. Jade sat beside me and put an arm around my shoulder. "It's okay, you know. She'll be fine here, better than at home now. Safer. You're doing the right thing."

I blubbered for another minute or so. Jade took my hands in hers, and part of my brain flipped to photographer mode as I studied her long, slim hands, at once delicate and strong, the elegant fingers unadorned, the smooth mocha sheen of her skin enhancing the soft peach of her blouse. Her voice brought me back to the moment.

"Once she's moved in, she'll find friends, and she can play in the garden all she wants."

The garden was one reason I'd wanted to get Mom into Shadetree. There was a lovely atrium with raised flowerbeds where residents could dig and plant to their hearts' delight all year round. This garden therapy program was overseen by the local Master Gardeners. Shadetree also had a resident cat and welcomed visits from several certified therapy animals. I'd have to start taking Jay for visits once he was certified. Other than having her mind back, what more could an old lady with green thumbs up to her elbows want?

I took a tissue that magically appeared in Jade's hand, wiped my eyes, blew my nose, and looked at the woman sitting beside me. Her nose was a bit doughy, her cheeks a tad too round, her forehead high and bare and creased, and her hair cropped tight to her head in a style more suited to a daintier, younger woman. But her eyes were the warmest shade of burnt umber, filled with humor and compassion and a hint of mischief. I wasn't looking forward to locking Mom up, but I was delighted to know I'd be seeing a lot more of Jade Templeton.

I looked around the room once more. "So, I'll go home and get her ready and we'll be back tomorrow morning."

Oh yeah, whispered Janet Demon into my left ear, *and won't we have fun.*

57

Jay couldn't come home. Dr. Douglas had
been in touch with vet toxicologists at the
Purdue vet school, and based on their
advice, he wanted to continue fluids and
vitamin K therapy overnight. I was already
depressed, and now I couldn't resort to my
therapy of choice. Some people go to
shrinks, some shop 'til they drop. I spend
time with my dog, often in the company of
other cynophiles and their own best friends.
The Zen of dog ownership, as it were.
Unfortunately, my spiritual guide was having fluid and vitamins pumped into him.

I called brother Bill and told him a little
white lie about a photo shoot, and he
grumbled but agreed to spend the evening
with Mom. I told him I'd be there about
ten. "And if you tie her up again, I'll make
you eat the chair she's sitting in." Bill is a
big guy, but I'm still the tough little sister
who made him eat the spider he dropped

down my shirt when we were kids.

"What are you talking about? I didn't tie her up!"

"I suppose she tied her own arm to the chair with the scarf?"

"Must have. She was wearing a scarf when I left."

I apologized for thinking the worst, and my fib about the photo shoot stirred up a little butterfly of guilt that fluttered around my brain but never landed. I needed to spend a few hours with people who knew what being dogless meant to me. I decided to take my camera along and snap a few pictures, so I'd be a fibber, not a big fat liar, a distinction that Bill and I honored as children.

Marietta never gets to work her own dog in group sessions, so I offered to call commands for heeling practice to give her the opportunity. She liked the idea for the first half hour, then put her dog in her office and took over. I got a diet pop from the machine and looked through the door into the back room. Connie and several other people were practicing with their dogs for the conformation ring. It may look easy, having a dog stand still for the judge and trot around the ring, but trust me, it takes a helluva lot of skill and hard work to make showing a dog look effortless.

I turned back to the obedience room and wandered over to the row of chairs along the wall. Giselle panted over to me. The chair she dropped onto heaved a metallic groan, but held. Giselle left a chair between us, and averted her eyes as she settled Precious on her lap.

"Hi, Giselle."

"You sent the police to talk to me, didn't you?"

"They're talking to everyone connected to Abigail."

"Not about Abigail. About your dog."

That got my attention. "What about my dog?"

"That police lady came to my house?" Her confidence seemed to flag, and she was back to inflecting statements as questions.

"And?"

The chair creaked as she shifted her weight, and Precious sat up and looked at her with big round eyes. "She asked if I knew anyone who'd want to hurt your dog?"

"Do you?"

"No?" She shoved her bangs from one side of her forehead to the other, and flicked a quick glance at me.

"Did you leave a basket of dog biscuits on my porch?"

"No?" She didn't ask how Jay was doing. "But you should stop poking your nose into other people's business. Someone could get hurt."

It occurred to me that an awful lot of people seemed to think it was okay to poke their noses into *my* business, and my hackles rose. "Are you threatening me?"

She shrugged. "I'm just saying?"

I glared at her. "When you have something sensible to say, come talk to me again." I walked into the ladies room, crushed the pop can in my hands with a growl and slammed it into the trash, and gazed into the reflection of my own angry eyes for a moment. I splashed some cold water onto my face, and forced myself to breathe slowly through my mouth while I dripped into the sink. I patted my face with a paper towel, crinkling my nose at the smell of wet brown paper. Squaring my shoulders, I forced the corners of my mouth upward to pump some smiley-face endorphins into my system, fished the can out of the trash so I could put it in the recycling bin, and pulled the door open.

The dogs in the group practice ring were sitting along one wall, their owners facing them from various distances, depending on how reliable the individual dog was. A few people, including Tom, were training jumps and retrieves in the other ring. I glanced toward the chairs where I'd been sitting, and there was Giselle, cuddling her tiny dog with one hand and shoveling chocolate chip cookies from the vending machine into her mouth with the other.

A frenzy of color drew my eyes to a woman coming in the front door. Her fiery hair stuck out from her scalp in startled spikes made brighter by the aqua shirt below them. Her eyes were wide and searching, her lips narrow and tight. Francine Peterson, Pip's breeder. What in the world was she doing in Fort Wayne on a Monday night? Marietta had told me Francine lived in Rochester, in the north-central part of the state, a good hour and a half from Fort Wayne.

Go poke your nose in her business, urged Janet Demon. *Ask if she needs any help,* urged my little angel. *Whatever,* I thought, getting to my feet.

"Are you looking for someone?"

She fixed me with a reptilian stare, and screwed her lips even tighter as she studied my face. "Greg Dorn."

"Oh, sorry, he's not here."

"Must be."

My scalp muscles contracted. "Don't

306

think so. I haven't seen him this evening. He doesn't come here much. Abigail did, but not Greg."

She was scanning the room again. "His car's parked out back."

"Really?" I hadn't seen it there when I pulled in.

She didn't bother to answer, just marched through the training room and out the front door. Tom and Drake strolled over to me, and Tom asked, "What was that all about?"

"She was looking for Greg."

"Who is she?"

I watched out the front window as Francine climbed into a beat-up cargo van. It was hard to tell if it was red or brown under the lights. I told Tom what I knew about who she was and where she lived. "She said she saw Greg's car in the parking lot."

"I'll bet she saw your car."

He shot me that damn smile. The ligaments in my leg joints loosened, but I managed to fend off the hormonal surge and stay upright. I was beginning to wonder if something was seriously wrong with me. To camouflage my reaction, I bent and gave Drake an ear scratch. "What are you talking about?"

"Abigail drives, er, drove a dark blue Voyager, right? At least that's what they always took to dog shows. You don't think Greg would let the dogs ride in his Mercedes coupé, do you?" He drew out the two syllables of coo-pay.

"Is that what he drives?"

"Oooh, yeah." His eyes looked like mine feel when I see a stunning photograph, or a stunning animal. "Silver-blue, black leather interior. Fine looking car." He probably saw my eyes glaze over, because his voice went from dreamy to resigned. "A perk of marriage to a bread heiress, I guess. About seventy grand." His eyes refocused on reality. "So anyway, I bet she associates him with the van, you know, from dog shows. Looks like your Caravan."

"Yeah, you're probably right." I glanced into the back room, thinking I'd say hi to Connie, but the conformation people had cleared out, so I walked with Tom toward a chair by the wall where he had left his training bag. Giselle must have thought we were heading for her, because she jumped up, grabbed her stuff, and bulldozed out the back door.

"What did you do to her?" asked Tom.

"She has an overactive imagination, that's all." We sat down, and Drake laid his lovely black head on my knee. His eyes were as soothing as warm dark chocolate, a shade deeper than his owner's eyes. I was beginning to think of Tom and Drake as the chocolate-eyed boys, all warm and yummy, and the thought stirred a hunger that had nothing to do with food. I stroked Drake's cheeks and silky ears to calm myself, and hoped I wasn't as transparent as I felt. A quarter of an hour slid by in small talk, and I bade Tom good night.

"Call me if you need me," he said.

58

"I need you," I told Tom, back inside Dog Dayz about three minutes later.

"Wow, that was quick." He faced me and opened his arms. "I'm all yours!"

Anger overrode estrogen, and my pulse didn't react at all. "I have four flat tires."

Tom followed me out the door and took a quick glance at my foundered van. "Yep, they're flat all right. Hang on." He took Drake to his car, came back with a flashlight, and made the rounds of the four useless tires. "Sidewalls have been slashed." Tom remained calm while I ranted in clear violation of my moratorium on four-letter words, then drove me to Mom's house.

I called Jade Templeton first thing in the morning and told her I'd have to postpone Mom's move until noonish. Then I called Detective Stevens and left her a message to call me. I knew it was a bit of a reach to expect a homicide detective to care about vandalism, but my gut told me this was linked to Abigail's death, and autopsy report or no, I no longer thought that was due to natural causes. I called Goldie next. I needed her to drive me to Sears to see about new tires, but she didn't answer either, so I called Connie. She said they had a light morning and her assistant could handle it.

Finally I called Bill and told him what was happening. He showed up at Mom's twenty minutes later and was still explaining how my tire situation inconvenienced him when Connie arrived. I placed one more call, this time to my road service for a tow, or rather a carry, since the poor car couldn't roll on four flats. "They said they'd be at the Dog Dayz parking lot in half an hour, so let's pick up some coffee on the way. I could use some caffeine."

We were getting back into Connie's car with steaming lattes and fresh muffins when my cell phone rang.

"Heard you had some trouble last night." It was Jo Stevens.

"How did you find out so fast?"

"Officer Hernandez knew I was working on the dog lady deaths. Since your tires were slashed at the dog training place, he thought there might be a connection."

"The dog lady deaths?"

"Cute, huh? Anyway, I want to come talk to you about it. Now a good time?"

"But I didn't call the police. Except for you."

"We know everything." The detective waited a beat, then laughed and said, "The owner of the place called since it happened in her parking lot."

Of course, that made sense. "Wait, but . . . You're investigating Abigail's and Suzette's deaths? I mean, officially?"

She didn't offer anything specific, but confirmed that there was now an official investigation. I told her where I was and where I was going, and she said she'd meet us at the Sears garage. She wanted to see the tires. "Don't let them take them off the car until I get there — I want photos."

"If I'd known, I'd have brought my camera."

"Anyway, be careful. See you in a few minutes."

Jo was waiting at the garage when we pulled in behind the tow truck. She took her photos and the mechanic began pulling the dead tires off the van. We needed a place to talk. The waiting room wasn't crowded, but there was a woman with four preschoolers and it was a tad noisy for conversation, so we walked into the mall and found a seat in front of Aunt Annie's pretzel place. I was giddy from the aroma of yeast and cinnamon by the time we sat down.

"Any idea who did this?" She studied Connie, who had popped a piece of gum into her mouth and now seemed intent on folding the wrapper into the tiniest packet possible.

"Not strong enough to accuse anyone, no."

Jo shifted her attention back to me. "No idea at all?"

I told her about my conversations with Giselle and with Francine Peterson. "But Francine wouldn't know my car and she'd have no reason to go after me anyway. And I just can't see Giselle doing it. Could have been random vandalism." But even I didn't believe that.

"All four tires?" Connie tossed the paper on the floor. "I *told* you not to ask so many questions." She folded her arms across her chest. "My money's on Francine."

"Why is that?" Jo asked, picking the gum wrapper up from the floor and tossing it into a waste container behind Connie.

"She looked pretty angry when she came in last night." Connie leaned across the table and tapped my hand. "Maybe she thought it was Greg's van, you know, Abigail's van. It looks a lot like yours." I recalled that Tom had said the same thing. "Or maybe she blames you for keeping her from picking Pip up at the show."

Jo was watching something to my left, and I followed her gaze. Good ol' Hutch was headed our way. "This kind of damage took some serious effort, and I'd say a fair amount of anger." She nodded at Hutchinson as he pulled up a chair. "Anything?"

A familiar odor tickled my nose, and Connie's expression told me she smelled it too.

"I checked the dog place's parking lot and alley. Found a chisel behind some trash about a block away. Looks about the right size." Hutchinson laid a bag on the table, "Evidence" stamped into the plastic and a tool of some sort inside. It could have been a chisel, for all I knew about tools.

"But how do you know . . ."

Hutchinson cut me off. "Look familiar to either of you ladies?" The smell was getting stronger.

Connie glared at him, and a warm wave rolled up my neck and face. "What are you suggesting?" I asked.

"Just asking a question, ma'am." He looked from me to Connie and back. "Either of you recognize this chisel or know who it might belong to?"

We shook our heads.

He held the chisel toward Jo and pointed to an area along the edge. "There's a nick in the edge of the blade, something caught in it. Could be a bit of tire."

Jo told her partner, "Dispatch called. We caught another case. You go get started and I'll catch up with you." She held out her hand for the evidence bag.

Hutchinson started to protest, but seemed to think better of it.

"And Hutchinson?"

"Yeah?"

"You need to clean your shoe."

"Huh?" He raised his right foot to check the sole, then the left. "Aww, shit!"

"Bingo."

When he was gone, I grinned at Jo. "You'd be a good dog trainer." She didn't say anything, but her lips twitched.

59

Detective Stevens and Connie and I stood looking at the tires from my Caravan. The holes were narrow slits, and clean. Exactly the sort of holes the sharp chisel in Hutchinson's baggie might make. Jo took some notes, then pulled her phone out and walked away. She was on her way back to us when a mechanic strolled over and handed her a piece of paper. "This was under the wiper." Jo took it by the edges, read it, and turned it so I could see. My stomach did a half-gainer as I read YOU COULD BE NEXT, printed in large black letters.

Jo pulled a plastic bag from a pocket in her notebook, slipped the warning into it, and zipped it shut. She gave me a look that made me think of Mom. "You call me if anything — I mean anything — strange happens again. Keep your eyes open and *be careful.*" I resisted the urge to glance over my shoulder right then.

When Jo was gone, Connie and I strolled back into the mall, figuring it would be better to walk than to sit in the gritty waiting room, even though the frazzled mother and her noisy mob had left.

"I'm worried for you, Janet."

"Tell me about it!"

We speculated on what the tire attack was all about. Was it possible that someone — Francine? — thought my car was Greg's? But why slash his tires? And what was she doing at Dog Dayz anyway? Giselle had left in a huff before I did. But why on earth would *she* do such a thing? And even if she wanted to, was Giselle ballsy enough to risk getting caught?

"Who would have a chisel?" asked Connie.

"I dunno." Didn't *I* have a chisel somewhere in my garage? "Lots of people do, probably."

"Francine would have one." Connie glanced sideways at me.

"She would?"

"She's a handyman, well, you know, handy woman. She has one of those odd-job businesses, like 'call-a-husband.' Abigail told me that."

"But that doesn't mean . . ."

Connie elbowed me in the ribs. I stopped

317

talking. Greg Dorn had just walked out of the Travelfair agency office with a packet of some sort in his hands. He was cutting across the mall at a right angle to us.

"I wonder where he's going?"

"Can't say I could blame him for wanting to get away for a while." I could have stood a getaway myself. "Should we say hello?"

But he had already disappeared into Macy's, so we walked on. Connie told me that Fly's breeder was going to take the dog back since Suzette's sister didn't want to keep her.

"She's up past Chicago, north of the city, actually in Wisconsin, I think. I guess she's willing to come get Fly, but asked Yvonne if she could meet her halfway."

"Yvonne?"

"Suzette's sister."

"I know that. But I thought Marietta was keeping Fly for a while?"

"Right. But I imagine Yvonne inherited her, so she's making the arrangements."

You could drive her part way. You've been wanting to take photos at Potowatomi again, whispered the helpful little angel on my right shoulder. Her devilish counterpart added, *Yeah, and you could do some more nosing around.* I made a mental note to call Marietta and offer to drive Fly halfway if her breeder could meet me. I might even take those photos.

60

Before I could volunteer to reunite Fly with her breeder, I had familial duties to fulfill. Moving Mom was not going to be a lot of fun. Tom offered to help, and I didn't try very hard to dissuade him. He had helped her gather a bouquet of at least fifty daffodils in yellows ranging from palest cream to darkest gold. Four or five branches of pussy willow added height at the center of the arrangement, which filled a big cut-crystal vase. Mom was humming something vaguely familiar and tying a big bow around the waist of the vase when I walked in.

"Hi, Mom. Beautiful bouquet."

"Yes." She stopped her work for a moment and frowned at me. "You're late, Alice." *Who in the heck is Alice?* Mom tilted her head toward me and lowered her voice. "The gentleman here is buying these flowers for his sweetheart. Isn't that romantic?"

Tom stood behind her, grinning.

"They're lovely. But why are you using Christmas ribbon with daffodils?"

"Oh, am I? I thought it was a nice contrast." She gave the bow a final tug and a pat, and stepped back for a better look. Yep, no question, the green, red, and gold plaid bow certainly contrasted with the spring flowers.

"So, Mom, how about we go for a ride?" I had to work to keep the emotion out of my voice.

"Oh, my, I don't know where my boots are." She adjusted a daffodil. "No, I don't think so, dear. Thanks, but I really don't like to ride without my boots. The stirrup leathers chafe my legs." Mom had been a competitive rider as a young woman, but I was pretty certain she hadn't been on a horse since before I was born. The sadness of that thought wrapped itself tight around my chest.

Tom leaned back against the kitchen counter and held me in his gaze, his eyes like a big, warm hug, while I regained control and plunged ahead. "No, Mom, not horseback riding. Let's go for a car ride."

"Oh, yes!" Mom clapped her hands together, twirled around, and lunged for her purse, which was lying on the kitchen table. "We can deliver the flowers! They'll be so happy to get them."

"So much for the sweetheart." Tom winked at me as he offered Mom his arm. "You bring the flowers, Alice. I'll take this lovely young lady to the car." Mom latched on to him with a giggle, and off they went.

Twenty minutes later we pulled up in front of Shadetree Retirement Home, and I was surprised that Mom remembered the stated purpose of our outing. I was even more surprised that she remembered my name. "Janet, dear, you take the flowers in. Your father and I will wait here." Ah, well, two out of three wasn't bad.

Tom hopped out and hurried around to Mom's door. He leaned into the car, unfastened her seat belt, and helped her out. "Upsy daisy, there you are. Shall we?" Once again he played the gallant, and she hooked her arm through his. I brought the flowers.

Jade Templeton met us at the front desk. "Ah, Mrs. MacPhail. It's so nice to see you. And what gorgeous flowers! Are these from your garden?" she asked, taking the bouquet out of my arms and setting it on the counter.

Mom froze, then scanned the lobby, a crease settling across her forehead. She pulled away from Tom, skewered me with a look, and declared, "I'm ready to go home."

"Why don't we take a little walk around?"

Jade emerged from behind the counter and started to put her arm around Mom.

"Leave me alone."

I don't believe I'd ever heard my mother hiss before, and another wave of guilt washed over me. I looked at Jade, then at Tom, for help. "Maybe it's not time yet. Not if she knows what's happening."

Jade tried again to take my mother's hand, inviting her for a "little tour of our home." Mom jerked away and hugged her purse to her chest with both hands wrapped so tightly around it that her knuckles went white.

"No. I don't know you."

"Not yet, but I'd like to get to know you." Jade took a step toward Mom. "Why don't I show you around and we can talk? Would you like to see the garden?"

No sale. Mom pulled away from Jade again and wove her arm through Tom's. He patted her hand. "Why don't we both take the tour?"

"No. I want to leave."

My eyes started to burn, and I needed to sit down. Tom signaled with his free hand toward a chair. He was reading my mind again.

"Let's walk around and see if we can find the exit."

That perked her up. She let her purse drop to her side, clutching the handle in her left hand and Tom's strong arm in her right, and off they went.

The lobby opened into a large common area. Two men were playing chess at a table in the center, and several ladies were gathered around a television at one end. A small gray and white cat lay curled on one of their laps. Another woman sat in a lounge chair, a vacant look on her face and a pink teddy bear upside down on her lap. Tom led Mom around the room, and I collapsed into the chair in the lobby. Jade patted me on the shoulder. "It'll be fine. This is the hardest part."

For once in my life, I was speechless.

As they approached me on their fourth lap of the lobby and hallway, Tom spoke to me. "What time do you have to pick Jay up?"

"They close at six."

He kept Mom moving, but slowed their pace. "Look, this is going to take a while. Why don't you call and see if you can pick him up and take him home."

"I don't . . ."

"Janet, you don't want to be without your dog again tonight and you know he wants to go home. Go ahead. We're fine. When you get back, we should be all settled in." I knew he was right, at least about the first part. I was going to need a warm, furry friend tonight. I had one at home, but two would be even better.

61

Ten minutes later I pulled into the vet clinic parking lot and took the last space. By the time I'd paid the bill, put a week's worth of vitamin K pills in my bag, and made an appointment for a follow-up liver function test, Jay was dragging the kennel assistant into the lobby, wriggling his bum off and "awoooing" a long list of indignities he'd endured since the day before. I'd never seen him so happy to hop into the back of the van.

Call me paranoid, but before I let Jay out I walked the perimeter of the fence and the entire backyard, back and forth in parallel tracks, looking for anything remotely out of place. Nothing showed up. Jay barreled into the yard, checked to see if Goldie was out, updated a few of his favorite sites, had an enormous drink from the bowl I keep under the spigot, and crashed under the patio table with a huge panting grin on his face. There's no place like home.

I sat with him, stroking his side with my bare foot for about five minutes before I got up and opened the back door. "Sorry, Bubby, but I have to go take care of other stuff for a while. Come on." Leo sashayed into the kitchen and bonked noses with Jay, and the two of them lay down side by side on Jay's favorite rug. I wanted nothing more than to stay with them, but duty called. "See you guys later. I'll bring something special home for . . ." I didn't dare finish the sentence — *dinner* would have them both up and hopeful. They are not opposed to moving the meal schedule up a few hours.

I was about to turn out of my subdivision onto Maysville Road when the car behind me blasted its horn several times. *You talkin' to me?* I glanced in my driver's side mirror and saw a neighbor I knew only by sight scramble out of the car and scurry toward me. Had she been a dog, I would have said she displayed classic avoidance behavior as she arced her path away from the back of my van before veering back toward my window. She had a hand clamped over her mouth and her eyes were enormous. I was already opening the door, my heart climbing into my throat.

"What?" My feet were on the ground and

moving along the side of my van. The neighbor held one hand over her mouth and waved me toward the hatch with the other. I rounded the back bumper and stopped.

The back of my van below the rear window was smeared with a thick black and red mess, and the air reeked with the coppery smell of blood. Dangling from the windshield wiper was a wet furry mass of gore.

62

I swallowed a mouthful of saliva, managed to keep my cookies, and stepped toward the van.

"Is it . . . ?"

I got a close look. "It's not real." My initial horror metamorphosed into red-eyed rage mingled with relief. "It's a stuffed toy." A stuffed blue merle Australian Shepherd toy to be precise. At least it looked like the blue merle version. It was hard to tell, saturated as it was with a mess that looked an awful lot like blood.

A thin nylon cord was tied around the neck, the other end fastened to the rear window wiper blade. The throat of the toy was torn open and the stuffing hung out, all of it sopping. There was an index card tied to the cord, but the side facing out was blank and I didn't want to touch it until the police arrived.

"But why?" She still had one hand over

her mouth, the other running through her short brown hair. Her blue eyes were enormous and her face an odd shade of mint green. "Is that supposed to be a joke?"

"Not exactly. I don't think so." We introduced ourselves, then she said, "My God, I thought it was a real puppy."

I pulled out my cell phone and dialed Jo Stevens' number as I asked, "Did you see anyone around my car?"

"No, I just came out. I did see someone pull away from the curb across the street from your house when I was putting some things in my car. I didn't pay much attention."

I signaled her to hang on while I told Detective Stevens what had happened and listened to her instructions. "Stay where you are. Pull off to the side of the road, but stay put. I'm near Georgetown." About half a mile away. "I'll be right there."

I explained that "some things" had been going on, and said the detective would like her to stay if possible, but she was on her way to work, so I got the information and thanked her again. "What do you remember about the car?" I asked as she was getting behind her own wheel.

"Oh, gosh, I didn't pay much attention. It wasn't a car, really. A van. Red, I think, or brown. Kind of ratty looking. That's really what caught my eye. It was rusty, you know, patches of rust, and didn't have any sign or anything like, you know, carpet trucks or plumbers or whatever."

"Did you see the driver?"

"Not really. I think he might have been wearing a red hat."

"He?"

Her forehead wrinkled, "To be honest, I'm not sure. I guess I was thinking a man because, you know, it looked like a work van. I figured you were having some work done on your house."

I nodded.

"I'd recognize the van if I saw it again, though. One of the rust spots was shaped like Texas."

She took off, and the police arrived a few minutes later.

"Oh, too sicko weird." Jo Stevens's re-action when she saw the mess about summed up my opinion. She put on a pair of latex gloves and carefully turned the note over. My mouth went dry as I read the cut-out words pasted to the paper to spell out in rainbow colors, "Back off, you nosey bitch."

"That would be you, I presume?" Jo removed her gloves and pulled out her pen

331

and notebook.

"I guess." It came out like a croak.

She looked me in the eye and said, "I agree with the first part. You need to back off whatever you're doing that's pissing this nut case off."

I didn't answer, but decided that since I really hadn't done much, I might as well *do* something to deserve all this attention. If Jo read my reaction, she didn't pursue it right then.

"We're going to have to process your car, so you'll have to leave it here." I explained that I needed it the next day to take Fly to her breeder, and was assured that I could have it all to myself in a few hours.

"Look, Janet, I don't like this at all." *You don't like it?* I thought. "I want you to be very careful until we get to the bottom of these threats. This," she pointed her pen at the toy, "is the work of a serious nut. A dangerous nut." Almost as an afterthought she asked, "Do you need a ride?"

She arranged for a uniformed officer to drive me to the nursing home, promising they would park my car in my driveway when they finished. I handed her my spare key. I also told her what my neighbor had told me, including her contact information, and that the stuffed toy was a now-defunct version of the one on my dashboard. It looked sort of like Jay must have looked as a puppy.

I kept the rest of my thoughts to myself. If I got my hands, which I realized were shaking as I settled into the police car, on whoever was threatening my dog, probably the same person who tried to poison him, the cops could well find themselves processing another dead body.

63

Three hours after I left them, Tom and my mother were still walking. I found out later that they'd been around and around the common area, up and down two hallways that led off it, and around the lobby I don't know how many times.

Tom was the picture of patience, and where my little old mother got the stamina was a mystery. Somehow Tom had convinced her that the door we came in was "in only," so they were still looking for the exit. Mom asked several people how to get out, with mixed results. Some didn't answer, one told her there was no way out, and at least three pointed in the general direction of the lobby door. Tom asked her every so often if she'd like to rest for a while, but she said no, she was fine.

At 4:52, Mom stopped a volunteer who happened by and asked her how to get out. The ever-so-helpful but not-so-observant young woman pointed to the lobby door.

"No, that's the entrance. I need the exit."

"You can go out that way too."

Mom stiffened. "I can?"

Tom tried to signal the girl to shut up, but she bubbled on in the affirmative.

Mom jerked away from Tom and swung her purse at him all in one unbelievably fast maneuver. "You tricked me! You son of a bitch! How could you? Get out! Let me out!" She kept whacking at him with her purse, her intent clearly to maim if not kill. Jade shot out from behind the desk, and another staff member came running from down the hall.

"Calm down," pleaded Tom, trying to grab the ninja purse, but Mom was too fast for him, landing a couple of good whacks to his shoulder and forearm. He stepped toward her and she backed away, swinging and yelling. One end of the shoulder strap on her purse tore loose, letting the business end of the weapon bob erratically from the remaining strap as it arced back and forth. The clasp popped open and the contents flew around the lobby, a billfold, pens, tissues, checkbook, and a lipstick scattering across the floor. I watched a quarter ricochet off a gilt-framed mirror and roll across the vinyl floor to topple by my toe.

335

I looked up in time to see Mom swing her handbag toward the top of the lobby counter. She let go of the strap, and the film in my head went to slow motion. I could see what was coming before it happened, could think *oh, shit,* but I couldn't stop the inevitable.

64

The gaping metal maw of the purse struck the vase dead on and the crystal exploded in a sparkling burst of water and glass, daffodils and pussy willows. Jade screamed and ducked. Tom pivoted away from the bouquet shrapnel, hooking a protective arm across his face. And my mother finally stopped.

My muscles slowly came back under my control and I jumped out of the chair. "Mother!" I crossed the lobby in two lunges, grabbed her by the arms, and shoved her into a chair. "Stay!" She sagged into the seat as if drained. Finally.

I turned back to Tom and Jade. "Are you guys all right?" Jade had picked up a phone and was calling for help, but she nodded at me.

Tom got the worst of it. He was drenched with water, and a daffodil was draped upside down across his shoulder. A fine trickle of crimson traced the center line of his right temple. "Oh my God, you're bleeding," I hurried to him and pulled a clean tissue from my pocket.

"I am?" He recovered more quickly than I did, and grinned at me. Looking at his hands, he asked, "Where?"

"Here." I pointed at his temple. "It's not bad. Just a nick, but it's bleeding."

"I'll live. What about your mom?"

"I guess she'll live too, although I'd like to throttle her."

Tom was already moving to Mom's chair, so I followed and pressed a tissue against the nick on his head. He took it from me with a nod. "Are you okay, Mrs. MacPhail?"

Mom didn't answer. Two young men had appeared with mop, broom, and bucket and had started to clean up the mess.

"Vacuum that after you get the water up. Do the whole room to be sure," Jade acted as if nothing were out of the ordinary. "Mrs. MacPhail, are you ready to go to your room?"

Mom jumped to her feet. "Yes. Let's go home, George," she called Tom by my father's name again as she took his arm. "Let's go now."

"Why don't we go see the room as long as we're here." Tom tried to get her moving toward the hallway.

No way.

"Why don't you take her home and bring her back later, when she's calmed down?" asked Jade.

"She'll never get in the car with me again after this," I fought back tears. "I don't know what to do."

Mom busily unfastened and refastened her blouse, one button at a time.

"Can you sedate her slightly to calm her down?" Tom asked Jade.

"Not without a doctor's order."

We were all quiet for a moment. "This can't be your first difficult admission." Tom used a no-nonsense voice that surprised me. "What do you suggest?"

"We could call for an ambulance and take her to the hospital for evaluation. If a doctor prescribes sedation, that will calm her. You can have them bring her back." Jade put her hand on my forearm. "Sometimes it's easier on the resident if family members aren't present at first. She may be more co-operative with strangers."

Mom seemed to have forgotten us and her buttons, and was watching the cleanup efforts. "Someone must have spilled something. People should be more careful." She smiled at me. "Do I know you?"

I turned to Jade. "Call the ambulance."

65

Twenty minutes later two EMTs walked in the door. One was the gymnast-looking little blonde who responded to Abigail's collapse. She nodded at me. "Our bus is here, Mrs. MacPhail," said Tom. "Shall we?"

"About time," Mom muttered as she walked out the door hanging on to Tom's arm. I tagged along behind and almost bumped into her when she stopped short. "That's an ambulance."

"It is! Come on, let's take a ride."

"I'm not sick."

"I know. We'll go for a ride. It'll be fun."

"George, I don't have time. I have to get to work."

"Work can wait. I'm going for a ride." He unhooked her arm from his and took her hand as he climbed aboard the ambulance. "Coming?"

She hesitated but then started forward. One of the EMTs, a muscular young man in blue scrubs, stepped up to help her in, but she slapped him away and climbed aboard on her own steam. Mom looked around, then surprised us all by lying down on the gurney.

I started to follow them up the steps, but Tom tossed me one of those winks. "Alice, you bring the car in case we need it there."

Right. So once again I found myself not the least bit reluctant to abdicate my self-determination for a while. By the time I walked into the emergency room the staff had told Tom to "just wait," and he and Mom were strolling around the waiting room.

"They say we need to wait for a doctor. They can't do anything since they haven't seen her in action."

"I owe you."

"Nah. It's okay. It was this or grading exams. This is more interesting." I stepped closer and laid my fingertips against his cheek, turning his head for a better view of his wound. It was barely visible now that the bleeding had stopped. "Think I'll need plastic surgery?" he asked, flashing that grin of his. I wanted to cry, or punch someone. I went to get Tom a cup of coffee instead.

When I got back, Sylvia Eckhart, hair pulled back neatly and not a speck of baby goo on her scrubs, was talking to Mom. I hadn't realized she was back at work, but knew that they could no doubt use her salary with two babies in the house. Sylvia placed a hand on Mom's arm. "Mrs. MacPhail, if you'll have a seat over here I need to take your temperature."

Mom jerked away from her. "I'm not sick!"

Sylvia did something to the thermometer in her hand. "We can't admit her against her will, Mr. MacPhail."

"I'm Tom Saunders, a friend. This is Mrs. MacPhail's daughter, Janet MacPhail." He tipped his head toward me, his hands occupied with trying to link Mom's arm back through his for control.

"Oh! Janet!" Sylvia smiled. "I didn't realize . . . I'm sorry, Janet, but we can't do anything if she's not showing any symptoms."

"Can you call Shadetree Retirement Home? Ask Jade Templeton, the assistant manager, how she was over there."

As I spoke, Mom apparently decided to help me along. She was squirming around, trying to get her arm away from Tom's grasp. When he wouldn't let go, she took a swing at him with her other fist, socking him in the shoulder and yelling, "Let me go!"

She leaned forward and tried to bite his bare wrist, and Tom let go. Mom pummeled his chest with both fists, shouting, "I don't even know you! Keep your grubby mitts off me!"

Sylvia shoved her thermometer into her breast pocket and reached for Mom's arms. "Okay, Mrs. MacPhail, everything's fine."

Mom rounded on her and gave her an uppercut, and Sylvia called out, "Need some help here! Now!"

Two orderlies came running from behind the swinging double doors and gently but firmly grasped Mom from both sides. They guided her back through the doors, and lifted her onto a gurney. Sylvia signaled me to come along, so I tagged close behind, leaving Tom in the waiting room.

A young, dark, sharp-featured man in a white lab coat appeared and began talking to Mom in a hypnotically silky singsong, asking questions and soothing her at the same time. *Must be the old lady whisperer,* quipped Janet Demon. She always responds to stress with a smart remark, this one in reference to "whisperers" who soothe troubled animals with gentle talk and body language.

When Mom had relaxed a bit, the doctor issued some orders to the nurse, then turned to me. "I am Doctor Patel. She is your mother?"

I explained, none too coherently, what was happening. Dr. Patel, in turn, explained that he had prescribed a sedative and would examine her when it took effect. He assured me that mine was not the first parent to resist nursing home care, even if it was the safest option for her. I felt a lot better when I watched them move my now-calm mother into a curtained examination area. Sylvia hugged me and said, "It'll be okay," and I returned to the waiting room.

"They've given her a mild sedative," I told Tom, as he nudged me into a chair. "Dr. Patel suggested we leave and let them examine her, talk to her regular doctor, and take her back to Shadetree."

"Sounds reasonable," Tom nodded. "I think Ms. — what was her name? — Temple?"

"Templeton."

"Templeton. I think she was right, your mom will probably cooperate better with strangers." Considering how often she mistook me for someone else, I thought I qualified, but I could see his point.

I walked out in a daze. Tom drove me home and offered to come in for a while, but I said I'd call him later. I just wanted to curl up in my bed with my dog and, if he was so inclined, my cat.

66

I slept deep and short, and by 5:30 the next morning I was enjoying the cool massage of dewy grass between my toes and the "pretty, pretty, pretty bird" song of the resident cock cardinal. This early morning stuff was getting to be a habit. Jay was back to his normal bouncy self and elated to spend the better part of an hour reading the tale of the night with his nose while I pulled a few weeds and tried to push the events of the past few days out of my mind. I couldn't.

My rendezvous with Virginia Scott, Fly's breeder, was set for 11:30 in Valparaiso, about two hours away. I showered, dressed, and still had half an hour before I needed to pick up Fly at Marietta's house. I decided to sort some more old photos. It was a good mindless job for a short time slot.

I had another half-filled shoebox of old candid photos I'd taken at Dog Dayz back when I still used film. A few went straight to the circular file. The others I put into piles by subject. As my pile of group photos grew, I put everything else aside and re-sorted those into two piles, one for photos with Abigail or Greg in them, and the rest. As I'd noticed in the photos I sorted the other day, whenever Greg was present, you could bet that Giselle would be there as well, in the background or off to the side. Some of these adoration shots went back years. For all Giselle's imposing size, her longing for Greg, so clear to me now, had been invisible.

Surely Greg knew? Or not. He's a man, after all. But what about Abigail? She must have seen it, especially if she spent time with Giselle, as Connie seemed to think.

I rolled my observations around in my mind until I noticed the clock on the wall. Five to nine. Time to go get Fly and head west.

I cruised along U.S. 30 at about five miles over the limit and made great time. This is a straight run across the northern tier just south of the interstate that fools out-of-staters into thinking Indiana is all flat fields of corn. By some miracle, I hit all green lights through Columbia City, Warsaw, and Plymouth. In Wanatah my luck ran out and

I sat behind a clean-emissions-challenged gray pickup with red cellophane duct-taped over the starboard brake light and a muffler a few inches too low and several decibels too loud. Why Indiana dropped vehicle inspections is beyond me.

The cows munching away in the big feed lot on the north side of the road distracted me from my impending asphyxiation. Give her a platinum wig and the little Hereford by the hay rack would be a dead ringer for the gum-popping clerk at the Clark station where I fill up my van from time to time.

I survived the toxic exhaust, dodged around the truck as soon as we got the green, and opened all the windows to clear the fumes. I pulled into the parking lot at the Broadway Inn in Valparaiso just before eleven. No sign of the white van with the Scotswool Border Collies sign on the side that Virginia Scott had described to me, so I got Fly and Jay out of their crates, and hooked them up to retractable leashes, and walked them in the grass edging the pavement.

Fly nibbled Jay's ear, bowed in front of him, spun around, and bumped his face with her tail, inviting him to play. After they twisted their leashes together for the third time, I put on my boring-old-fart-human hat and told Jay to jump back into his crate in the van. He gave me his best "I never get to do anything fun" look, but in vain. I walked a more sober Fly to the grass and then to a dumpster at the back of the parking lot.

When I turned back toward the parking lot, I found I was being watched.

67

A tiny dark-haired woman stepped from a white van parked beside mine. She barely reached five feet in thick-soled walking shoes, but she exuded energy and strength. She walked toward us, waving. "You must be Janet!" When we were ten paces apart, she knelt and opened her arms, and Fly nearly upended me to get to her. The dog was wooing and whining and squeaking, alternately slurping her breeder's face and rolling in ecstasy at her feet.

"You definitely must be Virginia!"

"Ginny, please." She wiped her hand on her jeans, and held it out, pushing Fly down with her left. "Thanks so much for meeting me here. I'd have come to Fort Wayne if necessary, but this saves me about five hours of driving. I appreciate it."

We chatted for a few minutes while Fly settled down a bit before Ginny loaded her into a crate in her own van. We moved both vehicles to the far side of the parking lot, under some trees and away from foot traffic but within sight of the restaurant windows so we could leave the backs open for air.

We ordered, and I gave Ginny a folder Yvonne Anderson had given me. She removed the contents and went through Fly's registration, veterinary and health-screening records, and various other papers, including a notarized letter from Suzette saying that in the event of her death, Fly should be returned to her breeder, Virginia Scott, Scotswool Border Collies.

"Leave it to Suzette to have everything in order." Ginny choked on the last two words. "Damn. It just stinks, you know?"

"I know."

"You were good friends?"

"Not really. I mean, I saw her all the time at training and at trials, and I photographed Fly a couple of times, but that's about it."

"She was a breeder's dream as a puppy buyer. Took great care of Fly and did everything she told me she'd do with her. More than everything. She was absolutely thrilled when she finished the OTCH and UDX." Ginny's eyes were red, and her little button nose was puffing up. "I can't believe it. It doesn't make sense." She blew her nose. "I don't believe it was suicide. Things were finally falling into place for her."

"Really?"

"Did you know she was getting married?"

"Not officially." I pictured the diamond ring I'd seen at Suzette's house, and flashed back to how weird she acted when I asked who the lucky guy was. I meant the stud dog she planned to use for Fly, but she must have been thinking of a different stud.

"She was very private about it. I didn't even know until last week, and we e-mailed almost daily. She said she'd been seeing this guy for quite a while but there were some things to deal with before they could make their engagement public." Ginny leaned forward and lowered her voice. "I wondered what things, but it wasn't my place to ask."

Alarm bells started clanging in my skull. Could Connie have been right after all about Greg and Suzette?

When she continued, Ginny's voice crackled with emotion. "The funny thing is, Abigail introduced them. Suzette's parents weren't happy about the marriage, so Suzette was having a tiny wedding. More of an elopement, I think."

"Abigail introduced them?" *Of course she did,* I thought. *She was married to the guy.*

"Yes." Ginny's voice seemed to be back under control. "They were friends long before they hit big time in obedience, you know, and still were, I think, despite the occasional sniping at one another."

"Do you think maybe things didn't work out? With the fiancé, I mean?"

"Possible, I guess. But Suzette wouldn't kill herself over a man. She was excited about breeding Fly. Her first litter and all. Besides, she would have made sure Fly was safe before she ever did anything to herself."

That certainly made sense to me. Then I remembered something else. "Someone told me Suzette bred Fly last year."

"She was going to. When it fell through, I encouraged her to wait until she finished Fly's obedience championship."

"That was probably wise."

"Guess so. But she was so excited about having a puppy of her own breeding."

"Why did the earlier breeding fall through?" I figured that if anyone had the scoop, it would be Ginny. Whether she'd tell me was another matter.

"The stud dog she was planning to use had close relatives with some serious health problems. The dog himself is healthy so far, but there are too many risks too close in his pedigree. Neither one of us knew about the problems until Fly was already in season, so there was no time to find a different dog." I knew that a responsible breeder would spend many hours investigating health and temperament and other traits of a dog's whole family before deciding on a match.

"How did you find out about the dog's problems?" I knew that it wasn't always easy to ferret out negative information about individual dogs and their bloodlines if the people in the know didn't cooperate.

"The owner of one of his brothers called Suzette. Said she'd heard about the planned breeding and figured the dog's breeder wouldn't divulge that there were problems in the line, and she thought Suzette would want to know." Ginny didn't say a word about DNA or suspect parentage. Maybe Abigail had kept that under her hat.

"What kind of problems?"

"The woman who called said her dog had CEA — collie eye anomaly — and she said there was another puppy from the same litter with inherited epilepsy. She said that their sire had produced puppies with epilepsy and eye problems in other litters, too." She put her napkin on the table and leaned back against the red upholstery of the booth. "So Suzette backed out of the breeding. The stud dog's breeder was furious. She sent Suzette a couple of nasty e-mails about what a fool she was, and threatened to sue her for slander if she talked about the health problems in her dogs."

"You can't slander an animal. Besides, attitudes like that hurt the whole breed."

"Right. But the breeder imported the dog's sire from Australia and his dam from Scotland. She had a fortune invested, all down the tubes if word got out. Anyway, Suzette said she didn't plan to launch a campaign against anyone, but she wasn't going to go through with the breeding."

Ginny picked up an unused spoon and balanced it across her index finger. "Next thing you know, the stud's breeder launched a campaign against Suzette and Fly. Posted to Internet lists and told people that Fly had health issues, and claimed that the stud owner refused to breed her dog to Fly, not the other way around. Very ugly."

Although I already knew that she was talking about Abigail Dorn and Francine Peterson, I had to ask. "So who owned the stud dog?"

She gave me a "not important" wave of the hand.

"It was Pip, wasn't it? Abigail's dog."

She hesitated, then nodded. "Suzette told Abigail about the issues in Fly's bloodlines. Fly's maternal aunt produced an epileptic pup. Only one I know of in the close family, but Suzette was determined to stay away from any dogs known to have close relatives with epilepsy." Ginny plunked the spoon onto the Formica table. "I mean, come on! All dogs carry the genes for something we don't want. You just don't double up on bad genes if possible. Pip is a fine dog, but not a good match for Fly."

"Makes sense to me." *Wow,* I thought. Another one who doesn't know about the really big obstacle to using Pip at stud.

"If everyone were open about these problems, we could get a better handle on them." She took a long drink of water. "Francine has always tried to cover up issues in her dogs. I think the lines Pip comes from actually are pretty healthy all told, but Francine used to have some serious temperament issues. In her dogs, I mean — she still has some of her own!"

I couldn't dispute that.

"Anyway, for years she denied that her dogs weren't perfect, then suddenly those dogs disappeared and she started over with new bloodlines." I wondered whether the dogs had actually disappeared, or if Francine had continued to breed them and fudged the puppies' papers.

"There's something you should know about Pip."

"What's that?"

"He's neutered."

"No!"

I nodded.

"Whoa!" Her eyes were enormous. "I bet Francine doesn't know that." She started to laugh. "You know, that sounds like something Abigail would do. Neuter the dog, avoid the hassle of telling Francine." She giggled some more. "And who could tell with the coat that dog has?"

We switched to more pleasant topics. Dogs mostly. After I got her mailing address and promised to send her the photos I'd taken for Suzette, Ginny and Fly drove west toward Chicago, out of the storm of murder and deceit. I headed the other way.

68

Jay and I spent a couple hours wandering along the Tippecanoe River and shooting photos in Potowatomi Wildlife Park. I'd hoped for a glimpse of an osprey or bald eagle, or a river otter like the one I spotted on my last trip, but there were no endangered-species sightings on my plate this time.

The sun was skimming the treetops by the time I pulled into my driveway. I let Jay out of his crate and he made a beeline for Goldie, who was deadheading grape hyacinths in her front yard. I thought he would dislocate a hip the way he was wriggling his butt.

"Where ya been?" She followed me into the house and I filled her in.

"Push those photo boxes out of your way," I told her as I scooped a cup of dry dog food into Jay's bowl.

She picked up a big old plastic dumbbell

that was standing on end next to the pepper grinder. "New kitchen tool?"

"Cute."

"Heavy sucker." She tested it against her biceps.

"Yeah. I have a lighter one I like better."

She clucked at me. "You really should start tossing things you don't use anymore. Give it to someone who can use it if you don't. Get rid of some of the clutter in here."

"Oh, okay, Mom. Sure thing." I made a rude noise as I took the dumbbell out of her hand and into the living room. I supposed I could have put it away somewhere, but I settled for the end table by the couch. I'd find a place for it later. Goldie rolled her eyes at me when I got back to the kitchen. "Something else?"

"I'm just suggesting."

"You never know when something like that will come in handy."

"Uh-huh." She tapped the side of one of the photo boxes. "May I?"

"Help yourself. Old photos from doggy school."

She popped the lid and flipped slowly through the photos. "Doesn't this look like fun? All those lovely dogs. Oops!"

Leo was straddling the box of photos and

head-bumping Goldie's chin. I stepped to the table and started to reach for the cat. "Hey, Mister, mind your manners. No kitchen table for you."

"I don't mind," Goldie protested, wrapping a protective arm about Leo's tawny body.

I looked more closely at Goldie's face and physique. Even in baggy sweats I could see that she had lost a lot of weight, and there were new hollows in her cheeks and the smudges beneath her eyes had darkened. "Goldie, are you really okay?"

"Oh, I'm fine." She hugged Leo and focused her eyes on the contents of the box.

I was about to press the issue when the phone rang. Jo Stevens lost no time on small talk. "I have an unofficial opinion from the coroner on Ms. Dorn and Ms. Anderson. Your friends were both poisoned."

"What?" My voice sounded shrill in my own ear. I mean, the thought had danced around my mind, but having it confirmed was something else.

"We're not sure yet about the source, but Mrs. Dorn had ingested lethal levels of some sort of alkaloids. And preliminary evidence suggests that Ms. Anderson was also poisoned."

"But we knew that. I mean, she took the

Tylenol."

"No, the medical examiner doesn't think so. The autopsy hasn't been done yet, but the M.E. took a quick look and thinks it was something other than acetaminophen."

I pulled a chair away from the table and sank into it, not sure my knees would hold me since they'd turned to jelly. An image popped into my brain. "Wait a minute." I started slowly, speaking more quickly as I continued. "That container I took from Abigail's setup at the show. The one I washed." A hot wave of embarrassment at my own stupidity crept from my chin to my cheekbones. "I thought it smelled funny." I tried to remember what I did with the contents of the bag. "I don't think I cleaned out the trash from the tote bag, you know, paper plate and napkins and stuff. I don't remember taking the plastic bag with the trash out of the tote bag. Maybe there's still something there."

"There was. They haven't run the tests yet, but the lab guy said there may be some traces." For a long moment I thought she might not tell me the rest. Then she did. "They lifted your fingerprints from the container."

69

Detective Stevens made my heart skip a beat or three when she told me they'd found my fingerprints on Abigail's food container, but I tried to calm myself. "Of course they did. I gave it to you." Then another thought hit me. "How did you know which finger-prints were mine? I've never even had a parking ticket!" I considered putting my head between my knees, but the urge to black out faded and curiosity, spiced with a dash of anger, to charge.

Detective Stevens' voice softened a tad. "Hutch, er, Detective Hutchinson, snagged a pop can you tossed. Anyway, we know how your prints got there. The question now is how the poison got there."

Neither of us spoke for a moment, and I could hear computer keys clacking through the receiver. A realization that had been flitting around the dark forest of my mind emerged into the light and landed with a whump. Someone I knew was a murderer. And there was something else.

"Am I a suspect?"

"Officially, yes, it's a possibility. But," her voice softened, "not really. And in view of the whole picture, especially your dog, I thought you should know about the possibility of poison."

"Thanks. Thank you." I thought I might have to run to the bathroom, but the feeling passed. "Sorry, I just . . . I guess we all suspected something, but having it confirmed . . ."

"It gets worse. That was indeed blood on the stuffed dog. Bovine." We were both silent for a moment. "We'll get to the bottom of this, but in the meantime, watch yourself, and your pets. I'll talk to you later."

"Wait! Do you have any serious suspects?"

"We're looking at some people. I can't go into that."

I had a couple ideas of my own. Too many, in fact, and I didn't like most of them one little bit.

Goldie waited, eyes wide, arms wrapped around Leo and chin resting on his back. I filled her in.

"Did she say what kind of poison?"

"Alkalines?"

"Alkaloids?"

"Sounds right."

"Hmmm."

"Hmmm?"

"Oh, you know, alkaloids are what make a lot of poisonous plants poisonous. Deadly nightshade, the hemlocks, Jimsonwe . . ."

"Hemlocks?"

"Yes, water hemlock and poison hemlock. Both are actually poisonous."

"Ohmygod! You showed it to me at Greg's house!"

"Not at his house. In the empty lot. But Janet, the stuff grows all over the place. Fields, along roads."

"I can't believe Greg . . ." The rest of the thought lingered, unspoken.

"Don't jump to conclusions. Besides, the policeman didn't say it was poison hemlock, right? Just an alkaloid."

"Woman," I answered, distracted by my muddled thoughts.

"What?"

"The policeman is a woman."

We sat in silence for a few minutes. Then Goldie chirped, "Did you get to go on your photo safari on the way home from Valpo?"

I told her about my side trip to Potowatomi Wildlife Park. She went back to looking through the box of photos while I talked, and pulled one out of the box as my saga wound down. "Whoa!"

"What?"

"Who's this woman with the daggers in her eyes?" She leaned toward me, pointing at a face in the photo.

"Giselle Swann. Why?"

"Oh, the look on her face stopped me. Could stop several big clocks, I'd say!"

I studied the photo more closely. Giselle did look angry. Or was that hatred on her face? Definitely more than her perpetual misery. I went to my desk and came back with a magnifying glass. "I want a better look." I focused on the enlarged image of Giselle. She was in the background, as usual, in the center of the photo. Abigail was in the forefront, looking at something or someone out of the frame to the left.

Greg was at the front right of the photo, near Abigail but facing the other way, smiling at another someone I'd mostly cut out of the shot except for the arm of a cable knit sweater and the end of a blonde braid visible at the shoulder seam. I scanned down the arm to the hand, held slightly away from the body, flexed upward, fingers reaching backward toward Greg. His own hand in turn reached out, the index finger nearly touching the back of the sweater owner's hand. And Giselle's ocular daggers were aimed outside the photo, just where the blonde braid must originate.

"Goldie, did you see any photos with this person in the frame?" I showed her the sweater and braid. I knew who it was, but wanted to be sure.

"I think so. Hang on." She flipped through several photos, pulled one out, and handed it over. Suzette was in the foreground, her blonde braid resting against the cable of her sweater. Two slightly out-of-focus figures stood in the background. Abigail and a redhead. Francine Peterson. I hadn't realized I had a photo of her, although how I'd missed her with that hair was a good question.

"Who's that?" Goldie tapped Suzette's image.

"Suzette Anderson."

"Oh! Isn't she one of the dead women?"

"Right. And this is the other one. Abigail Dorn. And," showing her the first photo again, "this is Greg, her husband."

She took it all in. "I'd say there was a love quadrangle here."

"That's what I was thinking."

"You know, I think I've seen that one."

"Which one?"

"Her." She indicated Francine. "Who could miss that hair?"

"When?"

She pursed her lips and shut her eyes for a few seconds. "I can't remember when it was, not long ago, but I'm sure I saw her at your house, when was that?" She tapped her fist against the top of her forehead. "Yesterday?" Another tap. "Yes, I'm sure it was yesterday."

"When?"

"Why, you didn't see her? I'm sure you were home. Your car was in the driveway."

70

After Goldie went home I nuked a frozen dinner and sat down to eat and check my e-mails. The pile of unread discussion-list digests was depressing, so I deleted them all unread, along with several opportunities to donate my life savings to Nigerian widows and to assist a friend who had lost her wallet while traveling in Europe between last night, when I saw her at Dog Dayz, and now. *Do people really fall for these schemes?* I wondered. Then I googled *poison hemlock.*

Goldie had been correct. The active toxin in poison hemlock was an alkaloid related to nicotine. *Coniine* to be precise, in case I ever made it onto *Jeopardy.* I didn't find much about hemlock killing people other than Socrates, but there was plenty of information on livestock poisonings. Assuming that it affects most mammals in similar ways, the signs of poisoning by poison hemlock sounded all too familiar. Within a couple hours of eating the plant, the animal becomes nervous and uncoordinated. Didn't Connie say that Abigail was a regular jitterbug before her class, and that she was stumbling around on her heeling pattern? Eventually the animal becomes unable to breathe, and its heart rate slows. A vision of Abigail's stricken face filled my mind.

The sites I checked also said that while the plant's toxicity is lower in the spring than later in the growing season, it's probably also more palatable when young, although they mentioned a "mousy smell" from the crushed leaves. So it would be easier to slip it into some . . . "Oh my God," I mumbled. "The cream cheese." I pictured the flotsam of Abigail's breakfast, including the remains of a bagel and remnants of a spread full of . . . what? I'd assumed it was spinach or dill or something. Yes, dill, I smelled dill, I remembered. And mice. The spread had made me think of mice.

I dialed Jo Stevens' number.

As her phone rang I read that the ancient Greeks considered hemlock a "humane" means of execution. How civilized. I wondered whether Abigail would agree.

Dog Dayz was hopping with people and dogs preparing for upcoming obedience trials, and all the usual suspects were there. Unless they were top ranked, and dead. Jay was full of energy and not so full of attentiveness, so we had a happy but not exactly accurate session. But what the heck, we do this for fun. If my dog sits a little out of position but acts happy, that's a perfect performance to my mind.

Sylvia Eckhart, her Cocker, Tippy, in tow, strolled over and asked after my mom. I filled her in, and she assured me that Mom's right to her chin had caused her no serious damage.

I was packing up my dog treats and other equipment when I saw Giselle Swann charging me from the direction of the back door. Her head was thrust down and forward, her face was magenta, her shoulders slightly hunched and her two hands balled into fat fists. *Look out,* yelled the little demon on my left shoulder. *She thinks your red sweatshirt is a cape!*

I faced her straight on. "Evening, Giselle."

"How could you?" She stomped her right foot as she pulled up in front of me. "How could you? How could you do that to me? Abigail was my friend!"

"Uh, what's the problem, Giselle?"

I noticed movement in my peripheral vision. Marietta Santini was speed-walking our way, no doubt hoping to prevent an all-out bitch fight. I use the term in the canine sense. Every breeder I've ever talked to says that if a fight breaks out in a multi-dog home, they'd much rather it be among dogs — males — than bitches. Boys fight for status, and they can certainly hurt each other, but tend to do a lot of posturing and pushing and then forget about it. When two bitches fight, each wants the other gone, one way or another. I, on the other hand, had no desire to fight Giselle, and didn't much care where she was.

She stood in front of me, puffing and shifting from one foot to the other, glaring not into my eyes, but somewhere in the neighborhood of my chin. I hoped it hadn't sprouted a new hair. "The police came to my house again. They asked me a bunch of questions."

"They asked me a bunch of questions too."

"Everything okay over here?" asked Marietta.

"You sent them, didn't you?" Giselle lowered her voice to a growl.

"Giselle, no one sent them." Marietta crossed her arms and cocked a hip. "They're investigating. They're talking to everyone who knew Abigail and Suzette. They talked to me, too."

Giselle shifted her glare to Marietta, then right back to my chin. "I know you told that detective to question me. You'll be sorry." She turned her head toward Jay for a moment, then charged out to the parking lot.

Marietta squinted and pointed the stiffened, splayed fingers of both hands at my face, cackling, "You'll be sorry, you and your little dog." She relaxed her limbs. "Weirdo."

"What in the heck was that all about?"

"Fear. Jealousy. Guilt. Hallucinations." She grinned at me. "Who the hell knows with Giselle?"

"Do you think she'd hurt a dog?"

"I doubt it." Marietta pursed her lips. "On the other hand, if anybody looked at my dog that way, I wouldn't let him out of my sight for a while."

71

Thursday morning seemed to bring, for once, a normal day. I stopped by the nursing home, but Mom was sleeping, so I didn't stay. Jade Templeton assured me that she was doing fine, and that it was sometimes better to let people settle in before visiting too often. *What difference does it make,* I wondered to myself, *when most of the time she has no idea who I am?*

Jade also said that Mom was enjoying the garden, and had assumed the role of garden director, telling the other residents as well as the staff how to plant, weed, water, and whatever. She might not know my name, but the Latin names of hundreds of plants were no problem. Other than that, it was business as usual for me — a five-mile walk on the River Greenway with Jay, phone calls, mailings, and miscellaneous. I skipped agility class, and by nine p.m. my brain was pooped.

I tried to focus on the boob tube before bedtime, but couldn't find anything I could stand to watch that I hadn't seen before, so I put on my old k.d. lang *Torch and Twang* CD, and lay down on the couch. I had my head propped on a couple of pillows, my feet tucked between Jay's cozy belly and flank, and my own belly blanketed by Leo's rumbling furry circle of heat. Despite my roiling thoughts and emotions, I must have been a picture of contentment as I opened my newly arrived issue of *Nature Photography.* But my brain wasn't ready to abandon current events, and when I found myself rereading the same paragraph for the fourth time, I gave up on the magazine and closed my eyes, my thoughts on the troubles in our little community of dog lovers.

Was Abigail right? Was Greg having an affair? Was he going to leave her for Suzette? But Connie said Abigail had hired a PI who said Greg wasn't fooling around. Maybe Abigail lied to Connie. I mean, if she was reluctant to say her dog was neutered, how would she feel about her husband's philandering? And where did Giselle fit into all this? Did she really think she'd get Greg if Abigail and Suzette were both out of the way? And what about Francine Peterson? Why in the heck was she lurking around?

The telephone shocked me out of my meditations. My limbs jerked, Leo flew off my belly with a yowl, and Jay leaped off the couch with a "Bfff," slid across the hardwood floor when his paws hit the throw rug in the center of the room, and gave me a "what the heck?" look. I made an effort to control my breathing, and picked up the receiver.

"Hiya!"

"Oh, Tom."

"You sound disappointed." He sounded disappointed.

"No, no! The boys and I were vegging out and the phone scared the bejeepers out of us. Sorry!"

We did the "how was your day" thing, and then Tom cut to the chase, inviting me to his place for dinner on Friday.

No, I thought. *You don't need that complication, not before these murders are solved,* but I heard myself ask, "Can I bring anything?" Meaning something I could pick up and pop open to serve.

"Yes. Drake says to bring Jay. Otherwise we're all set."

I hung up, and Jo Stevens's words came back to me. I had to watch what I ate.

I was halfway back to the couch when the phone rang again. Jay was already snuggled back into his corner cushion, and at the other end Leo was doing kitty yoga, back leg extended behind his neck, so it was just as well that I didn't need my spot back for a few more minutes.

Connie didn't waste any time on preliminaries. "I found out what Greg was up to at the travel agency."

"What are you talking about?"

"Remember when we saw Greg at the mall? Coming out of Travelfair?"

It took me a moment, but I remembered.

"Okay, so, he wasn't planning a trip. He was returning tickets."

"That makes sense."

"Yeah, it would if the tickets had been for him and Abigail," she replied slowly, with a tease in her voice. "Who do you think was going to Bermuda with him?"

"Tell me."

"Suzette."

"Suzette Anderson?"

"You know another Suzette around here?"

"How did you find this out, anyway?"

"Old high school friend manages the place. I bribed her with Abby Brown's chocolates." My salivary glands went wild at the thought.

"You're one devious woman."

"I prefer to think of myself as practical."

"You could have a bright future as a detective."

"You never know. If my wrist gives out from one too many Poodle trims, I might need a new career."

"You bring me anything from Abby Brown's?"

"I thought you were dieting?"

"I'm always dieting. Chocolate could be on my diet." Part of my brain was trying to recall whether I had any stashed anywhere. "So, anyway . . . Greg and Suzette?"

She didn't say anything.

"What about the private detective that Abigail hired?" I asked. "You said he nixed her suspicions that Greg was having an affair."

"Abigail could have been lying. Maybe she knew but didn't want to let on."

Someone was lying, that was for sure. "I had that thought too. Or maybe the detective had some reason to lie. Or maybe he was incompetent."

When I got off the phone I went back to the couch and thought about the latest news, leaning back against the Aussie-face tapestry pillow, my right hand stroking Jay's silky head, my left scratching behind Leo's ears. Who says I can't multitask?

72

I don't think of myself as a morning person, and was shocked to find I was up with the sun again Thursday morning. Jay and I went for an early walk to beat the heat, which was intensifying by the day.

The River Greenway led us into the rising sun, which danced among the leaves of tulip poplars, sycamores, black walnuts, beeches, and several species of oak and maple. A fine gray veil drifted over the murky surface of the Maumee, and the wooded banks fairly screeched as bluejays and crows called each other names. A farm field to the north of the trail showed a faint scatter of soft green shoots over the surface of the dark soil. Corn or soy beans, no doubt. Last year it was beans, so this was probably corn. We met only a handful of early joggers and cyclists.

A splash in the river caught our attention and I watched a pair of wood ducks paddle out of sight under some low-hanging branches. Cerise redbud and ivory dogwood blossoms, luminous in the morning light, danced beneath the hardwood canopy along the riverbank. An Indiana May morning at its finest.

The sirens of the river and woods urged me to linger, but I had things to do. Breakfast for Jay, and a quick shower, and I was on my way once more to Shadetree Retirement Home.

Jade Templeton met me at the front door. "Janet! So nice to see you. Mama is doing fine. She's out in the garden. I just came from there."

We walked through the common area where my mother had behaved like a berserker. Was it only three days ago? Two men played checkers by one of the floor-to-ceiling windows that flanked the French doors leading to the enclosed courtyard. An elfin little man with a fringe of white hair around his bald and spotted pate snoozed in a wheelchair toward the center of the room, and a cherry-cheeked woman with tightly curled too-black hair and an electric-yellow velour jumpsuit looked up from her book and fluttered her fingers at us. We exited the room through the French door.

Mom was busy at what appeared to be a

brand-new flower bed. It was raised for easy access for gardeners in wheelchairs, or folding chairs like the one Mom sat in. Great idea, I thought. I could use a little less bending over in my own garden.

"Hi, Mom."

She didn't react, so I touched her lightly on the sleeve. "Oh, hello. I didn't hear you come in, dear." For a moment, I hoped she might be lucid. But then she carefully wiped the fresh soil coating her old, familiar garden gloves onto her light blue sweatpants before pulling her hands from the gloves and extending one in my direction. "I'm Elaine Jones."

Jones was her maiden name. It hadn't been her legal name for more than half a century. I worked to keep my voice upbeat. "Mom, it's me, Janet."

She went back to planting her bedding plants, gloveless now. She seemed to have this plot of raised soil all to herself. Two women and a man worked companionably at another bed, and at the third, a young volunteer aid steadied a gentleman whose hands shook too much to plant his tomato seedlings by himself.

Mom's aesthetic abilities were intact, judging by the way she arranged the baby plants. I imagined the bed as it would be in a month. Plastic name tags identified the contents of the plastic containers, and there were no dainty pastels in mom's selections. I knew there would be no symmetrical rows for my mom, either. I watched her anchor the center of the bed with purple and pink cleome and tall white cosmos. Around those she planted sweeps of crimson zinnias, electric-blue ageratum, and clear-yellow French marigolds. A froth of white alyssum played in the spaces where the colors met, and the borders were edged in vinca vine and blood-red, purple, and white trailing verbena that would soon drape the outer edge of the box like a curtain on a Gypsy caravan. This tiny garden promised me a glimpse of the mother I used to know.

I watched her work for a little more than an hour, enjoying the warm sun and the Big Band music playing softly in the courtyard. I felt calmer than I had in many days, reassured that my mother would be happy here, at least in the warm months.

By the time I left, Mom was focused on patting handfuls of mulch into place around the plants. She acknowledged my goodbye with a dismissive wave.

Jade called to me as I walked through the front lobby. "Wait, child, I'll walk you out." She caught up with me and asked what I thought.

"She seems as happy here as she was at home. And she's safer."

"Your mama is a sweet lady. I wish I'd known her before."

I nodded.

"So, the reason I wanted to talk to you, your mama showed me some pictures of your dog, and she got all teary-eyed. Your dog and other dogs. She had a bunch of dog pictures, all in a little box. So I wondered — why don't you bring him to visit some-time. Your mama would like that."

"How strange." Jade looked puzzled, so I went on. "Oh, the timing. I've been plan-ning to do something along those lines. In fact, I'm taking Jay to Indianapolis on Saturday to be tested for his certification as a therapy dog. That will make him official, you know?"

"That's great then." Jade's smile was back. "We have some other dogs that visit, and our resident kitty, Thomas, but it's always nice to have one more. And your mama loves that dog. What's his name? Laddie, I think?"

"His name is Jay. But she thinks he's Lad-die, a dog she had before I was born. Sad."

"Oh, no, not sad." Jade wrapped an arm around my shoulders as we walked. "Memories of love are a measure of grace." She gave me a squeeze. "In the end, love is all that matters in our lives." She was right, of course, and who better to love than those who love us as our dogs do?

73

A message to call Jo Stevens was waiting on my answering machine, so once I got squared away, I picked up the phone, tagged the detective's voice mail, and thought about sorting and dumping some of the magazines and junk mail that had invaded my living room.

Thinking was as far as I got. Leo bounded in with a little yellow foam ball in his mouth and mrowled at me. I was bound by duty as a cat servant to sacrifice a tidy house in favor of play. Jay watched from the safety of the couch, more out of regard for his tender nose than for politeness. Leo is quite the defender of his little foam balls.

When the phone rang, I expected to talk to the detective, and was surprised by the voice at the other end.

"Janet, it's Ginny Scott. You have a minute?"

"Ginny! Yes, sure. How's Fly?"

"She's a sweetheart. Moved in as if she'd never been gone. Seems to be looking for Suzette from time to time, but overall she's fine. She's eating, so that's good."

"Great."

"I wanted first to thank you again for bringing her to me. I probably couldn't have picked her up for another couple of weeks if I'd had to go to Fort Wayne. That would be an all-day trip."

"Oh, no problem. I'm always looking for a good excuse to get to different places with my camera."

She jumped ahead to what I suspect was the real reason for her call. "Something odd happened last night."

"Oh?"

"Francine Peterson called. All friendly and gushy. Asked me 'How's that lovely bitch of yours?' I must be slow, but I hadn't a clue who she was talking about. I have six lovely bitches!"

Spoken like a true dog woman.

"She went on and on about how gorgeous Fly is. I was tempted to say something about all the trash she put out back when Suzette declined to breed Fly to Pip, but I held my tongue."

"That must have been hard."

"I guess I was curious about where Francine was headed. Anyway, I didn't say much. Just let her blather on."

"Did she have a point?"

Her voice turned to a snarl. "She wanted to buy Fly."

"Did she make you an actual offer?"

"Oh yeah! Very generous offer, couched in all sorts of crap about how hard it is being a responsible breeder and what a nuisance it is to take back an adult puppy that someone else has owned for several years, complete with a story about one she took back that caused chaos in her kennel." I was dying to hear how much the offer was, but Ginny was wound up. "I told her I don't consider my puppies to be nuisances, no matter how old, and that the only time there's chaos among my dogs is when I have a tennis ball or food bowls."

"I know this is rude, but I'm dying to know — how much did she offer?"

"Four thousand dollars."

"Whoa! You're kidding!"

"Nope. I was blown away. She talked about breeding her to Pip, so she must not know he's neutered. I'm sure she figured she could sell puppies from Pip and Fly for a pretty penny."

"I can't see Greg agreeing to that."

"She claimed she's getting Pip back."

I remembered the scene at Abigail's funeral. "I doubt that."

"Yeah, me too."

"I take it you turned her down."

"I'd as soon cut my arm off with dull thinning shears as let that woman get her hands on one of my puppies."

That seemed perfectly rational to me.

"I'm really not such a big gossip, but I can't stand Francine. I didn't care for Abigail, either, God rest her soul, but at least she was good to her dogs and responsible about breeding. But you're right there where the investigation is going on, and I don't know why exactly, but I thought you should know about this."

"Okay. I mean, I'm not involved in any investigating," I ignored Janet Demon rolling her eyes and whispering, *yeah, right,* "but I'll mention it to the police detective on the case. She'll know better than I do whether it's important."

74

Jay and Leo and I went out to the backyard for a game of tennis ball. We each have our special plays. I try to fake Jay out, and he gives me his "How lame is that, trying to fake out a dog?" look. Then I throw it, and he races across the yard after the bouncing yellow fuzz, and another ball of yellow fuzz flies out from under the forsythia jungle in the corner, races after the dog, counts coup on Jay's fanny, and races back to the leafy lair. Then Jay grabs the ball, spins toward the forsythia and charges toward the cat hunkered under its lowest branches, where he lets out a ball-muffled brrffff. Then he brings me the ball so we can do it all again.

I heard the phone through the open window and ran for the door. As I picked up the receiver, I glanced out the window. Jay danced from foot to foot at the back door, panting. His expression pleaded, "Wait! Wait! The game isn't over!" Leo was strolling along the fence line, showing how much he didn't care.

Jo identified herself. "We've confirmed that the chisel we found is the tool used to slash your tires."

"Did you catch the fiend who did it?"

"Not yet. But we lifted fingerprints from the chisel."

"That's good, right?"

"Only if we identify a suspect. Or it's someone with a record."

I must have looked disappointed.

"It's not impossible that the prints will lead us to the culprit."

"But not likely either, right?"

"Turns out this chisel is really high quality. You know anyone who would have reason to have a good chisel?"

"Not really."

Must have been something in my voice, because she pressed me, so I told her that I'd heard that Francine had a mobile repair business of some sort. "But judging by the beat-up old van she drives, I don't know how much she's into high-quality equipment."

Jo let a beat go by, then went on, her voice pitched slightly lower and faster. "Look, I have no hard evidence, but you and I both know that the tires are linked to the stuffed dog and that both are somehow linked to the two dead women."

My heart rate increased by half. "Wow. Hearing a cop put my thoughts into words makes them even scarier."

I excused myself to let the beasties in and to collect my thoughts. Jay guzzled from his water bowl, but Leo was nowhere in sight. Probably prowling the perimeter. I'd have to retrieve him when I got off the phone, but for now I got back to Jo. "It makes sense that everything's connected, but I don't know what I have to do with anything."

I heard a noise in the living room and walked to the doorway leading there from the kitchen. Leo was on the front porch, balanced on the ladder back of my rocking chair and patting the window with his claws. He'd have to wait a minute. My home is electronically challenged and I still have a phone with a cord. It didn't reach to the front door.

"You've had both the dead women's dogs in your possession, right?"

"Well, yes, but not for long. I had Pip for four or five days, but everyone knew that was temporary. And I had Fly for a couple of hours, in my car."

"Still a link. And you knew both of the women. And you seem to know all the other players." She added, as if she'd just thought of it, "And you take pictures."

"Pictures. You mean that someone thinks I've taken a picture of something that I don't even know I've seen?"

"Look, you need to be careful, okay? And not just about what you eat."

"What do you mean?"

"I don't want to scare you, but the bloody dog toy and the attack on your tires suggest more violence is possible than simply poisoning." Having watched Abigail suffer, I wasn't sure I'd call poisoning "simple," but I let that thought go and listened as Jo continued. "Whoever's doing these things is getting more desperate, so maybe you're on to something without knowing what it is. Frankly, Janet, I think we have a nutcase on our hands, so you need to take these threats seriously. Be careful, lock your doors, and watch Jay and Leo. And if you feel remotely threatened, call 911 first, then call me."

In my rush to get off the phone and go bring Leo into the safety of the house, I forgot to tell her about Giselle's hissy fit or Greg's travel plans or Ginny's phone call. I really had to start making lists. I stepped out the front door, but Leo was no longer on the porch. I called his name, which usually brings His Excellency in at a leisurely stroll. He can't appear to be obeying, of course, but he does come when called. Usually.

Okay, sometimes.

I went in, grabbed a can of salmon-flavored treats from the cupboard, and went back outside. I left Jay in the house — he was entirely too focused on the fishy smell coming from the can to be of any help. Why do cats have to pick the worst possible time to play games? Then again, Leo didn't know there was a killer on the loose.

I walked around the yard, peeking under shrubs and into other hidey holes, calling and rattling the treats, but no cat appeared. Today was evidently not a come-when-called day, and after a twenty-minute tour of the front, side, and back yards, I went inside. I popped a salmon treat between Jay's slavering jaws and told him, "The little booger was probably hunkered down out there watching me and laughing his furry little butt off."

75

The doorbell, followed by Jay's deep "boofs" from the direction of the front door, jolted me out of bed the next morning. The one morning in recent history that I'd actually slept until a decent hour, mostly because I'd been up several times during the night calling for Leo, and now some fool was ringing my bell. I glanced at my watch, pulled on a pair of sweatpants, and combed my hair back with my fingers. Turned out 6:49 was only a semi-decent time to get up, and obscenely early for a visitor. Panic clutched at my mind.

I should have used the peephole before opening the door since no rational person would come calling at that hour, unless they bore devastating news. I mean, what's the point of having a reasonably secure locking system that you open right up for bad guys? But it was way too early to think, so I slipped the chain, flipped the deadbolt, grabbed Jay's collar, and pulled the door open.

Detectives Stevens and Hutchinson were on my porch.

"Ohmygod. Who's dead now?"

Hutchinson had his badge out, as if I wouldn't recognize him. "Can we come in?"

I took half a step backward, holding Jay's collar and my breath. Jo Stevens smiled at me and shook her head. "It's not that kind of a visit."

Jay stopped barking and leaned into his collar, stretching his neck toward the detectives, sucking in their scent while his body vibrated from his wriggling tail nub to his shoulders.

Hutchinson glowered at Jay. "Call off your dog."

"Oh, for crying out loud." Jo pushed past him and stepped into the house, giving Jay a scratch under the chin. Her partner followed, puffing up his chest as he glanced at Jay.

"You don't like dogs much, do you, detective? I'll put him outside if he scares you."

"I'm not scared," he lied.

Jay was no longer interested in Hutchinson. He stood in front of Jo, eyes sparkling and fanny wriggling. She rubbed behind his ears.

I peered out the door before I closed it. "You didn't happen to see an orange cat out there, did you?" They hadn't. "Leo's been gone since I talked to you yesterday."

Hutchinson hitched up his pants. "Look, we're not here to chat about your pets. We have a missing suspect to find."

76

Jo glared at her partner but spoke to me. "I'm sure Leo will show up when he gets hungry. Probably needed a night on the town."

I wanted to agree with her, but Leo wasn't an on-the-town sort of guy. What would be the point, since he was neutered? "It's not like him." I led them through to the kitchen, let Jay out the back door, and surveyed the backyard. No Leo. "Coffee?" I asked, turning back to the detectives. My hands needed something to do that didn't ruin my cuticles.

"That would be nice," said Jo.

I got busy with the coffee scoop and asked, "Do you work every day?"

"Seems like it. We're covering for a couple guys who are off."

Hutchinson dragged a chair out. "Mrs. MacPhail, where is Greg Dorn?"

"Ms."

He harumphed at me.

"Why ask me?"

"He's wanted for questioning in the murders of his wife and his mistress."

I turned toward the detectives. "Mistress?"

Jo glowered at Hutchinson, the look on her face suggesting that she'd smack him if she had to, and he shut up for a moment. "We need to find Mr. Dorn. He isn't at home."

"We're not really friends, just acquaintances." I finished setting the coffee maker, moved a couple of photo boxes and some files out of the way, and signaled them to sit at the table.

"Did Mr. Dorn plan to leave the country?" Hutchinson was nothing if not slow.

"How would I know?"

"So you're not aware of any plans he might have had to leave the country?" Jo asked softly.

"Look, I don't know the guy that well. Saw him with his wife at dog events sometimes, and I took care of Abigail's dog for a couple of days. That's it. I'm not privy to his plans. I heard some rumors that he might have been planning a trip before. . . ." Suddenly my mind was spinning. Why would Greg kill Suzette if they'd been planning a Caribbean tryst? "Before?" asked Jo.

"Before what?" asked Mr. Charm.

"Well, before Suzette died." I sighed. "I heard that he cashed in some tickets he had for himself and Suzette. But I don't think . . ." I let Jay back in and served the coffee. "I can't imagine Greg killing anyone, especially his wife or Suzette."

Hutchinson pulled a beat-up spiral-bound notepad part way out of his shirt pocket. The end of the wire caught in the fabric, stretching out the bottom few coils and tearing the top hem of the pocket. He wrestled it free, tried to push the wire back into a coil, flipped the notebook open and scribbled something, and tried to pat the pocket flat against his chest. It defied his efforts, but Jay took the chest patting as an invitation and before I could intercede he had his front paws on the man's shoulders and they were nose to nose.

Everyone froze, and then I recovered enough to reach for my dog. "Jay! Off!"

But Hutchinson surprised me. His hands came up tentatively to Jay's cheeks, and he looked into the dog's eyes, and he said, "Nah. It's okay." His shoulders relaxed, and he slowly ran his fingers along Jay's copper cheek markings and, his voice softer, repeated, "It's okay."

Jo looked away from her partner and shrugged at me, then cleared her throat.

"Do you have any ideas about Greg's other friends, anyone who might know his whereabouts?"

"Sorry." Hadn't I just told them I didn't know him all that well?

"We haven't been able to locate any of his family." It was a statement, but there was a question in it.

"I don't think he has any family around here. I don't even know where he's from, now that I think about it. But how do you know he's gone? Maybe he just wasn't home when you were there."

"Oh, he's long gone." Hutchinson gently lifted Jay's feet from his chest and lowered the dog to the floor, then shoved his partially wired notebook back into his torn pocket. Jay sat beside him and rested his chin on the man's knee.

Jo explained. "We executed a search warrant early this morning." *Early? Had to be the crack of dawn,* I thought. "There's no sign of him. It certainly appears that he's gone out of town."

I watched several tiny bubbles spin in the whirlpool I stirred in my mug. "What about his car?"

"His car was there, and the van."

Jo carried her empty mug to the sink. Her partner stroked the top of Jay's head, and seemed reluctant to let the moment go. Finally he looked at me, his expression softer than I'd seen it. He seemed about to say something, then looked again at Jay, and stood up.

No one spoke on the way to the front porch, where I told Jay to lie down. "Are the dogs there?"

Jo looked at her partner, then at me, and shook her head.

"If the cars were there and the dogs weren't, I'd say he took them for a walk. How long were you there?"

"Forty-five minutes, maybe. We just came from there."

"Well, I bet he was just walking the dogs before work."

Hutchinson pulled a battered business card from his inside jacket pocket. "Call if you hear from Mr. Dorn or learn his whereabouts."

"Are you going to arrest Greg?"

Jo confirmed that there was a warrant for his arrest. Hutchinson's phone chirped. He bent and stroked Jay again, then headed for the car as he opened his phone. Jo watched him, and said, "That was interesting." She looked at me. "Cut him a little slack. His wife ran off last week with some biker dude."

"I didn't want to admit this to your partner. . . ." I said, and Jo turned and looked me in the eye. "I'm a tad scared. I mean, someone killed Abigail and Suzette, and I knew them both. I probably know the killer."

Jo completed the thought. "And the killer knows you, and doesn't know how much you've figured out." I nodded at her. "And whoever it is knows that you've been talking to us." She glanced at the black sedan parked in front of my house. "So be alert and be cautious, okay? And again, if you think something's wrong, call 911. Or me, if it's not an emergency." She bent and scratched Jay's chest. "If I were you, I'd stick close to this guy for a while."

I watched her get behind the wheel of the black car before I stepped back inside the house with my dog. We started for the kitchen, but I backtracked to lock the door.

77

As soon as I was dressed I called the AKC's
Companion Animal Recovery and left them
my cell number on the off chance that
someone would find Leo and scan him for
a microchip. He might even still be wearing
his collar and ID tag. Then I set out to look
once more for my cat. I drove first to Kin-
kos and copied a flyer I'd made with Leo's
picture and vitals. I handed them out at
Animal Control, then the Allen County
SPCA shelter, where I looked at the cats in
the holding areas and filed "lost pet" reports. Then, consulting the pages I'd ripped
from my phone book, I drove around to
every vet office north of downtown and
handed out more flyers. I've always thought
that putting a distraught face with a report
is better than just a phone call.

I tacked more than a hundred flyers to
every bulletin board and lamp post I could
find, and handed them out to my neighbors.

I even got permission from the principals of all but one school in the area to tape copies to the exit doors for a few days, since kids were more likely than most adults to notice an animal wandering around.

I couldn't think of anything else to do to help Leo find his way home, and I realized that I was close to Greg's house, so I decided to run by and see if there was any sign of the other lost boy. Just as the detectives had said, Greg's cars were both in the driveway. I parked on the street, and checked for lurking Yugos as I got out. Not a soul in sight.

I went to the front door and rang the bell. No barking. A newspaper was lying in its plastic wrapper at the edge of the porch, and I picked it up and looked at the date. This morning. I tried to peek through the decorative glass of the door, but everything was distorted, so I didn't learn much. There was no sign of movement inside the house, though, so after a few minutes I set the paper back down by the door and walked around to the side of the house and through the gate into the backyard. No dogs, no Greg. I climbed the bluestone steps to the patio and tapped on the French door, just to be sure. The umbrella was up on the patio table, and a plate and half-full glass of diluted-looking tea sat under it. Odd that Greg would leave them out if he left, but maybe he was tidiness challenged. Like me.

From the patio I stepped onto a lawn that felt like thick carpet beneath my feet, not a weed or errant leaf in sight. The flower beds looked as if someone had edged them inch by flawless inch with nail scissors. I walked toward a building about the size of a two-car garage at the back of the yard. Clay pots were neatly stacked along one side under a row of narrow windows, all in the shadow of an enormous ash that must have been on the property before the house was built. An overhang shaded a wooden porch along the front of the building. I stepped onto it and knocked on the door. As I expected, there was no reply.

I stepped off the porch and went to the front-most window on the side and tried to see in, but the interior was too dark to reveal its secrets. I tried the other windows, too, but got the same results. I stood and looked at the lake behind the yard for a few moments, then headed back to the house. The blinds were closed on several windows, but I did manage to peek into the master bedroom. Nobody home.

I was just rounding the front corner of the house when a cold spray of water hit me in the back and sent me scuttling forward. I turned and look, half expecting to see Greg standing behind me with a hose. Instead I found myself staring at an automatic sprinkler that had popped out of the ground and assaulted me.

"Perfect," I muttered, twisting as well as I could to wring out the hems of my pants and shirt. On a hunch, I opened the mailbox on my way by and sure enough, a hefty pile of mail hadn't been picked up. I glanced up and down the street, not sure what I was looking for, but all was quiet. Too quiet, I thought. No kids out playing, no forgetful old ladies out gardening. No signs of life at all.

I glanced at my watch and was shocked to see that I'd used up most of the day. My reflection in my driver's side window looked like a drowned rat. The perfect look for a dinner date. *Date? Who said this was a date?* But who was I kidding? I was really starting to like Tom, and guessed this was as much like a date as it could get. Oh, well, I'd worry about my hair when I got home. At the moment, I admitted to myself, I was more worried about Greg and his dogs and, of course, my cat.

78

I almost cancelled dinner with Tom to stay home in case Leo showed up, but Goldie insisted I needed to go and promised to check my yard every hour or so and to let Leo in and call my cell phone if he showed up. Still, by the time I changed out of my damp clothes and fixed my hair and face, I pulled into Tom's driveway a quarter hour late. Tom was in the open front door before I was out of the van. Drake sat at his side, holding the stay command but vibrating with excitement. He and Tom wore matching grins. Tom also wore his ever-popular just-right jeans and a white shirt, sleeves rolled to his elbows and top button open to reveal a hint of brown and silver chest hair. With a little air brushing, he could pose for the cover of a romance novel.

Tom ushered Jay and me into the house. I wanted to linger near the kitchen, where the aroma of simmering tomato and basil and something I couldn't identify wrapped itself around me like a warm embrace. But Tom wisely hustled everyone straight through to the breakfast nook, where he opened a sliding door and shooed the dogs out before they clobbered anything, especially us. They took off through the yard, careened around two Adirondack chairs set under an enormous pin oak, and zoomed away to the far end of the yard, each snagging one of a dozen balls scattered across the lawn. We stood on the deck and watched. I didn't know about Tom, but I wasn't interested in being slammed in the knees by my fifty-pound Aussie, let alone his seventy-five-pound Labrador pal.

"Gee, I guess they're glad to see each other."

"And I'm glad to see you." Tom moved half a step closer to me. I got a whiff of a subtle, spicy fragrance, and fought off an impulse to make him lie down. Lucky for him, he kept moving. "But I'm not going to run like a maniac around the yard. How about a drink. Wine, beer . . . that's probably all I can scare up except a dribble of Bailey's."

I followed him back into the family room, placed my order, and looked around while he disappeared into the kitchen. The room was tastefully comfy in a masculine way, and tidier by far than my place ever is. The deep-brown leather couch was well broken in but nowhere near shabby, and little Janet Angel whispered in my ear, *Good guy. He lets his dog lie on the couch.* A large nylon chew toy once shaped like a Y lay beside a needlepoint pillow with a black Lab on it, one arm of the Y-bone gnawed to a pointed nub and the other arm on its way to the same state.

"Here ya go." Tom handed me a bottle of Killian's Red, then grabbed the bone and tossed it onto a big round dog bed snuggled up against the side of an antique roll-top desk. He grinned at me. "Dogs!"

"Hey, you've been in my house. Toys-and-hair-are-us."

"Wouldn't have it any other way." He set his bottle on a coaster sporting — what else? — a black Lab. "Make yourself at home. I'll start the pasta."

One wall of the room had a red brick fireplace flanked by built-in bookcases crammed from hearth-to-ceiling with books and a few knickknacks. A rough-hewn mantle held a pair of pewter candlesticks and about a dozen bronze, brass, and pewter Labrador Retrievers of various sizes. A large, very good oil of a black Lab in a field on a snowy day, a faraway look in his eyes, hung over the mantle.

My mother always said that you can tell a lot about a person by the books on their shelves, so I took a look. Low across the left-hand bookcase was an eclectic assortment of poetry. This is a science guy? Above the poetry was a shelf of nature and travel memoirs, including some of my golden-oldie favorites — Eiseley, Erlich, Lopez, Dillard, Chatwin. Good stuff. Above that, it was all fiction, modern and classic.

"See anything interesting?"

"As a matter of fact, I do." I took a sip of my beer as I turned toward his voice and almost spewed it back out.

79

Tom was decked out in an oversized chef's hat and an apron that said "The chef is not responsible for dog hair in the food" under a comedic black Lab. He struck a pose, nudging the hat flirtatiously. "Like my outfit?"

"And me without my camera!"

"Christmas presents from my kid." He winked, and something just south of my stomach did a flip-flop. "Need another beer?"

Hey, drink up! Janet Demon was on alert. *You can blame the booze for anything that happens.* "I'm fine, thanks."

He saluted, and went back to the kitchen. I moved to the right-hand bookcase. There were tons of paperbacks, mostly thrillers, some sci fi, on the bottom shelf. A row of anthropology and botany journals, a number of field guides to trees, mushrooms and fungi, birds, bugs, and flowers, and several volumes on training retrievers. The next two shelves were home to ethnographic monographs, including such classics as Turnbull's *The Forest People* and Mead's now-controversial *Coming of Age in Samoa,* both of which I'd actually read in an anthro class way back when. The rest were more recent and focused mostly on Mexico, Spain, and Central and South America. I took another swig of Killian's, then went cold as I examined the top shelf. Book after book on poisonous and medicinal plants. *Run* was my first reaction. *Don't be silly,* whispered Janet Demon. *His interest is academic — he studies plants and shamans and such.*

I heard the back door slide open. "Whoa! Give me that! No sticks in the house!" I walked to the kitchen doorway. Jay and Drake had their muzzles deep in a big stainless-steel water bowl, slurping and dripping, Drake's thick tail wagging away, Jay's little nub wriggling. Drake quit first and settled with a grunt onto the cool vinyl floor. Jay flopped down next to his new buddy and sighed.

The table was set, informal and inviting. A rough-woven table cloth of robin's-egg blue flecked with bits of white, yellow, and red supported honey-colored stoneware plates. The plates supported dark brown salad bowls, and not-quite-matching dark brown rough-woven napkins underlay heavy stainless place settings. A handmade clay pot held a splashy assortment of blooms and foliage, garden and wild flowers mingled with greenery.

"You know, if the research and teaching doesn't work out, you may have a future as a restaurateur."

Tom wrinkled his nose as he delivered a wooden bowl brimming with dark and pale greens, crimson grape tomatoes, golden bell-pepper bits, and brown-black olives. My reptilian brain hissed something about how easy it would be to hide noxious herbs in a mixed salad, but was interrupted when Tom said, "I was a waiter — or what do we say now, server? — off and on in college. Enough restaurant work for me, thanks. I prefer to do my serving at home."

"Here I thought you were strictly a rough-and-tumble Labrador Retriever sort of guy. Figured you lived on beef jerky and trail mix."

"I have been known to eat baked beans out of a can, standing at the sink and watching hockey on TV." He cocked his head. "Does that restore my rough-and-tumble image?" *What the heck,* I thought. *So have I, except for the hockey.* "Would you like wine with dinner, or another beer?"

I figured I'd better stick with the beer. I can't mix my alcohol and pretend to be rational as convincingly as I could a decade or two ago.

Tom set a golden-brown loaf of warm, garlicky bread in front of the flowers, and served vermicelli topped with a thick sauce that made my mouth water.

"What's that fragrance that I can't place?" I asked.

"Wet dog?"

"Noooo. That I can identify, thanks. No, sort of, sweet? Like licorice?"

"Ah. Sorry, secret ingredient. You'll have to wait until I know you better."

Yeah! Shouted Janet Demon. *In the biblical sense.* I felt very warm.

Before he sat down, Tom set two bowls of freshly grated cheese on the table. "Romano on the left," he rolled the r, "and Parmesan on the right." He sat down, flicked his napkin open with his left hand, and tucked it into the neckband of his shirt. "I don't know why I wear white when I eat tomato sauces. You'd think I'd learn." He grinned at me and lifted his beer. "To us." I could drink to that, I thought, until he pushed the cheeses toward me and said, "Pick your poison."

80

Tom's eyes widened and a deep furrow dug into the spot between his eyes as soon as the word *poison* left his lips. "Bad choice of words. Sorry!"

For half a heartbeat I thought of forgoing the cheese, then decided that even if I were a failure at judging people and he was in fact a murderer, he wouldn't be dumb enough to kill me in his own home. Besides, he covered his own generous serving of pasta and sauce with a thick blanket of both the Romano and the Parmesan, rolled a fork full of pasta against a spoon, and gobbled.

The remains of the evening passed without major incident other than my periodic non-menopausal hot flashes. The sauce more than lived up to its aromatic promise, and my taste buds were ecstatic and my stomach over-extended by the time we cleared the table and let the doggy boys pre-wash the dishes before loading them into the dishwasher. What the heck, the steam sterilizes, and even if it didn't, I figure I'm more likely to catch something from someone handing me change in a store than from well-cared-for dogs licking some dishes. Apparently Tom agreed.

All the way home I could taste the good-night kiss Tom planted right smack on my lips, leaning in through the window as I fastened my seat belt. It was a simple brush of lips on lips, but I couldn't get it out of my head and was almost home before I knew it. Either I was entering my second adolescence, or I'd been celibate way too long.

I turned west off Maysville onto my own criminally dark street and once again cursed the neighbors who won't sign the street light petition. The moon wasn't up yet and the dark was impenetrable, and I barely saw the van parked on the wrong side of the street across from Goldie's house. "Shit!" I whipped the wheels to the left, missing the other vehicle by a foot or so. "What kind of idiot . . ." I let the thought subside along with my adrenaline level. Jay shifted in his crate, and I tried to see him in the rearview mirror, but the gloom was too thick. "You okay back there, Bubby?" His body thunked down in the crate.

I parked in the driveway, grabbed my purse, and walked to the back of my Caravan. Goldie's porch light popped on and her screen door banged. She came scurrying over, carrying two glasses and a bottle of Amaretto. "I brought the booze, and I want to hear all about it!"

"Any sign of Leo?"

"I'm sure he'll be back in the morning ready for a nice breakfast and some catnip. He's nobody's fool."

"No, I guess not," I said as I got Jay out of his crate. We were halfway to the front door when he turned toward the street, the hair standing out from his neck, ears pricked, nose thrust forward and twitching. Even with my limited human senses, I could tell that something was moving in the shrubs across the street. He whined softly.

"Come on, it's just a raccoon," I sped our progress toward my front door, my hand firmly wrapped around his collar. Goldie held my screen door open with her elbow while I wrestled with my keys.

"Whose clunker?"

I pushed the door open and ushered Goldie and Jay into the house. "No idea, but I almost creamed it on my way in." I glanced toward the dark street, then closed and locked the inner door. I could have sworn I saw a flicker of movement across the living room floor where shades of gloom fought for dominance, but Jay didn't seem to find anything amiss. I decided I was paranoid. *Of course,* whispered the little voice in my left ear, *that doesn't mean someone's not out to get you.*

81

Another morning arrived with no sign of Leo. Goldie promised again to check my yard and answering machine hourly and to call me if Leo showed up or if she heard anything, so I decided to proceed with my plans to drive the two-plus hours to Indianapolis for today's Delta Society Pet Partner test for Jay's therapy-dog certification. The tests are few and far between in our neck of the woods, and there was nothing more that I could do at home to find my missing cat.

If I'd had to pick a morning for a road trip, this would be it, except for the shadow that Leo's absence cast over my world. The sky was a soft, clear spring blue laced with delicate high-cirrus wisps. The long curve of I-469 that encircles Fort Wayne to the east ribbons through a twenty-mile stretch of farmland laid out like a massive quilt. The patches were newly tinted in the tender greens of sprouting corn, soy, timothy, and alfalfa, the fence rows stitched in willow, trumpet vine, and Russian olive. The whole green world still glistened under a sheet of dew that the morning sun had not yet lifted. I tried to remember the whole of e. e. cummings' poem of thanks, but it was buried too deep in memory, and all I could come up with was the beginning . . . *I thank you God for most this amazing day: for the leaping greenly spirits of trees and a blue true dream of sky.* Add a warm-eyed dog, and it was prayer enough for me.

I pulled into the parking lot at the church where the test would be held about twenty minutes before our appointment. We had the second time slot, so I fluffed up Jay's bed hair with a pin brush, pulled my tote bag from the front seat, and walked my dog to an enormous ginkgo in the grassy strip between the parking lot and the street. When Jay had watered the tree, we followed the hand-lettered "Delta Test This Way" signs through a bent-willow gate and down a winding path of red bricks laid in a herringbone design.

Pink and yellow columbines, white candytuft, electric blue forget-me-nots with sunny yellow eyes, and a riot of late-blooming daffodils in pale saffron, deep gold, oranges, and whites danced from the edge of the path to the church wall on my left, and right to a hedge of forsythia, gone green but for a whisper of gold still clinging here and there.

I checked in with the volunteer who was assisting the tester. My paperwork was all in order, so there was nothing to do now but wait. The assistant said the first pair had arrived a little late and they were running about ten minutes behind. I took Jay outside and pulled out my cell phone.

Connie answered on the first ring and asked, "Have you heard about Greg?"

I told her about my visit the previous day from Stevens and Hutchinson.

"They came here, too. Said they're talking to everyone from Dog Dayz. Must have been right after you saw them. I'm so upset. What do you think?" She sounded pretty calm to me, but that's Connie. "They seem to think Greg killed Abigail and Suzette. I know we talked about that, but really, I don't believe it." We were both quiet for a moment. "I guess we all have our breaking points though."

"I don't believe it either."

Her voice dropped to conspiracy volume. "But you know, he might have killed Abigail to be with Suzette, and Suzette found out,

so he had to kill her to keep her from ratting him out."

" 'Ratting him out'?"

"You know what I mean!"

Neither of us spoke for a moment, then
Connie said, "I'd put my money on Giselle."

I held the phone out in front of me, but
there was no text message indicating that
I'd heard wrong, so I put it back to my ear.
"Is there anyone you don't think is involved?"

"Oh, please!" I could almost see her roll
her eyes. "Giselle's in love with Greg.
Maybe she figured she'd do away with the
competition."

Giselle is a bit off, I thought, picturing the
witchcraft books strewn inside her car. *She
could have been into potions for more lethal
pursuits than love. She did get pretty testy
with me. But murder?*

"So I take it you don't know where Greg
is?" I asked.

"How would I know?"

Jay put a gentle white paw on my knee. I
massaged behind his ear and watched him
tilt his head into my hand and close his eyes.
Why can't people be more like dogs? I wondered, not for the first time. I told Connie
where I was and promised to call later.

82

When I walked back into the church, I saw the first pair of Pet Partner candidates, a frail wee man who looked like he could use a little therapy himself and his tiny mixed breed with long black stand-away hair like a Pomeranian on a long body slung low over short, bandy legs. The tester was wrapping up the paperwork. The little dog waved the long fringe of her tail and sneezed at Jay. She took a step toward us, her round little head tilted to her left and her bottom incisors gleaming from her undershot lower jaw. I asked if it was okay to pet her, and her owner beamed. "I should think so! Lulabelle passed her test!" He had dark, round eyes not unlike those of his companion. I grinned back at him, had Jay lie down, and knelt to pet Lulabelle.

Our test took about twenty minutes, and Jay sailed through. He wasn't happy about the part of the test in which a couple of people holler at one another, something that occasionally happens in therapy situations. But he responded as expected, staying where I told him to sit, and looking at me as if to ask why those people were so upset. When all the i's were dotted and the t's crossed, Jay and I backtracked along the brick pathway and headed for home.

Three hours later Jay polished off his supper, and we went looking for Leo again. I checked under and behind the shrubs, and into every nook and cranny I could think of in the backyard. Goldie leaned over the fence and said she'd walked the yard every hour to be sure the yellow guy wasn't waiting to be let in, but no luck. I told her I was going to try again to see if Jay could find Leo's scent trail. The old one would be getting weak by now, but if the cat had walked around the yard when we weren't looking, I should see some change in Jay's tracking behavior. At least I hoped so. Goldie said she'd like to watch and would meet us out front.

I took Jay into the house, snapped a retractable leash onto his collar, and grabbed the towel that lined Leo's favorite napping basket. Normally I'd put a tracking harness on Jay and use long line to run a track, but this one should take all of about forty-five seconds, so I stuck with the basics. On the front porch I held the towel for Jay to smell and gave him his tracking command — "Find it! Find Leo!" He gave the towel two quick little jabs with his nose, then sniffed around the front yard. We had only started tracking training a couple of months earlier, but I was sure he understood what I wanted, because, as he had two other times since Leo went missing, he followed his nose to a patch of ground between a pink shrub rose and the vinyl siding beneath the living room's picture window. It was one of Leo's favorite vantage points when I was working in the front garden.

Jay's eyes sparkled with anticipation. I slipped him a cheese-flavored training treat, showed him the towel again, and told him to "Find it." If I hadn't had a good grip on the handle of the retractable leash, I'd have been standing alone in the yard, because Jay took off again like his furry britches were on fire, nose to the ground and tiny tail wagging. As he had the other times, he raced around the side of the house, sticking close to the foundation. At the gate to the backyard he sniffed back and forth, made a quick about-turn, and shot across the grass to the edge of the driveway. He took a few more sniffs and a tentative lick, and finally sat down and looked at me as if to say, "Okay, end of the line, this is where I get my reward." Just like before.

I popped a couple more treats into Jay's mouth. Goldie folded her arms across her body and pooched her mouth out in a thoughtful *O*. "Is that what he did before?"

"Exactly. Except the first couple of times he did a lot more grass licking at the end of the track."

83

Goldie went home with a thoughtful look on her face, and I loaded Jay into his crate in the Caravan and slid in behind the wheel. I had a craving for a nice big salad, and Scott's grocery on Stellhorn has a nice big salad bar.

I swung by the vet clinic thinking I'd stop in and tell Connie we passed the Delta test. They're open Saturdays until 5 P.M., and Connie works a lot of weekends when she's not at dog shows. There were no empty spaces in the parking lot, so I pulled to one side of the lot, behind a row of vehicles, and let the engine idle while I dialed my cell phone. The receptionist said Connie had left for the day. I tried her house and cell numbers and left "call me's" on both voice-mails. Odd for Connie to be completely out of touch. As a professional show-dog han-dler, she liked to be available for potential handling clients.

I tried for a three-point turn, but there wasn't much room and I had to add a couple extra points to get the Caravan facing out again. As I maneuvered through the final backward leg, I noticed a battered red cargo van tucked into the corner space behind a shiny new conversion van. If it wasn't the rust bucket Francine Peterson drove, the two of them were littermates. I backed up a little further for a better look.

Why would Francine come to Fort Wayne for a vet? Then I noticed the license, not a plate but a temporary paper tag sheathed in plastic and taped to the back door.

You really are paranoid. There are lots of rusty old red vans. Janet Angel harangued me all the way to Scott's grocery store and then home, reminding me that, among other things, it's one thing to be careful, another to be obsessed, and I was treading darn close to the boundary. Then again, who wouldn't be obsessed with finding answers with two acquaintances dead, another missing, not to mention my cat, and my dog poisoned.

I grabbed my tote bag and salad, unloaded Jay, and locked the car doors. I even remembered to relock the front door when we got inside the house.

On the drive home I'd decided that if

anyone was likely to know where Greg was, it would be Giselle. Not that he would tell her, but she seemed to have an inclination for stalking so she might know anyway. I didn't relish a conversation with her after our last one, but decided I had nothing to lose, so I looked up her number and called. Just as she picked up, I noticed that my answering machine was blinking at me.

"I'll tell you what I told your friends, the police." Giselle's delivery was stronger than usual. "I have no idea where Greg is. And if I did know I don't think I'd tell you."

Okay then. For once she wasn't speaking in the interrogative. Maybe the police interviews were building her confidence. Or maybe she was just pissed, a possibility she reinforced when she slammed the phone down without saying goodbye.

I pushed the playback button for my message. The voice was female, I was pretty sure, but pitched too high, like a fake voice, a cartoon voice, and a little fuzzy, as if she was speaking through a wool muffler. "Keep your nose in your own business and your cat will find his way home. Keep sticking it where it doesn't belong and who knows . . ." The recording ran silent, and then the voice came back. "You might find more dead than

428

toy dogs." The ice in those words blasted like brainfreeze through my skull, but the taste in my mouth was definitely not ice cream.

I tried to wrap my mind around the threat as the machine whirred through the rewind. Then I replayed the recording, my gorge rising. I replayed it several more times, searching the voice, the inflection, for a clue to the speaker, but no bells rang. I hit the save button, and punched in Jo Stevens' number on my cell. By the time I had left her a message, my eyes were stinging and my heart was doing aerobics.

I considered calling Goldie, but changed my mind. Why worry her? What I really needed was a nice stress-reducing lavender bubble bath, so I rechecked all the doors, then ran a tub full of water as hot as I could stand it with double the recommended bubble bath. What did I care if it left bubble marks on the tile around the tub? I dropped my clothes in a heap between the toilet and the vanity, pulled my hair off my face with two alligator clips and a headband, and sank into the hot water. I was leaning back into my inflated bath pillow when the phone rang.

I decided to ignore it until I heard Goldie's voice. "I know you're there, Janet. Pick up the phone . . . Tum tee tum . . . Come on, Janet, pick up the phone . . ."

Goldie never hangs up if she knows I'm here, so I climbed out of the hot water, wrapped an almost-big-enough towel around myself, and shivered and dripped my way down the hall and across the living room. *Good thing I closed the blinds,* I thought. I reached for the phone, and heard the answering machine click off. Bzzzz. Goldie had hung up.

"You never hang up like that!"

"Oh, hi Janet. I thought you were in the bath or something."

"I was."

"Oh, dear. Are you covered?"

"Yes. With goose bumps."

She giggled. "That's not enough, dear."

"Very amusing. So were you checking to see if I was taking a bath?"

"My, my, aren't we grumpy." She clucked a couple times. "No, dear, let me tell you why I called."

Why didn't I think of that? I bit my tongue.

"You know," she seemed to be thinking aloud, "if I had to guess, I'd say Leo was bound for the backyard when he saw someone or something. With food. Remember how Jay was licking the grass?" She started tapping something against the phone. "You know what a social butterfly and chow hound, if that's the right thing to call a cat, he is. I think the trail ends because someone fed him something and picked him up."

84

Jay and I were out the door at four a.m. to search again for Leo before I left for my photo shoot near Culver. As I watched him work his nose along this end of whatever track he was following, Goldie's hunch about someone feeding and grabbing Leo echoed in my brain, and it rang true. I knew I should tell Detective Stevens about the threatening message on my answering machine, but was afraid she'd tell me not to make the drive. I'd made the commitment a couple months earlier, and at least one litter of baby Labs was supposed to be there for portraits. There wasn't much I could do at home, and Goldie had my cell number. Besides, I needed the money.

The Northern Indiana Hunting Retriever Club practices once a month at various ponds and lakes in a big rectangle from Michigan (the lake), south to Kentland on the Illinois side, east to the Ohio line around

Decatur, and north to Michigan (the state). I enjoy the variety of terrains contained in those ten thousand square miles, from the flat, rich farmland of west-central Indiana that once lay deep under ancient Lake Chicago, to the rocky ravines and rolling hills laid out by glaciers in the northern tier ten millennia ago, to the fertile soils farther to the east, once the bottom of the malarial Great Black Swamp.

My destination was a small private lake not far from Lake Maxinkuckee. I loaded my equipment and my dog into the van. I hadn't planned to take Jay, but I wasn't about to leave him home alone after that phone call. Besides, no one would begrudge him a swim when the retrievers finished. A little more than two hours later I pulled onto a grassy berm and parked behind a white Suburban. The back doors stood wide open and two Labs, a chocolate and a black, watched me from their crates, tongues lolling and tails thumping.

The air shook off the chill of night as daylight took hold, so I chucked my jacket, pulled my sweatshirt off, and put the cotton jacket back on over my T-shirt. I grabbed my tripod and my camera, popped the back of the van and checked that Jay had water, then struck out across the uneven field toward the shore some hundred yards to the east. The sun had cleared the tops of a clump of young willows weeping along the far bank of the pond, but dew still lay heavy near the ground, and the shin-high quack-grass and foxtail soaked my pants and shoes. Several people waved or nodded as I reached the group of some dozen retriever fans and twice that many dogs, mostly Labs, several Goldens, one Standard Poodle, a couple of Tollers, three Chesapeakes, a Curly, and three Flat-coats.

I had no more than set my camera bag on a canvas chair offered by Collin Lahmeyer, president of the club, when a mass of wet, dripping black hair and solid muscle jostled me. I looked down into two sparkling eyes and gently took the sodden goose wing offered in welcome.

"Gee, thanks, Drake." I examined the gift, and handed it back to the sopping dog. He liked it a lot better than I did.

"Drake! Come!"

The big Lab turned toward the voice, glanced back at me as if to apologize for leaving so soon, and ran to Tom. Together they came over, Drake at heel now, and Tom grinning. "Nothing so friendly as a wet dog, huh?"

I grinned back, running my hand down

my faded T-shirt and my well-worn jeans with the fraying seams. "And me all dressed up, too."

"Leo come home?"

"No."

"He's not in the habit of going awol?"

"Miss a meal of canned salmon? Not on your life."

"Maybe someone took him in."

"Or just plain took him." I told him about the message, and was on to Goldie's theory when we were interrupted by a sharp whistle. It was Collin, seeking everyone's attention. He explained to the assembled handlers that I was taking photos for possible sale to magazines, calendars, and books, then let me say a few words. I handed out release forms and business cards with my web address for those who wanted them, and promised I'd have the proofs online by the following weekend. A little foolhardy, but I find that a short deadline gets my fanny in gear. Besides, the sooner I post the proofs, the more likely people are to buy prints and CDs.

As I slung my camera case over my shoulder and picked up my tripod, Tom took me by the arm and said, "Call the detective."

"Okay, I will."

"Now, Janet." A flashback to Chet at his

bossiest made me start to bristle at Tom's words, but when I saw the concern in his eyes I knew that his tone was one of care, not command. I unslung my bag from my shoulder, pulled my cell phone from my pocket, and punched Jo's number in, thinking I might as well put her on speed dial. She didn't pick up, so I told her voicemail about the latest warning, then turned the sound off on my phone.

I spent the next three hours taking hundreds of photos of retrievers doing what retrievers do best — leaping into water, swimming, carrying training bumpers and birds, shaking water out of their coats and onto people, racing through high grass and brush, and generally being the happiest dogs on earth. Tom took Jay for a couple of walks so I wouldn't have to stop shooting.

The Lab puppies arrived mid-morning, and their breeder fastened three exercise pens together with clips to let the little guys take care of the Three P's of Puppyhood — play, pee, and poop — as nature dictated. There were eleven of them, six blacks, five yellows. They really were babies, only six-and-a-half weeks old, roly-poly, and utterly smoochable. I could hardly put them down long enough to take their pictures, but I forced myself and got some nice shots, singles and groups, and then the whole gang having their first swim outside a wading pool. People put their dogs in their vehicles, all wide open for ventilation, and came to enjoy the puppies. The breeder created a "buddy system," with a volunteer assigned to keep track of each puppy so none of them would wander off when they were out of the pen. As we wrapped things up with the puppies, Tom recommended that she check everyone for suspicious lumps under their clothing before anyone was allowed to leave, especially himself.

I stowed my equipment in my van, got Jay out, and let him run ahead of me to the lake. He and Drake greeted each other with polite mutual fanny sniffing before they bowed at one another and took off in big, joyous loops around the field. Tom stood at the edge of the lake and called to get Drake's attention, then pitched a fat stick far out over the water. Both dogs saw it fly, and hit the water running. Drake grabbed one end of the stick first and Jay got the other end, facing the opposite direction, and they swam in a spiral around one another.

Tom pitched another stick off to their side, and Drake let go of the first one in favor of the second. Jay made the bank, where he dropped his treasure at Tom's feet and shook the water from his coat. Tom raised his left arm to shield his face, and flung the stick back into the water. Jay went for it, swimming out as Drake came in with his prize. Tom threw Drake's stick far into the field this time, then did the same with Jay's when he delivered his stick to shore. For the next ten minutes, Tom kept the two dogs retrieving, sometimes on land, sometimes in the water. By the end all three were grinning, panting, wet, and dirty, and supremely pleased with themselves. Male bonding at its finest.

Tom offered me lunch at a nice little café in The Village at Winona, an artsy community south of Warsaw and about halfway home, but I took a rain check. I was hot, covered with muck and plant matter, and worried about Leo.

I should have stuck with Tom.

85

I left the retriever club training session and headed north into Plymouth on U.S. 31, stopped for a red light, and glanced at the signs at the intersection. If I continued north, I'd wind up in South Bend. Behind me to the south was Rochester. Why did that ring a bell? The light changed and I turned east onto U.S. 30. They were working on this stretch, I remembered, on Wednesday when I met Ginny Scott in Valparaiso, and the new blacktop surface was a vast improvement over the old bumpity bump concrete that was there before. I'd been telling myself for years that someday I'm going to take the Great U.S. 30 Road Trip all the way from Atlantic City to Astoria, Oregon. Abigail and Suzette's unexpected departures had me thinking that I should do the things I've always planned to do now, since we never know how long we'll have, and I decided as I drove that I should plan this road trip and do it, right after I took the first aid class I'd been planning to take since who knows when. I also remembered why Rochester sounded familiar. That's where Francine lived.

About five miles further east I found myself catching up to a semi that was actually sticking to the speed limit, probably because this stretch of U.S. 30 is notorious for its speed traps. Thinking I'd pass him, I glanced into my rearview mirror and my stomach contracted. The front grille of something big was barreling toward the back of my Caravan, closing the distance between us with alarming efficiency. I couldn't speed up without ramming into the blue and gold Alphonse Trucking logo blazoned across the doors of the semi, and a pale-gold Toyota Corolla blocked the lane to my left. The shoulder was filled with orange barrels still waiting for the highway department to pick them up. There was no escape.

I lay the back of my head against the headrest on the off chance that it would save my neck, and hoped for the best. There was nothing I could do for Jay except pray, and vow to rearrange my van so the crates would be in the center, away from a rear-end hit, if we got through this without injury. At least he was in an airline-approved crate, which was better protection than if he'd been loose.

We were approaching a crossroad. Could I make the right turn at 60 miles per hour without rolling over? I had a cinematic image of my van skidding sideways in a too-fast turn and going airborne over the drainage ditch that surely paralleled the pavement. These county roads all have them. No reason this one would be any different. And at this speed, that's where I'd land, in turtle position. We'd both be hurt. Or dead. I glanced once more at the mirror and realized that the turn option was moot. Whatever was behind us would make contact before we got to the corner.

I prefer not to close my eyes when I'm driving, but I couldn't see that it would matter much under the circumstances. My shoulders curled toward my sternum and my arms petrified against the steering wheel. *Please let the crate hold up, please let Jay be safe* ran like a mantra through my mind. My fingers started to cramp, and I couldn't stop my teeth from biting into my lip. Rubber squealed against concrete. *Please, please, please.* I murmured a slow count to give my spinning mind some traction, squeezed my eyelids tighter, and braced for impact.

86

By the count of three I was still rolling down U.S. 30, unscathed. I opened my eyes. A squeal of tires pierced the air to my left. The sound seemed to be moving away from me. I checked the mirror. Just open road. In my peripheral vision I saw the Corolla fall back, horn blaring but apparently unscathed. I turned to look. The speed demon had somehow squeezed between me and the Corolla without creaming either of us and was passing me on the left. The camera in my mind worked in spite of my fear, taking in a rattletrap old cargo van with rust eating the edges of the wheel wells. The back side door was dented, and binder's twine coiled through the handle to snake into the vehicle between the door and the frame. The driver was all but invisible behind a screen of dirty windows and reckless speed. My first impression was that it was a redhead. *Francine?* But doubt reared up. At that speed, without a clear view, I couldn't be sure. And anyway, how would Francine know where to find me?

We shot through the intersection. The cargo van shimmied back and forth in the left-turn lane, then rocketed through the intersection and veered back across the passing lane. It disappeared from my view in front of the eighteen wheeler.

Four miles further down the road I followed the Alphonse semi into a truck stop, pulled around the big rig, and parked in front of the store and restaurant. I had to will the muscles of my hands to unclench and let loose of the steering wheel, and my thigh muscles to relax. I turned off the engine, thinking I might have to toss my cookies. Instead I draped both hands across the steering wheel at twelve o'clock, pressed my forehead against them, and waited for the adrenalin to seep away. I had to check on Jay, but I couldn't get my limbs to move. All lucid thought faded as a visceral wave of relief rolled through me.

I was startled out of my moment of gratitude by a tap on the window. A wiry guy with a couple day's worth of whiskers was leaning toward me, a worried look on his face and an Alphonse Trucking cap on his head. I rolled down the window.

"You okay, ma'am?" He pulled the cap off, revealing close-cropped sandy hair that matched his stubble.

"Yes, thanks, I'm fine."

"That's good. An' just so's you know, I called 911 on that guy. Told 'em what he done back there. Damn fool like to kilt someone." He gave the rim of my open window a pat, and straightened up. "Don't know that they'll catch 'im. He turned off back there, pulled off on one of them county roads." He straightened up and took a step back. "More'n likely drunk."

"Him? You could see the driver?"

He ran his fingers and thumb up and down the sides of his jaw bone and thought about that. "No ma'am, I couldn't see that good. But dang fool driver like that more'n likely some young buck. Most women ain't that dumb."

A man of wisdom.

"You be safe now, ma'am." He touched the rim of his cap with two fingers, nodded, and walked into the truck stop store.

You be safe, I thought. *That's what I'd like to be.* But I was starting to wonder if we were safe anywhere.

445

87

Jay was fine. I walked him on the grass on the far side of the parking lot for a few minutes, then walked myself around the truck stop store for ten more, sipping coffee that I feared would put hair on my chest and looking at "scenic Indiana" ashtrays, mud guards with glittering buxom women, megaboxes of Milkduds, yard-long jerky sticks, and various other gifts from the road. Oddly enough, the coffee calmed me, and I finally got back on the horse, mine being a blue Grand Caravan. We were home, safe, an hour later.

I had hoped that Leo would also be waiting when I got there, but no such luck. I stripped off my mucky clothes and took a quick shower, pulled on some gray knit pants that have seen better days and a long-sleeved faded navy henley, and went to the kitchen to feed Jay. It was only three o'clock, and technically he eats at five, but what the heck. It had been a long day, and he isn't fussy about his schedule, as long as the food isn't late. Early is good.

While he snarfed up his kibble, I peeked out the back door and felt my heart rise at a hint of orange movement on Goldie's side of the picket fence. I opened the door and stepped onto the patio, calling. As soon as Leo's name was past my lips, though, I realized that I was looking at orange tulips swaying in the breeze. The hope that floated my heart for a moment dripped into heavy sludge around my ankles, and I went back inside.

Jay scoured the stainless bowl with his tongue, then nudged me in the pants pocket, so I let him out. I fished my cell phone out from under a bag of freeze-dried liver treats in my tote bag, slipped my feet into some grubby old tennies I keep for the garden, and joined Jay in the yard. I hit Goldie's speed-dial number, which seemed pretty silly when I could just walk over and knock on the door, but I was busy shaking the shrubs again. There was no answer, so I folded the phone and put it in my pocket. The elastic in the waistband was so old and frail I wasn't sure it would hold against the extra weight, but other than feeling an ominous little droop in the right side of my drawers, nothing happened.

Jay and I pottered around the yard for an hour before we went back inside. I considered checking the fridge for signs of food, but why kid myself? I wasn't going to cook an actual meal just for me when I could have a well-rounded dinner of English muffin with grape jelly followed later in the evening by cheddar-flavored popcorn. That gave me my grains, fruit, dairy, and veggie. A big hunk of chocolate and I'd have all the important food groups covered. Dark chocolate. Just last week I heard a doctor on National Public Radio say that dark chocolate is good for us, and if it's on NPR, it's good enough for me.

Restlessness was getting the better of me and I was in danger of doing some dusting when my cell phone rang. As I pulled it from my pocket and opened it, I had a quickie fantasy conversation with Leo, calling to tell me to pick him up at a cat house on West Coliseum, where he was being held captive as a sardine inspector. But it wasn't Leo, and I realized that I must be exhausted to be making up tales like that.

It was Giselle, which took me a minute to figure out from the marginally coherent bursts of English scattered between hysterical sobs and screams. "Calm down! I can't understand you."

"Okay," she squeaked. "I'll try?"

"Giselle?"

"Yes, yes, it's me, Giselle?" *Don't ask me!* I thought, another heartrending sob ringing in my ear. "I can't believe he's dead! I don't know what to do? There's blood, so much blood."

88

For a terrible moment I thought Giselle had found Leo, and my heart crawled into my throat. But then she said, "I'm at his house? Janet? I'm here, and he's dead, and . . ." She sounded like she might not be far behind him, whoever he was.

"Giselle, stop. Take a deep breath. Who's dead? What house?"

"Greg!"

"Greg? Greg Dorn?"

"Yes, yes, Greg Dorn! What other Greg?" Her voice pitched higher and faster as she spoke. "Greg's dead! I'm sure he's dead. What am I going to do?"

A chill swept my body. "Have you called the police?"

"The police?"

I reached for a tissue to wipe away the tears that were spilling inexplicably down my cheeks, and forced my voice to work. "Look, Giselle, you have to call 911. Get an ambulance and the police." Despite my lack of concrete information about whatever she'd seen, I clung to a scrap of hope. "He may not be dead."

"They'll think I did it!" she protested. "I didn't! I didn't do it!"

"Okay, look, don't touch anything. I'll be there in ten minutes. Wait for me, okay?"

"Okay." Sob. "I'll wait. I knew you'd know what to do."

Yeah, I know what to do. I hung up, wiped my eyes and nose, and wondered vaguely why I was crying for Greg. But it wasn't just for Greg, I realized, but loss and senseless death, and for my mom, for my poisoned dog and my missing cat, and my own fear of being hurt, and a boatload of other sorrows, great and small. I pressed my thumb and forefinger against the inner corners of my eyes, sucked up a lungfull of air, and, not so sure that Giselle would follow through, dialed 911. I gave them the Dorn's address, then found Jo Stevens' card on my desk and called the cell phone number she'd jotted on the back. I loaded Jay into his crate in the back of my van and took off.

I was a block from Greg's house when I realized I was still wearing my crappy don't-leave-home-in-these pants. Oh well, my undies were clean and free of holes, in case of incident. Like the elastic in my ratty old pants finally giving up. *Or murder?*

89

Sirens sounded in the distance as I popped the back hatch of the Caravan, now parked in a circle of shade in front of Greg Dorn's house. "You have to stay here, Bubby." Jay slumped onto his bed and lodged an appeal with the droopiest eyes he could manage.

Giselle sat on the top step leading to the front porch, her feet on the bottom step. Patches like big red plums blotched her face, and black streaks radiated down her cheeks from her eyes. Her bangs stuck up and out in all directions, as if she had been pulling at them in desperation. I wondered vaguely why they looked so rigid when Giselle's hair never seemed to benefit from hair care products. She shoved the last bite of a chocolate eclair into her mouth as I climbed the porch steps, sobbed at me by way of greeting, and ran a sticky hand through her bangs. *Ah, that's her hairdressing secret — the holding power of sugar.*

Giselle reached for another goodie from a white bag on the top step.

"Giselle. What happened?"

"I don't know?" She burst into ragged sobs, and followed up with a choking, coughing fit.

While I waited for her to recover I pushed the pastry bag out of the way and sat down next to her. A police car skidded to the curb. I reached over and took the donut from Giselle's hand. She'd gone limp at the sight of the police, and didn't resist. I handed her a napkin from the bag, and suggested she pull herself together, then got up to greet the fresh-faced officer who walked up to the porch. His nametag identified him as L. Baker. I wondered if he was old enough to drive. His partner, an older guy who might or might not pass his next annual physical, stopped back a few yards in the lawn.

"We have a call about someone being injured?"

I explained that I'd just arrived, and tilted my head toward Giselle. She had pulled her feet up to the step below the one she sat on and had her arms on her knees, her face buried in their ample bulk. "Giselle?"

"Mrmff?"

"Come on, Giselle, give us a hand here. Where's Greg?" I glanced at the cop. His expression was completely neutral, and he seemed perfectly willing to let me deal with the incoherent woman on the porch. "Giselle!"

"Back . . ." sob, gasp, "backyard. Sh . . . sh . . ."

I wondered why she was shushing us, but you never know with Giselle. The cop was watching the ambulance pull in and didn't seem to notice. "What happened, ma'am? An accident?"

"N . . . n . . . no. H . . . h . . . h . . . he . . ." She started to cry.

"Giselle, what happened to Greg?" I shook her arm enough to make her gasp.

"Blood. There's so much blood. Stabbed."

Baker turned, placed a hand on his holster, told the EMTs to stay put, and gestured for his partner to go around the house the other direction.

"Shed. He's in the storage sh . . ." Giselle tried, but she muffled the final word in more sobs.

I called after Baker, "She says he's in the storage shed." I had another thought, and ran a few steps after the cop. "Officer, there could be two dogs in the yard. Don't hurt them! They know me, I can get them out of the way!"

He nodded and gestured for me to stay

back. He had pulled his gun. I retreated to the porch with Giselle.

"I have to tell you something?" Giselle looked at me out of the corner of her eye.

"Yes?"

Before she could continue one of the EMTs approached and asked if Giselle needed their assistance. Taking in the crimson shade of her face and the sheen of perspiration, I understood his concern and asked if she wanted them to check her out. She shook her head.

When the EMT had retreated, Giselle murmured, "I sent you that e-mail." I had no idea what she was talking about. "I just wanted you to leave Greg alone, because . . ."

Oh, that *e-mail,* I thought. "The one telling me to butt out?"

She nodded. That explained why, at Abigail's funeral, Greg had acted as if he hadn't just sent me a snotty e-mail. He hadn't.

"Okay. Forget it." I let her relax for a moment, then asked, "Where are the dogs?"

"Hrmph?" She had retrieved the bag and was eating again, between sobs, and a blob of something gooey peeked over the edge of her lip.

"Pip and Percy. Where are they?"

She stopped chewing and turned wide

eyes my way. "I don't know?"

"Was the gate open when you got here?"

She dropped half a donut back into the bag. "No? I didn't think of that? I forgot about the dogs when I saw Greg?" She looked at the front window of the house, sniffing and gulping. "They should be barking, huh?"

90

A black Taurus pulled up behind the ambulance, and Detectives Stevens and Hutchinson got out and started toward us. Giselle had stopped sobbing and eating and sat hunched, rumpled and streaked with makeup, half her bangs now hanging in her eyes, the other half still sticking out at odd angles.

Jo wrinkled her forehead at Giselle. "Are they in the house?"

"Backyard," I said.

"Right." She turned toward the side of the house, looked around for her partner, and called "Hutch!" He was at the back of my Caravan, talking to Jay and stroking him through the crate wires. *Maybe there's hope for the guy.* Jo gestured to her partner to follow, and turned to me and Giselle. "You both stay put."

We sat in silence for about ten minutes. Jo finally reappeared with a pale-faced Officer

Baker tagging behind. Baker conferred with the ambulance crew while Detective Stevens pulled her notebook and pen from her pocket and joined me on the bottom step.

"Ms. Swann — it is Ms. Swann?" Giselle murmured her assent, eyes wide, and Jo continued. "Ms. Swann, I understand you found Mr. Dorn?"

Giselle nodded hard enough to throw tears into the air.

"Did you move the body, or touch it?"

"No?"

"Are you sure?"

"Yes, I never moved him or touched him?" She sucked in a ragged breath, and went on in a barely audible voice. "I just opened the shed, could tell he was d . . . d . . . dead." She punctuated her pronouncement by blowing her nose.

"And Janet, did you touch or move the body?"

"I haven't been back there. I just got here a few minutes ago. I've been here with Giselle."

"Neither of you touched or moved Mr. Dorn?"

How hard is this? I stifled Janet Demon — this was no time for a smart mouth. Giselle and I shook our heads.

"Right." She played twenty questions —

when did Giselle get here, did either of us see or hear anyone or anything unusual, could we think of anyone who might want him dead? I wasn't exactly full of useful information, and Giselle didn't seem to have anything to add.

"And what were you doing here, Ms. Swann?"

Giselle looked like she might swoon under Detective Stevens' scrutiny. "Huh?"

"Why were you here? And what were you doing in the shed?"

Giselle's face twisted and she sniffed and choked all at once, but then she regained some control. "I, you know, wanted to see if Greg needed anything?"

Jo Stevens continued to gaze at her, quiet, waiting.

"I went to see if maybe he was in the back, and I opened the shed, the door, you know, to the shed, to see if he was there, and. . . ."

"Was the door unlocked?"

"Huh?"

Jo softened her tone a notch. "Ms. Swann, was the door to the shed locked or unlocked?"

"Locked?"

"Yes, was it locked?" Jo apparently hadn't yet caught on to Giselle's interrogative affirmatives.

"Uh-huh."

"You have a key?"

"No? I mean, you know, I know where they keep, I mean, where he keeps it under the windowsill, and I, you know, thought Greg might be in there working or something?"

I wondered whether Giselle realized what she was saying. If Greg locked himself into his shed and didn't open the door to her, he was hiding from her. Assuming he was alive at the time.

Jo met my gaze. "It was locked when we were here looking for him. And he's been dead a while." She looked at the sky and shook her head. "Damn it."

Was he in there, dead or — worse — dying, when I was here snooping around the shed?

"Oh, man, I can't believe it, you know?" mumbled Giselle, addressing her knees as far as I could tell. She looked up at Jo and asked, "Can I go home? I can't stand this?"

"Not yet. We need to get your statement before you leave."

Giselle appeared to be on the verge of collapse, but agreed to wait to give a statement. She asked if she could get some tissues from her car and, permission granted, hauled herself up, using the wrought-iron railing for support. She grabbed her pastry bag and schlumped down the sidewalk to her car, which for some reason was parked across from the lot next door.

Jo called to Giselle, and caught up with her in a few long strides.

"Ms. Swann, why did you park over here?"

"Hunh?"

"Why didn't you park right in front of Mr. Dorn's house?"

"Oh." The confusion left Giselle's face. "There was a car there."

"A car?"

"A van really. Looked like, I dunno, a work van."

"Work van?"

"You know, like a plumber or carpenter or something. I figured Greg was having some work done?"

"Was there a sign on it?"

"A sign?"

The detective spoke slowly. "Why did you think it was a work van?"

"I dunno? It was kind of beat-up looking, you know? And the paint was faded, and it was one of those vans with no windows in back, like it's full of work stuff, you know, equipment?"

"Right." Jo jotted something in her notebook. "What color was it?"

"I dunno. Sort of b . . . b . . . brown?"

Sort of brown. *Could sort of brown be sort of rusty red?* I wondered.

Jo patted Giselle's shoulder. "Okay, try to relax, Ms. Swann. An officer will be with you in a few minutes." Giselle snuffled and coughed and seemed to study something on the ground.

Jo came back to the porch, leafing back through her notes, looking for something. I interrupted her. "Are you sure Greg is dead?"

"Oh, he's dead."

I started to tell her about Francine's red van, but she was dialing her cell phone. As she waited for a response, she flipped through her ratty little notebook, seemed to confirm something, and tucked it back into her pocket. "Ellen, we need a whereabouts on a Francine Peterson." *Great minds.* Jo gave a description of Francine's cargo van, the license number, and Francine's address and phone number.

"Giselle mentioned blood. I take it he wasn't poisoned like Abigail and Suzette?"

"We can't say he wasn't poisoned until we have the autopsy report, but I have a hunch he didn't *die* from poison." I waited for the rest, and got a taste of Jo's grim sense of humor. "I have a hunch that the chisel shoved through his eye took care of that."

91

Neither my legs nor my voice seemed to be working properly, so I let myself sink into a moment of silence on the concrete step while Jo once again scribbled in her little notebook. My vocal cords eventually recovered, and I told Jo that there was no sign of the Dorns' dogs, and that wasn't normal. I asked if we could check in the house, and offered to take both dogs home temporarily if they were there.

She called for Baker to clear the house before we went in, which was fine with me. I didn't relish a chisel in *my* eye. Officer Baker came out a few minutes later. "No sign of the dogs, but someone made a mess of one of the rooms. Looks like a home office. Down the hall." He pointed to the left, off the foyer.

I followed Jo through the glorious entry and down a wide hallway. I got a glimpse of my dream bathroom, complete with shower stall, huge Jacuzzi tub, skylight, and an antique fainting couch. Okay, the fainting couch isn't in my dream. But then, my dream bathroom isn't in my house. Now I knew why. The Dorns had it.

I almost bumped into Jo in the doorway to a room at the end of the hall. The Dorns' home office looked like a spring windstorm had hit it. A drawer marked "Dogs" stood open in the rosewood filing cabinet next to an antique desk that commanded the center of the room. Books littered the oriental carpet in front of the now-empty built-in floor-to-ceiling bookshelves. Crystal paperweights, pens, framed photographs, a leather blotter holder, and pads of paper and sticky notes were heaped on the floor at one end of the desk. A burgundy leather wingback chair lay on its side in front of the room's one window.

The top of the desk was hidden under file folders, some open, some closed, the contents spilling out. It looked a lot like my desk.

Beyond the mess on the floor was a wall covered with framed photos, many of them awards pictures taken at dog shows, obedience and agility trials, and, judging by the crook in Abigail's hand in a few photos, some herding trials. A couple of the photos had fallen, and some hung askew, the glass in one of the frames radiating across the image like a spiderweb of shards as if something had scored a direct hit.

I squinted at that one. It was one of the few non-show photos, a shot of Abigail and Greg in hiking attire, smiling and holding hands against the rocky red architecture of Monument Valley. Pip and Percy sat in front of them.

"Either Mr. Dorn had serious housekeeping problems since his wife died, or someone was looking for something." Jo followed my gaze to the photo. "Something significant about that picture?"

"Not really. But it must have been taken recently."

"How do you know?"

"Abigail wore her hair long and straight for years." I looked back at the short, curly style in the photo. "She just cut it, I don't know exactly, but not long ago."

"Well, if they weren't getting along, they sure put on a good show for the camera." She was right. They looked happy and relaxed with one another.

I looked back at the mess on the floor. "Can we see what the open folders are?"

"We can't touch the room until the crime scene techs finish with it." She eyed the desk. "Stay here." She tiptoed between the papers on the floor and read the label tab on a folder that lay open and empty on the desk. Then she retreated to the door. "It says 'Pip'. That's the dog, right, the big show star?"

"Yes, the Border Collie. Obedience star."

"Also a scribbled note, looks like 'DHA' or 'DNA.' Any idea what that might mean?"

Several possibilities scurried through my mind, so I let myself think out loud. "Parentage verification. Or checking for markers for certain inherited diseases, maybe, but I don't know the ins and outs of Border Collie DNA testing for disorders. I've heard that there may have been some question about the accuracy of Pip's pedigree, that maybe his breeder lied about his parents, you know, who they are. Maybe Abigail had his DNA checked against his parents, or siblings, or even offspring if he had any."

Jo listened intently. "You mean like paternity testing for dogs?"

"Exactly. Paternity and maternity. The AKC actually requires dogs who are bred a certain number of times to be DNA-ed so that offspring can be verified if a question comes up, or if a buyer wants to do that for some reason."

"Wow."

"Yeah, just takes a cheek swab, you send it in and the lab compares certain markers to relatives, or supposed relatives. Or in some cases they can look for disease markers."

"And if Abigail was doing this, it might worry someone?"

"Well, not if everything was on the up and up. But if his breeder falsified her application to register a litter or two, then yeah, if the DNA doesn't confirm parentage, she could lose her registration privileges and be fined, and they'd publish her name so there goes her reputation." I thought about Francine's nutty, almost panicky, behavior. "I've heard that Francine invested a lot of money in importing two dogs, well, you know, a dog and a bitch, to revive her breeding program. If she did lie about Pip's parents, and she was found out, she'd lose not just her rights and reputation, but a pile of money as well. And she'd be open to lawsuits."

Jo wrote madly for a few moments, flipping a page, another. Then she asked, "What else would be in his file that isn't there now?"

I thought for a moment. "Registration papers, health records, pedigree, his competition record, photos. Like that."

"Papers. Those would be valuable? Like if someone wanted to sell him or use him as a stud dog?"

"Well, sort of. But the papers are registered to the owner, or owners."

"And if someone wanted him for breeding?"

"But Pip's neutered!" I reminded her.

"I know, but you said Abigail kept that a secret, right?"

"Oh, I see." I thought about that for a moment. "But to register his puppies, the sire's owner has to sign an application. So stealing the papers doesn't mean much, unless someone forges the signatures. But Pip's well known in Border Collie circles. Everyone knows who owns him, and who doesn't, so . . ."

"Right." She wrinkled her forehead. "So what's this all about?"

I had nothing more to offer out loud, but I planned to find out what I could about litters and puppies that Francine had registered.

Jo guided me back down the hall, past my fantasy bathroom, and out the front door. "I'll put out an alert on the dog."

"Dogs." I corrected. "Greg also had a little Poodle named Percy." I started to give her a description, then ducked back in the door and pointed to a framed photo of the curly little guy.

I got Jay out of the Caravan so he could relieve himself while Jo called in the descriptions of the dogs. She walked to the curb and gave Jay a scratch under the chin before he hopped back into his crate. Jo told me she'd notify the shelters, and I offered to get the word out to the BC and Poodle rescue organizations as well. She told me to let her know if I heard anything.

I drove home in a deep, dark funk. Did someone really kill Greg and steal Pip and Pip's papers in hopes of using him at stud? Was Abigail about to reveal a more insidious secret entwined in the strands of her dog's DNA? If so, Francine stood to lose her reputation, her registration privileges, and some serious money. Greg would have to know about Abigail's suspicions, and Suzette may have been privy to Abigail's hunch as well. Now they were all dead. And with a flash of panic it occurred to me that Giselle, too, might know about Abigail's concerns, or the killer might think she did, and she might be in danger now. I pulled out my cell, found her number in my old calls, and left her a message to be careful.

It all seemed crazy. But then, anyone who kills three people is crazy by definition, right? Francine fit the crazy bill from what I'd seen. Did she have Pip and Percy? What about Leo? The thought made me shudder. And Greg's death? She might catnap Leo to frighten me off, and that had to be her in the cargo van scaring me out of ten years' growth. But why would she take Percy along with Pip? And if she didn't have the missing pets, where were they? The dogs could have wandered off through an open gate, although I'd have expected them to stay as close to Greg as they could. Leo could have wandered off, too, for that matter. I didn't want to believe that, but it was possible. I knew two things for sure. If I got him back, Leo was an indoor cat from now on, and I wasn't letting Jay out of my sight until someone got to the bottom of this.

92

As eager as I was to look into Pip's DNA records, I had other things to take care of on Monday morning. Jade Templeton and I had agreed on Monday for Jay's first nursing home visit, although his certification wouldn't be official until I had the paperwork back from the Delta Society. Jade understood that, but a local magazine was doing a story on Shadetree Retirement Home, and Jade was hoping to spotlight several life-enrichment programs going on at the home, including animal-assisted activities, garden therapy, art and music therapy, and a fledgling program in which preschoolers visited a select group of residents two days a week. Considering how welcoming Jade had been despite Mom's best effort to get herself expelled before she even moved in, I couldn't say no.

I'd tried to reach Giselle several times during the previous evening with no luck, but finally got through to her mid-morning. She said she'd be watchful and careful.

The magazine's photographer was supposed to be at Shadetree at 4:30, so in the morning I had tidied up the hair on Jay's tail, ears, and feet with my thinning sheers, smoothed his nails with a Dremel, and bathed him. Then the two of us headed over to Mom's house. Bill was already there, elbow deep in a beat-up cardboard file box.

"Gad, her files are like her cupboards."

I glanced at the wastebasket sitting next to the file box, filled nearly to the brim with paper.

"I take it she kept everything?"

"Even the envelopes everything came in. In no particular order, of course." He pulled a stapled packet of papers out, riffled through them, and got up. "Okay, finally, her long-term care policy." He looked closely at several pages, took a deep breath. "Thank God, it's paid up and current." He looked at me, relief palpable in his eyes. "I was afraid she might have let it lapse."

We spent the rest of the morning cleaning out files and putting together paperwork we might need soon. For lunch we had tomato soup and crackers on the patio, and caught up a bit. The tension of the past few months was gone, the decision about Mom made and action taken. It was nice to have my brother back, even if he could be a pain in the butt.

After lunch Bill mowed the lawn and tidied up the yard while I packed up the canned goods for him to take to the food bank, straightened the house up a bit, and finally headed home to prepare for our semi-official therapy debut. At four o'clock I made one final pass over Jay with a brush, tied a new red cowboy bandana around his neck, hooked up his leash, grabbed my tote bag, and we were on our way.

The sun hunkered behind a leading phalanx of gray thunder bumpers, and a hard southwest wind rippled the flag in front of Mr. Hostetler's house across the street, holding the stripes almost horizontal. The temperature had dropped twenty degrees since noon, and when I stepped out the door, I decided I'd better take a jacket. I put Jay in the Caravan and ran to the front door. As I fiddled with my key, I noticed two startling reflections in the full-length window flanking the door. The first was my hair. I'd forgotten to comb it. That was scary enough, but the other reflection made me forget to breathe.

A cargo van crept along the street behind me. I almost turned around, but thought better of it. I stepped into the house, grabbed my camera from its case on the coffee table, and gently parted the sheer curtains with the lens. The vehicle was more rusted maroon than red in this light. As it surged ahead, I clicked off three or four shots.

It didn't make sense, though. Why would Francine Peterson be hanging out in Fort Wayne, especially if she had killed Greg. She knew the police could be looking for her. And why harass me? I didn't have Pip, or anything else she could possibly want. Then again, the woman did seem to be a few pixels short of a complete picture.

"You did what?" Jo Stevens sounded angry.

"I followed it. Or tried to." I sat in my Caravan, still looking around as I spoke into my cell phone. "I couldn't find it."

"Are you *nuts*?" She scolded, then shifted to a lower-pitched, much scarier voice. "You see something, you call me or Hutchinson or dispatch, you got that?"

"Okay."

"Seriously, Janet. What were you going to do if you caught the van? This isn't funny — you want to end up like Greg, with a carpentry tool rammed through your brain?"

93

A huge raindrop splatted against my windshield, followed by another, and another. Not exactly a downpour, at least not yet. Just enough to smear the film of road gunk when I turned the wipers on. I tried the washers, but got only a few bubbles at the base of the windshield. *Note to self: check the washer fluid more often.* I turned the wipers off. I could see better through rain than through smeared road gunk.

Ten minutes later I drove through the South Anthony railroad underpass, a stretch of road I've always hated. The street dips beneath the tracks, and stone pillars split traffic into lanes so narrow that I swear they scrape dirt from anything wider than a bicycle. Decades of exhaust have coated the whole affair with a stinking black patina. It always makes me want to get in and out as quickly as possible, even in bright daylight. Two blocks further south I turned into the

Shadetree entrance and found a parking space close to the building — a good thing since the raindrop scouts were joined shortly by a cavalry of their friends. I didn't care if I got drenched, but I didn't want all my hard work on Jay's coat ruined before his photo op.

Jade skipped my usual hug, squatting to greet Jay with an ear rub and an "Oh, what a beautiful dog." Jay responded by gathering as many scent clues as possible from her face, and she giggled. "Those little whiskers tickle!"

"Is the rain going to ruin the outdoor shots?" I asked when she finished smooching my dog.

"All done except for the dog visit, and we'll do that inside." She led us into the common area, where fifteen or so residents were gathered. Their apparent awareness of their surroundings ranged from full to none. Mom was snuggled into a green high-backed armchair, flipping through the new issue of *Fine Gardening*. She glanced our way without any sign of recognition, and went back to her magazine.

Jay snapped his leash tight, his rear end wagging wildly. I let him take me to her, not a hint of hesitation in his step, though being a stranger to my own mother gave me pause enough for both of us. Jay laid his soft white chin across Mom's arm. She let the magazine fall to the floor, and tenderly cradled the dog's chin in her left hand, stroking his head with the other. "Laddie." Her voice was love itself, and my eyes filled.

The moment was brief, lost to the arrival first of an old gentleman with bushy silver hair and eyebrows that extended like wings past his temples, followed by another old man and woman. They paid me no attention at all, just reached out to touch the dog. I felt a light fluttering at my elbow, and turned to see a wren-like little woman with wispy gray hair and a sharp little nose. She chirped, "I like your dog," then turned and flitted away.

We made the rounds to visit other residents, and Jay tolerated wheelchairs, walkers, oxygen tanks, and palsied hands as if he saw them every day. Renee Koch, the reporter who was writing the article, followed along, asking questions of me, Jade, and some of the residents. The photographer clicked away, alternating his shots with peeks at his watch. I took a jab at conversation, but he didn't seem exactly thrilled with the subject matter, or with a jabbering woman old enough to be his mother.

I was saved the trouble of a polite withdrawal when an old man playing solitaire at a table by the window squealed "Ooh-ee! Looka that!" He pointed out the window, where a premature dusk had settled in under a dome of indigo clouds. Sheets of rain pounded the sidewalk in front of the common room, and sporadic bursts of wind shot the rain, clattering like BBs, straight into the window glass. A jagged electric gash tore the dingy sky, trailed within seconds by a rolling boom that made my teeth rattle.

The photographer checked his watch one more time, yanked a green poncho over his head and camera, and looked at the reporter. "Time to go."

Renee apologized to Jade for having another appointment.

"You could wait for the rain to let up, child!"

Renee turned to where the photographer had been, but he was already out the door. "It's okay. He'll pick me up under the overhang."

We watched her go, and Jade turned to me. "I am not letting you take that dog out in that rain." The emphasis of her concern didn't escape me. "You sit down." She steered me toward a couch next to Mom's chair. "I'll get us some coffee."

Mom was engrossed in her magazine,

although when Jay lay beside her and rested his chin on her foot she did bend over to stroke the top of his head. "What a good boy, Laddie." I may as well not have been there.

The rain retreated to a sprinkle twenty minutes later and the clouds dispersed, although the light was growing dimmer as evening came on. To the west another battalion of angry-looking clouds threatened to move in. I said goodbye to Jade while several residents told Jay to come back soon. I stopped in front of Mom. She grabbed the hair on both sides of Jay's neck, pulled him to her face, and kissed the space between his eyes. "I love you, Laddie." She still didn't look at me.

94

I was about to turn right out of the Shadetree parking lot onto Anthony when I saw a
line of red taillights creeping into the
underpass. They seemed to stretch a full
block, the last one in the lineup idling a
couple of car lengths past the intersection
north of the nursing home. The road was
alive with water, swirling and grabbing at
wheel wells, arcing away behind the cars
like long, fluid fins. If drowning is my
destiny, I'd rather not fulfill it in an oily
underpass, so I turned south on Anthony,
cut west to Lafayette, and then north
through downtown. The rain and wind were
picking up again by the time I turned east
on State, and night settled over the city like
a shroud.

The traffic lights were out all along State,
at Reed, Maplecrest, and Lahmeier, adding
to the challenge of the windblown obstacle
course. Cars slowed and wove back and

forth between lanes, dodging big tree limbs and crushing small ones. Three or four garbage cans rolled around the street, spinning this way and that, as if a giant cat were knocking them from one lane to another. I thought of *my* cat and hoped he was safe and dry.

So far people were civil, taking turns at the cross streets. I crept through the last uncontrolled intersection before my turn, inching up to 35 mph, which seemed to be fast enough for everyone except the vehicle on my rear bumper. Its brights bounced off my mirrors into my eyes, and I couldn't see what it was, but the height of the lights said truck or van or SUV. Big. For one paranoid moment I thought it was that cargo van again, and for some reason Connie's admonition that "it's not all about you, Janet" came screaming into my head. As much as that had stung, she was right, and not every wacko driver was out to get me. At least I hoped not.

I tried slowing down to get the fool to pass me. When that didn't work, I sped up to 40. All I could see in my mirrors was the blinding brightness. I used a couple of expletives when the lights followed me around the corner onto Maysville.

The turn onto my street was half a block

away when I put my signal on. I was tapping my brakes and hoping the jerk wouldn't hit us when a sheet of newspaper splatted against my windshield and diverted my focus from the truck on my bumper. I hit the down button on my window and reached into the maelstrom to try to pull the paper out of my way, but a morsel of newsprint tore away in my fingers, leaving the bulk glued to the glass. *Great! They'll find us dead in a papier-mâché car.* The wipers tore at the paper, shredding a little more with each swipe until I could see enough to make the turn if the nut on my tail didn't rear-end us first.

For a couple seconds, the lights stayed put, then suddenly swung to the left as I skidded around to the right. I checked my rearview mirror again, but there was nothing to see. I glanced over my left shoulder and got a quick impression of a big-wheel pickup. Not a cargo van. *What is it with idiot drivers lately?*

I pulled into the garage, turned off the engine, shut the overhead door, and leaned my head back against the headrest. I realized that I was panting, my lungs trying to catch up with my heart, and I forced my muscles to loosen as the tension oozed from my arms and legs. A headache had sunk its fangs into the base of my skull and was nibbling its way up the nerve paths to the top. The timer on the light from the overhead-door opener ran its course, and the garage went dark. Jay shifted in his crate and gave a little whine, bringing me back to the moment.

I got out and felt my way around the front bumper to the light switch on the wall. I didn't want to raise the overhead door again, so I popped the back of the van and let it rise slowly to a forty-five degree opening, the leading edge braced against the inner surface of the garage door, leaving an opening just big enough for me to crawl under to open the crate. Jay rolled his eyes up to look at the low-hanging hatch, and carefully hopped to the concrete floor. I slammed the hatch shut, and we retreated to the comfort and safety of the house.

I checked in with Goldie. Still no sign of Leo. I shed my wet clothes, toweled my hair, and put the kettle on for some tea. Blackberry sage, my comfort brew. Jay snarfed up his dinner in record time, but looked at me like I was nuts when I offered to let him out. I could see his point. The rain had lightened to a sprinkle, but the wind whipped the forsythia and lilac branches into a frenzy, and thunder rumbled somewhere to the west. I'd hold it awhile too if I had to go out there to pee.

I dialed Connie's number, but there was no answer. I wondered to her machine whether she'd heard about Greg, although I figured that Giselle had no doubt called her. There was nothing much on the television, and my headache seemed to be settling in for the night, so I decided to drug myself, take a nice relaxing lavender bubble bath, and hit the sack.

I fished around the bottom of my purse for some naproxen, but couldn't find any. Then I remembered the bottle I keep in my training bag, along with gourmet cheese-and-liver training treats, an emergency collar, and a lot of stuff I forgot about long ago. I started pulling things out of my bag and setting them on the end table by the couch, next to the old dumbbell I'd put there the previous week. Goldie would razz me again if she saw it still sitting there. I pulled out some notes and maps from tracking sessions. Several bungee cords — you never know when you'll need one. Finally I dug out the naproxen bottle.

I took two naproxens, went to the bedroom, and was pulling off my soggy pants when Jay started barking like a mad man somewhere in the front of the house.

95

Jay usually quits barking when I tell him "Quiet," but not this time, so I pulled my pants back up and went to see what was happening. He bounced around the living room window, his hair standing straight out around his neck, booming a warning into the darkness around us. I tried to see through the glass into the night, but couldn't make out anything except frantic branches and their shadows cavorting in the scattered lights.

"It's okay, Bubby. Just the wind." He gave me a "You can't fool me, I know you're scared!" look, but he quieted down except for an occasional soft *brffff.*

The adrenalin from the drive home had left me a bit woozy, and my head was about to explode, so I went to the kitchen and half filled a bowl with ice cubes and water, carried it to the living room, and set it on the floor by the couch. Then I trudged to the bathroom, pulled a washcloth from the towel rack, trudged back to the couch. I dunked the cloth into the ice water, wrung it out, and folded it in half. As I stretched out on the cushions, I lay the cloth across my forehead, pressing the soothing cold into my scalp line and temples, and lay as still as I could. Finally, the headache flinched and loosened its hold on the back of my skull, giving me some hope of a reasonable night's sleep.

Forty minutes later I was feeling a lot better, but the whine and clatter of the wind through the kitchen vent was making my nerves itch, so I dragged myself off the couch and down the hall to my bedroom.

My little respite on the couch wasn't nearly so relaxing for Jay. He had spent the entire time torn between lying next to the couch to keep an eye on me, as always, and running to bark at the kitchen door, then back to me every time I told him to be quiet, a most un-Jay-like behavior. The wind was making us both weird.

"Where's Leo, Bubby?" I asked my dog. I put on some old but clean sweatpants and a T-shirt and checked outside both doors once more. I was pulling the covers back on the bed when all hell broke loose. Something crashed outside the kitchen door, followed by a jarring wham into the door itself.

Jay barked frantically, looking at me for instructions as I ran into the kitchen. I held on to his collar and opened the door. "Leo?" I called, hoping against hope that he would pick this hostile night to return to us.

A maple branch sprawled across the patio, its main arm a foot or so in diameter, its smaller tentacles reaching toward the house. It saddened me to know that the big old tree was damaged, but I told Jay, "Look, Bubby, it's just a big stick." I closed the door and locked it, and decided to double check the front door while I was at it.

By the time I crawled into bed I was wide awake again, so I snuggled in and opened my book. Jay plastered his back against the length of my blanketed leg and heaved a sigh. The normal routine is for me to read and for him to fall fast asleep, but every few minutes he raised his head, ears swivelled toward the front of the house. I rested a hand on his flank. He rolled his hip tight against me, but kept his attention on the door.

A nearly imperceptible growl vibrated in Jay's throat, raising the hairs on my arms. I was about to get up and see for myself what was beyond the bedroom door when Jay rested his chin on his crossed paws, letting me off the hook. The storm was still roaring around us twenty minutes later when I stuck a piece of tissue between the pages of my book, set it next to the lamp, and turned out the light.

I was floating very near slumber land when Jay's barking jolted me back to full consciousness.

96

Jay stood on the bed, and it shook every time he let out a booming *buroof.* I should know by now to listen to my dog, but the shock to my adrenals had brought my headache back with a vengeance, and I took Jay by the collar and hustled him down the hall toward the kitchen. I flipped the switch for the hallway light, but nothing happened. *I told you to replace that bulb,* whispered the voice from my pompous side.

Jay tried to pull me into the living room, growling and barking, but I hauled him through the dark to the kitchen and out the door. "Go out and pee, and have a look around. Then maybe we can get some sleep!"

I groped for and found the light switch by the door, but it made no difference. No lights. *Storm must have knocked out a transformer,* I thought, until I noticed that Goldie's back porch light was on, as it often was all night. My circuit breaker must have tripped.

I turned toward the laundry room, felt my way past the kitchen table and chairs, hoping not to catch a toe on a chair leg, and followed the smooth surface of the wall into the gloom of the windowless laundry room. My fingers hit the cool edge of the dryer, drifted to the right, touched the wall, and ran over the vinyl wallpaper until they found metal. I felt for the pull ring and yanked the breaker box open, then realized that I had no idea which breaker was where. I needed some light.

I backtracked into the kitchen and slowly made my way to the counter. I opened the first drawer to the right of the sink and felt around, trying to remember whether anything sharp lay waiting to stab me. The biggest hazards in the drawer were probably a couple of pens. As my fingers closed over the hard plastic flashlight handle, I thought I heard something behind me.

I stopped, listening into the dark. *Must be the wind.* I picked up the flashlight and tried it. No go. *Note to self: replace flashlight batteries.*

I fumbled in the drawer again, and my fingers closed over a small cardboard box. I pushed it open and felt inside. Two matches.

Another note to self. Renew supply of matches.

Jay was raising hell outside the door. It wasn't his usual "let me in" bark, but more serious, a prolonged medley of deep-throated boofs and high-pitched squeals. "Quiet!" Knowing he didn't like the wind but puzzled by the panic in his voice, I hollered that I'd be right there.

My fingers fumbled further into the drawer and were rewarded by the feel of a cylinder about four inches long. I pictured its scarred red surface and blackened wick, and was glad I'd kept it though its tabletop days were done. As I'd told Goldie many times, you never know when something may come in handy. I put the candle stub in my pocket and edged back toward the laundry room. I was just starting to pull open the matchbox when a stunning pain knocked all thought out of my mind.

97

The pain severed any commitment I had made to clean up my language, and I swore like a lady pirate as I leaned against the door frame and bent to massage my poor little piggies. Jay leaped and banged against the kitchen door, barking and squealing, and the flap on the dryer vent clattered and whined erratically in the wind. I knew my headache was back when a fist of pain clutched my skull, unsheathed its claws, and sank them in.

Suck it up, MacPhail. I let go of my toes, straightened up, and tried to focus on the job at hand. I gently nudged open the matchbox. My fingertips caught one of the matches and pulled it out. I slid the cover over the inner box, felt for the striker paper, and stroked the head of the match along the rough surface. A couple of sparks, nothing more. "Crap!" I struck it again, harder. The head of the match snapped off, flared and arced like a fairy's comet, and fizzled before it hit the floor.

I dropped the useless bit of wood and carefully retrieved the remaining match from the box as I moved back into the laundry room. I held my breath and laid the head of the match against the striker. And stopped.

That sound again, a hint of sound really, not quite there, a whisper, like metal against cloth. I stepped backward out of the laundry room and listened. No sound, but something.

I backed further into the kitchen and inclined my head toward the living room, straining to hear. The kitchen window offered a dim glow, but not enough to reveal whatever the deep shadows concealed. Visions of maniacs danced in my mind, their heads aglow with incandescent red hair.

My cheek grazed something cold and hard. The phone. I picked up the receiver and pushed Goldie's speed dial button, listening for the ping ping ping of the electronic numbers. Nothing. I pushed and released the phone cradle, and listened. Still nothing. I knocked the cradle up and down a few more times. Dead.

Jay scratched and barked and banged at the door. I remembered the dead receiver in my hand, and plunked it back into the cradle. Never had the lights and phone both pooped out together. I felt along the top of the counter until I found my cell phone, but it was dead as well. I'd forgotten to recharge it. Again. A shot of panic flashed through me, and I wanted my dog beside me. If there were anything — or anyone — inside the house, Jay would know long before I would. Maybe he did know. Maybe that's what he'd been trying to tell me. My head throbbed and a razor of fear slashed into my gut.

I found the back door and pulled on the handle. It wouldn't open. The deadbolt had apparently slipped into place when I let Jay out, or maybe I'd turned it unconsciously. I grasped the deadbolt's knob and twisted, heard the click as it opened and caught. As I reached for the door handle, a new shock of pain bit into the base of my skull and coiled upward until my whole head was in its grip. It squeezed, and then the world went black.

98

I came to almost as soon as my face hit the cool vinyl. Jay was still outside the door, barking nonstop, his voice pitched high and verging on hysteria. I heard a shuffle and the squeak of a shoe sole on the vinyl behind me.

I scuttled across the floor on my hands and knees, trying to get to the back door, but froze at a bone-jarring report close at hand. It ended with the tinkle of glass shattering in the kitchen door and a sharp yip from outside. *Oh God, don't let him be shot.*

I ducked my head, cradling it in my left arm and wondering which throb would be the one that exploded my skull. Through the fog of pain and fear, my mind registered the sound of Jay barking again, loud and strong as ever. *Thank you, God.* I scrambled away from the back door, toward the living room.

"You'll be sorry you ever stuck your nose

in my business." The threat came in a snarl barely louder than a whisper. I couldn't identify the owner.

I wanted to ask who it was, but decided to shut up for once on the off chance I'd be invisible in the dark. If I could get to the front door . . . I heard Jay's claws scraping the back door, his frantic yips ripping through my heart. *Please don't let him get hurt.*

As I edged through the doorway from kitchen to living room, I got my feet under me and rose into a crouch. I figured I could move faster that way while keeping myself a tough target. I sprinted toward the front door. A blast from the gun, the bounce of the bullet off the steel front door, the muffled finale as the drywall absorbed the ricocheted shell. I stopped in my tracks, revised my exit strategy, and turned back into the room.

"I see you, you nosey bitch!"

I knew the voice.

Another shot sounded like a cannon in my small living room.

"How will killing me help?" She might be beyond reason, but it was the only weapon I had for the moment.

"Shut up!" Click. "Shit!" Click, click. A bunch more clicks.

A shadow flew across the room at me, snarling, "I don't need a gun to deal with you!" Then why did she seem to be raising one above her head like a club?

"You don't have to deal with me!" I took a step back, forgetting that the couch was behind me, and tripped, sprawling backward onto the soft seat cushions. "It's too late! You can't get away with it now."

"Yes, I can," she growled. All my senses were focused on the crazy woman in front of me, but some corner of my mind registered that the front door had opened. Or did I imagine it? Then she was on me, like pure energy. She planted a knee, sharp as a spade, against my thigh and pinned me into the couch. Bone pressed into my flesh, through it to my own bone within, and I wondered vaguely whether the bruise would show if I died in the next minute or so.

I saw her gun hand slam down toward my head, but was able to block it, wielding the tapestry pillow like a shield over my head. The impact knocked the pillow into my nose, filling my sinuses with bubbling pain.

I peeked from behind my shield in time to see her raise the gun once more, and was preparing to block her again when an inhuman caterwaul shocked the night, a wail calculated to turn blood to jelly. In the next instant the air in front of my attacker erupted in shadowy frenzy as the woman jerked upright, away from me, and whirled, her screams almost a match for the first one.

I dropped the pillow and tried to get up. Big mistake. She whacked with the gun at her own thighs, acting as if an army of fire ants had climbed up her pants, and in her flailing caught my brow bone with an elbow, sending a galaxy of stars cascading through my head. The gun thunked against the oak floor, the sound nearly lost in a stream of curses, snarls, and more howls.

"Janet?" Goldie's voice was almost drowned out, but I heard her.

"Here!" I panted, trying to get out from behind the maelstrom in front of the couch and onto my feet. I'd almost made it when I was smashed back into the cushions. A second set of snarls, pitched lower. I felt long fur against my hand. Jay. He'd un-latched the back door again.

The bones of my foe's rear end dug into my gut, and her arms windmilled in panic. Her left hand slapped at her thigh. A beam of light hit us, quivered away, returned. I was vaguely aware that it came from Goldie's hand, which was shaking too much to keep the flashlight steady, but steady enough to reveal the source of the blood-gelling screams.

99

Leo was locked on to my assailant's thigh, his fur standing straight out, ears flat against his skull, lips pulled back to let his fangs do their work, claws extended through cotton capris and into the flesh beneath. He sounded like he was possessed.

Jay had a grip on the intruder's arm just below the elbow and was trying to pull her off me, or her arm off her torso, whichever came first. Low, rolling snarls erupted from his throat, all business, primeval, like nothing I'd ever heard from him before. Blood ran down the attacker's arm where the dog had clamped on. It dripped and mingled with the gore that soaked the fabric of her shredded left pant leg.

The more Jay tugged on her arm, the more she pulled into me, knocking the air back out every time I managed to suck some in. I punched at her back as well as I could manage, pinned as I was to the couch. She shoved me farther toward the armrest. I braced my right hand against her and pushed, groping blindly toward the end table with my left, seeking a purchase, a way to pull myself free.

Leo let out a new unearthly sound, part growl, part battle cry, shrill hate and anger, as he dodged a blow to the head. He flinched and loosed the hold he had mid-thigh, swatted at the offending arm, and re-attached himself with a vengeance higher up. One paw slipped between the woman's legs and sank daggers into the soft flesh at the top of her inner thigh. The other flexed wide and gripped her buttocks. He worked his back claws like pistons, shredding the bloodstained cotton and ripping the skin beneath. The light beam danced erratically, but I saw my little tiger sink his fangs through the flimsy fabric once again, prying loose more barely human keening from the woman in his grip.

My head felt like a kettledrum, noise and heat and fear beating it raw. I pushed once more against the small of my attacker's back, and managed to slip partway out from under her. I had no plan, and acted on pure pain and reflex.

I extended an arm toward the end table, fingers flexed, and heard something fall away, clatter to the floor, and roll. The naproxen bottle. I pictured the table, trying to build a map in my mind, and reached further, feeling in the dark. My fingernail brushed something hard.

A long howl erupted from the body on top of me. My attacker arched and shifted backward, emptying my lungs again as she came down hard.

Something white flashed forward and down from behind my head, past my eyes. I heard a dull hard *thwack,* and then the world went slow. My bloodied foe stopped mid-scream, swayed for a moment, and, with a little shove from my right hand, toppled to the floor.

Leo released his grip and flew straight up, changed direction mid-leap, and came down running. His tail stood high and straight, fluffed out like a feather duster as he let out a yowl and disappeared into the bedroom. Jay gave the arm he held a test tug to be sure its owner was out of the fight, let it go, and jumped onto the couch, planting his paws on my shoulders and his elbows against my bruised ribs as he whined and licked my face.

"That'll teach her!"

I pushed Jay partway off and looked at Goldie, silhouetted like a spirit against the open front door, her long silver hair loose and wild, her free hand raised in a fist of victory.

I glanced at the body sprawled in the beam of Goldie's light on the floor in front of me and felt a pang of regret. As I tried to push Jay off the couch and raise myself into a sitting position, I realized I had something in my left hand. I felt its familiar shape and heft, moved it into the light, and waggled my big clunky spare dumbbell at Goldie. "I told you this might come in handy."

100

I got the lights back on and fished my cell phone recharger out of my tote bag, but before I plugged the phone in, Goldie said, "I already called that detective."

"You did?" Sure enough, I heard a siren somewhere in the night.

"She gave me her card a few days ago when she stopped by and you weren't here."

Goldie picked up a handful of bungee cords from where I'd left them on the end table. She rolled the intruder onto her stomach and secured her hands behind her back, then wound another cord several times around her feet. My attacker was waking up by the time Goldie propped her back against the couch and bound her knees together.

"What are you doing here, anyway?" I asked Goldie.

"Jay was raising such a ruckus at the back door, and your lights were out. I knew something was wrong."

The woman on the floor let out a string of expletives, ending with "hurts." Her clothes were torn and bloody, barely concealing the lacerated flesh underneath. She started to say something, but stopped when two uniformed police officers rushed in, Jo Stevens on their heels.

"Why, Connie?" I asked softly. She didn't answer. She tried to toss a strand of blood-soaked hair out of her eyes. I stepped toward her. She flinched from my hand, then let me push the hair behind her ear. I looked into her eyes, and a stranger looked back. Then she turned her head toward Jay, and her expression softened.

"I'm sorry I used you and Leo to scare that nosey bitch. I wouldn't really have hurt you."

A rocket of anger exploded in my mind. "Not hurt them? You poisoned him and kidnapped my cat! Did you take Greg's dogs, too?" I didn't realize that more people had entered the room, or that I had stepped toward her again until I felt the back edge of Detective Jo Stevens' arm cross my chest.

Connie continued speaking softly, ignoring me in favor of Jay. "Your biscuits weren't poisoned, sweetie." Jay cocked his head at her. "I would never do such a thing. I put mouse bait out in my garage. That's where the mouse came from. I put it in the pantry," she turned toward me and went on, "while you were putting the grooming supplies away. And Leo was perfectly safe." Conflicting emotions seemed to dance across her face, but I couldn't see anything like affection or friendship, and a sledgehammer of loss smashed into my heart. Then Connie's eyes filled with the light I knew and loved, and her voice went soft. "I thought I could scare you off. Should have known better, you're so damn stubborn."

I didn't know what to say to that.

"I took Pip and Percy so they wouldn't have to smell that bastard's body rotting or go hungry if no one found the sonofabitch for a while. I'd have found them all good homes."

Sorrow gnawed at me as I realized I might never have known what happened to my cat, or to Greg and Abigail's dogs. I looked at Goldie. "Where was Leo, anyway?"

"In that clunker van in the street. I heard dogs barking so I took a look."

"The van was open?" asked Detective Stevens

"Not exactly. One of the back doors was tied shut with twine. I squeezed my arm in far enough to unlock the front, and then popped the locks. And there was Leo, in a crate, looking like a wildcat. There are a couple more dogs there, too, and a bunch of luggage. That black and white guy you had here, and a Poodle."

Jo signaled one of the officers to go check the van.

Goldie continued. "Leo was a yellow streak to your front door when I opened his cage, and wild to get into the house."

"How *did* you get in?" I asked Goldie.

"Door was unlocked."

"No! I know I locked it."

Connie made a face. "Key under the geranium pot. How creative."

I looked at her, and tried again. "Why, Connie?"

Connie's face went livid. "I waited for that bastard all these years while he had his fling."

"Fling? Connie! Greg and Abigail were married more than twenty years."

She bared her teeth at me, twisting against her restraints. A siren sounded in the distance. "When they separated, I figured my wait was over." She snarled again, collected herself, and went on, "And then the stupid bastard ruined it all."

"What?"

"Stupid sonofabitch thought Suzette

killed Abigail," she hissed. "I thought *you'd* blame her for Abigail's death," she glared at Jo, "but the police didn't get it, and Greg got it wrong."

My head was spinning now as well as pounding. "But I thought Francine . . ." My thought trailed off. "You killed Abigail?"

Connie sounded suddenly like a woeful little girl. "I've loved that man all my life. I got tired of waiting. I thought when he moved out it was finally my turn."

"But they . . ."

"Yeah, yeah, I know." She shot me a look. "They were redecorating, for crying out loud."

Another question struck me. "Why do you have Francine's van?"

She looked at me like I was the village idiot. "I bought one like hers. And a stupid red wig. I knew if you kept asking questions, and thinking about it, you'd figure Francine did it because of the DNA tests. I knew you'd be on 30 that day, coming back from the lake. I just wanted to piss you off enough to make you blame Francine."

"You did my tires, too?"

I took her glare as a yes.

"And what about Greg? I mean, if you loved him . . ."

Her eyes went watery. "I went to see him.

Told him I'd waited all these years." She sniffed a couple of times. "I told him I killed Abigail. I did it for him, for us, and he just went crazy, started screaming that he thought Suzette did it. Then he started bawling like a baby. Said we'd have to turn ourselves in." She was talking very fast now. "He said he'd never loved me and he started to call the police, to confess about Suzette and tell them about me, and the next thing I knew the chisel was in my hand . . ."

Connie went quiet, Goldie and I exchanged looks of sympathy mixed with horror, and Detective Stevens directed one of the police officers to arrest Connie. As he stepped toward her and started to read her her rights, I asked, "Greg killed Suzette?"

Connie winced as she was pulled to her feet and cuffed, then nodded. "I think the chisel was meant to be there." Her voice had turned to a monotone that spooked me more than her screeching had. "Then you wouldn't back off, and I knew you weren't really sure about Francine, and that was a big problem. With Tom around you'd find out about me and Greg and put it all together." The venom was back in her voice. "You may be nosey, but you're not stupid."

I wasn't too sure about that at the moment.

An ambulance pulled to a stop in front of the house. The cops escorted Connie out the door for her ride to the hospital and then the jail. She resisted at the door and turned her face to me, a glint back in her eye. "I don't think you'll get Leo into a cat carrier for a while. But if you need to, he's a slut for sardines."

101

The sun nestled into the trees along the
Maumee River, and flights of crows and
smaller birds swooped over the brown water
and called to the coming night. Barely a day
had passed since Connie's arrest, and the
world along the river went on unchanged,
indifferent. Jay and Drake drew their retractable leashes full length as they searched
both edges of the Greenway path, back and
forth, back and forth.

"I didn't know Connie still carried that
torch for Greg." Tom spoke softly, and my
eyes filled. We walked in silence for a few
minutes, watching the dogs and reeling
them in whenever anyone else happened
along.

I elbowed Tom, trying to lighten my dark
mood. "So, Mr. Toxic Plants, what do you
think she used?"

"The police mentioned alkaloids?"

I nodded.

"And Abigail had coordination problems, and trouble breathing . . . Did anyone mention a funny smell?"

I thought back to Abigail's gear at the show, "I found cheese spread that smelled sort of mousy."

"Poison hemlock?"

"Very good. Yes. Goldie nudged that one out of her before they took her away. Connie made Abigail some 'special' spread for her bagels."

"And Suzette?"

"And was Greg really involved with Suzette?"

"No. Yvonne filled me in on that, too. Seems Abigail introduced Suzette to an old family friend when they were in the Bahamas last year, and they fell in love. Yvonne said their parents opposed the marriage. Hers didn't want Suzette going so far away, his had someone else in mind. So they were keeping their plans for a small summer wedding with close friends quiet."

"What about the tickets?"

"Yvonne said Greg and Abigail always flew separately, so Greg and Suzette were going on one flight, Abigail and Yvonne on another."

Tom guided me off the path to a bench overlooking a bend in the river. We sat, and the dogs lay down in the shade. Tom took my hand in both of his and traced the lines in my palm, sending a flight of butterflies spinning among my internal organs. I asked myself whether they were there because I didn't want to get too involved, or because I did, and I had no answer. Jay rolled onto his back and leaned his ribs against a sapling, and I envied him the simplicity of life in the moment. At least that's how we assume animals live, although I'm not always sure that's right. My philosophizing was interrupted when Tom asked, "And I take it Connie hadn't planned to kill Greg?"

"She seemed genuinely shocked that he wasn't thrilled that Abigail was out of their way, and angry that he'd spoiled it by killing Suzette and, worse, wanting to come clean to the police. She said it was satisfying to stab the son of a bitch with his own tool."

"Ouch."

"A little Freudian, huh? And very Connie. You know, she even bought herself an engagement ring. She said Greg gave it to her, but the police found a credit card receipt in her purse."

"What will happen to the dogs?"

Jay rolled onto his side, and Drake stretched himself so that one front paw touched one of Jay's.

"I spent today on that. Connie's dogs all have co-owners, so they'll take them. They're at the clinic in the meantime."

"And the DNA business?"

"Ginny Scott, Fly's breeder, talked to someone at the Border Collie registry and she said both they and the AKC were already investigating Francine. Apparently some of her puppies have been DNA tested and the results didn't line up with the dogs she claimed were their parents."

"What will happen to her?"

"She'll no doubt lose her registration privileges and Border Collie club memberships. What reputation she still had among BC people is shot. And Ginny said there's talk of a couple of lawsuits from other breeders who bought pups from her or bred to her dogs and now have pedigree disasters."

"Her dogs?"

"Ginny said Border Collie rescue groups are standing by to take them if necessary. They'll neuter them and find them new homes."

"What a mess." Tom shook his head and clucked softly. "And what about Greg and Abigail's dogs?"

The man was gaining hundreds of brownie

points in my book. To my surprise, few people had shown much concern for the fate of all the dogs affected by the murders and scandals. "They're at my house for now. Ginny is going to find Pip a home. And it turns out that little Percy is a certified therapy dog and visited a nursing home every week. You won't believe which one."

"Not where your mom is?"

"You got it. Jade Templeton wants him. She's wanted a dog for a long time, but didn't think it fair to leave one alone for the long hours she works. She loves Percy, so she'll adopt him and he'll be her dog, and he'll go to work with her. She has to clear it with the board of directors, but doesn't think that will be a problem. Their resident cat has worked out really well."

"Speaking of cats, is Leo happy to be home?"

I thought of my little orange man. "He curled up against my head and purred all night."

"Lucky guy!" Tom grinned and stood. "It's getting dark, lady and gents. We should head back." The dogs jumped up, and I eased myself into a stand, trying to ignore my aches and bruises and wondering how people on TV bounce back so fast from getting punched and shot and run over by trains. I was a wreck from a little couch wrestling.

My thoughts were cut short when Tom pulled me close, searched my eyes, and traced my lips with a touch as light as a whisper. He laced his fingers into my hair and cradled the back of my head, and then kissed me, slowly and thoroughly. Warring currents of lust and panic surged through me, and I didn't know whether to lie down right there or run like hell.

I barely felt the solid ground beneath my feet on the way back to the parking lot. My thoughts bounced around in my head like numbered balls in a lottery machine — *I don't want to get involved with anyone. Why didn't I shave my legs this morning? I can't get close and then go through the pain of losing him. This may be the man I've looked for all my life. I like my life the way I've created it. Change is good.*

Janet Angel and Janet Demon piped up in harmony, reminding me that life is like an obedience trial, and if I don't send the entry, I'll never get the title. *Of course,* I argued back, *I won't lose, either.* I thought of my disastrous relationship with Chet and the few uninspiring flubs since then, and of a photo I took years ago of two paths diverging in a wood of shadows and light.

Once again, Tom grinned and brought me back to the moment. "By the way, you owe me some portraits of my dog, and I intend to collect. So don't make a habit of putting yourself in harm's way."

Good thing I didn't make any promises.

ABOUT THE AUTHOR

Sheila Webster Boneham has been writing professionally for three decades, and writes in several genres. She has taught writing at universities in the U.S. and abroad, and occasionally teaches writing workshops. In the past fifteen years Sheila has published seventeen nonfiction books, six of which have won major awards. A long-time participant in canine sports, therapy, and other activities, Sheila is also an avid amateur photographer and painter. When she isn't pursuing creative activities or playing with animals, Sheila can be found walking the beach or salt marsh near her home in North Carolina. You can reach her through her website at www.sheilaboneham.com.